Praise for the novels of Michelle Sagara

"*Shards of Glass* is a spellbinding fantasy with a powerful tale of friendship at its beating heart. With vivid world building and compelling characters, this is a treasure of a book."

—Kylie Lee Baker, author of *The Scarlet Alchemist*

"[An] elaborate, magic-filled tale.... A treat."

—*Publishers Weekly* on *Shards of Glass*

"A puzzling, absorbing mystery.... Recommended for readers who have been caught up in the fantasy mystery trend, anyone looking for a way into Elantra without wading through its vast lore, and those who fell away from the series and are looking for a route back."

—*Library Journal* on *Shards of Glass*

"First-rate fantasy. Sagara's complex characterizations and rich world-building lift her above the crowd."

—Kelley Armstrong, *New York Times* bestselling author

"Sagara swirls mystery and magical adventure together with unforgettable characters."

—*Publishers Weekly* on *Cast in Silence*

"Sagara's remarkable Cast novels are a voyage of discovery into one young woman's fearsome destiny. Filled with time-release plot threads and intricate details, these books are both mesmerizing and unforgettable. If you're a fan of rich fantasy, this is the series for you!"

—*RT Book Reviews* on *Cast in Secret*

"This world feels so complex and so complete."

—*ReadingReality.net* on *The Emperor's Wolves*

"This magical thrill-ride is a treat."

t in Wisdom

Also by *New York Times* bestselling author Michelle Sagara

The Chronicles of Elantra

CAST IN SHADOW
CAST IN COURTLIGHT
CAST IN SECRET
CAST IN FURY
CAST IN SILENCE
CAST IN CHAOS
CAST IN RUIN
CAST IN PERIL
CAST IN SORROW
CAST IN FLAME
CAST IN HONOR
CAST IN FLIGHT
CAST IN DECEPTION
CAST IN OBLIVION
CAST IN WISDOM
CAST IN CONFLICT
CAST IN ETERNITY

And “Cast in Moonlight” found in HARVEST MOON

The Wolves of Elantra

THE EMPEROR’S WOLVES
SWORD AND SHADOW

The Academia Chronicles

SHARDS OF GLASS

Look for the next story in
The Chronicles of Elantra,
coming soon from MIRA.

MICHELLE SAGARA

CAST IN ATONEMENT

MIRA

/||MIRA™

Recycling programs for this product may not exist in your area.

ISBN-13: 978-0-7783-6972-1

Cast in Atonement

For questions and comments about the quality of this book, please contact us at CustomerService@Harlequin.com.

TM is a trademark of Harlequin Enterprises ULC.

Mira
22 Adelaide St. West, 41st Floor
Toronto, Ontario M5H 4E3, Canada
MIRABooks.com

Printed in U.S.A.

This is for Becca Lovatt, who not only tolerates writer neurosis
but has been so supportive with emergency deadlines
(and time off because of them).

This is *not* a thank-you for being a clever troll.

01

"Kaylin. *Kaylin.* It is time to wake up." Light flooded the room as curtains were drawn back. Kaylin had spent most of the evening, and much of the very early morning hours, with the midwives' guild on an emergency call. She—sensibly—pulled the blankets over her head.

Hope squawked; he'd spent most of the same time on her shoulder. He didn't pull the blankets over his head given his claws and the lack of opposable thumbs, but he did make clear that he wasn't interested in becoming more mobile yet.

"Kaylin, Imelda is making breakfast, it is almost ready, and she is expecting Lord Sanabalis to join us."

Us. Ugh.

"It is time to wake up."

Hope could sleep on Kaylin's shoulders; once she'd picked him up and put him there, he didn't have to move. He could grumble in his sleep—and was—but all movement was supplied by Kaylin, his theoretical master.

Hope snorted.

Kaylin had managed to dress, although she'd had to redo

buttons because the first attempt didn't match buttons with the correct buttonholes. She could hear Mrs. Erickson humming as she made her way down the stairs.

Mrs. Erickson was a hummer. Sometimes, she was a singer. She was a force of cheer and delight. Kaylin didn't *want* cheer and delight first thing in the morning.

"Why is Sanabalis visiting?" she asked Helen. "He's not supposed to check in for a couple more days."

"You will have to ask him," Helen's disembodied voice replied. Her Avatar must be with Mrs. Erickson. "I'm making a few adjustments to the kitchen. Imelda is the only one who actually uses it and I'd like to accommodate her needs."

"Did you wake up any of the cohort?"

"No. They don't require sleep. Mandoran is, however, in the kitchen with Imelda."

"Terrano?"

"He doesn't like to eat first thing in the morning, or so he says. But yes, he's in the kitchen as well."

"Did you tell either of them that Sanabalis is coming to visit?"

"Lord Sanabalis, or rather the Arkon, considering his new title. And no. Imelda did. Neither have chosen to flee."

Kaylin grimaced as she headed toward the front door. "He's here?"

"He is almost at the door," Helen replied.

"I don't suppose you could just answer it and let him in?" It was a rhetorical question. Helen *could* answer the door, but she preferred Kaylin, as the chief resident, perform that duty. Kaylin didn't understand why it was considered good manners, but understood that in Helen's mind, it was.

She therefore opened the door when Sanabalis knocked.

Sanabalis, being a Dragon, had eyes that shifted color depending on his mood. His current mood was orange with flecks of red, which was the outer edge of Dragon-safety color. Or rather, normal people's safety when confronted with Dragons. She froze when she met his gaze, and then got out of the way in a hurry, remembering to mutter a *please come in* as she did.

Hope remained flopped across her shoulders. If Sanabalis—ugh, if the *Arkon*—was angry, her familiar didn't think he was angry at Kaylin.

Helen's Avatar appeared in the foyer. "Arkon, we are pleased to invite you into our home. Mrs. Erickson has been in the kitchen all morning in anticipation of your visit." When Sanabalis opened his mouth, Helen added, "She insisted."

There was a hint of warning in the two words; Sanabalis raised a single brow before offering Helen the nod he hadn't bothered to offer Kaylin. "I am certain I will find it delightful."

"She *is* aware that Dragons don't necessarily eat what the rest of us eat?" Kaylin asked.

Helen smiled and failed to answer the question. "If you would join us in the dining room," the Avatar said to the Dragon, "we would be pleased."

The dining room was fancier than the usual gathering space used when the cohort chose to saunter their way down the stairs; the chairs were larger, and the tablecloth was lace; the plates were far fancier, as was the silverware—which was actually silver, at least by look.

Helen, not trusting Kaylin completely, ushered Sanabalis to his chair. Kaylin glanced around, intending to take the chair farthest from the Dragon. Sadly, that chair was already occupied by Terrano. Mandoran was seated closer to the Dragon, but Mandoran's experience living with Bellusdeo had made Dragons less intimidating to him. Probably.

Both Terrano and Mandoran were blue-eyed, which was natural given the presence of the new Arkon. Kaylin's eyes would have probably been a different color as well, if human eyes shifted the way most other races' did. She exhaled and took the chair to Sanabalis's right.

His eyes had lost the red flecks, but not the rest of the orange; she knew because he was staring in her direction. He hadn't come here to see Mrs. Erickson. He'd come to grill Kaylin about something.

She really wanted to skip breakfast and head to the Halls of Law early. Helen, however, did not approve of skipping breakfast, and Kaylin didn't need a lecture about the importance of the morning meal while a member of the Dragon Court was in attendance. She therefore had no easy escape route.

Mrs. Erickson came into the dining room, still wearing the apron she wore when she worked in the kitchen. She was carrying a large tray. Mandoran rose instantly to retrieve said tray. Mrs. Erickson beamed at him; she then removed the apron and hung it over the back of her chair. Helen caused it to vanish.

Mandoran set the tray where Helen indicated it should go—which was not on the table itself. It was on a small side table Helen had materialized for just that purpose. Helen then held Mrs. Erickson's chair out, and Mrs. Erickson sat. Mandoran returned to his own chair, his eyes less dark a blue.

Mrs. Erickson was a hard person to fear or dislike, as both Mandoran and Terrano proved. Annarion liked her. *Sedarias* liked her. The rest of the cohort largely kept to themselves, but over the past two weeks—the entirety of Mrs. Erickson's tenancy—Allaron had joined her in the kitchen as well.

The kitchen was Mrs. Erickson's happy place. She had always baked for the Hawks at the public desk in the Halls of Law, and she'd expanded that baking almost the minute she'd moved in. She liked to feed people.

Her former housemates, being ghosts, couldn't eat. Her current housemates could. And Mrs. Erickson was, in Kaylin's admittedly pedestrian opinion, an excellent baker. Today's breakfast, while not sweet, showcased that baking: pastry that contained breakfast-oriented meats and vegetables. Helen chose to serve.

Clearly this had been discussed before Mrs. Erickson entered the dining room, because Mrs. Erickson didn't jump up from her seat in a rush to be helpful. She looked like she wanted to, though.

Breakfast was not exactly a friendly, relaxed affair.

Kaylin ate quickly—she always did. Helen hated it when she talked with her mouth full, and arguments about what constituted *full* had never worked out in Kaylin's favor. As Sanabalis was two days early and most of his attention was on Kaylin, she wanted a mostly empty mouth.

Hope squawked.

Sanabalis exhaled a small stream of smoke. "My apologies for dropping in with little notice. Have you perhaps seen Lord Emmerian in the past week?"

Not the question Kaylin had been expecting. Given the presence of Mrs. Erickson's other ghosts, most of Sanabalis's concerns involved the dead. Emmerian wasn't dead, to Kaylin's knowledge; he wasn't close.

She blinked. "No, I haven't. Helen?"

"He has not visited in the past week, no."

"Why are you asking?"

Sanabalis exhaled more smoke, but notably no fire given the state of the food on his plate. "He has removed himself to Lord Bellusdeo's Tower, which was expected. He has failed to appear at the regular meeting of the Dragon Court, which was not. Lannagaros has attended all relevant meetings, and his duties to the Academia make him somewhat testy when present." A brief glimmer of a smile touched the new Arkon's face. "It does keep the meetings somewhat shorter."

"Can you not communicate with Emmerian while he's in the Tower?"

"Towers, very much like Helen, dislike the mirror network; they all feel it presents a security risk they are unwilling to take.

Given the subtle nature of Shadow, this is acceptable to the Emperor. Lord Emmerian has many other avenues to avail himself of the network, none of which have been used.

"He has been seen in the air above the fief of Bellusdeo, alongside Lord Bellusdeo herself." He lifted a hand to pinch the bridge of his nose. "We are grateful that races outside of our own do not fully understand the Dragon tongue. Were it not for the appearance of a third Dragon, their argument might have continued."

"Third Dragon?"

"Lannagaros believes it to be the Avatar of Bellusdeo's Tower."

Karriamis. That would make some sense.

"The Avatar intervened, and the argument—such as it was—retreated to a more private environment."

"The Tower itself."

"That is our assumption, yes. Lord Emmerian, however, has not yet emerged from that Tower."

"And Bellusdeo?"

Sanabalis didn't answer. It was the wrong kind of nonanswer.

Kaylin folded her arms and leaned back in her chair, tilting it onto two legs. "What's happening with Bellusdeo?"

"We are uncertain," the Arkon said. His gaze dropped to his hands, which were now folded on the table.

Hope squawked.

"Yes," Sanabalis replied. "That is the reason I chose to visit today, with little warning." He exhaled smoke for a third time before lifting his head. "Bellusdeo left her Tower—and her fief—and we believe she is coming to visit you."

"I won't be here—I have work."

"I have spoken with your extremely territorial and irritable sergeant; your work, today, will not involve your usual beat. You will, however, be paid."

"And my work, according to you, is?"

"Simply listen to Bellusdeo, and if at all possible, calm her or divert her attention from whatever it is that has her on the edge of rage."

Kaylin exhaled. "Dragons live forever, right?"

"Demonstrably not, but yes, we are Immortal."

"Could you just shelve this whole make babies thing for a few decades?" Or centuries. "She understands *why* it's essential for the race as a whole, but she never intended to bear children. She's accepted the responsibility—but not well. Emmerian is in the line of fire because he's the least unacceptable father candidate, but that doesn't mean she's happy about it.

"Could you just...wait until she truly accepts the need?"

"That advice has been given by Lannagaros," Sanabalis replied, his tone neutral. "But if that were her intent, taking the Tower she took was unwise in the extreme. The heart of her Tower is—was—a Dragon. I do not believe that he is content to, as you put it, wait."

"She's the lord of the Tower."

"Indeed."

"She gets to make that decision."

"That is the theory, yes. Her Tower cannot force her to do anything she does not desire to do. But her Tower cannot be rendered voiceless, to my knowledge. Karriamis is, no doubt, making his opinion quite clear. I am willing to abide by Lannagaros's advice. Others are ambivalent."

Others had to be referring to the Emperor. Emmerian knew better than to try to force Bellusdeo's hand. No, that was unfair. What he loved about Bellusdeo was what she was, who she was. He would accept her decision. The former Arkon had always pushed for patience and for a similar acceptance because he'd known Bellusdeo and her sisters as the children they had been in the Aerie. Sanabalis was neutral. Tiamaris, the youngest of the Dragon Lords, was likely neutral as well.

That only left the Emperor.

Kaylin exhaled. "I can't force Bellusdeo to do anything she doesn't want to do."

"Of course not. But Lannagaros feels Bellusdeo lacks friends. She has her Ascendant, but Lannagaros feels the Ascendant is liege, not friend. She will come to visit; she is on the way here as we speak. I apologize in advance for her temper." He rose. "I would like to see myself out before she arrives; she will not be best pleased to see me."

"You come to visit Mrs. Erickson regularly."

Sanabalis nodded. "How much of a difference do you think that will make to her in her current mood?"

None. None at all. Bellusdeo hadn't even met Mrs. Erickson. And using the old woman as an excuse left a bad taste in Kaylin's mouth.

"Should I go back to my room? I can visit with our new ghosts while you speak with your friend," Mrs. Erickson said, rising as well. She looked concerned but not nervous; having Sanabalis as a visiting guest had done much to alleviate any possible fear she could have of Dragons. Sanabalis, however, rarely lost his temper. The same couldn't be said of Bellusdeo.

"I don't think that's necessary," Helen told Mrs. Erickson. "Bellusdeo has more of a temper than the Arkon, but she has never once unleashed it around people who could not survive it. I am certain she will be fine."

Kaylin was certain Mrs. Erickson would be fine as well. Helen could prevent injuries when her various guests exited the self-control ramp.

"If you wish to depart," Helen said, turning to Sanabalis, "I will have to ask you to take the Tower exit. Bellusdeo has reached the perimeter of my space."

Sanabalis's shoulders slumped. "No, I will stay. I will not be seen scurrying up the stairs like a terrified hatchling."

Bellusdeo knocked on the front door, which did a disservice to the word *knock*. Kaylin had exited the dining room in a hurry, in order to head off her former roommate before she reached anyone else. Helen approved of this. Sanabalis remained in the dining room with Terrano and Mandoran, although Mandoran came to the dining room door.

Most of the cohort weren't keen on Dragons. They felt they owed a debt to Bellusdeo, but that debt amounted to cautious tolerance. Mandoran, however, genuinely *liked* Bellusdeo. Teela liked her. Terrano had warmed up a lot.

Angry Bellusdeo, however, was still intimidating, so it made good sense to try to avoid her.

Hope had pulled himself out of his lazy, wet-blanket slump across Kaylin's shoulders, and stood, wings folded, on the right one as Helen opened the door.

Kaylin got a face full of red-eyed, furious Dragon. It was almost a surprise when Bellusdeo opened her mouth and didn't roar in her native tongue. Or breathe fire.

"What happened?" Kaylin asked, as she moved toward the angry Dragon.

"Karriamis," Bellusdeo snarled, a little bit of fire framing the name she spit out. At least it wasn't Emmerian. "Karriamis is the heart of a Tower—his concern is supposed to be Shadow!"

"Karriamis is—or was—a Dragon, dear," Helen said, voice gentle. "But you are the captain of the Tower."

Bellusdeo's eyes didn't get any less red as she turned to Helen, whose expression was apologetic—but firm.

"I am the heart of this house," Helen continued. "I keep my tenants safe. I guard my perimeters. I was not created with the ability to choose my tenants—the Towers were. But I made some alterations, and I *can* choose now. Kaylin is my tenant. In theory, her role in my life is similar to your role in Karriamis's life. But we certainly disagree about some things. If it were up to Kaylin, she would wake up in the morning in just enough time to run out of the house in a panic.

"I believe breakfast is an important meal; I wake her and she eats breakfast. She *could* order me to stop."

"And you'd obey?" Bellusdeo asked, a hairsbreadth before Kaylin could.

Helen's smile was sweetness itself—and it was her only answer. No, of course she wouldn't obey.

"My dear, if Kaylin truly commanded me, I would have no choice. It is the same with Karriamis and Bellusdeo—but he is cunning. He, as I, will do everything within his limited power to maintain control over himself. In my case, I simply chose the right tenant. And in his, he chose the right lord."

Helen's Avatar froze, her eyes becoming obsidian spheres as they did when something demanded too much of her attention.

"Imelda?" Helen said, her voice sharper, harsher than her intent. She turned from Bellusdeo and the conversation they'd been having as if both were irrelevant, her eyes going to the dining room's door.

Mrs. Erickson stood in its frame. At her back, close enough to grab her and drag her to safety if necessary, was Mandoran. Terrano stepped through both Mandoran and Mrs. Erickson to stand in the hall. His eyes were blue, and they'd become larger than the Barrani physical norm. Sanabalis, Kaylin couldn't see, but maybe he thought it beneath his dignity to crowd around the door when there was no chance he could walk through it.

"Imelda, what's happened, what's wrong?" Helen moved toward the old woman who was clutching the frame of the door, as if it was necessary to support her very slight weight.

Kaylin had turned as well and froze.

Mrs. Erickson was crying.

Bellusdeo's eyes shifted color, darkening. Whatever had frustrated her so much that she'd stormed her way to Helen was set aside; she knew what the color of Helen's eyes meant. Danger. Fear.

Terrano stepped into the hall to allow Mrs. Erickson to enter it; she didn't. Her arm trembled and her tears continued to fall. Only when Mandoran gently caught her lifted arm, prying her fingers from the doorframe and offering the physical support the frame had provided, did she move.

She was staring at Bellusdeo. Her gaze never left the gold Dragon.

It was enormously awkward to attempt to introduce the former roommate to the current one, given the circumstances. Kaylin had been—and still was—certain that Bellusdeo would like Mrs. Erickson, but the weeping changed the nature of their first meeting. Instead of being polite and comfortable, it was raw and uncomfortable.

Bellusdeo didn't shed tears in public. Tears left other people feeling helpless—like they *should* be able to do something, but had no idea what, and anything they tried might make things worse, not better.

Kaylin understood this, because she felt that way herself.

Mrs. Erickson attempted to get her tears under control, and mostly failed.

"Imelda?" Helen approached Mrs. Erickson, glancing at Mandoran, whose arm was around the old woman's shoulders.

Mrs. Erickson shook her head. "I'm sorry," she finally managed to say. It took her three tries. She lifted a hand and attempted to wipe the tears away.

"This is Bellusdeo," Kaylin said, feeling far more awkward than she should have. "She used to live with us, but she has her own home now."

The Dragon snorted.

"And, Bellusdeo, this is Mrs. Erickson. She's living with us now."

Bellusdeo nodded. Her eyes remained red, but she approached Mrs. Erickson and offered an outstretched hand.

Mrs. Erickson took it, but her grip was white-knuckled. Any normal greeting was lost to the attempt to rein in tears. Or so Kaylin assumed.

Bellusdeo's eyes had lightened; her expression was one of concern. She didn't suffer from Kaylin's discomfort in the presence of tears. Or maybe her worry for this weeping stranger was greater than the fear she could somehow make things worse.

Mrs. Erickson's hand was almost clenched as she inhaled and tried to force her shoulders from their hunch. She opened her mouth, closed it, opened it again. The fourth time, she said, "I'm terribly sorry to be such a mess—but I must ask: Did you have sisters?"

Kaylin could see Mrs. Erickson's profile. She could see the place where the old woman's hand joined the Dragon's. But she could also see Bellusdeo clearly, and she could see the moment the orange-red of her eyes shifted into a much less normal color: copper.

This wasn't the question Bellusdeo had been expecting—if she'd expected a question at all. It wasn't the question Kaylin had been expecting, or had thought to expect.

Helen was utterly silent as well. Everyone was.

This time, it was Bellusdeo who struggled to answer. There were no visible tears, but the color of the Dragon's eyes implied their existence. "Yes. Yes, I did."

"Did they look like you?"

Bellusdeo glanced in Kaylin's direction, but it was brief. Mrs. Erickson was difficult to ignore in the best of circumstances; she was impossible to ignore now. "Yes. I had eight sisters."

"None of them survived," Mrs. Erickson said.

"No."

Helen stepped in, bracketing Mrs. Erickson on one side, as

if she needed to make clear to Bellusdeo just how precious the older woman had become to the house.

Hope squawked. A lot. Kaylin lifted one hand to spare the ear closest to his mouth.

Bellusdeo had frozen at Hope's unintelligible words—words meant only for the Dragon.

She lifted her head; her grip became as tight, as desperate, as Mrs. Erickson's—which would not be good for Mrs. Erickson.

"It's all right," Helen said. "I have her. She will not be injured."

Bellusdeo didn't seem to hear Helen's words, she was so focused. "You can see the ghosts of the dead?"

Mrs. Erickson nodded, and Kaylin realized that she hadn't been staring at Bellusdeo; she'd been staring at the ghosts of the Dragon's beloved, dead sisters.

"You—you can see them? You can see my sisters?"

"I can," Mrs. Erickson answered, without the hesitance or self-consciousness that usually accompanied that confession. "It's difficult; they're all overlapping. I can only tell that you're not one of them because you're holding my hand." She exhaled and added, "They're weeping or silent. I don't think they're aware of each other."

"Are they aware of me?"

"I think so, but I can't be certain—they're not speaking."

"If they did, could you hear them?"

"She can," a new voice said. Sanabalis had finally left the dining room.

Whatever had driven Bellusdeo to visit Helen was no longer her primary concern. It was no longer a concern at all. Bellusdeo looked across the hall to the new Arkon, but the color of her eyes didn't change much; flecks of red intruded on copper, but copper remained dominant.

"I've never seen this before," Mrs. Erickson told Bellusdeo. "But they can hear me speak to you. I... I'd like to try to talk to them. Can I let go of your hand?"

Bellusdeo was the one whose grip was tightest; she released it slowly. "Yes, I'm sorry. Please try to talk to them. Please ask them…" The words trailed off. "Please do whatever you can to help them."

"I can see that you're very worried about these ghosts, and I know what that's like. But—can I ask you not to speak to me while I try to listen?"

Bellusdeo nodded mutely.

Kaylin had never seen the gold Dragon like this before.

Kaylin glanced at Sanabalis; his eyes were practically welded to Mrs. Erickson and Bellusdeo.

"You've carried them for so long," the old woman said softly. "I won't take them from you—I don't think they want to leave—but…would it be all right if they could move a bit? They're overlapping so much it's hard for me to tell them apart."

Bellusdeo's hands, resting on her thighs, were white-knuckled. Kaylin was grateful Mrs. Erickson had asked to have her hands free. "Yes," Bellusdeo said. "Give them anything they want, if it is within your power. Anything."

02

"This may take a little bit of time, and I'm afraid you'll only hear my side of the conversation—and it may be the same conversation eight times."

Bellusdeo closed her eyes and nodded, lowering her chin. Kaylin almost looked away. She had seen Bellusdeo angry before—even enraged—and she had seen her upset. But it had never been like this.

The ghosts Mrs. Erickson could see—ghosts Kaylin couldn't—were Bellusdeo's sisters, dead on a world that had, slowly, lost its war with Shadow. It had been consumed, and Bellusdeo had wandered in the Shadows that led to *Ravellon* until she had arrived on this world—the world into which she'd been born.

Kaylin had seen the corpses of those sisters in the morgue of the Halls of Law. But Bellusdeo had somehow kept their True Names within herself, and those names, they'd become part of Bellusdeo's name. They were inextricable elements of the adult Dragon name that Bellusdeo had finally adopted.

Maybe that was why nine little Bellusdeos had been hatched in an Aerie that had been empty for centuries. To forge one Bellusdeo, golden Dragon, queen of a vanquished, lost kingdom. That was what Kaylin had assumed, when she'd helped her friend's name form and cohere.

But even if that were true, these nine Dragons had been sisters and friends for the entirety of their life. Bellusdeo's rage at the outcaste Dragon was fueled in part by the loss of those sisters and their many voices. She had seen their number diminish during the course of the war, and in the end, she had been the last survivor.

Kaylin was annoyed with herself. She had assumed that Bellusdeo, having emerged into her adulthood, her full name established, had somehow subsumed those names, had made them a part of her. That she was, if not joyful, triumphant.

True Names weren't people. She had seen the words in the Barrani Lake of Life and she *knew* this. The name didn't give the infant for whom it was selected the memories of that previous life; it gave them the essence, but the life lived was separate, unique.

This was the first time she realized that Bellusdeo was not okay. She wasn't fine. She wasn't whole. She wasn't, in this moment, triumphant. The loss of those sisters had wounded her, and the scars had been too deep to vanish with time.

Mrs. Erickson's voice was gentle, even coaxing. Kaylin had heard her speak this way with Jamal and the other children. She spoke a few words and waited, the essence of patience, until she received a reply. It was a reply that no one in the room could hear except Mrs. Erickson—and Helen if she were eavesdropping in the particular way sentient buildings could.

When Sanabalis cleared his throat, Helen moved toward him, lifting a hand. "Kaylin?"

Kaylin nodded and joined them. Mandoran seemed rooted in place, staring at Bellusdeo, his hands flexing because there was nothing he could do.

"Yes," Helen said to Sanabalis, although the Dragon hadn't spoken. "Imelda is a shaman. We don't call her a Necromancer in this house, although that would not technically be incorrect; there are too many negative associations with that word. As you're aware, she's received no training. Only the experience of having ghosts as childhood friends and lifetime companions.

"You mentioned the Academia, and I believe some research there is in order, if Mrs. Erickson can receive the appropriate permissions."

"She can," Sanabalis said, voice soft. "Lannagaros has a deep affection for Bellusdeo. If Bellusdeo wishes to escort Mrs. Erickson to the Academia, he will see her, permission notwithstanding. And Bellusdeo has never been one to ask for permission." He hesitated, his eyes a copper shade. "Bellusdeo did not know of Mrs. Erickson.

"Do you know why she chose to visit?"

Helen nodded. "Her visit is personal in nature; it does not involve external danger or political strife."

"Meaning you will not discuss it."

"No. I have not been forbidden such discussions; it is left to my own discretion. But I believe this is something Bellusdeo should discuss with Kaylin—if she even remembers it at all now.

"If you meant to continue with Mrs. Erickson's lessons today—"

"No. I can see that this is going to take some time, and if Bellusdeo is willing to wait, I will not interfere." His eyes shaded back to their natural orange. "What she is willing to say to Kaylin—or Lannagaros—she will not say to me. I am the Arkon."

"He was the Arkon, too."

"Ah, yes. But he was her elder in the Aerie, and he had a strong wish to provide her with a sense of normalcy or continuity, duties aside. I was not, and cannot; what she accepted from Lannagaros, she will accept from no other member of the Dragon Court. She would possibly be enraged to notice that I am witness to this, and I will never mention it in her presence."

Kaylin wanted to know why Bellusdeo, in a foul mood, had

marched to the house, but she was certain that the irritation had been overwhelmed by Mrs. Erickson—or by what Mrs. Erickson saw.

At the end of the first hour, Mrs. Erickson had managed, with patience, to speak with—not to—two of the sisters; Kaylin half expected her old roommate and her new one would still be in the hall at the end of the normal workday.

Sanabalis was worried about Bellusdeo, and he had already been concerned about Mrs. Erickson. "I will speak with Lannagaros to arrange a meeting between Mrs. Erickson, Lord Bellusdeo, and him. I will also inform your sergeant that you have, indeed, been seconded by the Imperial Court."

"You did that."

"I implied that it was possibly necessary. There is now no possible about it."

Bellusdeo's voice was a pure draconic rumble as she turned her head in Sanabalis's direction. "Mrs. Erickson," she said, her eyes red, "is otherwise occupied."

Her words were punctuated by fire.

Helen suggested that Mrs. Erickson and Bellusdeo retreat to Mrs. Erickson's room, and given the gouts of flame Sanabalis's interruption had caused, this seemed like the smartest idea. Helen also suggested that Sanabalis retreat for the day. His regularly scheduled visit was a few days away, and she suggested that Bellusdeo might be calmer at that time.

She didn't suggest that Bellusdeo would be absent.

"I should go to work," Kaylin told Sanabalis. "There's no way Bellusdeo is leaving, and whatever problem she was having before, she's forgotten it."

"If Helen agrees to mirror you should an emergency arise, I suppose that would be *acceptable*."

Which was *no*. Behind Sanabalis, Mandoran was shaking his head.

"…or I could stay home just in case something happens."

"An excellent idea," Sanabalis said, smiling broadly, his eyes borderline red.

That was tough, Severn said. He was at work. He clearly wasn't out on patrol, because his beat partner was trapped in her home. Babysitting a traumatized Dragon and an old woman who could see the dead wasn't Severn's job.

And that was unfair. But there wasn't anything Kaylin could *do* here, and she knew work would be piling up. Dragon Lord or no, life didn't stop happening just because she'd been seconded.

Bad things came in threes. Seeing friends shouldn't be considered a bad thing.

"An'Teela is approaching the front door," Helen informed Kaylin. Kaylin had taken a seat at the dining room table, beside Mandoran, whose eyes were an uncharacteristic shade of blue, and had been since Bellusdeo had arrived. The Dragon hadn't left, but neither of them expected she would anytime soon.

Kaylin glared at Mandoran as she got to her feet. "You knew Teela was coming. You couldn't give me a heads-up?"

"She was going to come anyway. She's worried."

"Why is it fine for her to worry about me, but a deadly insult if I worry about her? No, don't answer that. It'll just piss me off."

Teela wasn't alone. Tain had accompanied her. Teela's eyes were a darker shade of blue than usual; Tain's, while blue, were lighter in color. He offered Kaylin a sympathetic nod—from the safely behind Teela's back.

"I hear you had quite a morning," Teela said, pushing her

way past Kaylin, who hadn't had enough time to step out of the doorway.

Kaylin frowned. Teela's eyes had been dark blue before she'd invited herself in. Something other than Kaylin's situation was bothering the Barrani Hawk.

Tain joined them, glancing briefly at Teela.

"We have a case that was opened and closed just before you joined us as our mascot. It might be open again."

Kaylin frowned. "Caste court closure?"

Teela nodded. "As you're aware—sometimes loudly—caste court exemptions can be called when the crimes involve only the race over which the caste courts preside. Any member of the race itself, when affected by a crime, can demand an Imperial investigation, regardless."

If the investigation had been halted due to the caste court, it meant none of the victims of the crime had been willing to go against the caste court's decision. In Barrani exemption cases, the reasons for that were clear: anyone who spoke against the exemption usually had a fatal accident shortly thereafter. That murder, along with the prior crime, was also under the laws of exemption.

It was the reason there were very, very few interracial crimes at high levels of power.

"What did the Barrani do this time? Did you find someone else involved in whatever that crime was?"

"I didn't say it was the Barrani caste court but thank you for jumping to that conclusion."

"Come on—you know as well as I do that the Barrani are the worst exemption exploiters." Even in cases where the crimes involved other races, the caste court interfered: the suspected criminal wound up as a corpse, sometimes on the literal front steps of the Halls of Law.

"They are. It's expected of my people; it's the reason Barrani crimes are generally kept in check. Without the weight—and disapproval—of the caste court, the Barrani would feel far freer to act. We are a people who value power—and power must be visible to be acknowledged. Mortals are clearly less powerful; were it not for the Eternal Emperor, there would be far, far less safety from some of the Barrani than mortals currently enjoy.

"But in this case, a surprise exemption demand came from the human caste court."

Kaylin frowned. In all of the years she had dogged Teela's footsteps, there'd never been an exemption requested from the human caste court. "The Emperor accepted it?"

"He wrote the laws that were being invoked. Yes, he accepted it."

Kaylin glanced at Tain; his face was a mask, his lips closed. He did shoot Teela a subtle glance, but she'd clearly decided to ignore the silent opinion. Kaylin had known them for almost half her life; she knew Tain didn't want Teela to speak about this publicly. Or at least not to Kaylin.

"You think you've found someone who can stand against the exemption rules."

"It's a possibility."

"I don't disagree with your intentions—you know how much I hate exemption exceptions. But why are you pushing this when you never care about Barrani exemptions?"

Tain tapped Teela on the shoulder. "Not here," he said, voice low. "Why don't we go out for a drink?"

"Only if you two promise not to start a stupid brawl." It had been a while since she'd gone out drinking with Teela and Tain. The last time, Bellusdeo had joined them. And Mandoran. "But maybe that might not be a terrible idea. Do you mind if I bring company?"

Teela shot Tain an almost venomous glare, which was unusual.

Tain ignored it. "As long as it's the same company as last time."

"You're going to regret that," Teela murmured, but as she

exhaled, some of the tension left her shoulders. Until it did, Kaylin hadn't realized how strong it had been. "Fine. Ask Bellusdeo, if that's who you had in mind."

"About that..." She glanced at Tain. "Has Teela informed you about the morning's excitement here?"

"I inferred it, given her insistence that we visit Helen."

Kaylin filled him in on what he'd missed.

She'd gotten to the halfway point when Bellusdeo strode into the dining room. Helen sometimes brought the parlor to life when Kaylin had guests, but Teela and Tain didn't quite qualify. They therefore headed into the dining room, as it was the most common gathering spot in the house.

"We've permission to visit Lannagaros in the Academia," Bellusdeo announced.

The gold Dragon was wearing the large plate scales that formed armor when a Dragon was otherwise naked.

Had Bellusdeo been alone, Kaylin would have felt less concerned. Bellusdeo did not arrive alone. Mrs. Erickson was in tow.

"You don't plan on flying across the city—which is illegal—do you?" Kaylin asked, without much hope.

Bellusdeo grinned. Given the color of her eyes, no one voiced any further objections, but Bellusdeo grudgingly added, "Mrs. Erickson seemed quite intrigued at the idea of flying on Dragon back. Stop it. You'll make Mrs. Erickson feel guilty. The Arkon gained permission for the flight."

Hope squawked loudly.

Bellusdeo frowned, and glanced at Helen, not Kaylin.

"It's true, dear," Helen said—to the Dragon. Although her voice was soft, it could be heard clearly over Hope's continued squawking. "Your ghosts are not the only ghosts Mrs. Erickson is seeking to comfort, and the other ghosts have already proven dangerous. I am not certain why you wish to visit the

Academia immediately—you seemed somewhat opposed to it this morning."

Because Sanabalis had suggested it, of course.

Mrs. Erickson coughed. It was her way of interrupting. "If possible, I wish to learn more about my abilities—as quickly as possible. Bellusdeo agrees and has offered to escort me."

Hope squawked in obvious disgust and pushed himself off Kaylin's shoulder, heading up the stairs the Dragon had only half descended.

"He is going to remain near the other ghosts," Helen said. "He feels you will not be at risk at the Academia."

"But you can watch them, can't you?"

Helen's smile was complicated. It was as close to uncertainty as she got. "I would appreciate the help," she finally said.

Teela, dragging Tain, went in search of the rest of the cohort. Bellusdeo, Mrs. Erickson, and Kaylin went up to the tower that had the retracting roof. From there, Bellusdeo could take off safely.

Mrs. Erickson wasn't as unsettled as Kaylin would have expected. She had some difficulty climbing the Dragon, but Kaylin was there to help.

Technically, flying as a Dragon in the city was illegal without express Imperial permission, which was far less likely to be given in broad daylight, which this still was. The sun was edging toward the horizon, but hadn't reached it yet.

The streets below the Dragon's wings were a mass of wagons, emptier than they had been at the start of the day, headed toward various stables, some on the edge of the city boundaries, and some outside its walls.

Kaylin sat behind Mrs. Erickson. If Mrs. Erickson wasn't afraid, she wasn't accustomed to any of this. If she fell, Kaylin would feel both guilty and enraged. She did her best to watch for any instability, any hint that Mrs. Erickson might teeter over one side of the Dragon or the other.

Mrs. Erickson didn't notice. She was considerate by nature, but at the moment careful consideration had given way to awe and delight; were it not for her obvious age, she might have been a child.

Helen had said Mrs. Erickson's childhood must have been difficult because of her power. Given that Kaylin's childhood had hovered on the edge of starvation and cold, she hadn't thought much of it. But she wondered, seated behind Mrs. Erickson, if Helen might not have been right.

She wanted to ask Mrs. Erickson what she'd managed to achieve in regard to Bellusdeo's ghosts, but she couldn't have that conversation while on the Dragon's back; she'd be shouting at the top of her lungs, Bellusdeo was flying so quickly.

Whatever the reason, Sanabalis had seen fit to get Bellusdeo permission to fly in Dragon mode; he was the Arkon, and he had a direct line of communication to the Emperor.

Unless Bellusdeo had lied.

She wouldn't, would she? Not if she was carrying Mrs. Erickson?

Had Kaylin not been so physically tense, she would have wilted. It was Bellusdeo. Of course she would.

She didn't have much time to really build stomach-twisting anxiety, because at Bellusdeo's speed, half the city passed by in an eyeblink; taking off and landing took more time than the rest of the journey.

A second Dragon joined Bellusdeo as she approached the Academia; from the air, it could clearly be seen. That Dragon, red and slightly larger, was familiar: Lord Tiamaris, of both the Dragon Court and the fief of Tiamaris. He, unlike Bellusdeo, had no rider. He did have a voice, and a volley of Draconian thundered across the air that separated them.

Bellusdeo didn't even turn her head; Kaylin was certain she was aware of Tiamaris but considered his presence either an annoyance or irrelevant. Or both. She never stood on ceremony, but any situation when she felt someone was demanding behavior when they had no hierarchical right to do so never turned out well for the demandee.

Since they'd cut across the fief Tiamaris ruled, Kaylin felt a polite reply would have been in order. Bellusdeo clearly didn't; she sped up—which Kaylin would have bet was impossible—heading straight for the grassy quad at the center of the Academia's oval road.

Barrani and mortal students bolted in any direction that took them away from the quad's center as not one, but two, Dragons landed. The quad certainly looked a lot smaller when it was occupied by two gigantic Dragons.

"Get off," Bellusdeo said, in curt Elantran. The words rumbled beneath Kaylin; she could practically feel the two syllables. She slid off, and then turned to Mrs. Erickson, who was staring at Tiamaris, eyes wide.

"I've never seen a flying Dragon before today, and now I've seen two," she said. Kaylin offered her a hand, and then shifted to offer both open arms.

Mrs. Erickson managed to jump off—closing her eyes at the last moment as she collided with Kaylin. She didn't weigh much. Kaylin wondered if she'd been eating properly. And then grimaced and wondered if she'd been spending too much time with either Mrs. Erickson or Caitlin.

"This is the Academia?" Mrs. Erickson asked, when her feet were on solid ground again.

Kaylin nodded. "If I were you, I'd cover your ears," she told the old woman, lifting both of her hands to cover hers.

"Why?"

"Both Dragons have deeply orange eyes, which means they're about to start shouting at each other—in their native tongue."

"Oh, dear. Should I not have come?"

"It's got nothing to do with you—they'd be shouting at each other even if you stayed at home. Bellusdeo flew over Tiamaris's fief—obviously without warning or permission. She ignored him when he met her in the air. It was rude, and Tiamaris doesn't appreciate bad manners." She glanced at her shoulder; she'd forgotten that she'd left Hope at home.

She'd really gotten used to the little lizard over the past year.

Mrs. Erickson didn't raise her hands. Possibly because it would have been rude. Kaylin really needed to work on her delivery.

The argument sounded like a terrible storm—without the lightning—when the doors to the main building of the Academia flew open and a robed and orange-eyed man marched down the wide front steps toward the two Dragons. Kaylin lowered her hands instantly, although the Dragons were still going strong.

The former Arkon, the current chancellor of the Academia, did not condescend to join Bellusdeo and Tiamaris in draconic form, but he certainly didn't spare them the draconic voice; he *roared*.

Bellusdeo and Tiamaris stopped midroar, two Dragon heads turning in the direction of the chancellor, whose eyes were not orange as Kaylin had assumed at a distance; they were red with flecks of orange. The only thing stopping him from exhaling literal fire was the grass and trees in the quad; they probably wouldn't survive it, and they were part of the Academia. Which was his. His hoard.

"I will hear your reasons for this disgraceful behavior in my office. Now."

"Oh, dear," Mrs. Erickson whispered.

The two Dragons receded in size until they were plate-armored humans, at least in shape. One wore gold plate, the other red. They glared at each other, but when the chancellor turned and walked—heavily—toward the main building, they followed.

Bellusdeo, however, turned back to Kaylin and snapped, "Don't even think of avoiding this."

"I wasn't the one who broke the rules and deafened the students in the quad," Kaylin pointed out.

"And?"

She exhaled. "Fine. You go ahead. I'll lead Mrs. Erickson to the office."

"Do they not like each other?" Mrs. Erickson asked, as they walked—slowly and infinitely less dramatically—up the stairs.

"They care about each other," a new voice said.

Mrs. Erickson looked up as the building's Avatar—Killianas, Killian for short—appeared at the height of the steps, framed by an open door. He smiled, his smile so gentle it almost looked like a mask. Killian had a Barrani face, and Barrani didn't smile like this.

"I am happy to welcome you to the Academia." His smile deepened. "Yes, I am like Helen, although we have two different imperatives. Mine is the Academia, and the protection of the students who reside here." The smile dimmed. "I apologize; the chancellor is not generally in as foul a mood as he is today, but he is angry at the two Dragons, not at you."

"Or me?"

"He is mildly irritated with you as he believes you have some sway over Bellusdeo—but his ire is focused on the two Dragons. While he expects you to join them in the office, might I suggest we take a small tour of the building before we arrive there? It should give them time to calm down."

Or try to kill each other, but Killian would prevent the damage Dragons fighting would otherwise cause anywhere else in the city.

"Did Bellusdeo get permission to visit?"

"Permission is not generally required—for Bellusdeo."

"So that's a no." There were some days it didn't pay to get out of bed. No wonder Hope had disappeared.

"Yes, I noticed the lack of your familiar. It is unusual."

"Do you know if Bellusdeo intends to visit the Arbiters?"

"She is not entirely certain what she intends." He then turned back to Mrs. Erickson. "I apologize for the noise; I assure you that this is a highly unusual occurrence in the Academia."

Mrs. Erickson shook her head, smiling up at Killian. "If anyone should apologize, it isn't you. And I wouldn't have the courage to demand an apology from three rather angry Dragons. Should I wait, or is it safe now?" She glanced at Kaylin as she spoke.

"I'm a Hawk," Kaylin replied, knowing just who Mrs. Erickson was worried about.

"Yes, dear, but we're both only mortal."

It was, according to Killian, safe. Kaylin stayed by Mrs. Erickson's side through one change of classes, the only time that the Academia halls were full of loud, boisterous students. There were quiet students as well, but they didn't have to be avoided. Killian's Avatar remained by Mrs. Erickson's side, so the student body largely avoided colliding with her—if not each other—and the walk to the chancellor's office was orderly, if not silent.

Killian gently explained the Academia schedule as he walked. Mrs. Erickson always wanted to know everything, because everything was interesting to her. But maybe it would be—she'd become so accustomed to bringing home interesting stories to her children. To the ghosts that she had, with effort and at great risk, finally released from their captivity within the walls of her house.

Mrs. Erickson would never have trapped them there, but her life had been built around them; free of the responsibility of four dead, unaging children, she had to find a different life, a different path, for herself. It would have been hard for Kaylin; she imagined it would be all but impossible for a gentle old woman. But Mrs. Erickson approached life as if it were a gift, unasked for and unexpected.

"Evening classes are less numerous, but the first dinner has just let out, which is why the halls appear to be so busy. Some students will be heading for the late dinner hour."

Mrs. Erickson had never learned how to hide her joy; her eyes became almost luminous. For a person who was technically a Necromancer, she found joy in life in a way that Kaylin wished she could emulate.

Joy was a little less evident as they reached the chancellor's closed doors.

"Have they stopped arguing?" Kaylin whispered.

"They have stopped discussing their differences in their native tongue."

Good enough. She hoped that the room wasn't full of red-eyed, bristling Dragons; orange was the new gold.

The chancellor was behind his desk, that great divider that made clear to anyone who entered who was in charge here.

Bellusdeo and Tiamaris were seated—stiffly, given their armor—in chairs large enough to accommodate them comfortably, if one ignored the fact that neither wanted to sit in the first place. Eyes had remained orange, but barely.

The chancellor looked up as the door opened; Kaylin and Mrs. Erickson were bracketed by the doorframe. "Corporal."

Kaylin lifted a hand. "I'm off duty."

"Kaylin, then. Won't you introduce your companion?"

"This is Mrs. Erickson."

"Ah. Lord Sanabalis has mentioned her." To Mrs. Erickson, he added, "He believes you are a Necromancer. What do you believe?"

03

Mrs. Erickson was silent. Kaylin tried not to hover protectively around her; this was easier, because Bellusdeo was hovering enough for two. The gold Dragon, on the other hand, was hovering impatiently, which made her presence less comforting.

The chancellor had asked the question of Mrs. Erickson, and he seemed content to wait for her response; his glare made clear that no one else was to speak for her, but his voice had been almost gentle, if you took his general grouchiness into account.

Mrs. Erickson exhaled, well aware that everyone was waiting on her answer. Her hands remained by her sides, but her shoulders were slumped; she straightened them. "I think that's a bit harsh," she said quietly. "But all I know of Necromancers are children's stories."

"Which stories?"

"The ones in which Necromancers—evil villains, all—raised an army of the undead and used it to attack the hero."

"Ah. These are not stories we were told as children."

"Oh?" Her eyes brightened. "What stories were you told as children?"

"Stories about the terrible deaths of hatchlings at the hands of their infuriated guardians and parents."

She winced, but her lips then turned up in a smile because the chancellor was smiling fondly.

"The Imperial College is rather dry," the former Arkon said. "The word, to the scholars of the ancient, is a classification, a category. It does not, in theory, involve moral or ethical judgment at all. Judgment," he added, "is what we bring to it."

She nodded.

"To be fair, while we call it a classification, Necromancy has not been considered a practical class of magic such as would be studied in the Imperial College or the Arcanum; there is just enough historical information that implies something genuine at the root of the various stories children tell. You are therefore going to be of great interest to those whose studies encompass magical history." He cleared his throat.

Mrs. Erickson met his gaze head-on, although her hands trembled.

Bellusdeo roared. Her hands were fists, and her eyes were red.

Tiamaris roared as well, and not to be outdone, his eyes were crimson.

The former Arkon was clearly accustomed to this; his eyes, while orange, didn't darken at all. If anything, he looked slightly bored. "If the two of you wish to continue this...disappointing fracas, I suggest you do it outside." The doors to the office swung open—probably at Killian's behest. "And do not mistake me: I mean outside of the Academia grounds. Mrs. Erickson has come for a reason, but it is almost impossible to hear her at the moment."

Before Bellusdeo could speak again, the chancellor lifted a hand. "I am serious, Bellusdeo. You are always welcome in any home I call mine, but your interference is not."

"I'm the reason she came here at all!"

"Indeed. And I understand that she volunteered to accompany you. But there are some things to which she should not be exposed at any length, and a petty argument between my kin is one of them. And you, Tiamaris," he said, his voice far less gentle than it had been when he spoke to Bellusdeo, "as a lord of both the Dragon Court and the fief of Tiamaris, how is it that you have been drawn into a pointless, petty squabble in such a fashion?"

Tiamaris wisely failed to answer.

Red eyes faded to resentful orange. Had Mrs. Erickson not been present, Kaylin would have sympathized, even empathized. But she was, and the chancellor was right: she shouldn't be subject to screaming Dragons.

"Very good. My apologies for the interruption, Mrs. Erickson. Where were we?"

"You were speaking about Necromancers," she replied. She had lived with squabbling children—if ghosts—for all of her life, if one didn't count the past few weeks. She could probably pick out a petty sibling squabble from a mile away.

"Yes."

"I'm not sure if you know, but I live with a sentient building."

"You live with Kaylin," the chancellor said, nodding. "I am aware of Helen."

"Isn't she lovely?"

He blinked. Kaylin, expecting this, didn't. While she wouldn't be as gushing and effusive as Mrs. Erickson now was, she didn't disagree with anything the older woman was saying. The former Arkon weathered the inundation of happy, delighted praise for a full ten minutes before he lifted a hand.

Mrs. Erickson had the grace to redden. "Helen and I have discussed my abilities a bit. Helen didn't say I was a Necromancer; she said I was possibly a shaman."

The chancellor frowned. Bellusdeo frowned.

"Ah—she said it wasn't a common word, and it was used—

I can't honestly remember how long ago. One of her tenants had some experience with someone Helen called a shaman."

"That tenant was not from Elantra, then."

"I'm not sure Elantra existed at that time," Mrs. Erickson replied. "She didn't speak the same language that Kaylin and I do, but Helen can understand any language."

"Indeed. I spent some time in the Imperial College—as a lecturer," he added, in case there was any confusion.

Given the number of Imperial Mages Kaylin had met in the line of duty, she felt the clarification was justified; the Arkon—argh, the chancellor, damn it—was head and shoulders above those mages. Hells, they probably came up to his ankles, figuratively speaking.

"*Shaman* was not a term that was in use there."

"And *Necromancer* was?" Bellusdeo asked, the question sharp.

"No, not often; it was perhaps used as a humorous term, after exams. What did Helen say of shamans?"

"They can both sense and speak with the dead—the dead who are somehow trapped in our world. The dead who haven't, or can't, pass on. Shamans didn't raise armies of the undead in Helen's stories."

"And you have never raised an army of the dead."

"No," Mrs. Erickson said. There was a tiny hesitation before the denial.

"She hasn't raised an army of the dead," Kaylin said, voice flat. Since she was surrounded by Dragons, she attempted to keep irritation out of her tone.

"I did not imply that she had, but perhaps my humor was too dry for those accustomed to bombast."

Normally Kaylin would assume the dig was aimed at her, but given Bellusdeo and Tiamaris's presence, she couldn't feel singled out, even if she was the one who'd spoken up.

"Very well. Bellusdeo has asked—as a favor," he added, glaring at the gold Dragon, "that you be allowed to consult with the Arbiters."

"The librarians?" Mrs. Erickson asked.

"Indeed. They are a bit unusual, as librarians go. I must ask: Can you speak Barrani?"

Mrs. Erickson nodded. "Not well, and not a lot of it. I learned when I was a child. My parents had hope for my education. But I haven't had to use it very much in my day-to-day life. Will the librarians speak it?"

"It is the preferred language of speech when they deal with the student body. Arbiter Starrante may, however, be well enough versed in Elantran that he can speak it, should the need arise." The chancellor rose from behind his desk. His eyes were orange, but the color shifted almost imperceptibly as he looked at Bellusdeo. "I wish to know why you all but insisted that both you and Mrs. Erickson be given such permissions."

Bellusdeo, for once, was silent; her throat moved as she swallowed words without ever giving them voice.

It was Mrs. Erickson who answered. "If you've spoken with Lord Sanabalis at all, you'll know that I can see the dead."

"All of the dead?"

She shook her head. "Helen says that what I see are the remnants of the dead, trapped in the living world where they no longer belong. Not every dead person leaves such a ghost.

"But some of the dead are trapped, and those, I can see. I can speak with them."

"Go on."

Now, she glanced at the gold Dragon as if for permission; Bellusdeo nodded. "There are eight ghosts bound tightly to Lord Bellusdeo."

The chancellor froze; he placed one hand on the surface of the desk, as if to steady his weight. He, too, was silent for a long beat, his eyes practically glued to Bellusdeo, although his words—when he did speak—were meant for Mrs. Erickson. "Do those eight ghosts resemble Lord Bellusdeo?"

"Every single one of them."

"I see." The chancellor's eyes became copper, the Dragon color of grief. "I understand, now, the urgency of Bellusdeo's request. I will escort you to the library; the Arbiters have been informed that a matter of some urgency to the fieflord requires their attention. They have not been informed of what that matter is, as I myself did not know." His smile was careworn but gentle. "I won't make you explain it twice; I will hear it with the Arbiters."

Lord Tiamaris chose to leave the Academia, his conflict with Lord Bellusdeo either forgotten or paused. From the chancellor's expression, he understood that this was somehow personal for the other two Dragons, and Tiamaris had never been entirely comfortable with the personal.

Serralyn and Valliant were somewhere in the Academia, but neither showed up to interrupt the walk to the library. Kaylin couldn't tell if Terrano had made his way here, either; Hope wasn't on her shoulder, so she had no way of seeing invisible things.

Most days, she forgot about Hope, he'd become so much part of her shoulder. She was surprised at how much she missed his presence, given the way he bit her or squawked his displeasure in her ear. She wondered why he hadn't insisted on accompanying her; it made her uneasy. Helen had been worried about her new occupants. Not Mrs. Erickson, whom she seemed to adore, but rather Mrs. Erickson's new ghosts. Ghosts whose origins, whose forms while alive, were completely unknown.

Ghosts that had somehow taken possession of the new Arkon, Sanabalis, which was why Mrs. Erickson had had to move in with Kaylin; Sanabalis considered her a very real danger. She'd had no intent to somehow cause those ghosts to possess Sanabalis, but her intent hadn't mattered.

Kaylin shook her head; she'd come to a halt and didn't notice until Killian tapped her shoulder. "Sorry," she murmured.

"The Arkon is right to be concerned," he replied. Kaylin's thoughts were an open book to all of the sentient buildings she knew; whatever it took to both think and simultaneously mask those thoughts was a skill she was never going to understand, let alone possess.

"But Mrs. Erickson, like you, is an open book. I concur with both your assessment and Helen's. She has no ill intent. She is worried, at the moment."

"About Bellusdeo?"

Killian's smile was gentle. "Indeed. Her concern does not seem to be for herself. But she is worried that her presence, her possible power, will endanger others. At the moment, concern for Bellusdeo displaces that—but that fear has not been far from the surface since the Arkon's unfortunate possession."

"Are you allowed to tell me all this?"

"She is not a student," was the soft reply.

"Do you think the Arbiters will have anything useful to say?"

"Possibly. It is my hope that Arbiters Kavallac and Androsse will remain largely silent. They have been more fervent in their disagreement in the past few weeks; we have had to curtail all library visits during the worst of their arguments."

Kaylin winced; she had her doubts. She'd never been that lucky.

The library doors opened as the chancellor approached. Beyond them was the vast and endless library the Arbiters protected. The entrance was a portal, which usually gave Kaylin hives, but the library portal had never been normal. Not that she was complaining.

Starrante was the first visible Arbiter. At any other time, Kaylin would have worried about Mrs. Erickson's reaction—but the old woman had already met Wevaran, and she knew they were friendly. While she didn't lift her arms in the standard Wevaran greeting, she did offer him a normal, mortal one: she smiled and said hello in a bright, cheerful voice.

"I am Arbiter Starrante. Bakkon has visited to inform me of the recent events in your home. I see, in spite of the difficulty, you are well," Starrante replied, in Elantran.

"I am—I'm trying to adjust to all the changes in my life."

"Changes?"

"I'm living with Helen and Kaylin," Mrs. Erickson replied. "And her family of Barrani friends."

Those weren't the only friends. Starrante's visible eyes shifted slightly. "I hear that you have other…roommates?"

Mrs. Erickson nodded.

"They came from the Imperial Palace. Oh." She stopped and grimaced. "I'm not certain I'm supposed to mention them."

"It is safe to mention anything within the library; no harm will befall you. You are not the only person who has visited our library in some urgency in the past few days. We hope we may answer more of your questions than his, in the end."

Mrs. Erickson glanced around the library; books went on to infinity, shelves stretched so high it was hard to see their tops except at a great distance. "You couldn't find answers here?" She seemed confused.

"The library contains all books that have ever been written, many in languages that even scholars cannot easily decipher. But some things are never written. Some knowledge is not preserved in books; it passes from mother to child, master to student, and it is lost far more easily, hidden more completely.

"Nor do we know the contents of every book that abides here. There are some that we have not—or will not—touch; not all books of old are safe for unwary readers; some are not safe for even the most powerful."

"We're not here to talk about that," Bellusdeo snapped. She had chosen Elantran, possibly for Mrs. Erickson's sake.

The chancellor cleared his throat in warning.

Bellusdeo was good at ignoring warnings when she was distressed or angry; she was both, but the anger was the lesser of the two.

"I understand," the chancellor said, as he placed a hand on her shoulder. "But the Arbiters are older by far than either you or I, and their learning encompasses the whole of that existence. Treat them with the respect that knowledge deserves."

"In my experience," a new, and unwelcome to Kaylin, voice said, "Dragons have never understood the need for proper respect." Arbiter Androsse had arrived.

"And your people did?" The response was a low rumble. Although Kaylin liked Kavallac, this wasn't the right time for the Dragon Arbiter's arrival.

"Our people were accorded the respect due the powerful," Androsse replied.

Kavallac roared.

The chancellor sighed, and the Wevaran Arbiter's eyes shut, briefly, in one wave across the body. Lannagaros glanced at Starrante, who nodded.

"I believe," the chancellor said, with obvious disgust, "that we must retreat to my office for the time being. Arbiter Starrante will join us there."

"But the books are here—"

"I will need to confer with Mrs. Erickson in order to ascertain which books might be of interest."

Androsse surprised Kaylin: he roared as well. Even if the other two had something to contribute, they weren't going to get to it today.

Starrante arrived in the office by teleporting to it. He was in the room before the chancellor had managed to return there, but clearly he had the chancellor's permission.

"I apologize for my colleagues," the Wevaran said. He was

hanging in a space between shelves; Killian had obviously cleared it for his use. "Incidents in the Academia have caused heated disagreements which have not yet been resolved."

Given the personality of the two Arbiters, "not yet" might cover another century or two.

"They do not always disagree in this fashion, but when they really lose their tempers, the library is not safe for students. Or visitors."

The chancellor snorted.

"They're always like that?" Bellusdeo asked.

"No, as Arbiter Starrante implied. At the moment, minor collegial disagreements become major arguments at the turn of a sentence. If they were my students, I would consider strangling them or jailing them until they promised to behave like rational adults."

"I'm just surprised neither of them are trying to pressure you into choosing a side," Kaylin muttered to the Wevaran.

She could swear Starrante chuckled. "I was chosen as Arbiter for a reason. Not one of the three us could fall victim to such pressure. I'm perhaps not as...aggressive in temperament as either of my colleagues, but I am fully capable of defending myself. I am also the only Arbiter who is free to leave the library, although I am confined to the Academia grounds.

"In other words, I simply leave if the discussion is unproductive." He then turned to Mrs. Erickson. "I apologize again for their ill temper. I have done some research within the many tomes of our library, and I believe—although perhaps I am mistaken—that Arbiter Androsse has some slender experience with the field of study."

Mrs. Erickson nodded.

Kaylin assumed *field of study* meant Necromancy, but didn't bother to clarify; she didn't like the word. Or rather, didn't like it anywhere in the vicinity of Mrs. Erickson.

"He is, in my opinion, the most difficult to deal with. For

today, I wish to hear what brought you—personally—to the Academia. I am aware of your recent difficulties, and I believe we owe you at least that much, given the outcome."

"It's not about me, not exactly," Mrs. Erickson said. She had taken a seat, as had Kaylin; Bellusdeo was pacing, gold armor glinting in the room's light.

"Bellusdeo," the chancellor said.

She turned on the spot to glare at him.

"I understand your concern, but wearing a hole in the floor will not assuage it."

"You don't understand my concern," she snapped, rumbling, her eyes flickering between orange and red. The draconic undertone left her voice as she turned to Mrs. Erickson. "Tell him. Tell him what you told me."

"Will you be all right, dear?"

Bellusdeo's nod was shaky.

Mrs. Erickson turned her attention to Starrante. "You know I can see ghosts."

"Yes."

"I can't always tell the difference between the living and the dead."

"That must have been difficult when you were a child."

"Childhood was so long ago, I hardly remember," was the serene reply. It was as close to a lie as Mrs. Erickson could get. "I know now to check for simple things like shadows. Ghosts don't have them. Mostly. But it's not exact, and sometimes when the streets are too crowded, I make mistakes." She glanced at Bellusdeo and then squared her shoulders.

"Bellusdeo's ghosts have one shadow: hers. They're clustered around her, and they overlap. It makes Bellusdeo difficult to see at times."

"Are they always present?"

"I believe so. It's a bit hard to separate them. That many people don't usually all stand in the same place."

"Do you know their names?"

Mrs. Erickson hesitated.

"You have my permission to tell him anything you want. Anything at all," Bellusdeo said, voice low.

"They...don't think they have names."

Kaylin stiffened, her hands curling into fists in her lap.

"Pardon?"

"They don't remember their names. When I tried to ask, none of them could answer." She hesitated again, and then exhaled. "It was difficult to get answers because most of them were crying."

The chancellor looked to Bellusdeo. In a much softer voice than he had yet used when speaking to the Dragon, he said, "I understand, now, why you felt this matter so urgent."

Bellusdeo was silent.

He turned once again to Mrs. Erickson. "Are they crying now?"

Mrs. Erickson wanted to say no. Kaylin could see that clearly. But after a long hesitation, she nodded. "Not all of them," she added. "But yes."

"She can speak to them," Bellusdeo said. "She can hear them. I didn't even know they were there." Turning to Kaylin, she said, "You've never seen them."

"No."

"You could see the ghosts of the children in Mrs. Erickson's home."

Kaylin nodded.

"Do you think your familiar was aware?"

"I don't know—it's not something I would have ever thought of asking. But I've looked at you through Hope's wing before, and I've only ever seen one of you."

Starrante cleared his throat. "Was it your wish to learn more about Necromancy in order to speak with the dead Mrs. Erickson sees?"

Bellusdeo was silent.

"If I understand the very complicated coming-of-age procedure for Dragons, they are not dead. There should be no ghosts." When Bellusdeo turned toward the Wevaran, he said, "Our coming-of-age is also complicated, and it involves the deaths of all of our clutch mates in the birthing place." He held up a limb as Bellusdeo's eyes darkened. "I am not saying you were forced to devour your siblings. I am not implying that you are responsible for their deaths.

"Wevaran and Dragons are older races. With the Barrani, the process is simpler. With mortals, the process is simpler still, although mortals are ephemeral in comparison.

"The Necromancy you envision is a story meant to frighten the young or entertain an audience. It requires, among other things, a corpse. If such a school of magic existed, I believe it would prove ruinous for you, if it had any effect at all: You are not dead. You are not a corpse."

Corpse.

Kaylin said nothing.

"Mrs. Erickson can see ghosts; I will trust the corporal's observations in this regard. She cannot will them into being; she cannot give them physical form. If you wish her to somehow free the ghosts she sees—"

"I don't." Bellusdeo's interruption was sharp, instant. "I just want her to somehow make them visible to me. I want to be able to speak with them, as she does. I want to ask—" She stopped.

In as gentle a voice as Kaylin had ever heard Starrante use, he said, "I do not believe she can do what you desire. She can serve as interpreter, as she has clearly done, but she cannot somehow alter your eyes or their state to allow you to see them, hear them, or speak directly with them."

Bellusdeo didn't believe him. Or didn't want to believe him.

Kaylin's worry deepened. One word—one name—had come to mind and it stuck there: Azoria. Azoria An'Berranin.

Azoria hadn't had Mrs. Erickson's natural gift. She couldn't see ghosts. She could, however, make them. She had separated spirits from their bodies, trapping those spirits. Binding them somehow to both her will and the world in which Kaylin and Mrs. Erickson otherwise lived. Azoria could see spirits, those almost-ghosts, while their bodies still existed.

It wasn't Necromancy as Kaylin understood it—if *understood* was even the right word, given that anything she knew came from stories and reports made to the public desk of the Halls of Law, not reality. Azoria's magic had been a warped, twisted, subtle horror that no one but Azoria had clearly understood. Azoria was—thank whatever gods actually existed—dead. In Kaylin's opinion, she'd been so close to dead for such a long time, it was hard to think that she'd been alive when they'd first encountered her.

She certainly hadn't been Barrani by the end of that life.

Mrs. Erickson could see the spirits Azoria had extracted and trapped as ghosts.

But Mrs. Erickson could also see Darreno and Amaldi, and neither of them had been dead. Azoria had learned something different, something that overlapped Mrs. Erickson's natural skills. What would she have been capable of had she been able to possess Mrs. Erickson?

What had Azoria learned from manipulating the dead Ancient in the outlands?

Kaylin's head hurt. "Arbiter Starrante, tell us what you know of the historical roots of Necromancy." She spoke Barrani, although she'd had to hit Records to find the word for Necromancer in Barrani before she'd come to the Academia.

"Necromancy is an almost entirely mortal contrivance. We who are Immortal are blessed—or cursed—with True Names, True Words. Death for us is an ending that is different in all ways than the wise understood from death for your kind. But mortals have existed in the shadows and margins of all worlds for a very, very long time.

"Mortals have often been concerned with death, with dying, with the very nature of mortality itself. You are aware of the stories—and perhaps the truths—of their unending battle against their very nature. Some mortals struggle with the sense of ending; they do not or cannot believe that death itself is the end. From this belief arose many—but not all—mortal religions.

"The fact of ghosts, the fact of what Mrs. Erickson sees, provides some glimmer of truth in the belief that death itself is not an ending for mortals.

"I believe that those individuals who were gifted as Mrs. Erickson is gifted gave rise to the belief in the spiritual among mortals: she can see the dead." He lifted a limb before words fell out of Kaylin's mouth. "The Ancients are, and have always been, above our comprehension. Studies, in *Ravellon*, when *Ravellon* was the heart of all worlds, were done. Those who consented to aid in this research were mortals; the research was longer, by far, than a single mortal's life span.

"The gift itself is not a singular thing, as research showed. It is like any other magical gift: there is a greater—or lesser—power to be found in individuals. This is true of magical gifts in any individuals of any race. Some are more talented than others. Necromancy—and it was not designated as such, as it could not be taught or learned—was similar. Some were more gifted than others.

"But a few of the people who had consented to this long study—much of it lost, with *Ravellon*—felt that the dead they could see were not all of the dead; they were...displaced. They were trapped. There was a strong sense that the dead—the mortal dead—should not be here. In a few cases, what they called remnants were powerful enough to trouble the living, or to harm them.

"Understand that to the Immortal, the harm these ghosts

could do was minimal; it was hardly notable at all. Or so it was believed. But scholars are scholars for a reason; some become enamored of their chosen areas of research, even if that research yielded no obviously practical results. I have been accused of such focus in my time.

"Ah, but I digress. What remains of that research are the notebooks inscribed during some of the studies."

They were contained in the library. Kaylin didn't understand how new books appeared in the vast and endless archive, but she knew the Arbiters believed all books of any kind made their way to this singular collection.

"There were, during the centuries of research, three subjects considered of import and note."

Bellusdeo resumed her pacing. She was patient enough—barely—not to interrupt the Arbiter, but he clearly wasn't answering her questions.

"Mortals die. Their ghosts, in theory, should not have powers they did not possess while alive. But their lives were prescribed by the Ancients; we understood the boundaries of those existences because they were in front of our eyes, should we choose to look. The dead did not occupy that space. But perhaps the strength of their memories left an aftershock as they died. In all of the cases involving the subjects and their use of their power, resentment and rage fueled the existence of the ghosts."

Kaylin frowned, considering his words, and considering, as well, Helen's previous opinion. What he said aligned with Helen's brief comments.

But it didn't align with her experience. Jamal had not been the product of his death in the way Starrante's words implied; he had been a child, with the same sense of mischief and anger that children were less practiced at controlling. He had the same longing for company, the same desire to protect the people he loved, the same need for friends. He'd had friends: the other kidnapped and murdered children, Katie, Esmeralda, and Callis.

Was it because his death had been so unusual? His body had died fifteen to twenty years after he'd been separated from it, as had the bodies of the other three children.

She glanced at Bellusdeo and froze. The Dragon's eyes were a terrible color, a copper-tinged green.

Kaylin wasn't the only person to have noticed this; Starrante might have been the only one who didn't.

"No, dear," Mrs. Erickson told Bellusdeo, reaching out to touch the back of hands that had balled into fists. "They do not resent. They are not bound to you because they believe you were responsible for their deaths. They are sad, yes—but if they have one thing in common, it is their love for you."

"You can't know that," Bellusdeo whispered. She turned to the old woman without freeing her hands.

"I think I'm the only person in this room who can," Mrs. Erickson replied. "They are very, very concerned for you at the moment. They're afraid of the color of your eyes."

"They can't say what they feel—"

"One of them has just said she was angry when you stole… something, I'm sorry, I can't quite make sense of the word. She says it happened in the Aerie. Lannagaros gave you a…charm? Something protective. You broke yours in… I'm sorry, these are her words, not mine. You broke yours in a fit of temper. You didn't want to ask Lannagaros for another one, because you wanted to avoid a lecture. So you stole hers."

The chancellor's brows folded as he watched Bellusdeo; the Dragon's eyes widened, but the ugly green receded, leaving her eyes a copper-orange blend.

"She doesn't mean to embarrass you," Mrs. Erickson continued. "But she wishes me to make clear that I can hear them, and she felt that this incident would serve as proof. It is not rage that fuels their presence."

Bellusdeo returned to the seat she had vacated, lowering her chin until her expression couldn't easily be seen.

04

The chancellor's eyes shifted between Bellusdeo and Mrs. Erickson. Given the affection Lannagaros felt for the gold Dragon, Kaylin was surprised.

Mrs. Erickson wasn't silent; she was speaking in Bellusdeo's direction, but it was clear she wasn't speaking to the living Dragon.

"She wants to know what you want for yourselves."

"I want to know what they want at all. I didn't mean to bind them. I didn't mean to tie them down. If they were happy to be where they are, I wouldn't care. Kaylin's mentioned your ghosts—the children—but they wanted to be with you. They wanted to be with you for as long as you lived.

"Dragons live forever, unless something kills them. Mortals don't. I think your children knew that—but they wanted your company."

Mrs. Erickson shook her head. "They were trapped in my house. If they hadn't been trapped, I'm not certain my company would have had any appeal to them; they were children. They might have left my house and gone to where other children play."

"But they couldn't interact with them. They could interact

with you. They didn't stay with you because they were raging. They didn't stay with you because they wanted revenge."

Kaylin nodded. "They knew who had killed them, but they were terrified, not enraged. Bellusdeo is right: those children loved you. They were with you because they did."

"They wouldn't have stayed if they had the choice," Mrs. Erickson said, voice firm. "They didn't. They couldn't pass on until Azoria An'Berranin was gone. I have tried all my life not to be a harsh, judgmental person, but I do believe I hated that woman in the end. I was happy she had died."

Kaylin didn't understand the guilt Mrs. Erickson clearly felt; her words were a confession. Kaylin was very happy that Azoria was dead—well, dead and gone. She didn't consider herself a terrible person for feeling that way.

Maybe that was why she found it impossible to dislike Mrs. Erickson. All of the Hawks did. She was a truly gentle person. Kaylin didn't have that in her.

"And my sisters?" Bellusdeo whispered.

Mrs. Erickson's brow furrowed. "They're bound to our world, as the children were bound, but in a much more restricted space. They can't see each other. I think, had each of my four children been isolated that way, it would have been much, much harder for them."

"Why could your children see each other, then? If my sisters can't see each other, if they can't tell you what they want—"

"They can't, yet—but I'm sure they will," Mrs. Erickson replied. "But I do agree. If they could be made aware of each other in the way my children were, they would be happier."

"Can they—can they see me clearly?"

"Yes, dear. They can see you. They can see the world around you. One or two have distinctly unkind opinions about that world or the people in it."

"Can they see Lannagaros now?"

"I believe they can—but they're looking at me because I'm

present and I can hear them clearly." Mrs. Erickson then looked at the wall, or rather, at the Wevaran stuck to it.

"We wish to know how I can better use the gift I was given. I can see these ghosts, but I cannot touch them; they can hear me, but they cannot hear each other. It must be possible to create a space where they could at least have that. But I don't think Jamal, Katie, Esmeralda, or Callis became ghosts in the regular way."

"Neither did Bellusdeo's sisters." Kaylin's voice was soft.

Bellusdeo, pale, eyes fully copper, said, "They did. They died. My sisters weren't bound by enchantment. They were lost in battle, devoured by Shadow. They weren't like the children."

"How much did Helen tell you?" Kaylin glanced at Mrs. Erickson.

"She answered all my questions. She was hesitant. The privacy of her tenants is something she guards—but Mrs. Erickson didn't want that privacy, at least not with me." Bellusdeo swallowed. "They died in Shadow."

"You were absorbed by Shadow, but you weren't killed by it; I would never have found you, otherwise."

"I was the last," was the bitter reply. "The last and the strongest. I was the perfect warrior for Shadow's cause. I could go where they could not. Even here. The Towers could prevent my entry into your city because I bore the taint of Shadow, but not completely; I had the right to walk the streets of Elantra, as any other living being does."

"So they didn't transform you."

Bellusdeo nodded.

Starrante began to click as he spoke to himself. "Apologies, apologies," he said, in Elantran. "I forgot for a moment that you couldn't understand me. Shadow is corrosive. For Immortals, Shadow can blur the words that give life, rewriting them in subtle—or obvious—ways. When Shadow touches mortals who carry no such words, the transformations are writ in their flesh. It is not always so with the Immortal.

"Bellusdeo does not bear the taint of Shadow. If she did, she could never have become the captain of a Tower; the Tower itself would reject—or destroy—her."

"Perhaps," the chancellor said quietly, "this is a topic that could be discussed at a different time. Starrante is correct; Bellusdeo is free of even the hint of Shadow. She is not, apparently, free of the dead. Corporal? Your frown has been deepening enough your face may be frozen in that expression."

Kaylin shook her head. "Sorry, I was thinking about something."

"And that?"

"Bellusdeo once told me her sisters were killed by the Outcaste. He could travel to the empire she ruled before her adopted world fell to Shadow."

The chancellor's eyes were now orange. Kaylin considered her options. She understood that Lannagaros didn't want the discussion to touch on Shadow, Bellusdeo's long enslavement there, and the possible consequences; he did not want to deepen the gold Dragon's grief.

Given the existence of Mrs. Erickson and the existence of Bellusdeo's dead sisters' ghosts, Kaylin thought it was unavoidable. And she had questions that she felt, instinctively, were necessary to ask. But maybe they didn't have to be asked right now.

Bellusdeo said that her sisters had been killed on the world she'd once ruled. But their bodies had been found in Elantra.

Why had their corpses appeared in Elantra? The identical bodies had caused a stir, but they were the essential clues that led, eventually, to the gold Dragon's escape from *Ravellon*.

The sisters' names were the True Names that, combined, had become the name Bellusdeo now carried within her: a sign of her coming-of-age in Dragon terms. Had their bodies somehow been preserved because their True Names had been preserved?

That wasn't the way it was supposed to work.

The bodies found in Elantra had been almost pristine; there was no sign of the cause of their deaths. They looked as if they were sleeping; she would have assumed they were, but she knew Dragons, like any other living creature in this world, needed to breathe, and these bodies didn't.

She knew when it came to the nature of True Names as sources of life, she was almost entirely ignorant. She understood that they worked, because she'd seen the Lake of Life, and she knew what the Consort's actual job was.

True Names didn't preserve Barrani bodies. Tain's tooth, chipped in combat, had never magically become whole again. Barrani could be scarred, they could lose limbs, but the Hawks didn't see much of that because mortals couldn't really cause those injuries to Barrani Hawks.

She had no idea what happened to bodies when the morgue was done assessing them. Most would be released to families; those without families would be interred…somewhere. She'd never been too concerned with that part of the procedure, because it wasn't her job.

But even if the bodies had somehow been fully preserved—which she doubted—and even if they had some way of transferring True Names back to those bodies, they had no way of extracting those names. The names were part of Bellusdeo's name.

Maybe that was why these ghosts were now bound to the gold Dragon.

Bellusdeo would have accepted that—with immense guilt—had the ghosts not been weeping. She'd accepted the deaths of her sisters—and the structural change in the actual name at her heart—until the moment she'd met Mrs. Erickson in person.

But Bellusdeo hadn't come to Helen to discuss ghosts with Mrs. Erickson; she'd come in a terribly, almost red-eyed mood to discuss something else.

Kaylin cleared her throat. "I don't mean to change the subject—"

"Then don't," Bellusdeo snapped.

"—but you didn't visit Helen to meet Mrs. Erickson. You didn't visit because you had a ghost problem."

"Why I visited no longer matters. This is more important."

The chancellor exhaled a thin stream of smoke. "If you felt it important enough to visit Helen," he began.

"It isn't as important as this." Bellusdeo folded her arms, lifting her chin. "Nothing's as important as this."

"Very well. I assumed there might be difficulties with your Tower, and you wished Helen's input."

"It's not just the Tower. And I don't appreciate Kaylin's attempt to change the subject."

Since that was exactly what Kaylin had been trying, she winced but said nothing.

"I haven't spoken with Karriamis about Mrs. Erickson. I intend to ask him for information about Necromancy—or whatever it is we're dealing with—after we finish at the Academia. I've asked the Arkon for any information he has, and I've applied for permission to return to the internal mirror at the heart of the archives."

"I do not believe he wishes Mrs. Erickson to be in the presence of that mirror."

Bellusdeo clearly didn't care. "I'll be visiting with Helen for the foreseeable future. Mrs. Erickson hasn't had a lot of focused practice with her abilities, and even if the Arbiters can unearth practical, historical information, she's still going to need to attempt to use that information properly."

Arbiter Starrante came down from the wall. "I would, with permission, like to take Mrs. Erickson on a walking tour of the Academia campus."

The chancellor's brows rose.

"With your permission," Starrante added, half of his eyes turned toward Mrs. Erickson.

"I would love that," Mrs. Erickson replied, as if she meant it. She probably did. "But it's going to be dark soon—should we wait until tomorrow? My eyes aren't very good in the dark anymore."

Starrante's eyes—two of them—rose from his body and swiveled toward the chancellor, who seemed to be all smoke or steam, given his breath. His eyes remained orange.

Bellusdeo's were orange as well, but shading toward red. Kaylin expected a lot of red in the coming days.

"You have my permission."

Kaylin rose instantly. "We're going to head home, then." Her stomach hadn't embarrassed her yet, but it was dinnertime, and if she didn't eat something soon, it would.

"I'll take you both back," Bellusdeo said, turning toward the door.

"We can walk."

"I will take you home."

"Or not."

Helen had clearly been informed that Bellusdeo would be flying in; they landed in the tower with its odd, collapsing roof. Helen's Avatar was waiting for them. She moved immediately toward Mrs. Erickson, and the look she threw Bellusdeo was as critical as Helen ever got.

"Dinner is ready," she told them all. "Bellusdeo, will you be joining us?"

"I'll be back in the morning. Early." Which meant no. "Kaylin will be joining us at the Academia tomorrow."

Mandoran, Annarion, and Terrano were at the table when they reached the dining room. The rest of the cohort weren't.

"Sedarias is at the High Halls with Allaron and Karian,"

Mandoran told Kaylin as she pulled out a chair. "Everyone else is too exhausted by Sedarias to even look at food." He grinned. "How did the visit to the Academia go?"

"About as well as anything involving two Dragons in a snit."

"The chancellor doesn't normally engage in snits, according to Serralyn."

"Tiamaris and Bellusdeo. The chancellor stopped the snit from becoming full-blown hostility."

Mrs. Erickson didn't look comfortable with this description, but notably made no attempt to correct it. She'd spent decades around the police; she knew how they talked, and she'd learned to accept it with grace.

"Serralyn would have been here for dinner—she has questions—but she also has some sort of study period that's apparently urgent. She's speaking with Starrante now."

"About?"

"Bellusdeo and Mrs. Erickson. She's worried." He frowned. "Where's the limp lizard?"

Kaylin wondered that as well. He hadn't joined Helen in the landing tower, and he hadn't come to the dining room. She turned to Helen. "Do you know where Hope is?"

Helen's frown was similar to Kaylin's—uneasy. "Yes and no."

Kaylin began to eat. "Give me the yes after dinner and I'll go look for him. What's Starrante saying?"

"He's mostly venting frustration at what he considers the library's insufficient mandate for entry into the archive."

"He can't find actual books about Necromancy."

"Not direct ones, no. I mean, he's just said that it was a forbidden art in many places, or in many periods of time. If there were books, they would have been destroyed or hidden."

"That wouldn't make a difference to their presence in the library."

"No, not usually." Mandoran ate between replies, his brow furrowed. Kaylin saw the moment his eyes began to darken.

The cohort could speak to each other no matter how great the physical distance between the various members—that was what the name bonds meant. It was therefore hard to tell which particular member of the cohort was causing the stiffening of Mandoran's otherwise genial expression.

She glanced at Annarion. His eyes were generally blue—only Serralyn's were green on a daily basis—but they darkened as well.

Terrano, who had been silent, looked across the table to Kaylin. "That dinner you wanted to finish?"

Kaylin put her cutlery down.

"Torri says there's a lot of noise coming from one of the rooms upstairs." He set his own cutlery down. "I'll meet you upstairs." Before he vanished, he added, "I think Mrs. Erickson should probably come with us."

Kaylin turned immediately to Helen. "What's happening upstairs?"

"I am not entirely certain. But I believe Hope is part of the noise to which Torrisant refers."

Kaylin fell behind Mandoran and Annarion. She remained with Helen by Mrs. Erickson's side, an arm around the older woman's shoulders. No matter how quickly Mrs. Erickson moved, she was never going to run up the flights of stairs at the cohort's speed. Or Kaylin's, if it came to that.

In any other circumstance, Kaylin would have ordered Helen to take Mrs. Erickson somewhere safe. But if Torrisant was right, the noise was being caused by Mrs. Erickson's ghosts—ghosts that no one else could see. In theory, no one else should have been able to hear them either, but Torrisant had, and he'd alerted the cohort.

Terrano was nowhere in sight. Of course he wasn't. Knowing Terrano, he'd rushed into whatever it was making noise.

No wonder Sedarias worried more about Terrano than the rest of the cohort combined.

Mrs. Erickson said, "You can go on ahead. I'll be there as soon as I can."

Kaylin shook her head. She was certain that if the guests were involved, Mrs. Erickson was their only conduit; there wasn't much point in arriving before the newest of her roommates.

She reached the end of the stairs, turned toward the hall that had only one resident, and nearly ran into Annarion's back. Mandoran stood beside Annarion, but the halls were wide enough to accommodate more than two people standing side by side; they had clearly taken up defensive positions.

Torrisant was farther down the hall, and the two Barrani moved cautiously to join him; they stood three abreast. Kaylin looked between them. The gallery, with its balcony, looked normal for another three yards past the three Barrani men—but beyond that, it no longer resembled any part of Helen's house. The carpeting ended in a blur of blue and gold—as did the walls, rails, one half of a painting, and the ceilings.

Something that resembled a large, out-of-focus moon had taken over Helen's physical control of the space. Or maybe Helen had shifted space to contain whatever it was they were all staring at. Kaylin hadn't drawn daggers. Annarion had drawn sword, as had Torrisant. Mandoran had taken to leaving his sword in his room, where it was safe. Swords while within Helen's boundaries weren't usually a necessity.

Kaylin didn't think a simple sword—or a pair of daggers—was going to be of much use here, unless monsters suddenly emerged from the orb.

"Helen—what is that?"

Helen stepped between Mandoran and Annarion. "That," she said, her voice lower than its norm, "is Hope."

"He isn't alone," Mrs. Erickson said. She attempted to follow

Helen, but none of the three Barrani moved to allow her passage. They were silent; they were probably fielding questions from members of the cohort who weren't present.

"Kaylin, tell Terrano to retreat," Mandoran said.

Terrano was, as expected, in the thick of the unnatural. "Why are you telling me that? I can't even see him."

"Shout—he might listen to you."

Kaylin grimaced; it was Terrano—he didn't listen to anyone. "Helen—can you see him?"

"He is…very close to Hope; I believe Hope is attempting to isolate him."

"Please tell me he isn't actually trying to make contact with… whatever this is."

"I have never made lying to my tenants a practice." In a tone surprisingly similar to Mandoran's, she added, "Where else would he possibly be?"

"You can't pull him out?"

"I can," Helen said. "But I am containing the guests, and it is surprisingly difficult. Extricating Terrano would split attention I'm not certain I can spare."

"What is Terrano even doing?" Kaylin demanded, of the three backs.

To her surprise, it was Torrisant who answered—she couldn't remember him speaking much. "He's not completely stupid—he's got an anchor."

Anchor. She quickly reviewed the list of cohort members. Sedarias, Allaron, and Karian—another silent presence in the house—were at the High Halls. Serralyn and Valliant were residents in the Academia. Eddorian, alone of the twelve, had chosen to remain within the Hallionne Alsanis. That left only one straggler: Fallessian.

"Can Fallessian handle it?"

"He's trying." It sounded like *no.*

"Mandoran, what is he doing?"

"He's trying to phase into a plane which would allow him to talk to Mrs. Erickson's friends."

"They're dead!"

"None of us understand what that means right now. I mean, if they were dead, they'd be gone, right? But they're definitely here."

"Did Terrano call them out of their room?"

"No—they left it on their own."

Kaylin shoved her way between Mandoran and Torrisant; it was Mandoran who gave first. "Hope!" she shouted.

The moon, for want of a better word, moved.

"That is not a good idea," Helen said, voice far sharper than the norm.

Kaylin had seen Hope in three forms: the small transparent winged lizard that sat on her shoulder, the large transparent dragon she could—in emergency—ride, and the winged man, closest in appearance to an Aerian, who appeared when there was no room for a Dragon. She had never seen this form before; it was almost an orb of light, with indistinct edges.

"I'm going to try to talk to Hope," she told her companions. "I mean—I'm going to try to understand what he's trying to say to me. If he's trying at all."

It was Torrisant who gave her an odd look. He didn't speak, though.

She closed her eyes.

The marks on her arms began to glow; they were, for the moment, the only thing she could see. She'd learned that their glow's visibility had little to do with her actual eyes. The glow was subtle; it was hard to tell if the color was silver or a gray blue. Her skin didn't hurt, which meant there was no normal magic being used.

What she noticed, beyond the expected marks, was the sudden drop in temperature. It was cold. It was *so* cold.

It wasn't the first time she'd experienced cold like this—underdressed, no shelter in sight, almost resentful of the fact that death could come from something that had no will, no intent; it wasn't hunting her—it didn't notice her at all.

No. No—she wasn't that child anymore. She had a home, had income, had food. She wasn't trapped in the winter, her fingers and toes aching with a pain that would pass into numbness. She was with Helen. She was surrounded by friends. All she had to do was open her eyes.

Her marks flared suddenly, as if they'd been struck by fire; they were a gold almost eclipsed by orange, as if they reflected a Dragon's eyes. They had never been this color before, but everywhere the marks shone, the cold receded. She always resented their presence across over half her skin; for the first time, she wished they covered all of it.

Who was it who had told her she wasn't seeing her marks with her normal eyes? Terrano? Who'd said that to look at certain things she was unconsciously stepping to the side, stepping into a slightly different plane of existence?

Whoever it was, she wanted to thank them. Or strangle them. Which meant it was either Terrano or Mandoran.

She lifted her arms and realized belatedly that she could see them. She could see herself, her marks, and the darkness behind closed eyes, even if she'd opened hers, and she had. She could also see the white glow in front of where she stood. It no longer looked like a moon or an orb; she could see the faint outline of something draconic.

"Hope!"

You should not be here.

"Are you stuck there? Do you need help?"

You should not, he replied, in a more severe tone, *be here. Helen should know better.*

"I'm not the only person who's here—Mrs. Erickson is here as well. Can you see Terrano?"

Hope wasn't a Dragon, but his rumble was definitely a good imitation. *I am aware of Terrano; he is tied to Fallessian, who usually knows better than to join his brother in reckless action.*

"What are you even trying to do?"

Terrano attempted to knock on the door of the guest room. Helen had advised him against interfering with her guests—there is a good reason she has made their quarters in a separate hall—but he convinced her that he could do so safely. She created a space in which he could stand with Fallessian, adjacent to the guest room in some fashion.

Terrano and Fallessian could, with effort, occupy that space, but Terrano's attempt to somehow see and interact with these extremely unusual ghosts hadn't met with success.

Kaylin grimaced. "So he decided to take a walk."

He decided to attempt to approach them more closely, yes.

"Is that why you stayed home today?"

Yes and no. It did not occur to me that Terrano would be as foolishly reckless as he has been. I stayed because the guests were suddenly restless.

"How could you know that?"

I could hear them. I cannot tell you if they were afraid or angry; I could hear noise, murmuring, where there should be none.

"I can't hear anything but you."

Hope's silence was one of frustration.

"Can Terrano hear anything?"

Torrisant heard the disturbance first. It's a pity he doesn't join you more often; he is sensitive in ways his companions are not. Torrisant, however, is cautious. Terrano is not. When Torrisant declined to explore—he wished to alert Helen, and wait for her input—Terrano chose to investigate in his place.

"And Fallessian was just collateral damage. Are they safe?"

Fallessian is safe.

Kaylin cursed. "Where is Terrano?"

He is partially with me.

"And the rest of him?"

Occupies a space I cannot safely enter.

"Can I?"

Hope took longer to answer this question. *I am uncertain. I am aware of you; I am aware of your current location. It is not a location I could easily traverse; were it not for our bond, I am not certain I would find you at all.*

"Helen, can you hear me?"

"I can."

"Can you see me?"

"Not in the normal fashion."

"Great. Is this the same problem you're having with Terrano?" She added a few choice words after his name.

Helen clearly did not approve, given the tone of her response. "Imelda is not an officer of the law; she is unaccustomed to language such as this."

"She came to the Halls of Law every day, Helen. She must be used to it."

Helen chose to abandon the argument about appropriate language. "My difficulty seeing you is similar to the difficulty I have with Terrano."

"Can you see Hope?"

"Yes. He is not in his usual form, but he is clearly visible. I am only aware of Terrano and you because of the defenses against intruders built into my core."

"And Mrs. Erickson's guests?"

"I am aware of them as well, and in the same fashion. Imelda is attempting to gain their attention now."

Kaylin frowned. "Can Mrs. Erickson see them?"

"Yes. Yes, she can."

"What do they look like to her?"

"I believe they look like…people. It's how she managed to bring them to me in the first place."

Kaylin grimaced. She stood in a darkness alleviated only by the light of her marks; those marks were now a livid orange, as if her skin was on fire. But without the pain, which she appreciated.

"Hope says he has Terrano."

I did not say that.

"Hope says he's aware of Terrano, and he doesn't sound too panicked. I'm going to try to reach him."

No!

"No!" Helen shouted, at the same time as Hope, the two denials overlapping in tone and texture. "Please, Kaylin, allow Imelda to attempt to quiet her ghosts before you do anything rash."

"I can't see Mrs. Erickson."

"Just please remain where you are."

"I'm not trying to reach her ghosts—I'm just trying to find Terrano."

"The two, at the moment, are entwined. We do not know what these so-called ghosts are; we don't know what they can do. What we do know is they were capable of possessing the Arkon.

"Death for the endless and Ancient is not death as we perceive it. Death for mortals is finite and irreversible."

Kaylin hesitated, remembering the corpse of the Ancient, trapped in Azoria's enchantments. Nothing about that being, when finally freed, was dead in any fashion Kaylin understood. Jamal and his friends had been: they were ghosts; they couldn't interact with living people, with the sole exception of Mrs. Erickson, and that was more because she could see them; it was her power that allowed contact, communication.

If these ghosts, these words, were dead in the fashion of that Ancient, they weren't dead in any way that Kaylin, a mortal Hawk who had seen her share of corpses, understood.

Did words die?

Did they perish, unspoken?

Or did they remain, waiting for new readers, new speakers, to give them life again?

She heard murmurs as she listened—as she realized she was

focused on listening—in this dark place; they sounded like a crowd of people at a great enough remove that the words they shouted were indistinct, blurred.

The marks on her arms grew brighter, orange and flickers of red giving way, at last, to gold and white. As if she had finally reached the outer edge of the crowd, words broke through the murmur of the crowd.

To her surprise, they were spoken by Mrs. Erickson.

05

"No, you aren't in a prison here." She paused—the pause was long—before she continued. "I'm sorry, I don't understand how you were trapped in the altar. I don't think the Arkon was responsible for your captivity—I don't think he was aware of your presence at all."

The crowd's volume rose, but the words remained unintelligible.

Kaylin needed to be closer to make sense of what was being said, but neither Hope nor Helen believed it was safe for her to move. She was a corporal now, not a private—or worse, a mascot. She could assess their concerns. She could sit on her impulse. She didn't have to rush ahead.

She had always trusted her instincts; they'd kept her alive. But learning how to differentiate between impulse and instinct was way harder than it should have been.

"I live here as well," Mrs. Erickson continued. "I brought you here because it would be safest—for both you and the rest of my people. We aren't what you are, and we aren't what you were. I'm not certain people like us could survive you. We don't... Pardon?"

Kaylin strained to hear what Mrs. Erickson heard.

"No, dear—I'm not like you. I'm not as you were, even when you were alive. Alive? It means..." Mrs. Erickson exhaled. Clearly this wasn't something she'd ever had to explain to the dead of her acquaintance.

For the first time since she'd started listening, Kaylin heard a single word. A word that she hadn't heard before but was nonetheless familiar. Oh. It was a True Word. A word spoken in the first language of the Ancients.

To her great surprise, Mrs. Erickson repeated the word, syllable for syllable; her voice rose at the end, making a question of it.

"Then what is death?" Mrs. Erickson asked.

A second word, more carefully spoken than the first, emanated from no known source. This one, Mrs. Erickson didn't repeat.

"Hope?"

This is beyond us, Hope replied.

"Us?"

Helen and me. I think it's beyond Terrano.

"Not me?"

You are Chosen.

"I don't even know what that's supposed to mean!"

No. His voice contained a glimmer of amusement. *No more did any other being who was granted the marks of the Chosen in their time. Words have meaning. True Words have immutable meaning. But I have come to believe that the granting of those marks was the Ancients' sole attempt to give flexibility to a language that had none.*

"What do you mean?"

To my knowledge, no two people who were Chosen made use of the marks in the same way. The marks were the same; the uses were fundamentally different. Their meaning relied on the individual who bore them.

Kaylin's frown was the thinking frown. "Wouldn't that make them like True Names?"

Why?

"The Barrani Lake of Life contains a finite number of names.

Those names are used to breathe life into Barrani infants. But when the Barrani to whom they were given dies, the name returns to the Lake. The name might be chosen by the Lady for another infant, but the child retains no memories of the past life. The lives might be markedly different. If the names are True Words, would that make sense?"

True Names are not malleable; if they are altered, they lose meaning. And the bearer of them loses their life.

"Yes, but the life itself is different. You can't just give a child a name and expect them to be the exact same person as the prior bearer. So…the words at the heart of Immortal people are flexible; they'd have to be."

They are not.

"Their meaning isn't clear in the way True Words are. I mean—the lives wrapped around them are different, right? So they can't somehow mean the same thing."

Hope was silent.

"So maybe the marks of the Chosen are like that? That's the type of flexibility the Ancients sought?"

Perhaps. It is something to consider, but I fail to see the relevance.

"When I saw Mrs. Erickson's ghosts, I didn't see what she saw—but I did see something. They looked like words to me. Like the words on my skin. I could see her ghosts—the ones she lived with—and they looked like the children they'd once been. Amaldi and Darreno weren't actually dead—I could see them with your help, but not on my own.

"But I'm not certain the Ancients had a concept of death that is anything at all like ours. And by ours, I mean Dragons, Barrani, Aerians, Leontines, humans—any of us. Dead is dead. It's absence. It's empty space. But the corpse of the Ancient we found still had power, and Azoria was using it. And when we freed him, he wasn't dead. He wasn't dead by any measure I understand. To the Hawks, to the law, he'd be considered alive; he could speak, he could interact."

Her frown deepened. "The ghosts that are in the hall now possessed Sanabalis."

You should really call him the Arkon. You are going to have to get used to it.

"He's not here and you know who I mean. I mean, how can it be disrespectful when he can't hear it?"

I will leave this discussion in Helen's capable hands.

"Fine. The thing that's worrying me right now—I mean, besides the fact there's a miniature moon in my hallway—is the possession of Sanabalis. If what I saw were the ghosts of words—and how does that even happen?—does that mean they could possess Sanabalis because they are words? Were they somehow displacing his True Name? Interfering with it somehow?

"What if they somehow just replaced those words? What would happen to him?" Her hands tightened as she considered the possibilities she really hadn't had time to consider, she'd been so distracted with ghosts and Azoria. "Tell Terrano to leave. Right now."

He asks me to point out that he cannot, at the moment, move. Both Helen and I are preventing it.

"Just let him leave!"

We do not wish him to "accidentally" overlap with Mrs. Erickson's guests.

This was reasonable. "You can't prevent that?"

We are not even certain what we would be preventing. Helen doesn't deem it worth the risk to Terrano. If his state—and theirs—were concrete and separate, we would have immediately done so.

"Terrano's attachment to his True Name is the most tenuous of all the Barrani I know. I think it's more dangerous for him."

And it is safe for you?

Kaylin squinted as she looked at her arms. "Yes. Yes, I think it's safe for me. I have the marks of the Chosen." She hesitated, and then said, "But that's not why I think it might be safer. I don't have Words. I think the only people who are guaranteed some sort of safety are Mrs. Erickson…and me."

Because you are mortal?

"Because we don't need Words to live, yes."

Very well. Terrano is not, as you guessed, corporeal in any of the traditional senses. Fallessian is, but he is tightly connected to Terrano. I do not believe he will attempt to maintain that connection if Terrano is returned to your plane of existence.

"Good. Sedarias would murder us slowly if we managed to lose Fallessian here."

Terrano did not, as it happened, go away. Kaylin offered a few choice words—in two languages Mrs. Erickson wasn't likely to know—as the most difficult, reckless member of the cohort appeared in front of her. He had a rope of gold tied around his waist. At any other time she would have snickered; it was something used on foundlings when they went on their very rare field trips.

But she thought the rope was gold in color for a reason. "That rope better not be Fallessian."

"Nice to see you, too."

"How did you get here?"

"We were almost in the same place," Terrano replied, shrugging. "It's darker here than I'm used to, but I could see a pretty blazing light, and I followed that."

"Instead of listening to Helen and Hope?"

"She's your landlord and he's your familiar. I don't have to listen to them." He reached for the rope around his waist; when he touched it, he shouted and lifted his hand as if it had been burned. "You talk to him," Terrano snapped, glaring at Kaylin.

His eyes were black with obsidian flecks.

"Can he hear me?"

"He can hear me, I can hear you, so even if he can't hear you himself, he'll hear what I hear. I'm certainly hearing what everyone else thinks." Given his expression, she could imagine what the cohort's opinion was.

"Fallessian, Hope feels it's not safe to be anywhere near these ghosts. Mrs. Erickson is talking with them now. I can't understand most of what they're saying; I can understand Mrs. Erickson." She hesitated again, exhaled, and said, "I think the ghosts are words. True Words—possibly closer to True Names than the spoken language of the Ancients.

"I'm not certain what they'll do to True Names. I think it's possible that the reason they could possess Sanabalis was because they could almost fill the same space as his name. I don't really want that to happen to any of you; I think Helen's probably already moved Mandoran, Torrisant, and Annarion to someplace safer.

"Mortals don't have those words. We don't need 'em to live and breathe. We don't live forever because we don't have them—but I don't think they can possess either me or Mrs. Erickson."

"Fallessian wants to know what they can do to the marks of the Chosen, if you think they can just shove important words to one side. That's not how he put it," Terrano added, "but that's what he means."

"I don't know. But… I think the worst they could do is join the marks on my skin. There's nothing in me that they can displace."

Hope said, *That is not entirely true. You carry a True Name within you. Your life does not depend on it, but it is there.*

Kaylin forgot about it, most days. "I don't think it works the same way. Look: if it disappears, I'm still going to be Kaylin Neya. I'm still going to be a corporal. I won't become some sort of weird undead vampire the way Barrani do or can.

"Just…let Mrs. Erickson talk and let me listen. I think the two of us are going to be safe." She hoped.

Mrs. Erickson's voice was low and gentle. "But you could leave your room. You did. You aren't in your room now. If you don't want to stay in your room, you can join me—I don't stay in mine. But you have to learn to be a bit careful here. There are other people living in this house, and your presence can affect them.

"Your presence seems to have affected the house itself—which won't harm you now, but can harm the others, because they aren't like you." Mrs. Erickson's voice was soothing, gentle. Always had been. "I will come visit you. You can come visit me."

"Mrs. Erickson—can the ghosts even see the other tenants?"

"They can see me," she said. "And they're aware of the others, but…not the way they are of me. I believe they're aware of you right now as well."

"Do they see me the way they see you?"

"I don't think so. It's difficult to understand what they're saying. I do understand the words, but not the way they're using them, and sometimes the words they speak are indistinct, too soft or too broken to hear properly.

"But they don't mean any harm," she added quickly. "They're confused and they're lost—and I think they're cold. They can't get warm."

"Can you lead them back to their rooms?"

There was a long pause. "I'm not sure I can. I can't see their rooms. I can't see the hall anymore."

"Do you see a small moon in the hallway?"

"Yes."

It was what Kaylin saw. She could hear Mrs. Erickson clearly, but couldn't see her. The only thing she could see was the miniature moon—and Terrano.

"Can you see me clearly, Terrano?"

"More or less."

Kaylin exhaled. "I really, really want you to get out of here." She held out her hand, palm up.

Terrano placed his palm across hers, and she tightened her

fingers. She then dragged him toward her, until he was practically standing on her feet.

"Teela's not sure this is smart."

"Teela's certain that everything you've done until now has been reckless and foolish," Kaylin countered. "Being uncertain is a big improvement."

"Fair enough."

"Can you let go of Fallessian?"

"I'm not holding on to him. Fallessian's willing to let go; Sedarias isn't willing to have him let go. Where are you going?"

"I'm going to find Mrs. Erickson. I think there must be some overlap in the space."

"Helen doesn't think so."

"I can hear her."

"Helen thinks that's a function of her voice—you can hear what the dead hear. Mrs. Erickson is standing in the hall beside Helen's Avatar. She hasn't phased into a different plane of existence. What she sees is normal, everyday house—with a giant orb in the way. And the dead."

"You're saying that it's her eyes and her voice that are perceiving different planes of existence, not the rest of her?"

"Seems like it to me. Helen won't let me study her eyes—she thinks it's rude."

"Wherever we are isn't where she is. I'm trying to move to where she is."

"How did you even get here?"

"I closed my eyes, okay? I closed my eyes and I could see the marks of the Chosen clearly. When I opened my eyes, I was here, in the dark."

"You saw the ghosts, back in the palace."

"I saw them only when Mrs. Erickson came in contact with them. But I didn't see what she saw. Come on."

"She doesn't need rescue."

"Who said I was trying to save her? It's you I'm worried about."

Terrano grimaced. "Just in case this changes your mind, Sedarias approves."

Kaylin rolled her eyes. She and Sedarias didn't see eye to eye on much—but where the safety of friends was concerned, Kaylin had no arguments.

"Teela thinks you're an idiot, though."

Kaylin would not let go of Terrano's hand; he only tried to wriggle free once. She turned to face the orb, listening for Mrs. Erickson's soft voice. As she did, she could almost hear the ghosts of dead words. No, that wasn't right. The words weren't dead. They were just words.

How could the words be ghosts?

What had they occupied before, when they were what passed for alive? Was it only the body that was missing now? Were they confused because of that absence? Were they trying to find a different body, a new form?

She'd asked herself variations of this a dozen times and was no closer to an answer than she had been when she'd started. But she felt as if she was almost touching one that remained frustratingly out of reach.

Helen said that shamans—not Necromancers—helped the trapped dead, or the echoes the living left behind, pass on to wherever it was they were meant to go.

How did words pass on?

Mrs. Erickson had wanted to free Jamal and the rest of the children, but had had no idea how to do that; her biggest fear of her own death had been deserting those trapped, captive children. But she hadn't helped them to pass on. Once Azoria was dead, they could leave. They could go wherever it was the dead were meant to go.

These words clearly couldn't—but maybe there had never

been a place for them to go. Kaylin wondered if she could gather them up and dump them in the Lake of Life.

Absolutely not, Hope snapped. *They are contained for the moment, but it is tiring. Do not add to the burden by being reckless.*

Kaylin held on to Terrano as she closed her eyes. When she opened them again, she saw darkness—but it was subtly different. In that darkness, as if she were a ghost herself, Kaylin could now see Imelda Erickson. Mrs. Erickson's shoulders weren't bowed; she stood straight, and her eyes were an odd color, given that the rest of her was colorless.

Mrs. Erickson's arms were extended, her palms facing upward, her forehead slightly creased with concern. Kaylin watched her carefully. She could see the moon—but in this space, it wasn't an actual orb. She could see Hope in a state she'd never seen him in before: half Aerian, half serpentine. And she could see the words as they canted forward, as if to fall into Mrs. Erickson's open hands. They were transparent, but their shapes overlapped; they were larger than any of the marks of the Chosen—but the marks of the Chosen could detach themselves from her skin, becoming larger, or far larger, in different circumstances.

Mrs. Erickson was focused on those words, and on her own—the ones she spoke, the ones she offered as comfort. Her eyes widened as Kaylin approached her, Terrano in tow.

"Kaylin?"

"Yes, it's me. I have Terrano as well."

"My goodness—you aren't... You didn't die, did you?"

"Not that I'm aware of."

"You did disappear."

Kaylin nodded. "I think, given the way the words are leaning, they'll follow you. They can hear you; I'd guess they can't easily hear the rest of us."

"They don't want to stay in the room Helen built for them. They find it very cold, very empty."

"It was designed to be manipulable by Imelda's guests—but I've never had dead guests before. I suppose it isn't surprising they can't fully control the space."

Kaylin couldn't see Helen.

"Hope?"

I concur. They desire to follow Mrs. Erickson. If we can ask Mrs. Erickson to keep an eye on them, we may survive this. As Kaylin watched, the various mismatched parts of her familiar shifted in place until he was once again the version of himself she knew best. The words were far larger than his form; he flew and landed on Kaylin's shoulder; she could feel his claws pierce fabric around her collarbone.

She blinked several times as reality reasserted itself: she was standing in the hall that led to the residents' rooms, and the hall itself no longer contained a glowing orb.

The cohort was absent, with the single exception of Terrano; when Kaylin realized the words were gone, she let go of his hand.

She then turned to Mrs. Erickson, whose cupped hands contained the shivering words—just as she'd done when she first carried them to Helen.

Mrs. Erickson looked worried for the words she saw as people; she looked pale to Kaylin's eyes, but that could have been a trick of the abundant light. "I'm going to take them to my room," Mrs. Erickson said, looking up briefly to meet Kaylin's gaze.

Kaylin nodded.

She liked having a room of her own but felt that Mrs. Erickson might need company.

"She won't, dear," Helen said. "They mean her no harm."

"They took over part of the hall when they meant her no harm. I'm not worried about her safety—I'm worried about the safety of everyone else."

Helen nodded. "I am informed that Serralyn has been doing some research which she hopes might be of use. In the meantime, I can strengthen the envelope of protection around Imelda's quarters. I know you feel Imelda is a civilian, but technically so are most of the cohort. You cannot stop her from trying to help these ghosts—it is her very nature.

"I am sorry my own containments were not up to the task. I cannot see them as you—or Imelda—see them; I can see what you see, but Imelda's vision, as it relates to these dead, is impassible to me."

Kaylin exhaled. "Do what you can to keep Mrs. Erickson's room habitable for her." She stared at the words she couldn't read, couldn't pronounce, hoping to consign them to memory. "I'll head back to the Academia."

"The Academia?"

"The Arkon—the former Arkon—had some schooling in True Words, and I'm almost certain the Arbiters understand them. I need to know what these words actually mean." Her stomach started to rumble. "I also need to finish eating."

Hope was once again draped across her shoulders. She was almost embarrassed about having missed him, he could be such a pain. She'd spent most of her life without a familiar of any kind and would have sworn she'd be fine if he simply chose to leave. Apparently she didn't really know herself as well as she'd thought.

Hope squawked.

She fed him from her plate. As far as she knew, he didn't need to eat—but he enjoyed it sometimes.

Mandoran and Annarion came down to finish their interrupted dinner; to her surprise, Torrisant and Fallessian joined them. Terrano did not.

"You heard them first, right?" she asked Torrisant.

He nodded.

"Can you still hear them?"

He glanced at Annarion, who shrugged: *Up to you.* She didn't expect an answer; Torrisant and Fallessian both avoided anyone who wasn't part of the cohort. "Yes."

"They're in Mrs. Erickson's room right now."

Torrisant nodded. "I can hear them as a murmur. I can almost make out syllables."

"You knew there was a problem because you could hear something?"

"The syllables grew louder and faster."

"Can any other member of the cohort hear them?"

Mandoran said, "No. Serralyn's frustrated. She'd like to be here when things are going, as she put it, pear-shaped. But there are things she's doing at the Academia that she can't just drop."

"Why can Torrisant hear them? Sorry," she added to Torrisant. "I'm used to talking about you in third person because you almost never come to meals."

Torrisant shrugged; the gesture was far less fluid than Mandoran's. Kaylin realized he was trying to fit in, somehow; he was trying to be more Elantran. "I'm not certain."

Annarion raised a brow at Torrisant, who grimaced. "My family is Immolan. Nine hundred years ago, give or take a few decades, we were a family of scholars and mages. We had some power in the High Court, but we weren't a largely political family. Most of the time."

"But you got sent to the green with the rest of the cohort. I mean—wasn't that about gaining power?"

"It was about gaining power to fight the Dragons," he replied, voice low. "It wasn't about gaining power in the court itself."

Mandoran snorted. Loudly.

"We weren't!" Torrisant snapped.

"Torri isn't the most politically canny of our number," Mandoran said.

"Speak for yourself."

"I am. I'm not interested in politics, especially not ours. But I'm aware of the undercurrents and the jostling for position. You weren't sent to the green because Immolan wanted to contribute powerful soldiers to the war effort. You were sent because powerful soldiers meant more power for Immolan." Mandoran folded his arms and tilted his chair onto its two back legs.

Torrisant glared at Mandoran. "It doesn't matter, does it? Immolan's fortunes fell during our long absence. They're part of the High Court, but they have no reliable power."

Before Kaylin could ask, Mandoran said, "They're remaining neutral. They don't support Sedarias. But they don't support any other member of Mellarionne either; they consider the fight for the line to be irrelevant to their interests."

Kaylin glanced at Annarion; he ate. But he ate without looking at either Mandoran or Torrisant; he had opinions but was trying to remain neutral.

"Let's go with Torrisant's opinion for now," Kaylin said. "If they were a family of scholar mages, did they hope to increase your power so it would be useful in that regard?"

Torrisant nodded stiffly. He was—no doubt—arguing silently with Mandoran.

"Did you have to be tested in some way before you were chosen?"

"I wasn't the main branch at the time. All of the families who owed allegiance to Immolan produced their children to be tested."

"And it was a magical power test?"

"It was—but Immolan's tests are unusual, and highly secretive."

"So you passed—or failed, depending on how your parents felt about it?"

He nodded.

"And I suppose there's no way to know whether or not you'd have hearing this sensitive if you hadn't been exposed to the *regalia*."

"Sedarias highly doubts that this sensitivity is useful," Mandoran added.

"Can I ask a different question?"

Torrisant nodded.

"Why did you not go to the Academia with Serralyn and Valliant?"

Mandoran and Annarion both winced.

Fallessian, who hadn't spoken once, stood. "Immolan was a family of scholar mages—but Torrisant had no desire to become a scholar. Not then, and not now. He was abandoned—we were all abandoned—by ambitious parents, or parents who were too weak to have a choice.

"Torrisant won't go to the Academia because he doesn't want to give Immolan, and his mostly dead ancestors, any advantage from that ancient decision. We are people, not tools. We get to decide what we make of our own lives. Maybe if we'd had a choice, as Sedarias did, we'd feel differently. We didn't, and we don't. Torrisant won't become what they wanted him to become.

"None of us will."

"Sedarias is An'Mellarionne."

"Because that's what Sedarias wanted—and wants. She wasn't there for Mellarionne. She was there for reasons she chose. We support her because this is what she wants. And without Sedarias, the cohort might not have existed at all."

Torrisant lifted a hand, and Fallessian fell silent. His eyes were a dark blue; he was angry. Kaylin hoped his anger wasn't directed at her. "Helen is our home now. She may consider us to be your guests, but we consider ourselves to be tenants—with the same responsibilities you shoulder.

"She saved Annarion and Mandoran when they first arrived. She offered us shelter and sustenance when we joined them. Even now, she does what she can to protect us, and most of us are truly grateful."

"Most?"

"Terrano has never liked external protection." Mandoran shrugged.

Torrisant continued. "These guests destabilize Helen; they threaten the security of our home. What I was not—and will never be—willing to offer Immolan, I will offer Helen. While we believe it would be best if she ejected the guests she has accepted, we know that she—like you, her primary tenant—will not do that. But there is a danger. If I cannot fully hear or understand the words, I hear enough. If such words can be frightened, they are; if such words can have ambition or will, they do.

"I believe they want what Helen gave to us; they cannot perceive her attempts to offer them shelter in the way we did and do." Torrisant exhaled. "I will, if you intend to visit the Academia again, go with you. But I will not apply to join Serralyn and Valliant.

"And for what it's worth, Serralyn's family would have considered her tenure in the Academia to be a contemptible waste of time; Valliant's family would have been embarrassed, if not humiliated, at his choice to remain there. Had either of their families intended that fate for them, I am certain they, too, would have rejected the Academia." He looked at his untouched food, and then rose to join Fallessian. "Helen will inform me when you are ready to leave."

She turned to Helen. "I'm going to try to get some sleep after dinner—but I'll be heading to the Academia after work."

"You are going to the Halls of Law?"

Kaylin nodded. Sanabalis wanted her to deal with Bellusdeo. Bellusdeo had Imperial permission to accompany Kaylin. And Mrs. Erickson needed to spend time with the ghosts she'd brought home—not Bellusdeo's sisters. "I don't think it's a good idea for Mrs. Erickson to leave the house while the ghosts are so unstable."

Helen nodded in silent agreement.

★★★

There was no emergency in the middle of the night. Kaylin slept without interruption, woke up on time, and dressed quickly, then headed to the breakfast table. Mrs. Erickson was absent. "Helen?"

"She spent much of the night awake speaking with her newest ghosts, and she is not—in her own words—as young as she used to be. I therefore chose to let her sleep. Bellusdeo mirrored."

Kaylin winced.

"She intends to accompany you to the Halls of Law this morning. She is not highly pleased to have any delay in her return to the Academia; she believed you would be heading there, instead of the Halls of Law."

"Doesn't she have a Tower to captain?" Marcus accepted Bellusdeo because the gold Dragon had insisted, with vehemence, that she was no part of the Imperial Dragon Court, but he was never going to be happy about Dragons.

"I believe she had an argument with either her Tower or Lord Emmerian, and felt that finding a different occupation for the day would allow her to rein in her temper."

Great. Angry Dragon in the Halls of Law.

"But Imelda did make baked goods yesterday. She asked that you deliver them to the front desk if you have the time; they won't last another day."

06

Bellusdeo was at the door before Kaylin had finished eating. Mandoran finished quickly so he could offer Bellusdeo his particular brand of support, which meant mostly friendly sarcasm. Her eyes were fluctuating between gold and orange—but the gold, in Mandoran's presence, was stronger.

Annarion was distracted; he didn't join in. But he'd never been prone to the same friendly teasing as Mandoran.

"You're sure Mrs. Erickson is okay?" Kaylin asked Helen, as she stood.

"I'm certain she's exhausted—and she feels guilty about it. I've tried to explain that, in my opinion, she is utilizing power she doesn't understand to communicate with these particular ghosts, but she feels 'just talking' shouldn't have this much of an effect. And she had been planning to visit the Halls of Law today—she hasn't seen the Hawks at the front desk for a while now."

Bellusdeo frowned, her eyes shading instantly to orange.

"Mrs. Erickson is fine. She's just tired."

The gold Dragon crossed her arms.

"I'll explain it as we walk to work. I'm on a winning streak for timely arrival, and I don't want to break it."

"Because you'll lose a bet?"

"Something like that."

Mandoran said he was bored enough that walking through the Elantran streets with a Dragon as a companion seemed far better than being stuck in the house—no disrespect to Helen.

"Fine. You carry the basket."

"The basket?"

"Mrs. Erickson baked for the Hawks; I think she'd've accompanied me to work if it hadn't been for last night's excitement."

"Which you're about to explain," Bellusdeo added, voice and expression grim. Ugh. Of course it was. Mrs. Erickson was her only conduit to her dead sisters. Mrs. Erickson's untrained powers might—just might—be able to somehow free them, just as Jamal and company had been freed.

Kaylin didn't expect Bellusdeo to care all that much about the other ghosts. Which made sense. Bellusdeo was no longer living with Helen, so her experience with the danger these ghosts presented wasn't visceral.

As they walked to work, Kaylin attempted to change that. The walk was therefore slower than usual. Mandoran was quiet, which wasn't like him; words would have deflected Bellusdeo's attention, where silence drew it.

By the time they'd reached the Halls of Law, Bellusdeo was caught up on anything she'd missed. She didn't set aside her own request of Mrs. Erickson, but understood that the old woman's safety might be at risk. There were just too many things that were overlapping Mrs. Erickson—most of them were questions, not answers.

Hope didn't snore, but it wouldn't have surprised Kaylin if he started today; he seemed floppier and more exhausted than usual. She wondered what she would do if he ever got sick. Wondered if there were anything she *could* do. Wondered, last, if Hope could die, or if Hope were even alive in any meaning of the word Kaylin, as a Hawk, understood it.

It wasn't a comforting thought.

She knew he'd hatched from a very odd egg, but still wondered where he'd come from, and why he'd come to her. It wasn't just the marks of the Chosen. He'd even eaten one of them. Or maybe it was the marks, because he *had* eaten one of them.

Hope squawked, but it was a pathetic squawk; it barely rose above the sound of the people in the streets.

Kaylin clocked in on time. She then turned to Mandoran and liberated the basket of baked goods Mrs. Erickson had sent before heading to the public desk, where Rybatte was on duty. He was one of the older Hawks; he'd lost three fingers on his left hand, and unless there was a terrible emergency, he was on permanent desk work.

"I hear you covered the desk in my absence," he said, glancing at the basket. "That's from Mrs. Erickson?"

Kaylin nodded.

"We haven't seen her around much this past week. Did she injure herself?"

"No—but she's living with me, and she's just settling in. I keep an eye out."

"And gain weight?"

"How many cookies can I eat in a day?"

Rybatte laughed. "One of the only perks of this rotating desk is her baking. She's come in with some pretty wild stories—but mostly, they're mundane."

Kaylin grimaced. "She meant to come in person today, but she was just too tired."

"You're making her work?"

"Not intentionally." Kaylin set the basket on the desk, lifted its lid, and discovered that it wasn't cookies today, it was muffins. She took one. "I'll tell her she's missed."

The door behind the desk opened. Bridget stood in the frame. "Tell her she's free to come visit without forcing the people on desk duty to write up a report."

"She misses her daily routine," Kaylin replied. "But I think she'd feel guilty if she came for no reason."

Bridget took one muffin out of the basket, considered the contents, and took another one. She left the two on the desk and took the basket instead. "I'll send the empty basket to your desk."

Severn didn't appear to notice that Bellusdeo had shouldered her way into their two-person patrol. He offered the Dragon a nod as if she were a natural third partner. Mandoran, in theory, headed home. In practice, he pulled a Terrano, and trailed them as if he were an invisible shadow.

Elani street wasn't a danger. It was annoying, sometimes enraging, but that was the reaction of anyone who wasn't interested in fleecing the gullible of money. And if she were being fair—which was difficult, especially when she passed Margot's shop and saw the small lineup outside the closed door—Evanton's store was here, and some stores that sold jewelry and clothing were interspersed with the seeing the future, cures for baldness, and communicating with the deceased.

Kaylin wondered what it would be like if Mrs. Erickson could set up a small store here. She probably wouldn't have nearly the clientele that Margot had fostered, because Margot was young and, in some eyes, beautiful, and Mrs. Erickson was old. But Mrs. Erickson's gift was genuine.

And Mrs. Erickson couldn't see ghosts that weren't there. She didn't have a way to communicate with the dead on command; she could see ghosts anchored to the places not even death let them escape, but she couldn't magically bring them here, to Elani, where the grieving and desperate came.

Why was so much of life about death?

Hope squawked; it was his complaining squawk, not his alert one.

Bellusdeo's eyes were orange with flecks of gold; she agreed with Kaylin's general disgust about the merchants on Elani street. But her gaze was often aimed beyond the city streets.

"Why did you come to visit the other night?" Kaylin finally asked.

"I needed to get out of the Tower for a bit."

"Who were you arguing with?"

"Why do you think I was arguing with anyone?"

Kaylin rolled her eyes. "You generally don't need to get out of the house unless you want to prevent yourself from murdering someone. You can't murder the Tower."

"Some days I'd like to try. Karriamis is a smug, arrogant, condescending—" She bit back the rest of the sentence.

Some days. So it wasn't Karriamis. "Lord Emmerian is living in the Tower, isn't he?"

Bellusdeo's jaws snapped shut. It was a wonder she didn't crack her own teeth, and her eyes' gold flecks changed to crimson flecks.

Kaylin lifted a hand. "You can say anything you want about Emmerian. I can't, not publicly—he's a member of the Dragon Court."

Bellusdeo exhaled a stream of smoke from her nostrils.

"And I'm the worst person in the city to come to for any relationship advice. Trust me on this."

"I don't want advice," the gold Dragon snapped. "Not about Emmerian. I can deal with Emmerian."

"The Emperor values him. Hells, I value him. He's the only Dragon I've met who knows how to be consistently considerate."

"I know. And I hate it."

Dragons were definitely not human. "How could you hate

that? Don't touch the small dragon," she added, when someone whose gaze was welded to Hope approached.

"He never, ever says what he's thinking. He always takes time to find words; if it weren't for the color of his eyes, I'd have no idea how he feels about anything."

"That's generally considered a good thing— Hey, I'm serious. Don't touch." Before Kaylin could say it a third time, Severn intercepted the large hand—which was attached to an equally large man. Severn's silent intervention was far more effective than Kaylin's spoken warning, which irritated her immensely. She was at least as dangerous as Severn—possibly more so, given her visceral reactions—but it was always Severn people avoided offending.

Ugh. This was life. It was life as she'd experienced it as a child; it was life even when she wore the Hawk's tabard. She wasn't as tall, or as large, as Severn, and people didn't immediately equate her with danger. She could hate it all she wanted, but unless she stepped out of line and beat the crap out of the stranger, she couldn't change it. Even if she did—and she'd be back down to private from corporal—it would change exactly one person's reaction.

Hope surprised Kaylin; he sat up, his body rigid. When she continued to walk, he squawked, loudly, in her ear. She sighed. "I think Hope wants us to check in with Evanton."

Severn nodded. Evanton was part of their regular patrol.

"Why does he want us to visit the Keeper?" Bellusdeo asked, her eyes losing the crimson flecks.

"I don't know—you can ask him."

Bellusdeo raised an eyebrow in Hope's direction, and Hope squawked. Bellusdeo's expression grew thoughtful, neutral; her anger, her ire, at Emmerian was pushed aside.

"What did he say?"

"He thinks Evanton wants to see us."

★★★

Evanton was sitting behind his long desk, a glass over his right eye. He looked up as the door chimed entry. In the Elani merchant shops, exterior doors weren't warded; it was seen as discouraging possible customers.

"Corporal. Corporal." Evanton was seated on a bar stool, which made him seem taller than he actually was. "It's good to see you. Did Helen pass on the message?"

"I'm working. If you sent it during my patrol hours, I haven't heard it yet. It's better to contact me through the Halls of Law during normal working hours."

"Perhaps. It's not safer, and I prize safety."

"Where's your apprentice?"

"He's in the garden. I should be there myself, but he is adept at calming the elements, and it is good practice for him."

"The elements needed calming."

"Indeed. They have been unsettled for the past few weeks."

Kaylin glanced at Severn. "How many weeks?"

"I see by your question you have some idea of what the root cause might be."

"We had a bit of difficulty with an almost-dead Barrani woman."

"Barrani are born to cause difficulty; I fail to see how that would disturb the elements."

"When I say almost dead, I mean she probably should have been dead. But she'd somehow tapped into the power of the green."

"In the West March."

"No, she was here—but I'm given to understand that the power of the green is more pervasive than a simple physical location."

"And the fate of that almost-dead Barrani?"

"We got rid of the almost."

"Might I ask her identity?"

"I'm not sure if you'd know her, but Azoria An'Berranin is what she was called while she lived."

Evanton was, in theory, human; he had lived well beyond the normal measure of years because he had become the Keeper of the garden in which the heart of the elements resided. His job wasn't actually running a store—which the cobwebs and dust clearly signaled; it was keeping the world functional. It was holding the elemental forces together in such a way that they didn't escape and turn the world to ash, drown it, or bury it. A new addition to the garden was the Destroyer of Worlds. The name was not decorative.

Kaylin sometimes whined about her job, but at base she loved it. She did not envy Evanton at all.

Evanton's eyes widened. "Did you say Azoria An'Berranin?"

Kaylin nodded.

"When did this happen?" His tone was sharper. "Let me guess: two weeks ago."

"Around then."

Evanton exhaled heavily. "There have been disturbances in the past month. Small disturbances, but the elementals have been progressively less happy. Two weeks ago, there was a sharp increase in aggression—with us, and with each other. It has calmed down somewhat, but they are still uneasy.

"I would invite you into the garden, but you are not guaranteed to survive it, at the moment." His frown reworked the many lines of his face. "I suppose I should not be surprised that you had some hand in this."

Life, Kaylin thought, was never going to be fair. "I didn't do anything except stop Azoria."

"Stop her from doing what?" He paused, turned to Bellusdeo, and offered her a surprisingly graceful bow. "Apologies; my manners are terrible. I see you are accompanying the corporal on her rounds today. Corporal?"

Bellusdeo nodded. She had genuine respect for Evanton. Most days, so did Kaylin.

"From harming an old woman who's a regular fixture in the Halls of Law."

"Azoria had an interest in an old woman? I find that almost difficult to believe."

"You knew her."

"I met her on prior occasions. Had I imagined you would ever come in contact with her, I might have warned you to avoid her at all costs." His frown shifted. "Your instincts are generally good, and the warning itself may have been irrelevant. She is dead?"

Kaylin nodded. "I would say she's been almost entirely dead for centuries."

"Corporal, I have had a very trying month."

Kaylin glanced at Bellusdeo. The gold Dragon's eyes were orange, her expression neutral. "It's a bit of a long story."

"Do your best to tell it in coherent order."

Evanton listened as she began. She focused on the past events and failed to mention Bellusdeo's sisters at all—if the gold Dragon wanted him to know, she'd tell him, and if she didn't want him to know—well, Kaylin wasn't the Keeper, and could survive far less ire.

He interrupted many times.

"You found two people Azoria An'Berranin had imprisoned in a painting."

Kaylin nodded. "They're still alive. I think they're in the High Halls right now. They were imprisoned when Elantra didn't exist; they were slaves. Elantra as a concept interests and frightens them." She hesitated, and then said, "I was thinking that they might find a home in the Academia, but that's not up to me."

"How did you find them?"

"Mrs. Erickson found them. They were, to her eyes, ghosts:

people she could see and speak with, that no one else could see and speak with. I could see them only when Hope lifted a wing and placed it across my eyes. It's why I thought they might not actually be dead."

"Mrs. Erickson saw the dead in the palace?"

Kaylin nodded.

"You could not?"

"Not easily, no—and I can't see them the way she sees them. To her, they look like people. I'm sure she could describe age, facial features, gender, if asked."

"Interesting. What did you see?"

"I see words. I see True Words. The size can vary, but the shape of the words don't. Before you ask, no, I don't recognize their meaning. But when they possessed Sanabalis..."

"These ghosts possessed the current Arkon?"

Kaylin nodded. "I can't explain that part. It's true, they did—and they let him go because of Mrs. Erickson. She was pleading with them; she said they were very upset and afraid."

Evanton pinched the bridge of his nose. "Where are these ghosts now?"

"In my house."

"They reside within Helen?"

"Yes. It's been a bit tricky."

Evanton's final interruption—if one didn't count criticisms of Kaylin's architectural knowledge and therefore description—came when she talked about the outlands to which Azoria's painting of herself had been connected.

Evanton was human at base, so the color of his eyes didn't change, but his expression became an iron mask as he took in what she had to say.

"I would ask you what you've done, but your answers would be frustrating—at best. You found a dead Ancient in the outlands—one bound by Azoria; she had shaped the words, or some of the words, at the heart of the corpse into a language that had nothing to do with them: her own words, her attempt to rewrite her own name."

"That's what I think she was doing. I can't ask. I don't think her ghost, for want of a better word, lingers. Mrs. Erickson could ask her if it did, but..."

"But you feel protective of her."

Kaylin shrugged.

"Have you returned to speak with the Ancient who is not, by any stretch of our own concept of death, dead?"

Kaylin shook her head. "We went to Mrs. Erickson's house to help her move the few items she wanted to keep, but she's been living with us since then. I'm not sure she's gone back; she's getting used to Helen. Who adores her."

"Does the house Azoria occupied still stand?"

Kaylin fell silent.

Evanton's brows creased. "Do not tell me you have not checked."

"I've been a little busy."

"Be more productively busy." He pinched the bridge of his nose again. "I would like to meet Mrs. Erickson."

"But you never leave your store."

"I leave it very infrequently, it is true. But I have an apprentice now, and I believe it is necessary. Also: you should have that house checked. If it is still connected to Mrs. Erickson's humble abode, her house should not be sold to anyone else."

The only thing, beside Bellusdeo's sisters, Kaylin had purposely left out was the single moment when Mrs. Erickson had chosen to command Azoria An'Berranin—and Azoria, dead, had had no choice but to obey. Mrs. Erickson had done so only with Jamal's permission; she had promised him, or perhaps all of the children, that she would never use that power.

Which meant it was power they thought she did have: the power to command the dead.

Given that most people couldn't even see the dead, it hadn't seemed like all that much of a danger to Kaylin; sure, Mrs. Erickson could order ghosts around, but the ghosts couldn't do anything.

But as Evanton had reminded her, at least some of the dead weren't dead in the normal way. And some of them had possessed Sanabalis—a living Dragon. If Mrs. Erickson could command those ghosts, she could do a lot of damage. The fact that she would never, ever do it would count for very little.

"When did you want to visit?"

"I will speak with Helen and arrange a time."

"Could you come after my work hours? I mean, tomorrow or the day after that."

"That could be arranged, yes. I believe I understand some part of the unease the elements have been feeling—but not all. In the meantime, arrange to visit Mrs. Erickson's empty house."

"I'm going to have to do that after hours—we still have the rest of our patrol and any resulting paperwork to get through."

"I believe you will be allowed to inspect that house as part of your legal duties."

"You've never met my sergeant."

"As it happens, I have—when he was much younger. But as you say, you have work to do and I have interrupted it. Do not let me further detain you."

"Academia tonight," Bellusdeo said, after Evanton's door was firmly closed behind them. "He can visit Mrs. Erickson some other time."

This didn't come as a surprise to Kaylin. Bellusdeo had no desire to harm—or even cage—Mrs. Erickson, and she assumed speaking with the ghosts of her beloved sisters would cause no harm. Her sisters—her weeping sisters—were the highest priority to the gold Dragon. Kaylin understood it. But she was far less certain that Mrs. Erickson would be safe. "I think I should revisit her home; Evanton's going to have more questions that I can't answer, and maybe I can get ahead of a couple of them."

"I'm not certain that visiting her house will supply answers to those questions."

Probably not. "Not visiting will mean he has fewer questions and way more criticisms. But if I'm going to her house, I think Mrs. Erickson should come with us."

"You're against this?"

Kaylin shook her head.

"You're afraid she'll be too tired?"

"Normally I wouldn't be—she walked to the Halls of Law hauling her basket of baked goods every single day. But...the new ghosts have been acting up, and I think she's been calming them. They remind me of newborn infant schedules. She's exhausted. But yes, Academia this evening. I just don't want Mrs. Erickson to be overwhelmed or intimidated. I promised Jamal I'd keep her safe."

"You don't intend to bring her to the Academia?"

"I would have—but we had an incident last night and right now she's living in the same rooms as the ghosts we brought back from the Imperial Palace. The cohort will be at home; if we need to ask Mrs. Erickson questions, Serralyn can ask Annarion, and he can ask Mrs. Erickson.

"If it gets more complicated than that, we can ask Bakkon to serve as interpreter and go-between for Mrs. Erickson and Starrante."

"We?"

Kaylin grimaced. "You, then. Bakkon is a Wevaran who lives with Liatt, the fieflord, and she's probably going to be more willing to negotiate with Bellusdeo the fieflord than with me."

"She won't interfere with Bakkon," Bellusdeo replied. "If you gave yourself more of a chance, I think you'd approve of Liatt."

"Her streets aren't that different from Nightshade's."

"Neither are the warrens. You approve of Elantra because you didn't have to live in them."

Kaylin clenched her teeth, swallowed, and accepted Bellusdeo's words as truth.

Severn didn't choose to join them at the Academia when the work shift ended. *Bellusdeo is with you, and I have some research to do.*

Bellusdeo wasn't interested in dinner. She allowed Kaylin to grab something from a market stall toward the end of the shift, but otherwise herded her, insistently, toward the bridge that entered Tiamaris. That bridge had become the safe focal point of all Elantrans who had interests in the fiefs, possibly because Tiamaris's money was spent on rebuilding whole sections of the lands he called his own.

Bellusdeo was on good behavior; she waited until she'd set foot in Tiamaris before she shed her human form and demanded Kaylin climb up on her back. Kaylin wished she hadn't. She didn't want the two Dragons to continue their interrupted argument. If they did, she wanted to be safely elsewhere first.

Tiamaris, however, did not arrive, and Bellusdeo bypassed foot traffic—most of it crossing the bridge back to Elantra at the end of their working day—as intended.

She landed in the quad; students moved quickly out of her shadow as it grew larger over their heads. Kaylin had just enough time to dismount before Bellusdeo shifted into her human form; she wore golden plate armor. Clothing existed that could magically survive the transition to and from draconic form, but it was expensive and Bellusdeo clearly didn't consider it worth the bother.

The former Arkon was waiting for her when the doors to the building opened.

"Mrs. Erickson is not with you today."

Kaylin exhaled. "We had a bit of trouble last night. She's exhausted."

"I believe it was Mrs. Erickson who was to be the recipient of the librarian's research."

"Serralyn is here, and classes are over—I thought she could serve as a go-between. We have Annarion on the other end, ready to go."

"Or I could do it," Terrano said. His voice was quite clear; the rest of him wasn't.

Kaylin poked Hope, who squawked, but did lift a wing to cover one of her eyes. "Or Terrano could do it, if Serralyn is busy."

"Oh, she's not," was the cheeky reply.

"Given Mrs. Erickson's friends, don't you think you might be needed at home?"

Terrano shrugged. "I think she has things under control for now."

The chancellor's eyes were orange, but he ignored Terrano.

"He is not ignoring Terrano," Killian said, as disembodied as the most difficult member of the cohort. "But he considers Terrano to be like mice or cockroaches; persistent but not ultimately immediately dangerous."

"Easier to get rid of, too."

Killian's Avatar was waiting for them in the building proper. He took the lead, bypassing the chancellor's office entirely as he led them to the library. One or two students exited that space. The Barrani student threw a glare in Kaylin's direction; she was the only safe target for his obvious displeasure.

"Did they throw out students who had appointments?" Kaylin asked.

"That is what appears to have happened, yes, although you could ask the librarians."

No wonder she was hated. "Serralyn's not coming?"

"She's actually in the library," Terrano replied, grinning.

The library doors opened. Killian turned to Bellusdeo and said, "The librarians will see you now. I ask that you remember that books are flammable."

"Given the way Androsse and Kavallac fight, those books must be indestructible," Kaylin said.

"They are part of the library itself; Lord Bellusdeo is not."

Kaylin hoped to see Starrante. He was present and waiting.

Sadly so were the warring librarians; Androsse was to the left of the Wevaran, and Kavallac to the right. The Dragon librarian offered Bellusdeo and the chancellor a nod, the type that would pass between equals.

"Corporal," she said, skipping that gesture of respect as she addressed Kaylin. "We have spent the past mortal day researching the tomes that might contain information."

"What she is failing to say," Androsse added, "is that we were forced—for the first time in some decades—to shift the passage of time between the Academia and the library. More time has passed within the confines of the library. Serralyn is on her way now. She has been helping us as she can; she doesn't yet have the proper range of languages to access some of the older works, but we are arranging for a broader range of languages in future. We have been pleased by her intuition, even in the absence of concrete linguistic skills."

Bellusdeo stepped forward. "Have you discovered any salient information?"

"Serralyn says maybe." Terrano delivered her opinion before she had arrived to do it herself.

Androsse was ill-pleased to have his work so easily dismissed or reduced. Kaylin, however, thought that was for the best—Bellusdeo was hovering at the edge of her limited supply of patience.

To no one's surprise, it was Starrante who began the research progress report. "We have uncovered different accounts of both ghosts—as we will call them, with the understanding that the term is not entirely technical—and those who might exorcise them. We have also found two separate accounts of what would be referred to as shamanism, where those accounts overlap exorcism and ghosts.

"What we have not found—and we did warn you—is a better account of what constitutes shamanism. Much of the learning that passed between master and student was not consigned to written words. Shamans themselves seemed to be mortal in nature; we could uncover no knowledge of a similar discipline among the Immortals. The closest we have come involves the tending of the green in the West March, and those who study and serve the Warden there—but such endeavors do not touch upon the dead.

"Kaylin? You have questions."

Kaylin exhaled. "Yes, but it's not going to decrease your workload."

"It is very seldom that intelligent questions have that effect." Starrante gave her the benefit of the doubt; Androsse clearly considered the questions of a mere mortal irrelevant for the most part. Kavallac's expression was neutral enough Kaylin couldn't tell what she was thinking.

"You know about the Keeper?"

Half of Starrante's eyes blinked. "We are aware of the position, yes."

"Did you ever meet any of the people who held that position?"

"I did not, no. Some of my distant kin did—but they are gone now." Starrante turned eyes in the direction of the other two Arbiters.

"I met the Keeper before I was chosen as Arbiter," Androsse said, sounding slightly less bored. "The current Keeper is not the same individual."

"No. The current Keeper is mortal. Or was mortal, before he became the Keeper. He's old now."

Kavallac rumbled. "Why are you asking this question? I perceive there is a reason for it."

Bellusdeo didn't consider that reason to be as urgent as her own, but she didn't interrupt the older Dragon.

"I spoke with the current Keeper while on my regular patrol for the Halls of Law." Kaylin hesitated, which was what she should have done before she'd asked the first question. But anything that unsettled the Keeper—or, to be fair, the elementals for whom he had responsibility—could cause problems on a worldwide scale.

Kaylin understood why Bellusdeo was frantic. In the gold Dragon's position, she'd've felt the same way. But her sisters were already dead; their lives couldn't be saved. Kavallac cleared her throat. Loudly.

"The Keeper has noticed a disturbance in the garden he tends; the elementals have been unsettled for half of the past month."

"And you feel this is relevant to our research."

Kaylin sucked in stale air. She didn't like to talk about Mrs. Erickson, and in specific the current difficulties her abilities had brought to Helen. But Mrs. Erickson was at the heart of the research, the very strange ghosts, and Bellusdeo's pain and guilt. They were entwined.

"Mrs. Erickson found ghosts in the heart of the Imperial Palace. She managed to talk those ghosts into coming home with her—with us. Those ghosts were capable of possessing the current Arkon. I mean, that's already dangerous, but I think Mrs. Erickson has those ghosts under control for now."

"Ghosts of which race?" Kavallac asked.

"That's the problem. I could, with effort, see them. Terrano, with effort, can see something. But they don't look like they were ever alive in any way I understand life—not to me. Mrs. Erickson sees them as people. Normal people. Upset and uncertain people. She could coax them into my house, and Helen has tried to create rooms or containments for them."

"And that has worked?"

Kaylin grimaced. "It's a work in progress."

"This is relevant, then."

"More than relevant, sadly. But these ghosts were in the Imperial Palace; there were many ghosts in the phased house attached to Mrs. Erickson's home, but they were all human, or had been when they were alive." She inhaled again. "I think the elementals in the Keeper's garden had become at least peripherally aware of the work Azoria An'Berranin was doing before her death; something about her work had begun to overlap our world, although she did most of it from a pocket space."

Starrante clicked as Serralyn came into view; she made a beeline for Starrante and stood just in front of him—as Robin, one of the Academia's human students, often did when in the Arbiter's presence.

"What work, then?" Starrante said, his eyes lifted from his body.

"I'm sure she kept notes. Not all of those notes might overlap our current research—but I think some probably should, if notebooks make their way here." Kaylin inhaled and then exhaled slowly.

Starrante clicked for a long moment before replying. "That will depend. The library boasts a collection of all written endeavor—but that writing occurs in what you would consider our reality. Your reality. The extensive search might take too long," he added, "to be of use to Mrs. Erickson."

Kaylin shook her head and decided to lay all of her remaining cards on the figurative table. "Azoria found the remnants of a dead Ancient in the outlands. She was using their corpse, and the power inherent in it, for some goal of her own."

07

The silence that followed was so complete, even breath didn't disturb it. Eyes flickered, shifting color as the statement was absorbed. Even Bellusdeo was staring at the side of Kaylin's head. The chancellor, like Kavallac, was still, his eyes a red-flecked orange.

It was Androsse who recovered first. "What exactly do you mean by a dead Ancient?"

It was a damn good question. Kaylin glanced at Terrano. She wanted him to answer it. He was tight-lipped. Serralyn was silent as well, her eyes a dark blue. *Great.*

"Did Bakkon not mention it?"

"I am not certain Bakkon was aware of it; I am certain he would have had much to say, otherwise," Starrante replied. His eyes were also red, and half of them had extended to their full height.

Kavallac's rumble contained no words. When she found them, they were curt and visceral. "Answer the Arbiter's question, Chosen." Not Corporal, Chosen.

"I don't fully understand it myself. Azoria had created a space adjacent to our world; it existed beside a small bungalow in an otherwise decent neighborhood. That bungalow was occupied by Mrs. Erickson, who now lives with me. Azoria was clearly capable of creating pocket spaces with ease; I think—and I'm not certain—that she began to experiment while the High Halls wasn't fully active, as it is now; she certainly understood how to reach what I call the outlands.

"I think she must have started with paintings, and she refined them; she could draw power from trapped, living Barrani. She could, I think, draw power from their True Names, even if she couldn't read them or speak them."

"Barrani are not Ancients," Androsse said, eyes narrow.

"You knew Azoria."

"He did," Kavallac said, the words tinged with anger. The two were prone to heated arguments, which no rational person wanted—but if they started, the meeting in the library would be over. Bellusdeo wouldn't get access to the fruits of their reluctant research, but Kaylin wouldn't be on the hot seat, being interrogated.

"I don't know how she found the Ancient, but it was clear she could already manipulate the matter of the outlands to some extent. But by this point, I think she understood how to draw power from True Names, from True Words—and I think the Ancients are fully stuffed with them. I think it's their blood—literal blood." She hesitated and glanced at the former Arkon. "The ancient mirror at the heart of the Imperial Palace—"

The chancellor lifted a hand. "There are things about which we do not speak in the presence of outsiders."

Kaylin couldn't decide if that meant the Arbiters, the cohort, or her. The Arbiters were the power in the room, if *room* was the right word, but she'd leave the library, and the chancellor remained part of the Dragon Court, which included the Emperor, her ultimate boss, who was also not trapped in the library.

She had seen that ancient mirror, and had seen the fragments of its past, its creation: the blood of Ancients had been shed there, to give the mirror power.

That wasn't the way mirrors were created now.

And calling it a mirror was wrong; it was just convenient, a way of understanding its function. It could be a mirror. But it could also be a graveyard. It was from this mirror that the ghosts of words had risen when Mrs. Erickson had walked into the cavern.

Kaylin understood death. It was the worst part of her job: murder, the collection and dissection of corpses, the need to find the killer to bring them to justice—or at least prevent them from making more victims. She'd seen Barrani corpses, had stood beside Red in the morgue when he examined human corpses.

No experience with death made sense of either Mrs. Erickson's ghosts or the being Kaylin had found in the outlands: the Ancient, who, while dead, could still speak.

"The Ancients were sometimes called the lords of law and the lords of chaos," Androsse said. "You have seen their work in the races that populate your city; you have never seen the grandeur of their labors as it once existed in *Ravellon*. The Ancients created the Towers that exist to this day in your fiefs.

"They created the Academia. They created this library—the finest of their achievements, the repository of all learning, the remnant of dead worlds, and the evidence of worlds that have not yet come to their end. But they have deserted us, their many, many children; they have left the worlds an empty, mundane place. We assumed, we eldest, that they had left to create different worlds, different planes; that they had chosen to walk in a fashion that we, lesser in all ways, could not survive.

"And you tell us that one is dead? They are deathless, Chosen."

"Azoria had bound them. I freed them. I think she was attempting to drain their power. She'd already managed to do this with her own people—Barrani—and there was a power in this Ancient that far exceeded her own kind's.

"I think she was trying to create a new language, a different truth—at least for herself. I think she was trying to change her True Name."

"Azoria did not—and would *never*—have the power to bind an Ancient!"

"Not a living one, no. But a corpse? A body?"

Androsse looked scandalized; it was the first time Kaylin had seen that expression on his face. He then turned to Kavallac. "It appears you may not have been entirely mistaken about Azoria."

Kavallac exhaled smoke. "You have always been too appreciative of boundless ambition." Her voice was quieter, less rumbling, as she accepted Androsse's no doubt extremely rare peace offering.

"But after I broke the words she'd tried to create, the Ancient woke. They said they were dead. I'm not a shaman—you've done your research, right?—so the dead don't speak to me the usual way. This one did. I think... I found it hard to talk to them. I wasn't even certain my voice could reach them. But they said they were dead because they had fulfilled their purpose."

"What purpose?" Androsse's voice was a snap of sound.

"I don't know. I didn't ask. I think...if they're truly endless, death is about change, to them. But I didn't ask a lot of questions."

Androsse was a pot of simmering frustration, but it didn't boil over. "I am uncertain that I would be able to properly question such a being, so your poor effort must be forgiven." By his tone, very reluctantly. "Has Mrs. Erickson interacted with the Ancient?"

Kaylin shook her head. "I'm not sure the Emperor would approve of that, either."

The chancellor agreed, but Kaylin was now thinking. If the ghosts Mrs. Erickson was babysitting came somehow from the blood of the Ancients, if they had been trapped in, part of, the ancient mirror at the heart of the Imperial Palace, maybe the Ancient themselves would be able to help Mrs. Erickson. Or help the ghosts.

"Mrs. Erickson doesn't use power consciously." But even as the words left Kaylin's mouth, she hesitated; Mrs. Erickson had used her power consciously—after getting Jamal's permission. She had promised Jamal she would never do something again. Which meant she'd done it at least once in the distant past.

Bellusdeo cleared her throat in full draconic fashion. "She spoke to the ghosts of my sisters deliberately."

"Yes—but she spoke to them the way she'd speak to any of us. I mean, anyone alive. When she was younger, she couldn't even tell the difference. The dead don't look like corpses to her. They don't look the way they did at death. She meant to speak to them, yes—they were upset and isolated, and she's the type of gentle soul who reaches out. I don't think she can stop herself."

"It's why you like her so much," the gold Dragon replied. "And I understand why you're worried for her." Bellusdeo swallowed.

The chancellor very gently placed a hand on her left shoulder. "The research done here, the research done by Helen, will help Mrs. Erickson to better understand—and help—your sisters."

To Kaylin's shock, Bellusdeo turned toward the chancellor. "Lannagaros—I know. I know. But she said they were weeping. I survived. I was the only one who survived. My name is their name."

"It is all of your names," was his quiet reply. Kaylin had never seen Bellusdeo look so young. "It has always been thus. We are expendable. The mothers of the Aeries are not."

"Then why are they weeping? Did I do this to them? Am I doing something now that I'm not even aware of?"

"I cannot answer that question. But I remember you. I remember all of your sisters. They were the most difficult hatchlings in the Aerie—possibly in any Aerie. Perhaps it is why I can tolerate Terrano; he reminds me of your sisters. Mrs. Erickson did you no kindness, but she wants to help. And if I understand what has happened, she doesn't know how. It would be safe for her to interact with your sisters, and if it brings you comfort, you might ask Helen if you can visit more often.

"But you are a Tower lord now. You cannot simply abandon your fief. I promise that the Arbiters are giving their research their full attention; if not before, certainly now. But this is new to us. You will help your sisters, but if Mrs. Erickson's power is not understood, unintentional damage might be done. The consequences of that power have already been seen once. The Emperor is aware of her existence; he is aware of her lack of malicious intent.

"But tidal waves and earthquakes have no malice. We are attempting to understand whether or not she is, or will be, a cataclysmic disaster, and the Arbiters have thrown all of their vast powers of research into that very question. I understand your urgency—but inasmuch as it is possible, be patient. You have duties to the living that I fear you have been neglecting; concentrate on those. You cannot drag the corporal to the Academia every single night until you have answers."

Kaylin was grateful for the chancellor's intervention. Bellusdeo quieted, but her eyes were pure copper, shadowed and dark.

"What has research unearthed?" It was the chancellor who asked, taking the reins of the discussion from Kaylin's hands.

"If we assume that Mrs. Erickson is not a Necromancer, very little."

"And if you assume she is?"

"There is more information. It cannot, we are informed, leave the Academia; it should not leave the library."

"Forbidden studies, then."

"Indeed. There are more recent studies and documentation

about the field of Necromancy; it was once a studied ability in the Arcanum."

Of course it was.

"When he says recent," Kavallac added, "he refers to a period of four and a half centuries ago. It was not well understood, and the study was forbidden by the Emperor when he took power. It was not that Necromantic magics were feared—it was the experiments surrounding that study that caused issues. One Barrani Arcanist destroyed a small human village in order to have necessary experimental materials.

"We were informed that that threat was ended. The criminal is dead." Her tone made clear that her only regret was her inability to be the cause of that death.

Androsse, however, didn't care.

Kaylin thought, watching him, that his current intensity was unusual because Androsse cared only about the fate of the library. She thought he'd let the world burn, and find amusement in the chaos and destruction, as long as that destruction didn't touch the library at all. Yet he cared, in some fashion, about the dead Ancient. The speaking, walking Ancient who was not, in any way Kaylin's life experience had defined the word, dead.

She shook her head; Androsse's stare was like a physical threat, it was fastened so grimly on her. He had no desire to discuss Necromancy now; all of his attention was on the dead Ancient, and therefore the person who'd been stupid enough to mention it.

Kavallac was less focused, or perhaps she wished to annoy Androsse. She continued. "Necromantic abilities were not as reliable in study as they were in story, but the Necromancer could, with effort and will, force bodies to move; they could, with the same effort, command those moving corpses. Not all of the bodies rose; not all of the bodies could mimic the movements they had once had in life. The research was done on human corpses, and I believe some Leontine corpses as well."

In spite of herself, Kaylin was curious. "How many of the corpses could the Necromancer animate?"

Androsse chose to join the conversation. "A third of the villagers. The third that could be animated rose immediately upon Necromantic command. But the commands obeyed were rudimentary; movement, very simple tasks. Nor did the magic preserve the bodies."

"Mrs. Erickson has had nothing to do with corpses."

"No? Very well, no. It is my suspicion that the Arcanist who studied this discipline was lacking what Mrs. Erickson has: the ability to see ghosts, to see the echoes of the living. Were Mrs. Erickson to make the attempt—"

The chancellor cleared his throat, Dragon style.

Androsse was annoyed.

"It is *forbidden*, Arbiter. What you choose to do in the confines of the library is beyond the mandate of Imperial Law. Mrs. Erickson is not."

"Those studies hint at the absence of natural talent," Androsse replied, voice cool. "The researcher understood the forms but did not have the ability. It is possible that Mrs. Erickson might have that ability."

"She is an old, mortal woman," Bellusdeo said. "She'd probably faint at the sight of a corpse. Regardless, the chancellor would not allow her to participate in any such experiments. The Emperor has forbidden them entirely." And so did the gold Dragon. "If it's possible that her natural talent would supply what the Arcanist lacked, it remains irrelevant."

"If there is no study, there is no further understanding."

Bellusdeo turned to Starrante, as almost all of the students who came to the library did. There were exceptions, of course; some were so terrified of spiders that they couldn't get past their terror. "Arbiter, the studies about shamans?"

"They are not direct studies; they were personal biographies, personal stories of interactions with those who claimed to be shamans. It is difficult to gauge their authenticity; biographic information is often far more emotional than clinical. There are those in Elantra now who claim to be able to confer with the dead."

Kaylin's expression immediately soured as she thought of Margot and the rest of the Elani street vultures. Yes, there bloody well were. "Did they use crystal balls?"

"Do not bring your contempt for Elani street into this." A flicker of orange shifted the copper in Bellusdeo's eyes.

"Some, indeed, used those focal elements. They may have been necessary for the shamans to exercise the full range of their powers; it is the reason many mages depend on wands or staves," the chancellor said.

"If we ditch those—" Kaylin kept the grimace off her face with effort "—is there anything left?"

Starrante's eyes had once again settled into his body. "There are three. But they are not technical in nature; indeed, they are also, at core, emotional. They are not, to our eyes, different from those incidents that involve crystal balls, herbal remedies, or similar elements.

"In all of these stories, the shaman in question behaved very differently from Necromancers; they did not insist on the presence of corpses, although two did conduct their activities at gravesides. I believe, however, they chose to do so to draw as clear a line as possible between the living and the dead, so that the living might, at last, be freed from the darker elements of human grief."

"Did those who wrote about this actually see the dead?"

"Where herbal remedies were used, yes, but it is highly likely that those remedies made the recipient far more suggestible. We cannot be certain that what they saw was not a product of their own fear or longing. In most cases, the shaman, the medium, was the conduit to the dead. Mrs. Erickson has no artificial ceremonies, but it is possible that the shamans thus noted in these texts did not require them, either; I believe they were meant as gestures of respect, something the living might better appreciate.

"But in one case—and I think this is the closest example we have found to Mrs. Erickson—a young woman appeared at the door of a wealthy lord's manor. She did not go to the trade entrance; she simply knocked at the grand front doors and waited. The author of this account was a child at the time and heard the noise—he came down the stairs to find his mother and father at the door.

"His mother was weeping; his father was furious; he summoned guards to have the woman either driven away or killed. The mother, however, countermanded those orders, as she was the lord of the manor; she ordered the guards to apprehend her husband, or to stop him from interfering.

"The young woman then spoke to…thin air for some time. That thin air was, purportedly, what remained of the child's sister, who had run away from home."

To Kaylin, it didn't sound like biography. Her expression must have contained some skepticism.

"You are wondering why we believe there is some grounding in fact in this incident."

"I am, sorry."

"The woman who ordered her husband apprehended on that night wrote many, many volumes in her life, which was markedly long for a mortal. None of those volumes were fiction; many were magical engineering manuals. She was remarkable, and although she was often accused of flights of fancy, even those whimsical flights of fancy proved grounded and true in the end.

"All information is sifted, evaluated. We look at the surrounding cultural context, the contemporaries of the author. It is part of the reason research can be so time-consuming. We might find something that seems promising, but attempting to verify it in an objective fashion can easily increase our time by an order of magnitude—if only that.

"Everything we present to you has been vetted in this fashion. There are thousands of stories involving the dead; most are, as you suspect, unverifiable. They are relegated to fiction."

Kaylin exhaled. "But the author of this biography wasn't the shaman in question."

"No. The woman's written forays into her personal life were very, very few. The author of this incident was her son. It was an interesting biography; his childhood provided personal insight into a scholar and mage of some power. He was spare with his words, which gave the illusion that he embellished very little. As her child, he was mentioned in contemporary sources, but not to any great extent; beyond this, very little is known about him.

"But the timing of this recollection and the timing of the death of the lord's husband—and daughter—overlap exactly. She did not write about ghosts. She did not write about shamans. But she did write about the discovery of her daughter's corpse, and she did write about her husband's execution, the latter in some detail.

"And I have lamentably digressed."

Androsse rolled his eyes.

"The child's father caused a bit of disturbance; he attempted to kill this strange visitor, and he became increasingly unhinged. He had not been friendly to his son, and his son had craved—as human young do—approval and affection, neither of which was offered. The father's love, such as it was, had been for the younger sister. The boy had resented her, and had tried very hard to keep his distance, because he loved her and hated her, both.

"But she ran away from home one day. The servants could not find her. She was equipped with rings that might be easily traced with magic, but no invasive magics—such as slave seals—had been cast. The ring was found, but it was no longer with the boy's sister.

"And the shaman who came to the front door, the shaman who asked—in an eerily neutral voice, as the son described it later—to speak with the lord, carried the word of the dead. She spoke a single name, and the lord grew still. And then the lord commanded three things: that the woman be allowed to enter, that she be treated as an honored guest, and that her husband be incarcerated.

"The stranger was odd; she would turn to her right and she would speak; the boy could hear the murmurs as if they were half a conversation. The lord had questions for her, and the boy followed at a discreet distance; he wished to hear what was said, but knew he would be sent back to his room if he was discovered.

"He eavesdropped, and perhaps his mother allowed it—or perhaps her thoughts were occupied with tragedy and its consequences. He said that this experience shattered everything he had thought and known: The sister he had resented and envied was dead. Her body was in the manor. The father was not a man without power, and it had not occurred to the lord to be suspicious of him, except in a desultory way."

"What do you mean, desultory?"

"She had food tasters, among other things. She did not immediately choose to trust the stranger, but the stranger continued her one-sided conversation, and it was clear to the lord that if this woman was a terrible, predatory sham, she was either the actual murderer or she was speaking the truth. The shaman knew things about her daughter that could not be casually known.

"She tested the stranger; her son remembers that clearly. She asked questions, seemingly at random. The woman did not even need to convey the questions to the ghost; the ghost, unseen, unfelt, could hear them. She conveyed the answers. On occasion, his sister's ghost appeared to argue. He could imagine—he said—the stamp of her foot, the waving of fists, even the squeal of frustration.

"He believed she was there. Abandoning caution and secrecy, he burst into the small room; the guards stopped him, but they did not have time to eject him. He believed his sister was present. He believed the stranger. And he needed to tell his sister something: that he loved her, that he missed her, and that he was sorry about their fight, sorry that it was the last living thing he'd given her.

"The shaman turned to him; he was surprised because she was only barely adult. But she smiled and said, 'Your sister says, *I'm sorry you're an idiot.*' As final words went, they were perhaps not a comfort, but they were real. *I was jealous of you. I didn't* want *to be loved. And I couldn't tell you. Take care of my dog.*

"He, too, believed the young woman who said she could speak with the dead. And envied her."

"Some people are garbage," Kaylin said, teeth on edge.

"I cannot argue that. But this particular incident—I feel it is something Mrs. Erickson could do now. The lord questioned the young woman. The shaman refused to speak about anything but the desire of the ghost she had accompanied. If she had a greater power, there was no evidence of it. The power that she used was similar to Mrs. Erickson's, except in one regard: she could bring that ghost home."

"Mrs. Erickson did bring the ghosts from the palace to her new home," Kaylin said. "The children to whom she was most attached had no desire for vengeance; if Mrs. Erickson had attempted to take them to confront their killer, they'd've done everything they could to prevent it.

"The ghosts of those children were bound to Mrs. Erickson's home."

Bellusdeo said, "And my sisters are bound to me."

"For now," Kaylin told her former roommate. "What we

need to discover is why, and if that binding can be broken in any way."

The chancellor's head swiveled as he turned a brief, warning glare on Kaylin.

"Chancellor," Arbiter Kavallac said. "I believe it is now time to discuss what coming-of-age means to Dragonkind. Lord Bellusdeo is clearly in possession of her adult name. Bellusdeo, how many sisters did you have?"

"Eight."

"Eight? Impressive. That would have been a cause for celebration in the Aerie of my own youth."

"Why?"

"Because there were nine of you. Nine in total."

Bellusdeo blinked.

"Perhaps your Aerie did not discuss the details of what coming-of-age means. You were fragile at birth, in a way that your brothers were not. In our Aerie, we were separated for our safety; the young hatchlings are far too rough. We were taught the use of sword, and of magic; we were educated in several languages, and in theories and modes of governance. The boys were not; they would have shredded books and burned desks—at best.

"I had four sisters; it was considered auspicious. Do you know why?"

Bellusdeo was mute.

"Lannagaros," Kavallac said, voice louder. "How lackadaisical was your Aerie?"

"I remind you that we were embroiled in a war, Arbiter. Bellusdeo and her sisters were partially educated, but they were chaotic. Had they the ability, they would have been far more like Terrano than it appears your own sisters were."

Kavallac exhaled a small plume of fire. "Let me explain, then—perhaps you were taken from your Aerie before the difficult discussions had begun."

Bellusdeo nodded, her eyes an odd color.

"My sisters and I were not the same person, although we were identical in form; small blemishes, some scars—the intrepid had insisted on exploring the entirety of the Aerie, and when permission was denied, they went anyway—were the only distinguishing differences. We had personalities of our own, and when we were young, ambitions of our own, daydreams of our own. We pursued similar fields of study but chose to specialize in those that suited our abilities.

"And when we were almost of age, the Aerie's first mother called us into her presence. We had wondered why, if there were five of us, and if other Aeries had similar numbers of female children, there were, even then, so few female Dragons.

"And we learned. She had called us for that reason." Kavallac's lips curved in a gentle smile. "The day she was born, there were three girls. I was one of five. As we five, the three were not of one mind, not of one body—not then.

"We watched our brothers leave the Aerie; we watched them gain the skies. We watched them fight and injure each other to prove their fitness." Her grimace made clear what she thought of that. "Did we envy them?" She looked at Bellusdeo. "Did you?"

"They could go to war."

The Arkon coughed but didn't otherwise interrupt. Kaylin understood why. This was a conversation between two Dragons, one an Arbiter who would never return to the life she'd been born to, and the other, the only remaining hope of Dragonkind.

"Would you care to explain, Lannagaros?" The use of his name, not his title, added texture to the question.

"They could not, as you put it, go to war. Not as they were; they would descend entirely into bestiality as war became personal territoriality. I have never understood why you were born as you were; I—we—were not. We lacked the substance of an adult name, an adult form. To us, the human form is a sign of adulthood."

Kaylin lifted a hand.

Bellusdeo grimaced.

"I thought you didn't have a name. I mean, at birth."

Kavallac and the chancellor exchanged a glance. Kavallac spoke first. "I was not born as you are born," she said. "If you wish to clarify, do so; it is not relevant to this discussion otherwise."

"The corporal has a tendency to interrupt if she is confused or realizes that she does not understand," the former Arkon said.

"I thought Kaylin had no desire to become a student; it seems to me that this tendency could flourish in the Academia."

Great. Just what she wanted: a dozen condescending and dismissive professors who could look down on her and treat her as if she was stupid. No, thanks. She managed, barely, to keep this to herself.

"Male Dragons live, from birth, without names." The Arkon glanced at Kavallac; she nodded. She meant him to continue.

Bellusdeo's eyes narrowed. She opened her mouth, but Kavallac shook her head, a gentle motion, almost a request.

"When we come of age, we search for our adult names. We are not guaranteed to find them, and if we do, we are not guaranteed to survive the finding. You have tales of Dragons, children's stories. Perhaps you believe that they arose from ignorance and fear; you have met Dragons. You know what we are.

"But it is our belief that your tales contain a kernel of truth. There are those who could not, or did not, find the names by which they could bind the bestial and the intellectual. They became a danger because they lacked that essential self-control." The chancellor exhaled. "Yes, Corporal?"

"Are you saying it's the human form that gives you that?"

"No. I am saying that our ability to hold that form, to truly master it, is the proof that we have developed that self-control, that awareness. We went in search of names that would prove that we had the awareness, the impulse control, necessary to join our kin, to join a flight, and to take war to our enemies without descending into primal instinct and competitiveness better suited to beasts."

Bellusdeo was frowning, but it was a more measured frown; she was clearly thinking about the chancellor's words.

"I was born in a different era," Kavallac said, when it was clear the chancellor had no more to add. "War was not ever on our minds, and the survival of Dragonkind was never in question. None of us bear the burden that you now bear." She exhaled smoke, her eyes a blend of copper and gold. "I could not have carried it." When she turned to the chancellor, her tone was far less gentle. "I could not carry it, and I had been taught everything that might have been of aid."

"They were lost far before that education would have begun." The chancellor's expression was neutral, but his eyes had shaded to copper. Copper with flecks of red; it was an unusual combination. "And I was responsible for them as a minder, not an educator. Before we lost them, the Aerie mother was responsible for their teaching, but those lessons were in their future, not their past."

Kavallac nodded, the copper in her eyes almost glinting. "Perhaps, even if you were taught what we were taught, the experience would not be so easily conveyed; it would be secondhand." She turned once again to Bellusdeo. "I realize this is not the reason you have traveled to the library, but your situation is unique, and perhaps it will be of aid to you, regardless.

"Lannagaros is not wrong. The Aerie mother, your mother, was responsible for teaching what must be taught. But it could not be taught to children, and you were—all of you—children when you were lost to your Aerie. We were not lost in the same fashion. We were schooled almost as the Academia students are schooled now; we had classrooms, not caverns. Our lessons were lectures; we did not learn to hunt, and we certainly did not learn to kill.

"But we grew, almost as mortals grow, although not nearly as quickly. And when we came of age, we were summoned, at last, to the Aerie. We were excited, I confess; we felt that the journey to join our kin, our kind, had finally begun.

"The mother of our Aerie told us two things on that first day: That we would form an Aerie of our own when we at last laid our clutch, and that there would be only one of us at that time. Only one would remain."

08

Bellusdeo's eyes were full-on copper; the Dragon was unusually pale. Armor didn't bend as easily as cloth; she was therefore upright, rigid.

Kavallac waited until Bellusdeo nodded before she continued.

Kaylin glanced at the chancellor; his expression was a mask. Hard to tell whether or not this had surprised him; his eyes remained predominantly copper.

"As you now imagine, this was a shock to us. Were we meant to kill each other? Were we meant to compete in a complicated duel to the death? We would not do it. If I desired, on any given day, to strangle two or three of my sisters, I would never, ever kill them. If I trusted nothing else, I trusted them. We were not to spend time with our brothers—and perhaps Lannagaros has done us a favor, for his explanation makes clear why."

Kaylin lifted a hand.

"Corporal."

"If Dragons finding their adult names, their actual True Names, is expressed by the human form, and girls are born as humans..."

Kavallac's nod held grudging approval. "Serralyn, my apologies, but I will ask you to leave before I continue; I should not have spoken so freely."

Serralyn swallowed, nodded, and immediately walked through the portal Kavallac had created with a simple gesture. The Barrani student wasn't a fool—she had no desire to hear secrets of Dragonkind. Not as a Barrani.

Kaylin glanced at the portal and moved toward it, but it winked out of existence before she could reach it.

"Not you, Chosen. I am told you were present when Bellusdeo at last transcended her childhood. You have some understanding of what I am about to say, and your unusual nature—the marks of the Chosen—might have a role to play in Bellusdeo's difficulty that the wise cannot foresee."

Kaylin glanced at Bellusdeo for permission. The gold Dragon failed to see her until Kavallac answered the question she had asked. "Yes, Chosen. No Dragon is adult without possession of a True Name. Every Dragon of your acquaintance has achieved that fusion: word and being.

"But the male Dragons and their arduous process is not the process I faced; it is not the process Bellusdeo and her sisters faced. It is not something that was discussed with the fathers or the other adults within the Aerie."

Kaylin knew she didn't know enough about Dragons, but this wasn't something taught in racial relations classes. If it had been, she'd've paid more attention. "You...you had names. From birth."

"We had nascent names. The immature name I was granted at birth is not the name I now possess. We were never to speak of them, to offer them to others; they had the power that names have. Perhaps the Ancients who created us wished to lessen the threat of youthful folly; we could come into possession of our adult names—and the danger a True Name can present—when we were of an age that that youth would not count against us.

"It is not the way Barrani names work; nor is it the way Wevaran names work. I do not know the process by which Arbiter Androsse's kin wakened—and that is entirely irrelevant to this discussion." This was a warning to Androsse, who lingered in the area. She offered no like warning to Starrante.

"So on the day we were considered of age to join our mother, and she told us that only one of us would survive, it was not the welcome step into adulthood we had anticipated. One of my sisters, who tended to be more vocal and more immediate in her reactions, said as much. We lacked the full vocal cords of our adult people, but our voices were higher pitched, and hers carried. The mother simply nodded.

"We asked if she had killed her siblings. She had not. And, Bellusdeo, you have not killed your sisters, either."

"Then why—" the gold Dragon's voice was low, shaky "—are they weeping? Why are they trapped and bound to me?"

Kavallac's inner eye membranes rose, but the muted color was copper. So much sorrow in draconic eyes today. "There are accidents in the Aerie. I mentioned that some of my siblings had scars, did I not? Our bodies in childhood are frail—they are not the bodies of the male children. One of my sisters did not survive. Our people are not famous healers with reason.

"We went from five to four, and the mother grieved; her wails shook the Aerie for the entirety of the day." Kavallac exhaled, bowing her head in remembrance before she continued. "We had not yet finished our lessons, our classes. But in those classes, we were— Ah." She frowned. "Lannagaros, this cannot leave the library. Do you understand? I am willing to speak of things that would never have been spoken of in your presence, because I perceive you are our young queen's sole emotional support, and the rest of the Dragon Court is appallingly ignorant."

The chancellor nodded, bowing his head as if to the greater power.

"In her presence, we learned each other's True Names."

Kaylin's brows rose into her hairline before they descended again.

Bellusdeo hesitated, and then said, "Did you not learn them before this?"

"It was forbidden."

"Rules that can't be enforced shouldn't exist."

Kavallac chuckled. "You ignored those rules. Of course you did. You knew the True Names of your sisters."

"It was easiest."

Kaylin wondered if this was why Bellusdeo could tolerate the cohort so well. They had made the same choice that she and her sisters had, if for different reasons. She stopped. Were the reasons that different, after all? The girls were born frail; they were raised separately for their own safety and survival. They did not leave the Aerie often—if at all—because they had no wings. They couldn't fly.

"That was a disturbing lesson, but necessary. We thought, at the time, that it was to promote either closeness or caution. It opened up a world to us; we had lived together as the closest of kin for all of our lives—but we became far, far closer as a result.

"Our mother told us that the reason we were born as we were was to learn, to absorb, to have different interests, different passions, different ambitions; to accumulate magical knowledge, historical knowledge—everything individuals who were nonetheless closely connected would have.

"She asked us what we were willing to lose, if we were willing to lose anything at all. She asked us if we could imagine murdering—that was her word, and I feel in retrospect that it was far too melodramatic—our sisters. We had already lost one, and the grief of that taught us everything we needed to know about loss. We could not countenance another such loss—let alone becoming the cause of it."

Bellusdeo nodded. She had no words.

"She left us with that question, and with the discussions that arose from it—the desperation, the certainty that only one of us could survive, the discussions about which one of us it would ultimately be. We criticized each other's choices, and we elevated them as well—the choices we had not, by inclination, made ourselves. We called for votes, we called for consensus—it was a tumultuous, difficult period. We did hate our mother then.

"We eventually came to a decision: we chose. We had experienced loss and grief and we did not want to be the only survivor; we did not want to live with that loss in isolation." Kavallac lifted her face; she was smiling, and there was a serenity to that smile that was rare.

"I had no choice," Bellusdeo whispered. "We had no choice. We had gone in search of our adult names, as we were taught." Her eyes flared a deep, almost shocking red.

"Taught by who?"

"A…male Dragon." The loathing in her words transformed grief to the crimson of rage. "He taught us how adult names are found and made."

"That is not how our adult names are made or found," Kavallac replied.

"I know. I know that now." Bellusdeo's voice was low, almost a whisper.

Kavallac glanced at the chancellor. He said nothing, but his eyes had shifted from grief to anger, the rage slower to arrive than Bellusdeo's.

Kavallac lifted a hand—as if she were, in truth, Bellusdeo's mother, and not an Arbiter of this endless library. "When I speak now, I speak as a single person. But every single one of my surviving sisters is with me. I am multiple.

"On the last day of our childhood lessons, the Aerie mother guided us and explained to us how the mothers of the Aeries come of age. Our names merged—it was fraught and terrifying at the time. But when we emerged from our final lesson, there was, as our mother had said at the beginning, only one of us. But that one was all.

"I could handle a sword. I could read multiple languages. I could cast spells from different schools of magic. I could sing. I could write music. I could remember all of our lives as if they had been only one life: the sum of us, the sum of our childhoods. That is how we who are mothers emerge into the world as adults.

"And I could, at last, become a Dragon; the skies were no longer beyond my reach if the adults would not condescend to carry me."

Bellusdeo was silent. When Kavallac's voice died into stillness, she continued to listen, as if clinging desperately to a glimpse of a vanished, lost home.

It was Kaylin who was therefore left with questions it was awkward—or worse—to ask. She would have waited, would have asked them of the chancellor later, when Bellusdeo was absent. But the chancellor wouldn't have answers.

She swallowed. No one wanted to talk about their own mistakes, but especially not the life-altering tragedies. And Bellusdeo had been the queen of her empire, a ruler who could not display weakness or uncertainty where it might be seen by her subjects.

Kaylin cleared her throat. She could ask to come back to the library later. She could. But while it was far safer to ask the questions behind Bellusdeo's back, it felt wrong. How, she didn't know. Safety was best, and it wasn't like she'd be using any information against her friend.

She decided on a half measure. She tapped Bellusdeo on the shoulder. "Can I speak to you in private for a minute?"

Bellusdeo frowned. She was no doubt considering what might require privacy. But she was unsettled, enraged, and there was only one thing that could cause that. She might have made a good Hawk. She understood, and nodded.

* * *

They stood surrounded by books about three city blocks away from the library's only other occupants.

Kaylin inhaled. She was afraid of angering Bellusdeo, and she was afraid of causing pain. Had she not felt viscerally certain that her unasked questions were important, or would be, she would have shut down the line of thought and walked away from it permanently.

"I don't have Immortal memory," she began, speaking slowly. All of her possible words seemed like the wrong ones, but that was the topic, not the words themselves.

"Stop it."

"What?"

"Ask. Just…ask. I obviously trust you enough that I won't assume malice, and I am an adult. I ruled an empire, a world. I was not in the habit of torturing or murdering my counselors when they brought up unpleasant topics."

"It's about the names. You said you were guided in the creation of, the finding of, your adult names."

Bellusdeo nodded.

"All of you? Were all of you guided the same way?"

"Yes."

"But you had names. Not adult names, but names?"

"We did."

"And you were namebound."

"Mortal memory cannot be this bad. Were you not listening to Arbiter Kavallac?"

"I was—but she never did what you did. She never met the Outcaste. She was never a denizen of a world that was falling to Shadow. I want to ask her how…how that might have affected you. How having something that could be a placeholder for an adult name—while you were all separate individuals—could have affected the…merging."

"Did you know?"

"No, not before—not before your True Name fully emerged. But I understood it while I was—while I was helping you. I understood the rightness of it. I understood what had to happen."

Bellusdeo, pale, looked up.

"I want to ask her what might have happened had you and your sisters—without the guidance of a mother—found adult names and forms individually."

Silence. Bellusdeo closed her eyes, her hands by her sides. They weren't fists, but fists might have been better; there was so much unsaid it felt like an unbearable weight had descended on the Dragon. Kaylin had no way to carry it.

"What answers? What answers do you think she'll have?"

"I don't know. But… I'm a Hawk."

The sentence made no sense to the Dragon; her eyes opened, her brows folded, and she turned to Kaylin, eyes orange. "Believe that we all know that. What does that have to do with this?"

"Sometimes the questions we ask—the incidental questions, the unrelated questions—lead to answers. If Kavallac has no answers, she's a Dragon, she was raised differently, she understands adult names. The possible ramifications might lead her to questions we'd never even think to ask, and the answers to those questions might be what we need."

"You didn't ask."

"No."

"Why?"

"Because this isn't an investigation for the Halls of Law. It's…" Kaylin trailed off. There were some words she just wasn't good with. She'd never be good with them. At heart, she was an orphan from the fiefs. Yes, she was a Hawk, and she'd made that define her because it was better than being a helpless, useless fiefling, with no money, no purpose other than survival, however survival could be attained.

Bellusdeo had once been a queen, an empress. She had led

wars. She was the heart of the future of Dragonkind. She, too, had fought for survival. But never the way Kaylin had. There were thousands of people like Kaylin in the world. There was only one Bellusdeo.

"What is it?" Bellusdeo had never been famous for her patience, at least not in this world.

"I think of you as a friend. I don't have family, so my friends are important to me. I know there are things you don't want to talk about, and things you want kept secret. This one—the Outcaste—is the biggest one.

"If you don't want Kavallac to know, I don't want to mention it."

"Even if you're a Hawk?"

"Even then. I won't ask without your permission."

Bellusdeo exhaled smoke, her eyes flecked now with red. "How pathetic do you think me, Corporal?"

Kaylin flinched, but held Bellusdeo's gaze with her own. "I don't think you're pathetic at all."

"You must, if you feel that even the mention of the Outcaste will cause so much damage."

It wasn't only the damage to Bellusdeo that she was worried about. She almost asked if Bellusdeo considered her a friend, but couldn't. She couldn't force those words out of her mouth. She didn't want to look pathetic. She regretted her life choices, or at least the ones she'd made in the last five minutes.

"Ask her. At this very moment, hiding my own folly seems almost irrelevant."

They returned to the Arbiters and the chancellor; the four were speaking quiet Barrani. Bellusdeo would hear the words at this distance, but Kaylin wouldn't, the difference in their hearing was so marked. The words stilled as Bellusdeo approached. Or as Kaylin did.

Kavallac turned to the Hawk.

Kaylin began. "Dragons who are male are born with the physical prowess of your race. They find their adult names—and forms—somehow. It's not necessary that I know," she added, as the Arbiter's expression shifted. "I want to make sure I understand what you've said. The girls are born almost like Wevaran are born: they have parts of what must become the adult name—and when they achieve that, they gain the physical prowess; the emotional and intellectual strength is accessible at birth, but they have to grow into it."

"Yes."

"What happens if, on a distant world with no mother to guide them, the girls reach the age of maturity in terms of human form without somehow merging with their sisters?"

Kavallac's eyes had shaded from copper to orange. "They would remain as sisters."

"What then happens if a Dragon—a male Dragon—teaches those sisters how to form a True Name in the way that the male Dragons are forced to search for one? Assume the male Dragon had a vested interest in the results but possibly didn't know that the women are born with some fragmentary elements of a name."

Her eyes, predictably, adopted flecks of red. "I perceive that this is not a theoretical question."

"No. It's not."

Kavallac turned to Bellusdeo, who had adopted a familiar posture which Kaylin recognized only belatedly: it was how she stood when Kaylin was at work and the gold Dragon was shadowing her. Bellusdeo met Kavallac's gaze in silence; the investigation was in the corporal's hands.

Kaylin looked to Starrante, who was huddled, legs drawn into his body, all but two of his eye stalks housed there as well. "Has that ever happened to your kin?"

"We cannot leave our birthing place," was his slow reply.

"Not until we are complete. We are not Dragons; our design predates that race."

"If, in the birthing place, there was a way for the hatchlings to find, to build, an adult name the way Dragons do, how would that affect the gaining of a name?"

"You ask a complicated question. I have no immediate answer."

Kaylin nodded, and returned to Kavallac. "I have the same question for you. If the immature sisters could be guided the way the male hatchlings were, what effect would that have? If the sisters—all of the sisters—could fully transform into their draconic shape, would there be any need to merge?"

"I am not an Ancient, Corporal. I am considered wise, but I did not design our race; I did not bring Dragons into being. I cannot, without some meditation, begin to answer that question. Were there other circumstances you wish me to consider while I reflect?"

"The sisters," Kaylin replied.

"How so?"

"They died. They died before they could merge the nascent names to form a whole."

Kavallac's mouth opened soundlessly. To Bellusdeo she said, "Impossible."

"It's not impossible. We found their bodies—we found them here, within Elantra. It caused a bit of a stir because the bodies were identical; it was like the same person was dying over and over again."

"Corporal, I assume you are good at the duties required of a Hawk. I am—I was—as good at the duties required of a Dragon. Bellusdeo, as she stands before me now, is whole."

"How can you be so certain of that?"

"Lannagaros?" Kavallac said.

The chancellor was silent, marshaling words. When he spoke, he spoke quietly. "What she sees, I see."

"And the first time?" Kaylin demanded. "When you met her again?"

He shook his head.

"But…she could become a Dragon. You saw that."

"Yes."

"Did you not think something was wrong at the time?"

"I sensed no taint of Shadow. I sensed no hint that she was not as she appeared to be. But what she appeared to be at that time was a child. A familiar child. I was very frustrated by her in my youth—she and her many sisters—but very fond of them as well. We assumed they were dead, and we grieved.

"It is the gifts unasked for that move us most deeply, and her presence was that. If she could not be the future of the race, she could not—but she was nonetheless Bellusdeo." He turned to Bellusdeo then. "I wished for your happiness. Even now. We lived as a race without a future before; we survived it. I did not feel the pressure to become something other, to become something you had no desire to be, was reasonable."

Kavallac's expression made clear she did not agree. "What do you see when you are in her presence now?"

"Bellusdeo," he replied.

The Arbiter's eyes narrowed. To Bellusdeo she said, "Is your name now the one you retrieved with the aid of someone who did not understand?"

"No."

Kavallac exhaled smoke, her eyes more red than orange. "This is not the discussion I thought we would be having; you have given me much to consider." None of it, by her tone, pleasant. "I understand the question of Necromancy or shamanism is critical to your well-being, but there is too much now wrapped up in those questions. Allow us—or allow me—to retreat for now; there is far too much to research and consider.

"What you have asked, Corporal, is dangerous; it is possibly the reason that the Ancients, in the end, abandoned a race with the duality ours contains."

"Bellusdeo," the chancellor said, his voice gentle in the way it was only for the gold Dragon. "Will you not tell her the rest?"

"This is a Hawk investigation, for the moment—at the Hawk's request."

This was going to be a day in which Kaylin deeply and continually regretted her life choices.

"Kaylin, do continue," Bellusdeo added, when Kaylin failed to open her mouth.

She lowered her chin, her eyes now skirting various sets of feet. It was the only way she thought she'd be able to continue under the weight of different stares.

"Arbiter, when you lived in the Aerie, did you ever have to contend with outcastes?"

"No." The word was a vibration of sound that encompassed anger and denial.

"But you were aware of Dragon outcastes from other Aeries?"

"Yes." The single syllable took far longer to speak than Kaylin would have liked.

"I don't know if the chancellor has spoken to you about the early days of the Imperial Dragon Court."

"He has not."

Kaylin looked up from people's feet, swiveling her head toward the chancellor. His eyes were a deep, dark orange as they met hers. She really wanted him to take that part of the discussion and fill it in; he remained silent.

"One of the Dragons in the Imperial Court—in the Emperor's flight—is outcaste. He was not while he dwelled within the Aerie; he was considered a Dragon during the Draco-Barrani wars. But in the early attempts to investigate the heart of the fiefs, something he encountered there changed him."

"Lannagaros?"

The chancellor nodded.

"Very well. Continue."

"He was an adult Dragon; he understood the methods by which adults attained their True Names and forms. But he could traverse *Ravellon*, even after the Towers rose. And through *Ravellon*, he could traverse the portals that stood there—those that had not been destroyed, those through which Shadow traveled to devour worlds."

Kaylin met the Arbiter's gaze. Her early training took over. "Bellusdeo was lost to a different world: he found her—and her sisters—there."

"You are telling me that it was an outcaste who guided the nine children to incorrectly adopt their adult names?"

"Yes."

Had the library ceiling opened up to a storm of lightning bolts, it would probably have been more comfortable—she'd be forgiven for running away and dodging.

"Lannagaros."

"We did not—we could not—know."

"Does the Outcaste survive?"

It was Kaylin who answered. "Yes. And his name—I've seen it. He showed me. I don't think I could even begin to say it, to think it, because it's so complicated. It's like the name of a small world."

"You saw his name."

"He was fishing. If I tried to somehow use that name, to read it, the attempt would form a bridge between us. My will versus the will of an outcaste Dragon. I didn't take the bait."

"Perhaps one of the few moments of maturity and wisdom in your long career," the former Arkon said.

Kavallac exhaled fire—a small amount. Kaylin could feel its heat, although it didn't reach her. Hope squawked loudly, pushing himself up to stand at attention on Kaylin's shoulder. He clearly resented having to make the effort.

Kavallac coughed. "My apologies, Corporal. It appears that even the ancient and wise are not shorn of emotion. This is not the news I anticipated. Almost, I want to leave the library to confront the danger that faces the remnants of my race."

Which was impossible.

"Bellusdeo was guided to find her so-called adult name by a Dragon who understood the process—but did not understand how that process was different for Bellusdeo. She attained an adult name, and the fullness of the prowess of her form. As did her eight sisters, if I understand what I have heard." This time, she looked to Bellusdeo for an answer.

Bellusdeo nodded.

"And you knew those names."

The gold Dragon nodded again.

"I will not lecture you—as no doubt your mother would—about the folly of sharing your adult name; to you—and your sisters—it would be a simple, natural progression of the relationship you had shared to that point.

"I would be concerned—ah, far more than I am now—were you not Lord Bellusdeo of the fief of Bellusdeo. No Tower built by the Ancients would accept you as captain were you to be tainted by Shadow; indeed, at least in the case of the Tower you now occupy, I do not believe you would survive the encounter.

"But you are, to me, whole. Tell me, do you remember your lives?"

Bellusdeo frowned.

"Do you remember the lives of your sisters as if you were, singly, each of them? Or is your memory formed of your personal experience with each of the other eight?

"I told you that we were born as five, and one did not survive. I do not have her memories or experience; she was not part of the whole that I became. But I can remember each element of the four of us as if I personally lived it. I can trace the thread of each life as if it were my own.

"When you achieved your True Name, none of your sisters were alive."

"No."

"But the name you now bear is not the one you found for yourself under the guidance of the Outcaste."

"No."

"How, then, did you come by that name?"

Bellusdeo's hesitation was brief; Kavallac would notice it. "Is it relevant?"

"Yes. Because you have what you should not have if all of your sisters were dead before you achieved it. You should not possess the strength of name you clearly do.

"And perhaps that is why the ghosts that none of us, with the exception of a single, mortal woman, can see are weeping and lost. If you are now driven to somehow quiet the pain of the dead, it is an answer that will lead to necessary questions."

Bellusdeo said, "I will consider it. Understand that my attention, my power, has been turned toward the threat of Shadow, the heart of *Ravellon*, and the creatures that reside there, hemmed in on all sides."

Kaylin shook her head. "The Outcaste can—and has—left *Ravellon*. The Towers don't seem to be able to prevent his passage. He lives, as far as we can determine, in *Ravellon*, but whatever he consumes there, he can hide from the Towers."

Kavallac's eyes were blood red. So were Starrante's; Androsse's were midnight blue—moonless, midnight blue.

Kaylin exhaled then. She understood that Bellusdeo's silence was meant to protect her. Since she'd dragged the Dragon into a corner to ask permission to even mention the Outcaste, she understood it—and it was a relief.

"I helped," she told Kavallac. "I helped, with the power of the marks of the Chosen."

09

It was the former Arkon who broke the silence that descended in the library. "You never do anything the easy way, do you?" His eyes were orange, narrowed, and familiar; Kaylin might have stepped back in time, and interrupted his work in the archives of the Imperial Library.

"I hardly see how it's her fault," Bellusdeo said, her tone the same tone Kaylin would have heard had she never taken command of a Tower.

"You have always been far too indulgent where the corporal is concerned."

"Indulgent? Hardly. Your facility with language has diminished due to the stress of the responsibilities you have undertaken. Perhaps, if you wish to be critical, you might try *protective*."

"Overprotective."

Bellusdeo snorted. "I fail to see why Kaylin is being blamed for taking the more difficult path—it's not as if she chose it."

"That is true; I will not argue it. But just as Mrs. Erickson is a genuine threat absent any malicious intent on her part, Kaylin rivals Terrano for the chaos she causes, also absent malicious intent. If she had not been involved with Mrs. Erickson, Mrs. Erickson would never have been offered assessment by the Arkon, and the ghosts—which possessed the Arkon—would never have wakened. Kaylin would not have encountered Azoria. Were it not for Azoria's long research, she would not have encountered what she considers to be a dead Ancient—"

"Further research is required on that front," Androsse cut in.

"Mrs. Erickson would not now be living with Helen; were she not, Mrs. Erickson would never have encountered you. Had this not happened, you would not be aware that the dead that you loved are bound, in misery, to you.

"And she has only just begun."

Bellusdeo grimaced. "I will not fault your observations, but will counter them. It is true there would be no possession of the Arkon by unknown, foreign bodies—in theory dead as well—but had she not found Azoria, Azoria would have succeeded in becoming a threat to the Empire that none of us could easily counter.

"If she is without intent, her instincts have guided her to the greater benefit of all of us. If it weren't for Kaylin's stumbling, the Academia would not now be your hoard."

Kavallac's frown was impatience personified as her eyes narrowed on the chancellor and Bellusdeo. She returned her attention to Kaylin. "You aided Bellusdeo with the marks of the Chosen? What do you mean by that, exactly?"

"What I said. If you want technical details, I don't have them. Sometimes the marks of the Chosen react to events in ways I can't predict. Sometimes, the power from the marks is accessible."

"Accessible?"

"The only deliberate way I can use the power is healing. I've been able to do that since the marks first appeared on my body. I've used the power of the marks in other ways—but not without intent most of the time."

"Explain."

Kaylin shook her head. "Some of it's private. I'm known as Chosen—but the first time I heard that word, I'd had the marks for years. Someone knew that those marks existed, somewhere, in the fiefs where I lived. And many children were kidnapped, tattooed, and murdered because of it.

"The library is huge. You've said that anything written—notebooks, diaries, things like that—can somehow be found here. I don't know how. That many books from that many worlds should be the size of a world. But—I've never asked for research on the marks of the Chosen. Maybe you could find books that involve those marks. Research on their use. Or private journals of those who were marked before me.

"I knew Bellusdeo's name wasn't complete, but I can't tell you how or why."

Bellusdeo coughed. "There was one other element of the name that did not involve my sisters' names."

Kaylin nodded. "Maggaron. Your Ascendant."

"Lannagaros?" Arbiter Kavallac said, the word a question and a command.

"Norranir. I know little of the Norranir, but they have some ability to repel Shadow. They did not have Towers; if the Ancients graced their world with anything other than its creation, it has not been mentioned. But there was some resistance in the Norranir before the fall of their world.

"They are here, now, in the fief of Tiamaris; I am certain they will move to the fief of Bellusdeo in time. They live, always, nearest the borders that face *Ravellon*."

"They are Immortal?"

"No."

"But they have names?"

"Again, I am not an expert in the Norranir. The closest you will come is Lord Bellusdeo, and her time has not been spent in scholarship, either in that world or this." He turned to Bellusdeo. "I believe we have necessitated a longer period of research for the Arbiters. There is little more that we can contribute at the moment."

Bellusdeo's nod was tight.

A door appeared to their right. Kaylin waited for Bellusdeo to move toward it, but the gold Dragon was still.

"Arbiter Kavallac," she said, voice soft, eyes copper, "as you suspect, we lacked a mentor; we lacked a mother. Children demonstrably survive without such parenting; we survived. Perhaps, had we the guidance a mother offered, the outcome of our war would have differed."

Starrante lifted his arms, weaving them in a dance before the gold Dragon. "It would not, Lord Bellusdeo. Perhaps your individual fate would have differed—but the fall of the world cannot be laid across your shoulders."

"I was queen."

"And perhaps because you were queen, the fall of the world was slowed."

"You are being kind to me, Arbiter."

"No. You are being unkind to yourself. We will retreat now—I fear we will cause some unrest among the students—and we will inform the chancellor of any further questions our research necessitates."

Kaylin thought he was done, and headed toward the free-standing door they had summoned.

Starrante wasn't done. "Kaylin. If you intend to return to Mrs. Erickson's former residence, be cautious. I do not advise you to attempt to explore whatever may be left of Azoria's home. If you must explore that home, avoid the path that leads to the dead."

Bellusdeo's eyes were narrow, but copper gave way to orange with flecks of red. Kaylin was certain that would be their optimal color until her sisters were somehow either happy or free.

She'd heard the story Starrante told, of the woman who had

come—at the side of a dead girl—to accuse the girl's murderer. The author hadn't seen what had happened to his sister, because he couldn't see his sister at all. But the Arbiter was right. Mrs. Erickson could have done exactly what the nameless young woman had done. And perhaps that was her way of bringing peace to a dead girl.

Or perhaps it was her way of preventing any other such deaths at the hands of this one man—the man who should have been the girl's protector, her father.

Kaylin had no idea who her own father was. Fathers hadn't figured prominently in her life, except in one way: they were a source of envy. Maybe not all fathers were worthy of envy.

"You did well," the chancellor said.

Bellusdeo didn't answer. Instead, she turned to Kaylin. "He's talking about you."

What? "Me?"

"Yes. I realize I very seldom offer praise, but you did well. The Arbiters are intimidating, powerful presences; if you are standing in their library, you are at their mercy. The rules that govern the Academia do not govern the library. When the Arbiters close their library for research purposes, it is rumored to become a very, very odd place—a place that can be inimical for the survival of anyone who is not an Arbiter or a book.

"But I have never seen that expression on Arbiter Androsse's face before. If he were like Starrante, he might be moved to leave the seat of his power. You unsettled him. You unsettled all of us," he added, "but Arbiter Androsse has no experience with the chaos that is a constant presence where you are involved.

"I am uncertain how we should proceed from here."

"You don't have to proceed," Bellusdeo said, in Elantran. "This isn't your problem. It's ours."

Ours. Meaning hers and Kaylin's. Kaylin, who was mortal, and wasn't nearly as learned, as wise, or as powerful as Lannagaros. Or Bellusdeo.

"Evanton wants to visit us at home. By us, I mean Mrs. Erickson."

"Now?"

"Tomorrow." Or later, if she was lucky.

"Corporal."

"She's a really nice, really gentle old lady. I don't want her to be thrown into the deep end. I want her to spend time with Helen, to bake, maybe figure out what she wants to do when the dead aren't—" She stopped the rest of the words from falling out of her mouth, because Bellusdeo was listening.

"Perhaps," the chancellor said, "you might ask Mrs. Erickson what she herself wishes. There are too many things entwined with Mrs. Erickson at the moment."

"It's not her fault."

"No; I believe it is probably—somehow—yours. You have not been keeping up with magic lessons—"

"It wasn't my fault this time! You saddled Sanabalis with the position of Arkon! He's been busy!"

"I suggest you attempt to be more flexible and accommodating. There are other alternatives to his lessons, and you do not wish the Emperor to decide that your ability to understand and harness the power of your marks is of far more relevance to the safety of his Empire than fulfilling your duties as a Hawk."

Aside from the one moment in the meeting with the Arbiters, Hope remained draped across Kaylin's shoulders for the entire day. Bellusdeo offered to fly Kaylin home; it was late when they emerged from the library. Since the gold Dragon's version of offer was essentially command, Kaylin accepted.

It was far too late for dinner. Even if it hadn't been, Bellusdeo was not in the mood for more conversation; she dropped Kaylin off in Helen's landing tower, and headed to her own Tower.

"Is Mrs. Erickson sleeping?" Kaylin asked, as she headed for the stairs.

"She is. Her ghosts seem to be quiet as well. How was the Academia visit?"

Kaylin grimaced. "I don't even want to think about it tonight."

"That's good, dear."

Kaylin slowed her usual rapid descent of the stairs. "What's happened? Did the midwives' guild mirror?"

"Ah, no." After a brief pause, Helen said, "But you do have a guest, if you feel you are up to a visit."

"If it's Evanton, I'll see him."

"It isn't, but he did get in contact with me. I took the liberty of asking Mrs. Erickson if she would like to meet him."

"Did you explain his day job?"

"In very broad terms, yes. She was curious and she agreed. He'll be coming for dinner tomorrow, unless you have objections."

She did, but she didn't have any reasonable ones. "No, it's fine." Two more stairs. "If it's not Evanton, who exactly is it?"

"Lord Emmerian," Helen replied. "I believe he is talking with Mandoran in the parlor if you'd like to join them."

Of the Dragons, Emmerian was definitely the calmest. He was also the most considerate, which she found surprising on occasion, given the rest of the Immortals in her social orbit.

She went to her room to change before she headed downstairs. Or rather, bounced off Terrano, who was waiting for her. His eyes were bluer than they usually were.

Emmerian hadn't visited since the last disaster of a visit, which had involved the cohort, an enraged Dragon, and Helen's interference. "Is it bad?" she asked.

"Not in the way you're thinking. Look, of the Dragons, Emmerian is usually the least offensive. I would have bet he had no temper at all—but he does. It's just less easily triggered."

"Helen said Mandoran's with him now?"

"He is. The Dragon's worried, but not in a bad way."

"What's a good way of worrying?"

"He's worried for, rather than worried about."

Ugh. "Is this relationship issues?"

"We think so. He's keeping the conversation afloat by discussing Shadows and life with a Dragon-based Tower."

"That doesn't sound like a relationship problem."

"He hasn't mentioned the captain of the Tower once. And given that she's now Lord Bellusdeo, that probably takes effort."

Kaylin slowed. "You know I suck at relationship issues, right?"

Terrano shrugged. "You can't be as bad as Sedarias."

Helen's Avatar was waiting outside of the parlor door.

"Is he drinking?"

"Which he?"

"Never mind. Do you know why he came here?"

"Yes."

"And you're not of a mind to share."

"I believe Emmerian will speak of his concerns—it's why he chose to visit. But no, dear. If I can hear thoughts—and I am surprised at how clear his are at the moment, as he's usually much more careful—but he is a guest, and entitled to some privacy. If there is a danger present in those thoughts, privacy has less priority." She opened the door.

Emmerian stood when Kaylin entered. Mandoran didn't. Kaylin was grateful for the latter; bowing was a strata of manners that made her feel underdressed and ignorant.

"Please don't," she said, as she headed toward one of the chairs. Helen had chosen to decorate tonight's parlor with large upholstered chairs that had very soft cushions. Kaylin could spend all day on her feet, but preferred not to have to do it at home.

Emmerian sat only after Kaylin did. Mandoran had taken

the opportunity of the Dragon's bow to make pleading eyes at Kaylin. She mouthed *Bellusdeo* at him, and he nodded. Mandoran probably didn't care all that much about Emmerian, but he did like Bellusdeo; he considered her a friend. Most of the cohort seemed to avoid friendships that didn't involve True Names and centuries of history. Mandoran was more flexible.

"I'm sorry I was so late to return. I was at the Academia."

"Are there problems there?" Emmerian asked.

"No—the librarians are doing a bit of research on our behalf."

"Yours?" The word was slightly sharper.

Kaylin exhaled. "Ours. Some of it involves our newest roommate, Mrs. Erickson. Some of it involves our former roommate, Bellusdeo."

The Dragon tensed, although the tension was subtle.

"Have you met Mrs. Erickson?"

"No, not yet. Helen said she was trying to catch up on the sleep she's missed because of her guests." His eyes blue, he nonetheless smiled. "The Arkon says she is charming and kind."

"Was that all he said?"

"He has some concerns which were, of course, shared with the Imperial Court. The Dragon Court," he added. "But he does not feel, at this juncture, that she would be best served by a stay in the Imperial Palace. He expected that she might have some difficulty adjusting to both a new home and new wards."

It took Kaylin a minute to realize that wards referred to the ghosts Mrs. Erickson had carried from the palace to Helen.

"Is the Academia research an attempt to better understand Mrs. Erickson's gift?"

Kaylin nodded. "In part."

"What concerns does Bellusdeo have?" The heart of his curiosity.

"Have you talked to her about it at all?"

"She has not been resident in the Tower. Karriamis has informed me that there is a problem, but would not disclose its nature."

No wonder he'd come here.

"It isn't a problem that's life-threatening or world-threatening."

"I'm not certain that statement is terribly comforting, dear."

"Probably not. It's personal, for Bellusdeo." Realizing that this probably wasn't comforting either, she added, "It's not about you. She's not angry with you or worried about you, or upset at something you've done."

Helen cleared her throat.

"That I'm aware of."

"Is it something you feel you cannot speak of to me?"

"To anyone," Kaylin replied, regretting it. "Anything discussed was not to leave the library—under no uncertain terms." She exhaled. "I don't have a lot of leeway—she's probably going to be following my Halls of Law schedule closely. And this isn't mine to talk about." She wanted to. She trusted Emmerian with anything related to Bellusdeo.

But it wasn't her trust that mattered here. It was Bellusdeo's.

Emmerian knew.

"I think she's not willing to talk to you about personal things because she's not ready to be a mother."

Emmerian swallowed and nodded.

"But inasmuch as she trusts any Dragon, she trusts you. Are you living in the Tower?"

"It is my current residence, but I am expected to fulfill my duties to the Emperor."

"I'm not the person you need to talk to right now. I think you should talk to the chancellor. He won't be able to tell you what to do, but… I think he understands Bellusdeo better than any of us, except maybe Helen.

"I only know her as she is now. The chancellor knew her in the Aerie. She remembers, and I think she's as comfortable around him as she is around anyone. She didn't expect to be here. She didn't expect to have no empire and no war into which she could throw her entire existence. The Tower is a start—but I'm not sure it's a good start." She felt guilty even saying this much.

Emmerian was silent.

"That's not what I mean," she finally continued. "It's a war that has to be fought—but it's almost like she thinks there's nothing else she's any good for now. She can't rule. She can't govern. The Empire is the Emperor's hoard, and he's a Dragon. She spends some time with the Norranir—but they're the people I think she feels she failed.

"She was never raised to be an Aerie's mother. She didn't think of parenthood at all. But she was a queen, and she understands why, if there are no other Dragons, she has to become that mother.

"But I don't think she'll be able to do that until..." Ugh. "Talk to the chancellor."

Emmerian nodded.

"Look, I trust you with Bellusdeo. Even the cohort does. Some of them might pity you, but they trust your intent. So does Helen. I'm certain the chancellor does as well.

"But it's what I said: this isn't about anyone else's trust. It's about hers. And she's just too raw right now."

Emmerian was not much happier than he had been when he'd arrived.

"She never intended to be a mother," Kaylin told him, voice soft. "But she intended to live with her sisters forever. Right now, it's the sisters that matter to her. Mrs. Erickson matters because of her sisters. We're trying to work through it all now, but Mrs. Erickson doesn't know what she can do, either.

"If you can, wait. Wait, listen if she talks—and she probably won't. She can only barely contain her rage at the Outcaste, her rage at Shadow. There's not a lot of space left. Maybe if she could have become our Emperor, it would be different; she's responsible enough that ruling would absorb all her time, all her attention. But she can't have that, either."

Emmerian nodded, but said, voice as soft as Kaylin's, "It's not because of her ability to repopulate our race that I was drawn to her. We survived believing that there would be no more Dragons. We could survive the lack." He swallowed. "She chose me because I was the best choice out of all the bad choices she was offered—but it was a choice she didn't want to make. I want that to change.

"And, Kaylin, you are correct. She doesn't speak. She won't talk about anything but Shadow."

She did, or had. But maybe not now. Maybe not especially now.

"Well, that was awkward," Mandoran said, after Emmerian had cleared both the door to the manor and the fenced gate that surrounded it—the true boundary of Helen.

"It was," Helen replied. "It is far easier for Bellusdeo to spend time with you because you want nothing from her; you have nothing you feel you could, or must, give."

"Maybe he should try that."

"If he could, I believe he would. Being a Dragon complicates things enormously; I believe she is the hoard he desires. That desire is not always destructive; it is what bound Tiamaris to Tara so strongly. Tara is what he desired—and Tara needed exactly that drive, that totality of commitment. It is not clear that Bellusdeo either needs it or would accept it.

"I like Lord Emmerian, and I am worried for him. I am worried for Bellusdeo. I believe the Tower is her true home in this world, but I think she moved out a bit too early."

Kaylin glanced at Helen.

Helen's smile was gentle. "She was at home here, with you—and with the members of the cohort who were willing to interact with her. She was learning to live in the world she now inhabits, if slowly. Those lessons didn't have time to take root and fully blossom."

"But..."

"There is a reason she came back, a reason she wanted to speak with—or to—you." Helen hugged Kaylin gently, drawing her away from the door. "Perhaps she would have gone to her sisters, had they lived. I think the best thing we can do for Bellusdeo now is to untangle Mrs. Erickson's power and ability. It was unfortunate that she saw the ghosts of those beloved sisters in the state they were in. But Emmerian and Bellusdeo have no chance if they remain trapped as they are."

Kaylin leaned into Helen. "Evanton wants to speak with Mrs. Erickson. And it's not about her sisters."

"I know. But now, sleep. You have work in the morning, and Evanton in the evening, unless there is some other unforeseen emergency to interrupt his visit."

There was no unforeseen emergency, or at least not one that woke Kaylin up in the middle of the night; she slept like a log. Why logs were supposed to be great at sleeping, she didn't know, but didn't think about it too much; Hope was her wake-up call, and he was loud.

It was funny; she'd've said that the absence of Hope would be a blessing, but the relief she felt at the grouchy dragonlet's presence made clear that she would have been wrong.

Mrs. Erickson was not at the breakfast table.

"She is sleeping. While her guests are not as extreme in their concern as they were yesterday, they are still vibrating their fear. She speaks to them and calms them, but communication with them is still somewhat difficult; she can hear them, but I believe the translation that comes with her natural gift leaves something to be desired.

"Regardless, they hear her clearly, or perhaps hear her intent clearly." Helen was worried. Of course she was. Kaylin was worried as well.

Kaylin could—and did—wake up at any hour of the night when there was an emergency, but she was younger than Mrs. Erickson, and lack of sleep didn't affect her as badly. She could go days without much sleep and still function.

"Not entirely well, dear."

"Well enough for government work."

Helen coughed. "Bellusdeo has just arrived."

"Again?"

"I believe she intends to shadow you while you work. And I think this is for the best, before you argue against it."

"I know." Kaylin finished breakfast and rose to meet the gold Dragon.

Kaylin started the morning, Bellusdeo in tow, writing the standard patrol reports. It was her least favorite duty, but once it was done she would finish the working day with the actual patrol. She didn't understand why reports had to be filed if nothing had gone wrong, and viewed them with the same distaste her sergeant did. Marcus, however, felt that if he had to file reports, everyone had to file them. No one argued.

The worst thing about the Barrani Hawks, in Kaylin's private opinion, was that they filed their damn reports perfectly and on time. It was seriously annoying.

"Don't look to me for sympathy," Bellusdeo told her. "Severn appears to file his reports on time."

"Why can't I just add my signature to his reports? We saw the same things."

"That is something you'd have to take up with your sergeant. I personally never required unnecessary reports, but I'm sure the Emperor has his reasons."

"Sadism."

"Is she whining again?" Teela said, from across the office. Kaylin hadn't been that loud, but Barrani could hear everything.

Bellusdeo's eyes lightened, and she left Kaylin to the tail end of her report. "Of course. It's how we know she's awake."

Hope snickered. Kaylin flicked his snout. She then finished writing her report.

Elani street offered no further emergencies. Evanton was working in his storefront, and looked up when the Hawks paused in front of his window; he waved them off. If he had more words, he intended to save them for his visit to Kaylin's house.

Only one mirror message had arrived at Kaylin's desk by the end of the day: it was from the Academia. Apparently, the Arbiters had a few further questions. Killian at the Academia had as dim a view of mirrors and the mirror network as Helen did, but understood that communication, when attempting to attract students, was a necessity.

Kaylin forwarded the questions to Helen. She wouldn't be able to answer any of them tonight.

"Did you want my company at dinner?" Severn asked.

"If you want to join us, you can. I don't expect there will be much difficulty."

"Bellusdeo?"

"I'm joining them," the gold Dragon told Kaylin's partner. "I don't care if you're there. Helen's not likely to mind, and Mrs. Erickson will be fine with it. I expect we'll get a number of cohort members as well—not many of them have met a Keeper." She spoke using the same tone orphanage supervisors used when talking about kids at the zoo.

Kaylin finished work on time and rushed home; she talked Bellusdeo out of arriving the "efficient" way, and was forced to march, at speed, back to Helen. If Bellusdeo had chosen to break the laws governing Dragons in the city, she was likely to survive it—but her clothing wouldn't; she'd have to join dinner in her natural armor. Severn chose to accompany them. Hope squawked, but it wasn't the annoyed or angry squawk, so she assumed he approved—not that disapproval would change anything.

Helen was waiting in the frame of the open door. She smiled at Severn, and offered Bellusdeo open arms; Bellusdeo walked into them, wordless. Helen matched her silence, but gently disentangled herself and drew her into the house.

"Evanton has not yet arrived," she told them. "I expect him soon. Would you like to wait in the parlor?"

"Depends. Is it empty?"

"It is. The dining room, however, is not; I believe most of the cohort in residence have chosen to welcome our guest." Which meant Sedarias would be present.

Kaylin wondered if Bellusdeo would be more comfortable if most of the cohort were elsewhere. But... Evanton wasn't coming to see Bellusdeo; he was coming to speak with Mrs. Erickson. At least one cohort member should be present; if Evanton wanted to hear about Mrs. Erickson's home—or the parts that Azoria had controlled—the cohort had better memory.

The cohort had causes of their own. Telling them to leave—when they lived here—because Bellusdeo might be uncomfortable didn't feel right.

"Mandoran did suggest a quieter dinner might be appropriate," Helen said.

"But he's still coming to dinner."

"Yes, dear—but I think he hopes to be a buffer of some sort, if a buffer becomes necessary."

Hope snorted.

Kaylin turned to Bellusdeo. "Did you want to join the zoo immediately, or wait in the parlor?"

"Best begin as we mean to continue," the Dragon replied, a glint of steel in her orange eyes.

The dining room was not a zoo. The cohort—in best dress, except for Sedarias, whose standing in the High Court elevated best to ridiculous amounts of jewelry and expensive cloth—were seated at the table. There were no floor cushions scattered around the room, and no cohort-size huddle of bodies reclining on them.

Left to their own devices, the cohort reminded Kaylin of Leontine children; they sought physical contact and absorbed it as if it were oxygen. Plated food was often eaten on the floor, passed among the cohort if they were hungry. They mostly shared a room, although Helen did have individual rooms available for use, should any of them desire privacy.

Today, however, they were all seated. Barrani tended to look perfectly groomed no matter how much effort they did—or did not—put in; the only exception Kaylin could immediately recall was Teela, in the wake of life-threatening combat.

Teela was absent.

"She will not be joining us unless something, as she put it, goes catastrophically wrong. Serralyn and Valliant have likewise chosen to be absent, although there is some chance that Serralyn will arrive before the Keeper leaves." Helen's voice was very soft; Kaylin assumed that she'd chosen to speak privately. "Yes, dear."

A swift glance around the table showed blue eyes to a man, although Sedarias's were darkest, Mandoran's lightest. Terrano's even had flecks of green in them. Neither Mandoran nor Terrano became darker eyed when Bellusdeo walked into the dining room behind Kaylin.

Nestled between Terrano and Mandoran was Mrs. Erickson. She'd come down early—of course she had. Kaylin thought her color was off—she was a bit on the pale side—but she seemed happy to be at the table. Kaylin hoped that would last. Maybe the reason Mandoran and Terrano seemed more at ease was Mrs. Erickson herself; they were speaking with her, and she was listening and smiling in that open way that encouraged talk.

If she found the rest of the cohort intimidating, it didn't show. She wasn't dressed as formally, probably because she didn't have much in the way of formal wear—but Kaylin wasn't, either. The cohort didn't care the way they might have had Mrs. Erickson been Barrani; they didn't expect much from mortals.

Maybe that was unfair. Kaylin thought Mrs. Erickson an older version of Caitlin; it would take the determination of a special sort of person to dislike her. There was a reason the dead children had been so worried about what would happen to her if they moved on to wherever it was the dead were supposed to go.

"No," she was saying to Terrano, "I haven't managed to make it back to my house yet. Things have been so busy here, I've barely visited the Halls of Law."

"She did send food," Kaylin pointed out. "And I did bring the empty basket home. Bridget told me to thank you—and to tell you you can visit the front desk at any time, without making her privates write long incident reports."

Mrs. Erickson's smile was one of gratitude and embarrassment.

"They just miss the food," Terrano said.

"That she went through the trouble of baking. There's nothing wrong with appreciating her because she feeds us."

"Us, is it? So all the time you come home ranting about front desk work and how you shouldn't have to do it—"

"People who do the work get to complain about it."

"Given how much you complain, you should be dead from overwork."

Helen cleared her throat.

Terrano glanced at the Avatar, and then folded his arms, his mouth a mutinous, thin line. Mrs. Erickson gave him a sympathetic glance, but no words.

"Kaylin, I believe your guest has arrived."

Kaylin rose. "I'll get the door," she told the almost silent table.

10

Helen, mindful of Kaylin's extreme dislike of door wards, had created a wardless door. Evanton knocked on it, and Kaylin answered. He was wearing an actual jacket with matching pants, a shirt, and shiny shoes. She blinked. What had she expected? Evanton in his working apron, with a jeweler's glass glued to his eye?

"I apologize for being a bit late; the garden was unusually active today."

"You're not late," she said, moving out of the doorway. "Come in. Oh, I think I should warn you. Our entire household was so excited about meeting the Keeper in person that everyone who lives here is joining us for dinner."

"Ah."

"And Bellusdeo."

Evanton, living up to his reputation as a man who did not desire social company, turned to Helen. "If I visit again, I would prefer not to do so for dinner."

"They understand what the Keeper is," Kaylin told him. "They're going to treat you with respect."

"There are many questions I cannot—or will not—answer. I hope respect precludes aggressive curiosity."

★ ★ ★

"This," Kaylin said, as they entered the room, "is Evanton. He's the current Keeper of the elemental garden."

Everyone—except Mrs. Erickson—rose. Mrs. Erickson followed, noticing that all of the others had left their chairs. Kaylin exhaled. She hated formality, because she was so bad at it; she wanted to tell the cohort to sit when their names were called, because she had to introduce them all, and Evanton might have some chance of remembering their names. Evanton, being human, if not exactly mortal, had a normal person's memory.

"These are my housemates. Sedarias An'Mellarionne, Terrano Allasarre, Annarion Solanace, Mandoran Cassarre, Allaron Boranin, Torrisant Immolan, Fallessian Torcannon, Karian Reymar. Bellusdeo, you already know. And this is Mrs. Imelda Erickson."

"Pleased to meet you," Mrs. Erickson said, smiling.

The rest of the cohort offered Evanton deep bows; Terrano's was sloppier than the others as he seemed distracted.

"Teela is good friends with them, but she's busy tonight, so she won't be joining us."

"Unless something catches metaphorical fire," Terrano added, grinning.

There must have been some law of nature that kept Terrano's and Sedarias's moods balanced; when he grinned, she frowned.

Evanton's seat was at the head of the table, not exactly close to Mrs. Erickson's. Helen didn't rearrange the seats—and the people sitting in them—to change that.

To Kaylin's surprise, Evanton started the conversation. "I admit I'm surprised to see that Kaylin has so many housemates. How did you meet her?"

Silence gathered at the table; Kaylin was certain the cohort were now having an interior group discussion about how to answer that question. Terrano even opened his mouth three times but shut it without ejecting words.

It was Sedarias who answered. "We met in the West March. Kaylin had been sent there to participate in a rite known to the Barrani as the *regalia*." This was a highly sanitized version of the events that had led Kaylin to the West March, but Kaylin understood why; she had no desire to correct it.

Evanton nodded. "It is not normally a rite offered to mortals." His answer surprised Kaylin; it made clear that Evanton knew about the *regalia*.

"It is not. If you know Kaylin at all, you know she frequently crosses lines she cannot perceive." Sedarias's smile was reserved, but genuine.

"Oh, I do. I absolutely do. She has certainly interfered with the garden in the past few years, denying me the peace and quiet of a tranquil sunset. I'm not certain the marks of the Chosen are not responsible for much of her interference. It is probably why she has managed to survive."

"She interfered with the garden?"

"She added another element to the whole."

Every set of blue eyes turned to Kaylin.

"It was that or have the world end," Kaylin said.

"Indeed," Evanton agreed, smiling. "But she met you in the West March? All of you?"

"We were imprisoned in the Hallionne there," Sedarias spoke slowly, as if measuring each word. "She freed us. But our period of confinement had been many centuries, and the world itself was not the world from which we had been sequestered. We are grateful that she offered us a home, and that Helen was willing to allow it. We are all exceedingly fond of Helen."

"I found them because of Teela," Kaylin added. She found lies—even lies of omission—difficult because it meant she had to sift every word before she actually spoke. "They were Teela's only childhood friends. Or her only surviving friends."

"And how long have you been resident in our fair city?"

Sedarias answered this more readily. "Not long. These days

have been much occupied with the High Halls; they have been radically altered—although some merely say they have been restored."

"I was aware of the change—it was quite sudden." His gaze narrowed as it once again returned to Kaylin. "Perhaps, at a later time, you can tell me the story around that restoration, for I perceive that you understand why the change occurred."

Terrano rolled his eyes.

"And, Mrs. Erickson, forgive me if I seem intrusive, but I would be interested to know how you met Kaylin as well. I assume she did not free you from a prison."

Mrs. Erickson nodded.

To Kaylin's surprise, Helen brought food into the dining room. Usually she just caused plates to magically appear, but today she was determined to be more formal. She began—at the head of the table—to put plates in front of the various diners.

Mrs. Erickson wasn't raised with fourteen forks and spoons and knives, but she didn't look too intimidated. Kaylin did, but she'd learned manners—with Bellusdeo—and could now eat without using the wrong utensil, even if she resented the need for all of them. A fork was a fork, right? Why did there have to be so many of them?

Why could Severn use all of them so naturally he might have been born with utensils in his hands?

"I first met Kaylin in the Halls of Law," Mrs. Erickson said, smiling. She liked the Halls of Law. Kaylin loved her job, but conversely didn't love the office as much as a lonely old woman whose only friends were ghosts had. "I visited the front desk frequently."

"The front desk?"

"It's the desk where the officers listen to the concerns of private citizens." Mrs. Erickson looked at her food, and then looked at how others were eating before picking up a small fork.

Kaylin expanded Mrs. Erickson's overly positive explanation.

"It's where people report vampire sightings, werewolf sightings, missing dogs, cats, and the occasional person. Oh, also arguments with neighbors over fences, in the hope that there's no further crime that will need to be investigated."

"You met Kaylin while she occupied that desk? And you befriended her?"

Mandoran and Terrano snickered; even Bellusdeo's eyes lightened, although they wouldn't reach full gold this evening.

Mrs. Erickson's smile was gentle. "Of course I did. She's a Hawk, and she takes her duties seriously. And I suppose I should confess that I was there to report the findings of my various ghostly friends as well."

"Which no one took seriously, I assume."

"There were few occasions when my reports would be considered urgent—but Kaylin did take my concerns seriously."

"She just wanted the baking," Mandoran pointed out. "Mrs. Erickson is a really good baker, and she always brought baked goods with her when she made her reports."

"Oh, it's not just that—the Hawks were very helpful. I broke my leg, and I live alone—it was the Hawks who came to check in on me when I didn't show up."

"And how—if it is not too intrusive to ask—did you come to live with Kaylin?"

Mrs. Erickson glanced at Kaylin, as if for permission.

"I asked her if she was willing to live with Helen and me."

"Not the rest of us?" Terrano's grin was practically contagious.

"I may have forgotten to mention it's a package deal."

"I'm quite happy to be living with all of you," Mrs. Erickson said, smiling. "And Kaylin asked me to join her because she thought I would benefit from Helen's company."

"And that is the only reason you chose to accept?"

The silence was brief, but it was clear Mrs. Erickson was now less comfortable. She once again looked to Kaylin. This time

Kaylin kept her voice soft as she spoke to her newest housemate. "Everyone in the house knows already. Bellusdeo knows. I'm sure Sanabalis—ugh, the Arkon—would discuss the matter with Evanton if Evanton could be moved to visit the Imperial Palace."

Evanton's snort made clear that this wasn't going to happen anytime in the near future.

"It's a bit of a long story," Mrs. Erickson then said. "And if everyone else already knows it, I'd hate to take up their time by repeating it."

"I'm certain they won't find it boring," Evanton replied, his tone taking on some of the steel he reserved for difficult customers.

"I won't," Terrano said.

"I wouldn't mind hearing it from a rational point of view," Mandoran added. "I mean yours, in case that wasn't obvious. Kaylin swears too much."

Mrs. Erickson's smile deepened. "Well, she is a Hawk."

Evanton did eat, but his gaze was now focused on Mrs. Erickson. She had one of nature's quiet voices. If the cohort had not fallen silent, it would have been harder to hear what she had to say.

She spoke about the children first: Jamal, Esmeralda, Callis, Katie. Evanton nodded; he did not interrupt her almost nostalgic musing. Only when she spoke of the beautiful artist who had painted the Swindon family's portrait did his eyes narrow, but he nodded regardless.

Mrs. Erickson, having spent so much of her time telling stories of her daily life to the children trapped in her house, had a good sense of narrative. When Kaylin tried to tell people what had happened, she often had to backtrack, to fill in things she hadn't mentioned earlier. Most people did. Mrs. Erickson didn't.

"Kaylin got involved because some of your friends—friends

that no one else could see—were interested in her Corporal Handred."

"Yes. But Kaylin could see them, and she didn't think they were ghosts." Mrs. Erickson's smile deepened. "They were worried that Severn was somehow a servant to Azoria, but they didn't say that at the time."

Severn, as usual, said nothing.

"Pardon me for interrupting. Please continue."

"I think Kaylin will have to tell this part of the story," Mrs. Erickson replied, almost apologetically.

"It's what eventually led us to Azoria An'Berranin," Kaylin said. "Because the two Barrani we met weren't dead; they were trapped, their bodies separate from the rest of them in paintings Azoria had created when she lived in the High Halls. The detritus of her life there had been preserved by the High Halls itself. But we believe she was capable of creating those odd pocket cells because she had tapped into the power that the High Halls—that any sentient building—uses to create and sustain themselves."

"And Kaylin believed the children in your home were ghosts."

Mrs. Erickson nodded.

"They were ghosts whose bodies died some ten to fifteen years after they did," Kaylin added.

"Pardon?"

"Something else possessed those bodies. We're not certain if it was Azoria, although that's the most likely. Each of the four bodies eventually met their end through the justice system; they had, to a person, murdered their families. Before that, they'd been caught for breaking and entering, petty theft."

"I see. Please, continue."

This was the hardest part for Mrs. Erickson, but Kaylin thought it was possibly the most important. "Kaylin believed that I had magical potential." She said this as her shoulders began to sink. "I'd been tested, as an older child. The results of that test were negative."

"Why were you tested?"

She tensed but shook her head. "My parents—my mother—thought I might have talent."

"For what reason?"

"I don't know." Her voice was very small now. "But I was told I didn't, and I went home. Kaylin, many decades later, disagreed with the testing. I went to the Imperial College," she added, as if that meant anything.

Evanton's expression matched Kaylin's for a brief moment.

"Kaylin's a Hawk. The Halls of Law works with mages from the Imperial College. She approached a member of the college—one of the Dragon Court. I believe he is now the current Arkon. The Arkon agreed to reassess my possible abilities."

"It is difficult to say no to the corporal when she very earnestly pursues a goal. I have tried, in my time. Very well. The Arkon chose to test you personally."

"Yes."

"And his conclusion?"

Mrs. Erickson once again fell silent. This time, when she looked to Kaylin, Kaylin could see the ghost of a young girl in her eyes. Afraid of being judged. Afraid of being useless or disappointing. It made Kaylin wonder if anyone could ever outgrow those feelings.

She once again took over. "The test wasn't finished. It wasn't really started. When Mrs. Erickson entered the room in which the tests would be done, she found new ghosts. They weren't human ghosts. They weren't ghosts of any race I'd recognize. They'd been trapped until they sensed Mrs. Erickson entering the room. And they possessed the Arkon."

Evanton, being human—at least to start—didn't have eyes that changed color; they did change shape as his brows rose.

"She didn't, obviously, tell them to possess a Dragon. But…

they could. I'm not sure what would have happened if not for Mrs. Erickson's intervention; she could speak to them, they could hear her, and she could coax them out of Sanabalis. The Arkon wasn't keen on letting Mrs. Erickson return home—because the ghosts she'd talked into abandoning Sanabalis were now following her.

"But the Dragon Court is aware of Helen; Bellusdeo lived here until very recently. They trusted Helen with Bellusdeo's safety, and they didn't think Mrs. Erickson was an intentional threat. Sanabalis was willing to have Mrs. Erickson live with me."

"And the ghosts?"

"They live with me, too. The only person who can communicate with them is Mrs. Erickson."

"Tell me, Chosen, what did you see, if you saw the ghosts at all?" Evanton's question was somber.

Kaylin exhaled. "Words. True Words."

Evanton was silent as he considered what he'd been told. "Mrs. Erickson, I would like—if possible—to be introduced to your new friends."

The old woman was surprised. "I'm not sure you'll be able to see them. Kaylin can't, without her familiar's interference."

"But she could see the children clearly?"

Mrs. Erickson nodded. "She could speak with them as well. She could hear them."

"Do you see these ghosts as words?"

"No. They look like people to me. Younger people. They aren't as visually clear; to my eyes, they look like what ghosts would be expected to look like in stories. My usual ghosts looked like people to me—hair color, eye color, skin color."

"I see."

"But why are you asking?"

"Ah. Yes, I suppose I should answer that question, inasmuch as it can be answered. I am what the ancient world knew as the Keeper of the elemental garden. It is my duty to calm the elements upon which the stability of the world depends; the elements have will, and desires, as any living thing does. Left to their own devices, they would burn, drown, or bury everything in their need to display their primal abilities.

"The garden was created by the Ancients to contain the heart of the elements, and to allow them to coexist in relative peace. But the elements, if housed in the garden, are only theoretically constrained there; they exist in the world. Mages who summon them touch some part of their awareness.

"The elements are contained—but they are not the only things the garden can shelter. It is a liminal space; its edges touch the world in which we live, and the places in which elements of our world are based. The elements, as an example, are aware of the green in the West March; they are aware of the reformation of the High Halls; they are aware—peripherally—of *Ravellon* when it stirs.

"I, as Keeper, can be aware of those things, with greater or lesser effort. Often it is the restlessness of the elements that indicates that something has gone wrong or will soon go wrong. The ability to sense such things is a function of the office itself.

"The reason I wished to meet with you is a direct result of that. When Kaylin dropped by my store, she was accompanied by Lord Bellusdeo. Lord Bellusdeo is much occupied with concern for her dead. One thing led to another, but when Kaylin mentioned that she had a new housemate, I thought it possible that some of the uneasiness in the garden might be indirectly related to you.

"Let me emphasize that: indirectly. Kaylin can be very annoying at times, but her instincts are good. She clearly holds you in great affection. She does not consider you a threat or a danger; indeed I believe she feels that you should be protected from all threats or dangers. She therefore considers questions surrounding you and your abilities to be of lesser import unless those abilities might have immediate, pragmatic use. She is interested in solving Bellusdeo's difficulty, as an example.

"The name Azoria An'Berranin is not unknown to the elements, which is not generally considered a good sign, at least in my job. I believe there were perturbations caused by that woman, who I am assured is now dead. I would like to hear about that," he added.

Kaylin fell silent, joining Mrs. Erickson.

Terrano took up the rest of the story because no one else wanted to touch it. Kaylin's reasons were no doubt different from Mrs. Erickson's, but Evanton was right about one thing: she wanted to protect the old woman who baked for the Hawks and whose company Helen so enjoyed.

Terrano, however, hadn't seen everything Kaylin had seen.

He had, however, seen the dead Ancient.

So he could speak about the events—could speak about the trapped, enslaved dead that Azoria had gathered in the home that was magically attached to Mrs. Erickson's small bungalow. He could speak about Azoria's end. He could not speak about Mrs. Erickson's promise to Jamal, or rather, her attempt to get him to make an exception.

That promise, Kaylin didn't know—but given events, she was certain her guess was right. Mrs. Erickson had promised, sometime in her childhood, not to command the dead. Not to use the power of command. It was the one thing Kaylin didn't want anyone else to know—not yet. Not when the question of Necromancy hung in the balance.

Evanton listened without interruption and without further questions. All of the interruptions came from the cohort as they tried to add clarity to Terrano's chaos. Both Mrs. Erickson and Kaylin kept words to themselves until Terrano was done.

Evanton's gaze had moved from speaker to speaker, but when Terrano was finished, it returned to Mrs. Erickson. "You have not, by chance, sold your house?"

Mrs. Erickson shook her head.

"Very well. If it is acceptable to you, I would like—with your company, of course—to visit that house."

Mrs. Erickson seemed surprised, but not upset. "It would have to be in the evening—Kaylin has work during business hours. Oh, but she said you had a store, so you must as well."

Evanton could close the store at will, and frequently did; Kaylin often wondered why he bothered to run a shop. Then again, she had daggers that made no sound at all as they were drawn from their sheaths, courtesy of Evanton's store. Teela had taken her there, the first time; it would be years before Evanton's store became part of her regular beat. When she'd first started tagging along with the Hawks, she'd shadowed Teela and Tain—and the Barrani didn't get put on Elani.

She shook her head. "When did you have in mind?"

"Tomorrow," was Evanton's prompt reply.

"I'd like to join you," Bellusdeo said. She had spoken very little, absorbed in listening.

Evanton frowned. "I am uncertain that it will prove of interest to you." This was the polite way of saying no.

"I am certain it will," Bellusdeo replied, rejecting the rejection. She smiled.

"If she's going, I'm going," Terrano then said, his grin deflecting the glare Bellusdeo turned on him.

"It really isn't very interesting," Mrs. Erickson told them both, her hands in her lap, her head slightly bowed.

Terrano shrugged. "I've seen at least half of it before. It was certainly interesting then. Serralyn asks, if we're taking visitors, if she can join us as well."

"Of course!" Mrs. Erickson said, clearly pleased at the prospect.

Evanton's expression had become his front desk why-are-you-bothering-me-now look. But he accepted what he could not easily change—not without argument. "Fine. I will come here tomorrow to pick up Mrs. Erickson."

★ ★ ★

When Evanton excused himself—early, as he was an "old man" who required some rest—Bellusdeo hung back. The cohort dispersed. Mrs. Erickson remained by Bellusdeo's side until the hall contained the Dragon, Kaylin, and the old woman.

"Are they still crying?" Bellusdeo asked Mrs. Erickson, when the last of the cohort were out of sight. Being out of sight guaranteed nothing where Terrano was concerned, but Kaylin assumed the gold Dragon knew this.

"No, dear."

"Are they happy?"

Mrs. Erickson shook her head. "It's hard to get them to speak much, but… I think they are at least now aware of each other."

"Are they aware of me?"

"They're aware that you exist, they're aware that you are alive. But they feel as if they can't reach you."

"They can't," was the Dragon's flat reply. "I've listened. I've tried to speak of what I remember of their lives—and mine, in case it lessens the sense of isolation. But I hear nothing. I see nothing." She exhaled. "Karriamis, the heart of my Tower, would like to meet you as well, but says it isn't urgent. Nothing he has done—and Towers are far, far more flexible than I had initially realized—has allowed me to see or converse with my dead.

"I understand that the Keeper's concerns take precedence." Bellusdeo swallowed. She opened her mouth, but no further words followed.

"Kaylin works during the day, but I don't," Mrs. Erickson told the gold Dragon, her voice gentle. "If you want to visit, I'm sure Helen would be happy to see you, and I would be happy to try to further converse with your sisters."

Bellusdeo nodded. "I just— I want to know why they're in so much pain. If I understood it…"

"I'm used to talking with ghosts," Mrs. Erickson said, placing a hand on Bellusdeo's shoulder, as if the taller Dragon were the frailer person. "I do miss it, sometimes. Perhaps you could visit tomorrow during the day, while Kaylin and Evanton are occupied with work."

Bellusdeo nodded.

Kaylin lay in bed in the dark, staring in the direction of the ceiling.

"This is so messy," she said.

Hope, seated on his pillow, squawked.

"Do you know what Evanton is afraid of?"

Squawk.

"I just don't want anything bad to happen to Mrs. Erickson. The rest of us are used to fighting; we're trained for it. And we're not physically fragile. She can't be the source of Evanton's worry. She just can't."

Squawk.

"She can't, can she?" Kaylin turned on her side and poked Hope. "Can you keep her safe?"

Hope failed to answer. She'd grown accustomed to the familiar; his squawks, while wordless, had tone. His silences had texture. "Is protecting one old lady something I have to make sacrifices for?"

The air around the familiar grew cold, as if the translucent form was now composed of ice. She could see mist in the air as the cold expanded.

You understand the danger, Hope said. *She is like a tidal wave, an earthquake. Knowledge will not change the threat she poses.*

"But she doesn't! I swear she's never hurt a freaking fly—she'd probably try to catch it and let it go outside her house!"

Yes. That is your conflict. But you know that she is a Necromancer. You saw it, when she commanded Azoria. She has that power, and it is bound and contained by a promise she made to a dead child. If those children were sent to watch her, to spy on her, they grew at-

tached to her, and it is because they did that she never dreamed of becoming what she might become.

"That promise holds weight to her."

Yes. But, Kaylin, promises can be broken in emergencies. Promises can be broken when the cost of keeping them seems, in the moment, too high. Think. There is a reason Azoria was interested in Mrs. Erickson. There is an Ancient who claims he is dead living or standing in Azoria's figurative backyard.

There are ghosts who can possess Dragons—the Arkon, in fact. These would be at her control; they would obey her, should she choose to give them commands.

If you wished to keep Mrs. Erickson safe, agreeing to accompany her to her home with the Keeper in attendance was not the wisest option. But if you wish to keep the rest of the world safe—as the Keeper does—it might be necessary.

"Starrante didn't mention Necromantic activity in the few stories he found credible."

No. And you have gone out of your way to hide what you believe.

"I have no proof."

Mrs. Erickson understands that the abilities Jamal sealed by her promise are dangerous enough that she, too, has failed to mention them. Terrano, you will note, edited his account slightly to leave out the one salient point. I believe the cohort is fond of Mrs. Erickson; they know you are.

Kaylin was now cold, but that was purely physical. She wrapped herself more tightly in her blankets before she continued. "Could she somehow use that ability—the ability to command the dead, rather than communicate with them—to somehow free Bellusdeo's sisters?"

Hope was silent for long enough, she thought he wouldn't answer. *Perhaps, but the question you must ask yourself is: Will removing the dead injure—or kill—Bellusdeo?*

"She's alive."

She is. But she is alive because of your intervention. What you did defied common sense; it is accepted because you are Chosen. Perhaps Bellusdeo is whole because you bound the dead—dead you could not see yourself—to her. If you unbind the dead, will her name survive?

11

Bellusdeo arrived punctually; Kaylin was just finishing breakfast. Mrs. Erickson had cooked it—she liked cooking, and Helen was perfectly happy to see the kitchen used. She looked better this morning, less exhausted and fragile.

"The ghosts were quiet last night?"

Mrs. Erickson smiled. "I wouldn't say *quiet* is the right word, but they were far less anxious, far less upset, than they were a few nights ago." She looked up as Bellusdeo entered the dining room; the Dragon was wearing actual clothing, which meant she'd more or less walked.

Maggaron had accompanied her. Before she'd moved out, he spent much of his time in the larger-than-human-size rooms Helen had created for his use; since she'd moved out, he lived in the Tower, although Bellusdeo said he spent much more of his time with his people, the Norranir. His height and build marked him clearly as other, and people were generally apprehensive when confronted with the differences between their builds and his; had he been a dwarf, it wouldn't have caused issues.

But the phrase *gentle giant* suited Maggaron perfectly. Because the Norranir had moved into the fiefs, to be near the border of *Ravellon*, people in the rest of the city just hadn't gotten a chance to get accustomed to Norranir in the city streets.

"I won't be accompanying you to the Halls of Law," Bellusdeo said. "But I thought I could visit Mrs. Erickson while you were working. It was her suggestion," she added, sounding a tiny bit defensive. "And Maggaron needs a break from Karriamis and Emmerian."

Maggaron, as usual, was silent, although he did smile and nod in Kaylin's direction.

Hope was once again on Kaylin's shoulder as she left home.

The workday had only one interruption. Marcus called her to his desk, which was never a good sign; his eyes were dark orange, which emphasized the lack of great distress. But when he spoke, he spoke first in choice Leontine, adding a couple of scratches to the latest attempt at a new desk.

"You've been sent a message," he said.

Kaylin had her own mirror, which meant the message had come from some variant of on high.

"Lord Lannagaros has requested your presence at the Academia." Which would explain Marcus's mood. He had never been happy at interference from the Dragon Court.

"Did he say it was an emergency?"

"He has indicated that while it is not a matter that directly requires active duty at this time, it might become one. He did not speak as the chancellor of his fancy school; he spoke as a Lord of the Dragon Court. Unless and until it is considered of import to the Halls, you will visit his school on your own time."

"I can't go tonight. I have an appointment I can't miss after dinner."

"Not our problem."

"Yes, sir."

"I expect not to hear from the Academia in future unless there is a need for intervention from the Halls of Law. Am I clear?"

"Yes, sir. Permission to speak?"

"Lack of permission has never stopped you."

"Please inform the Arkon that my visit will be delayed tonight at the request of the Keeper. He'll understand what it means."

She understood why the former Arkon was worried. She truly did. But did he really need an intermediary when he was dealing with Bellusdeo? Bellusdeo liked him, trusted him, and listened to him as much as she was willing to listen to anyone. Kaylin wasn't an expert in anything; the librarians were far, far more learned. He probably just needed someone to absorb grouchiness because he never snapped at Bellusdeo.

Severn chose to accompany her home.

"Do you think something's going to go wrong?"

He glanced at her. "You're taking Mrs. Erickson, with the Keeper, to her former home. I'm certain Evanton wants to examine Azoria's mansion. What could possibly go wrong?"

Kaylin grimaced but accepted this. "Terrano and Serralyn are coming as well. And Bellusdeo."

You're worried that Terrano will be the usual agent of chaos. And Bellusdeo is not quite herself.

Kaylin shrugged. It was true. "We could ask Terrano to stay home, but he wouldn't do it, and we'd just end up with even more of the cohort joining us. Mrs. Erickson does seem to like them, and when they interact with her, they've been good, but I'm not sure Evanton won't object. If it were up to Evanton, no one but he and Mrs. Erickson would be going."

"And you."

"He's not certain Mrs. Erickson would be comfortable on her own. He wouldn't want me, otherwise. He thinks I'm like Terrano."

"No comment."

"You're coming, too, right?"

"I'm your partner."

"We're not going as Hawks."

"I'm your partner," he repeated.

Evanton was punctual. Mrs. Erickson and Bellusdeo were not. They did come down for dinner, but on the late side, and both were silent. Bellusdeo was copper-eyed; she took the chair next to Mrs. Erickson, who looked at her with open sympathy—something Kaylin wouldn't have dared.

Evanton didn't join them for dinner. He waited in the parlor, with Helen.

Terrano did join them; Serralyn sat beside her cohort member, her eyes the blue of worry as she gazed at Mrs. Erickson and Bellusdeo.

It was a really silent dinner, the awkward kind of silence where everyone trapped in it is trying to think of something—anything—to say that won't make things worse. Kaylin hated it. She hated feeling useless. Her friend was clearly in pain, given the color of her eyes, and she should be able to do something. But making a joke to lighten the mood? No—that would probably be seen as not caring. Saying anything sympathetic when there was nothing practical she could do? Not helpful. Saying anything seemed so fraught; saying nothing made her feel helpless.

Mrs. Erickson didn't say anything, either. Maybe she'd done all her talking during the day, while Kaylin had been scowling at Margot's storefront on Elani street. Maybe her presence, the fact that she was the link between the dead and the living, was all of the comfort required.

Kaylin concentrated on her food. She wasn't certain that anything that happened tonight—and she was silently crossing her fingers hoping that nothing would—would change Bellusdeo's situation. What they needed to do was find some way to free the dead who were trapped. At least Jamal and the rest of the kids had been trapped in a house; Bellusdeo's sisters were trapped, in isolation, by Bellusdeo herself. She had no say in it, and neither did they.

She cleared her throat. "I received a message today. Well, no, Marcus did."

Bellusdeo lifted her gaze.

"The chancellor wants to see me."

"Have the Arbiters found anything more useful?"

"The message was sent to my sergeant—or possibly the Hawklord—so I didn't have a chance to ask questions." Kaylin grimaced. "I'm to arrange a meeting and head there on my own time. For now."

"For now?"

"I think the subtext was: or the Dragon Court will second my services if I'm tardy. Which, predictably, Marcus hates. I did ask that the chancellor and Arbiters be told that 'tardy' in this case is due to a direct request from the Keeper. That should keep them off my back for at least a day."

"Optimist."

"I'm not certain that Evanton will care to be blamed for this," Helen's voice said; her Avatar was with Evanton in the parlor.

"Is any of it a lie? I didn't complain about Evanton at all. I just said—"

"I heard you, dear. Very well. We can't change the past. I will inform Evanton that there is rather more pressure on your time than anticipated."

"He's important," Kaylin said, voice flat. But he was important because anything that could give Mrs. Erickson any hint on how to use the powers she was born with would help Bellusdeo.

"Do not be certain of that," Helen said, her voice a private whisper.

Mandoran, of the cohort, was fondest of Bellusdeo. Kaylin wasn't surprised when he joined them. Evanton wasn't pleased, but didn't argue, probably because it wouldn't have done any good. Mandoran was easier to ditch than Terrano, but not by much.

The sun was in the process of setting as they made their way to Mrs. Erickson's home. Her absence had not caused weeds to run amok on her lawn, which made Kaylin wonder who'd cut her lawn when she lived in the house. Maybe she'd done it herself. Maybe the neighbor had done it until Azoria had interfered with his mind.

Mrs. Erickson hadn't decided what she would do with the house she no longer inhabited. She had no Swindon relatives to whom she might leave the bungalow, but it had been her home—hers and the ghosts'—for all of her life. Yes, she'd moved in with Helen, but Kaylin was almost certain she would have stayed in the familiar confines of her house if not for the current Arkon and her new ghostly friends. She wasn't ready to let it go, yet.

Until Helen, Kaylin had never owned a home—had never really dreamed of owning one. She'd had no advice to offer. But she suspected that if she were Mrs. Erickson, she'd hold on to the home, even if she couldn't live in it, for as long as she could.

Evanton noted the size of the houses to either side of Mrs. Erickson's, but it was polite, perfunctory conversation; the moment his foot hit the narrow walk that led to her front porch, his gaze rose to the roof—and above it.

Kaylin poked Hope, and Hope, disgruntled, whacked her face with his wing, but left it in place. In the growing evening street light, she could see the faint trace of another building resting above and beside Mrs. Erickson's house.

Evanton frowned at Hope before he transferred the frown to Kaylin. He raised a brow, as if to ask if she could see what he could see; she nodded. "You are certain she is dead?"

"Absolutely certain."

Mrs. Erickson let them into her house. "I'm sorry," she said. "Let me find a lamp."

Kaylin shook her head. "I'll handle lighting for now."

"Oh?"

"I've been reminded I need practice."

"And you listened?" Evanton asked. "I'm almost impressed with your teacher."

"He's a Dragon."

"What is that supposed to mean?" Bellusdeo demanded. She had left Maggaron with Helen, given the size and composition of their unusual party. Maggaron attracted attention from much farther away than the cohort or Bellusdeo herself. Kaylin felt bad for him. His height wasn't his fault. The effect he had on people wasn't his fault, either. But there was nothing he could do about it. She'd've brought him along. She'd assumed he'd be joining Bellusdeo.

Bellusdeo insisted on being practical.

Maggaron accepted it. Kaylin knew she'd've been either hurt or angry, or probably both, in his place.

"He isn't worried for me," Bellusdeo had said. "The Keeper and the cohort, as well as the Chosen, will be my escorts and guards should the need arise."

"But what about him? What about *his* place?"

Bellusdeo hadn't understood the question. To be fair, it didn't seem like Maggaron had, either. Maybe it was just a human thing.

She rethought her position when she entered Mrs. Erickson's house; the ceilings weren't of a height Maggaron could easily manage without walking on his knees.

"This is where I lived," Mrs. Erickson said, almost apologetically. "I know it isn't much."

"It is larger than my own humble home," Evanton replied. "The storefront takes up much of the living space, and your halls are wider."

"And less creaky," Kaylin muttered.

Evanton asked no questions until Mrs. Erickson opened the closed door to what had been a family room or a parlor. He did, however, reach out to place a staying hand on the old woman's shoulder. "Corporal."

Bellusdeo said, "Let me check."

Hope squawked. Loudly.

"You realize she's mortal, right? The marks of the Chosen don't change her essential nature?"

Squawk. Squawk.

"Fine. Your familiar wants you to look first."

"That might be a problem," Serralyn said, in a quiet voice.

Bellusdeo exhaled smoke. "I honestly do not understand how Terrano has survived. Were I Sedarias, I would have strangled him by now."

"She'd have to catch me first." Terrano's cheerful voice came from the interior of the darkened room. Kaylin had chosen to lift a mark from her skin and send it ahead of where they walked, at roughly chest height. It had been a steady, and strong, source of light, until she'd reached this room.

"She's too busy avoiding assassins," Mandoran added. "If any one of us could murder Terrano, it's Sedarias."

"I don't understand," Kaylin said, as Mrs. Erickson and Evanton stepped aside. The hall wasn't large, and jostling for position took a bit more time. "Azoria's dead."

"You have experience as a Hawk," Evanton said. "You are aware that there are enchantments that survive their creators. I believe you have even encountered them." He wasn't impressed.

This was true. But if Kaylin died this second, she was certain the light in the house would be extinguished. And she knew if summoners died, their summoned elements would vanish. It was only if the summoner lost control—and survived it—that the elements raged wildly.

"It's simple. Some magic is like carpentry. If the people who built Mrs. Erickson's home died, the home would not collapse; it is a house. Time and wear occur naturally, and if a home is not kept in decent repair, it will eventually crumble—but its existence is not linked to its builder's life force. Again, you have had experience; you should know this. I begin to wonder what kind of teacher the Arkon is."

"Rather, wonder what kind of student Kaylin is," Bellusdeo said.

"Ah, yes, I forget myself. It is a habit of the old. Perhaps the Arkon is struggling with the raw materials available. Very well. There was an issue with this room—or so I was told—and I would like to examine the structure of this particular enchantment."

Kaylin nodded. "We're going to need a different lamp, though—my light might not cut it here." She turned to Serralyn, whose eyes were blue. "Has Terrano stumbled into anything dangerous?"

"Not yet. Sedarias is arguing with him now."

"Tell him to listen—Mrs. Erickson's home isn't large, and I don't want angry Sedarias to descend on us all. Again."

Serralyn sighed. "It's Terrano," she added. She'd really gotten good at employing the fief shrug. "He says the enchantment is still present."

"The painting?"

"Yes. I thought it would change, but it hasn't. He can see the flowers in young Mrs. Erickson's hair clearly—but they don't look like flowers. Not the way he's examining them."

"What do they resemble?" Evanton asked.

"Vines, maybe? Nothing you'd consider normal vines, though. Tendrils."

"Terrano is unharmed."

"Yes, but…he's not quite here. The room and the painting were designed to be active or effective here, where we're standing."

Evanton cleared his throat. "The corporal has her familiar,

and the marks of the Chosen. I would like to examine the painting with my own eyes."

Serralyn swallowed all further argument and nodded.

Evanton entered the family room, closely followed by Kaylin. Hope could, in an emergency, erect a potent barrier against magic, and she wanted to make sure the elderly Keeper was within range if it went off. The shield was always centered on Kaylin.

Evanton didn't notice—or if he did, he kept his usual dour remarks to himself. He moved toward the painting of the Swindon family—mother, father, and twelve-year-old daughter, Imelda. Around the room lay shallow wells of darkness; if they'd been light, they'd be pooled at the foot of a standing lamp. She frowned as she considered this. What would the equivalent of lamps be like for darkness?

Thinking this, she looked up.

Hope squawked.

Above her head were circles of darkness, more distinct, more sharp-edged; the darkness on the floor seemed more like inkblots in comparison. "Terrano, can you see the ceiling?"

"If that's what you want to call it, yeah. What can you see?"

"Black circles. They seem to be evenly spaced, and I think they match the dark blotches on the floor."

"Can you see anything near the painting?"

She shook her head. "Not besides Evanton, no." She moved around—or as much around as she could—the dark areas. The floating mark she was using for light dimmed as it crossed the blurry perimeter of the dark patches. She still hated this room.

"Is it safe for Mrs. Erickson to come in?" Bellusdeo asked; she stood in the doorframe, Mrs. Erickson behind her.

"No," Evanton replied, before Kaylin or Terrano could. "You said the children were afraid of this room?"

"They were," Mrs. Erickson replied, her voice soft. "Not at the beginning, but toward the end. They couldn't even speak of it unless they thought I was going to open the door or enter the room. I found their reaction heartbreaking, so the room was neglected while they were alive." She coughed. "I mean, when they were still with me."

Kaylin understood the mistake. Mrs. Erickson didn't see the dead as dead—she saw them as people.

Perhaps because she first saw the dead—invisible to almost all of the living—when she was a child and she couldn't tell the difference between them and the living, she'd learned to treat everyone as if they were a person, even if they were invisible to the eyes of most.

"They were exceedingly fond of you," Evanton said, his voice so soft Kaylin almost missed it. "Did they tell you why they feared this place?" He stood in front of the painting itself, and an odd glow enveloped him; had he been walking in daylight, it would have been too subtle to notice.

"No—as I said before, even mention of it would cause them to freeze in place. They wouldn't come back from terror unless I could change the subject. They pretended that I didn't know, and I pretended that I wasn't worried—it was much harder in the later years."

"The painting appears to be a family portrait. Are you attached to it?"

"I barely remember what it looks like after all these years," Mrs. Erickson replied—untruthfully, in Kaylin's opinion.

"It is not, as you must know, a regular painting. There are obvious magical elements—I shall call them pigments for the moment—involved at the heart of the family portrait, but even absent those pigments, there is magic in the weave of the canvas itself."

Bellusdeo's voice was a draconic rumble. "What type of magic?"

"I am not a scholar, Lord Bellusdeo. I am fully capable of sensing the magic; I am, in some circumstances, capable of working with it. Were this painting not rooted in place, I would suggest that you take it with you to the Academia, where actual scholars might better answer that question." He turned toward the door but didn't otherwise move. "I do not believe this painting can be preserved. The manner of its creation is entwined with every element of it, and given the painter, I do not believe it is entirely safe."

"Could you take it to the garden?" Kaylin asked.

"It is true that if it is contained in the garden, it would be safe—but I am uncertain that it would be wise. There are things this painting is rooted in that do not belong in any garden."

"Can you uproot it?"

"I can, but it is not without danger."

"To whom?" Bellusdeo asked; she was annoyed. She knew, intellectually, that Evanton was the Keeper, but she also knew he was an older man. Older, and far more fragile than a Dragon, or even a Barrani.

Evanton turned back to the painting, his hands loosely clasped behind his back. "To anyone who resides within this house—but that would only be the start." He exhaled. "I believe this room should be locked for the moment, but if anyone was wondering whether or not Azoria's former abode is still active, I can say with certainty that it is. You said that you entered her home when you attempted to leave by the front door, yes?"

"Yes," Kaylin replied.

"Part of the grounding for this painting, in this place, is in that abode. I believe we should examine it."

"I'm not certain the door will open into Azoria's mansion."

"Ah. I believe it now will." Kaylin didn't like the sound of that.

Serralyn, silent until that moment, said, "Bakkon would like to join us, if that's okay."

Evanton frowned. "The Wevaran?"

"Yes. Arbiter Starrante contacted him. He came to the Academia. He can arrive here, without passing through the city streets, because I'm here; he attached a thread to me. He won't interfere if the Keeper doesn't wish it, but there are things he would like to examine. We didn't have a lot of time the last time he was with us."

"Given our current company, I cannot see how it would be harmful," Evanton replied.

"Have you met a Wevaran before?"

"No. I am aware of the Wevaran, of course, but I have not personally encountered one before. I find their language taxing. Come, let us continue."

Kaylin accepted that her understanding of what a Keeper did was imperfect. Worse than imperfect. She should have guessed some of it; Evanton had enchanted her daggers. Enchanting daggers had nothing to do with the husbanding of the elemental garden—and that control was imperfect; she'd been in his shop when it suddenly flooded. But... Evanton knew Wevaran? Evanton could see magic of a type that Kaylin couldn't see? Kaylin was very sensitive to magic, to magical sigils, to the traces of the work of mages; it was one of her biggest strengths as an investigator where magical crimes were involved.

Evanton's entire posture had changed by the time he left the family room; he had insisted that the door remain locked—and implied that it was fine with him that Terrano was stuck inside the room. "That boy gives me a headache."

Terrano, of course, wouldn't remain stuck in the room for long—if he'd even remained inside it. Hope's wing trembled against her eyes, but he didn't lower it; he stood, alert, on her shoulder as Evanton made his way to the front door. "Do not tug the Wevaran thread until we've opened the door into Azoria's mansion."

"I'm not sure it will open into the mansion." Mrs. Erickson's voice was soft, but her hands were clasped together as if in prayer. "It's only ever done that once, when Azoria was still alive."

"I am certain it will," Evanton said.

"Oh? But why?" The old woman was curious in spite of her anxiety. Or perhaps because of it.

Evanton's expression gentled instantly when he turned to answer her. "A strand in the magical weave that surrounds the finished painting is meant to open that door. I caused it to activate."

He hadn't touched the painting. He hadn't lifted a hand.

"What activated the door the last time it opened?"

"Azoria, of course. She had far more control over her creation than a simple old man like me." Evanton approached the door and opened it. To no one's surprise, it opened into the foyer of Azoria's mansion.

He turned to Mrs. Erickson, and offered her his arm. Mrs. Erickson accepted it. They stepped into the mansion together. Evanton then turned back. "Serralyn, it is safe to call Bakkon now; I am uncertain that he will be able to track his own thread after you cross the threshold."

Serralyn nodded, lifting a hand to touch a slender, glimmering thread Kaylin was certain she wouldn't have seen without Hope's wing. The light brightened beneath her fingertip.

Bakkon, the Wevaran who lived in Liatt's Tower, appeared, his legs landing so silently he might have been weightless. He lifted his front legs, waving them delicately in a more complex than usual Wevaran greeting.

Evanton nodded, rather than raising his arms in turn; one was occupied by Mrs. Erickson.

The Keeper moved farther into the foyer to allow everyone else to enter; if the door that led to Azoria's former home was magical, it hadn't increased in width.

"I am Evanton, the current Keeper," he said to the Wevaran, in Barrani. "Can you make certain the door remains open?"

"I am honored to meet you, Keeper," Bakkon replied, a faint

click between syllables as he lowered his body almost to the ground. "I will do what I can."

Can we just move a piece of furniture over the doorjamb? It's what we did last time, Kaylin said to her partner.

We can, if you think that's wiser. Severn didn't trust the door, either.

Everyone except the Wevaran entered the foyer; Bakkon's body was large enough that the door was a tight squeeze until he turned sideways. Kaylin had expected him to portal between the two living spaces. "I apologize for intruding. I wish to examine this space for my own reasons."

"What might those reasons be?" It was Evanton who asked. Fair enough; the Wevaran—like the Barrani and the Dragon—seemed to hold the Keeper in high regard.

"When Azoria was alive—if that word can be applied to what she had become—the space felt very familiar to me."

"Oh?"

"It felt like a breeding ground. A Wevaran crèche, if you will."

Kaylin grimaced. A Wevaran crèche was a place where many, many small spiders hatched, their sole purpose to eat their brethren until only one remained.

"Do you believe Azoria found one, or do you believe she created it?"

"I am uncertain. I believe it must be created; our birth homes existed for one purpose only. I could not now return to mine; none of us could, once we emerged. We believed—without proper research, I confess—that our emergence destroyed the area."

"Did all birthing grounds produce a Wevaran?" Kaylin asked.

Bakkon's eyes swiveled in her direction—well, two of them.

"It is a worthy question," Evanton said. "I would be pleased to hear your answer."

"No. Perhaps one fifth failed to produce living Wevaran."

"Did the spaces collapse? I assume they failed because the final Wevaran killed each other." Kaylin's tone was full-on Hawk.

"They did not vanish; they did not become unmade. We do not know whether or not all of the hatchlings died. We simply knew that they had failed to produce living kin."

Kaylin's frown deepened. "Did you have birthing grounds? Places you laid your...spaces?"

"Not in the sense that the Dragons did. Understand that we did not lay eggs. We created spaces in which the very young might be stirred to life. But those spaces might be, on the interior, very like this one."

"What do you mean? Wait, do you remember the place you were born?"

"I do. I admit it did not resemble the Barrani architecture of these halls, but it was not a place of darkness; it was not restricted. We are not like humans; our young are not carried and ejected when they are viable. We find spaces, cracks between planes, and we lay our eggs there. We are not like human families; we are not like Barrani families. We do not number our descendants, nor do we prioritize them.

"If they emerge, we treat them as kin. If they do not, we do not grieve."

Kaylin turned to Evanton. "Did you know this?"

Evanton frowned. "Was it relevant to my duties?"

"Probably not."

"Have you finished?"

"I just have one more question."

"Then ask it; Wevaran are notoriously patient with genuine questions, regardless of their practicality."

Kaylin nodded. "When you lay these eggs, do you lay them in the outlands? Is that the crack between planes you mentioned?"

Bakkon chittered in Wevaran, which no one present could understand, but it continued for a couple of minutes before he stopped. When he spoke again, it was in Barrani. "I am not familiar with the word *outlands* as you use it, but I believe I understand the question.

"You are speaking of the potentiality from which the Towers, the Academia, the Hallionne, and all sentient buildings draw their reality and assert it?"

"Yes."

"The answer is yes. Yes, we do. I am aware that Wevaran biology is not well understood by most races, and certainly not modern races. But birth is complicated for both the child and the parent. The laying of...eggs, in your analogy, is not a simple act. It is not a compulsion to procreate or create, as it is for many living beings. We require words—True Words—to become. We require True Words to emerge."

So did all of the Immortals. But the Barrani had the Lake of Life. The Dragons... Kaylin wasn't certain what the Dragons had; she knew they had to achieve their full name to become adult, but she'd never carefully considered the how or the where; they had no Lake of Life in the fashion the Barrani did.

"True Words don't just exist in the outlands, do they?"

"No, of course not." Bakkon paused. "Tell me, Corporal—or any of you who are not my kin—what do you think the outlands is? We called it potentiality for a reason. You speak. You communicate. You use words. But True Words and your words are not the same. There is a power in True Words, a subtle tapestry of immutable essence and life itself. True Words are not alive."

Kaylin glanced at Mrs. Erickson. Mrs. Erickson's ghosts looked like words to Kaylin, like True Words.

"Bakkon, were True Words alive once?"

12

"I fail to understand your question," the Wevaran replied, his eye color implying that Kaylin had surprised him. No one else was surprised; they knew what Kaylin had seen when she looked at Mrs. Erickson's ghosts. But they knew, as well, that Mrs. Erickson didn't see them that way.

"True Words are the source of life, of life force, for the Immortals. Things I've seen in ancient Records imply that they were the source of life for the Ancients as well—almost their literal blood."

Bakkon stilled, but said nothing, waiting.

"Blood isn't alive, but it's part of being alive. I assumed True Words were sort of like that. Or like a heart. The heart doesn't exist separate from us unless we're dead—but at that point, it's not beating. But did the Ancients once have a language that was actually alive? Were words sentient in some way?"

"Why are you asking this question?"

Kaylin opened her mouth and closed it again. "I think you should speak with Starrante," she finally said. There were follow-up questions that Bakkon was likely to ask that she didn't want to answer. And it was her own fault for asking the question she'd asked, for thinking out loud without considering possible consequences.

Ghostly words led to questions about Necromancy, which was fine, and possession—of Dragons—which was not.

"You understand that the purpose of True Words is communication. It is, among those who can speak and hear the language, a way of making meaning completely clear. These words exist outside of cultural contexts and the social enclaves that arise around them. Were these words to somehow have a sentience, a life, an existence of their own, how could they serve that function?

"What lives knows change. In the case of the Immortals, that change is slow and oft cumbersome—but life is change. Think: if you cannot change, you cannot learn; knowledge alters our views, our understanding, our grasp of the world." His tone was slightly condescending, which Kaylin had to struggle not to take personally.

"The Ancients were not hoarders of knowledge; they attempted to teach their creations. Our ability to understand what they taught, to even perceive it, was flawed. Were Ancients to walk now, it would remain flawed; we are not what they were. We cannot be what they were; it has been tried. The results have never been good."

"That is true," Evanton said, cutting the conversation short. Or shorter. "If you have investigations to make that do not require our assistance, we have investigations of our own. We will leave you to your work and continue with ours."

Serralyn looked to Kaylin, who shrugged. "Evanton's always like that. Do you want to stay with Bakkon?"

She hesitated, her expression shifting at what was clearly an internal conversation. "Yes. I'll stay with Bakkon."

"Meaning we're stuck with Terrano?"

Her smile was sunny.

★★★

Evanton, growing more impatient by the minute, led the way. Azoria's front foyer was grand, the floors perfect gray marble, the ceilings very high; light was cast by the chandelier that occupied the ceiling's height. If it fell, people would die. There were no paintings in the foyer. Evanton wanted to see the paintings, or what remained of them after Mrs. Erickson's first visit. But he paused at the two statues, facing each other from the sides of the foyer. He frowned.

"You didn't mention statues." He turned to Terrano. "Were there statues present when you arrived the first time?"

Barrani memory was better—by far—than Kaylin's, but it hadn't been that long.

"I don't remember statues," Terrano replied, his tone utterly neutral. His quiet response chilled the mood in the foyer. Completely.

The statues appeared Barrani, although they were pale, almost alabaster, the color of skin and hair made irrelevant by the material the sculptor had chosen. Both had long, flowing hair; both wore robes that seemed almost rustic; both wore slender crowns of leaf and vine, not the jeweled tiaras of the powerful and the rich. The robes were voluminous; it was hard to determine gender. Both stood, hands by their sides, chins level, as if they were looking at each other. Or looking for each other.

Mrs. Erickson said, "Azoria is dead."

This wasn't much of a comfort. Mrs. Erickson understood that death wasn't necessarily the end.

Evanton glanced to the side. "You believed that Azoria's research had something to do with the extensive use of the dead."

"Oh, I don't know very much about her research," Mrs. Erickson replied.

Kaylin grimaced at the Keeper. "We're not certain what the goal of that research was. Azoria was Barrani; she had eternity, if she were careful."

"And?"

"It's mostly mortals who break things in an attempt to become Immortal. I don't think she was necessarily trying to extend her life."

Terrano coughed.

"You think she was?"

"I think she was, what's the word? Intrepid. I think she was intrepid. She was willing to experiment."

"Clearly."

"With her own life. With the source of her life force: her name. She wouldn't be the first. If mortals go down the wrong paths in their desire to be Immortal—and they do—Immortals, taking immortality for granted. They don't want eternity because they already have it.

"They want freedom. They want the security of an existence free from the threat of enslavement, which is what True Names represent. If that wasn't her goal, forbidden research—at least among our kin—revolves around that. How do we get names that no one else can bind us with?

"Even if she wasn't looking for that directly, if she performed other questionable research, that would form the underpinnings of any extrapolation."

Evanton exhaled. He walked toward one of the statues; it was taller than anyone present; it might have been taller than Maggaron. Kaylin's frown deepened. The foyer of Azoria's home hadn't been this large, had it?

She turned to Mrs. Erickson; when Evanton approached the statue, Mrs. Erickson had failed to follow, her hand sliding off his arm and falling to her side.

"It's probably a good idea we're here," Terrano said, in an uncharacteristically grim tone. "The foyer wasn't this large the first time. Serralyn says it's possible that without Azoria's will to shape it, the building is slowly transforming."

"This doesn't look like drift to me."

"Not to us, either. I think Bakkon's worried."

"The dead aren't supposed to have power. This can't be Azoria, can it?"

"I'm not the person to ask, and before you continue, I have no idea who is. But Sedarias is now worried."

Great. Just great.

"She's not mad at you—not yet; she was certain Azoria was gone as well."

"What if it's not Azoria?"

"I think that's what she's worried about."

"Her worries can be explained on your own time," Evanton said. He'd left the statue he'd approached and was walking a straight line to the second statue, which brought him in range of their conversation.

"What do you think he's looking for?" Terrano whispered, when Evanton stood in front of the second statue, chin lifted, hands clasped behind his back.

Kaylin shrugged. *Severn?*

The statues look the same to me as they look to you through Hope's wing.

The rest of the foyer?

The same as well. Hope clearly thinks there's something here that might require visual aid—but whatever it is, it's not in the foyer.

She watched Evanton's back and posture. *I'm not so sure about that.*

Evanton stood in front of the second statue for at least five minutes; it felt longer, but she knew when she was forced to be inactive, time seemed to elongate. She'd become better about not fidgeting over the years, mostly because it annoyed Teela.

"You said there was a gallery?" Evanton asked.

"There was. It was where the ensorcelled paintings were hung."

"Do you believe it to still be in the same location?"

Kaylin shrugged. "Only one way to find out."

"Two," Terrano said, grinning. He vanished.

Bellusdeo glared. To be fair to her, she was glaring at everything that happened to cross her gaze, it was just that Kaylin was the last person it reached. "I didn't object to his presence, but I hoped you could keep him in line."

Mandoran coughed. A lot.

Bellusdeo's eyes narrowed, but their color didn't darken. "Will he be safe?"

"He's Terrano. Nothing's managed to kill him yet."

The gold Dragon exhaled steam. "Tonight might be a first." But she glanced at Mrs. Erickson. "Or not. This place looks different to you, doesn't it?"

"My memory isn't very good," Mrs. Erickson replied. "And we were in a bit of a panic the last time I was here. But…yes. It looks different. The ceilings are different, and I'm not sure I like the look of that light." She gestured in the direction of the chandelier. "But I like Terrano—I don't want anything bad to happen to him."

"If it does, it won't be your fault. You had nothing to do with this place."

Mrs. Erickson nodded as if she agreed. She didn't. The dead here, the ghosts of the children who had been her lifelong friends, the artist and the boys and girls who had become permanent interior fixtures—they had been entrapped by Azoria because Azoria's interest in the very young Imelda Erickson had been so focused.

Mrs. Erickson was mortal. It was clear—somehow—that Azoria could inhabit living bodies, the bodies of the people she'd imprisoned. It was also clear that the spirits, the souls, the essential nature of the living people, had been ejected from those bodies, as if the body was a simple vehicle. If Azoria had suspicions about Mrs. Erickson's power, Kaylin didn't understand why she hadn't chosen to eject Mrs. Erickson from her own body and take over.

But she hadn't. Perhaps her control of the bodies frayed, or her sense of self disintegrated with the passage of time; the physical body of each of the children in Mrs. Erickson's house had eventually been executed for a series of brutal murders, all occurring roughly at the age of twenty-five.

It wasn't guaranteed that the inhabitant of those bodies had been Azoria; it wasn't guaranteed that it hadn't.

If she'd considered Mrs. Erickson's power possibly useful, she must have been trying to make certain her tenure in that body would be stable. But Mrs. Erickson's body was mortal, like Kaylin's, and Mrs. Erickson was, well, old.

Evanton is also old, Severn pointed out.

Yes...but Evanton is the Keeper. I'm sure there are enchantments that have extended his life while he looks for the next Keeper.

Which implies enchantments can extend mortal life.

Evanton's been around forever. Don't you think if it were that obvious, every mortal Arcanist ever would be flocking to his shop to attempt to kidnap and dissect him?

The Arcanists wouldn't. There are enough Barrani in the Arcanum that the role of the Keeper would be protected. There's no point in immortality when the world has been destroyed.

Kaylin wasn't so certain. There was an annoying breed of mage that believed that rules only applied to other people; that they were, and would remain, the exception. Reality—even reality as strange as the garden—was for other, lesser beings.

I don't think Azoria would've been foolish enough to remove the Keeper. She would've certainly been aware of his existence.

"Terrano says the gallery is still here. Sort of," Mandoran informed them.

Kaylin frowned. *If Azoria intended to occupy Mrs. Erickson's body because of Mrs. Erickson's innate power, she had to know that Mrs. Erickson would age and die, just like the rest of the mortals.*

Severn nodded.

That means the question of mortality suddenly becomes relevant, no?

It does. Perhaps some of her experiments with the spirits of the living were an attempt to preserve their innate power.

Kaylin shook her head. *I'm not sure that's the way it works.*

I agree—but Azoria was not a woman given to acceptance of that fact, especially where mortals were concerned. Mortals lived without the need for a True Name.

Yeah, but we can't live forever.

The ghosts could. Had Mrs. Erickson passed away, the children would have been trapped for eternity.

Kaylin flinched.

The gallery, as Terrano had informed them, was not the same gallery through which they had walked previously. Paintings hung across its walls, and statues adorned its alcoves. The statues were new, which was concerning, but it was the paintings that drew the eye.

Azoria had created paintings such as these in the High Halls; it was in such paintings that she had trapped—and suspended—living mortals. If stasis could be considered immortality, Amaldi and Darreno had effectively been Immortal. They just hadn't experienced the passage of time, unless and until they were released from their prison.

Kaylin had sometimes wondered why people were obsessed with living forever. What kind of lives had they led that made eternity seem appealing? When she'd first come to the Hawks, she'd wanted the exact opposite: an end to what seemed unending pain.

Severn tapped her shoulder.

Sorry. You know I don't feel that way now. She shook herself and returned her attention to the paintings. They had been portraits, at one point. Paintings of mortals. But the frames were so dark they might have been composed of obsidian—and the images were no longer of people. Had the paintings simply become the backgrounds that Azoria had painted, it wouldn't have been so disturbing.

They were landscapes, yes—but not the landscapes or interiors that had graced Azoria's work. Some were almost like the building they were currently investigating, but some were not. The only similar thing she had seen was in her brief foray into *Ravellon*. Which made things far worse.

But here and there were verdant, brilliant greens—trees or very tall plants, beneath oddly colored skies. And some were the gray, roiling clouds of the outlands.

The paintings looked almost like windows.

Kaylin lifted a hand to touch a canvas; Hope squawked. Loudly.

"Do not make me breathe fire," Bellusdeo said, her voice louder than Hope's.

"I just wanted to see if they were still canvas."

"See with your eyes."

"I don't know why people say *I'm* reckless," Terrano, invisible, muttered. "I wouldn't touch these with gloves, armor, or a ten-foot pole."

Kaylin rolled her eyes. "We believe you."

"I don't," Mandoran said, his words overlapping Bellusdeo's.

"I was being polite. Terrano, what does the painting at the end of the gallery look like?"

"It's the only one that looks the same—but it's a fair ways off now. I don't think there are more paintings, but...there are more sculptures."

Kaylin nodded; she could see that. The sculptures were similar to the ones that now graced the foyer.

"These sculptures were not here the first time you had the misfortune to visit?" Evanton asked.

"No."

"I would like the Barrani boys to pay attention to every detail in this mansion, their memory being better than ours. Or," he added, glancing in the direction of the Dragon, "Lord Bellusdeo could do the same. I feel hesitant to command her as if she's a simple errand runner. I'd have you do it," he added to Kaylin. "I pay taxes. Taxes pay you. But your memory is worse than mine."

Bakkon and Serralyn had not entered the gallery; that left Mandoran and Terrano as the errand boys. No one in this hall felt safe. Azoria was dead, in theory, but the hall had changed. Either something else had moved in, or the hall was somehow reverting to an earlier shape and form.

Kaylin doubted it was the latter; the hall was larger, and far grander, than the home that Azoria had constructed; she couldn't imagine that the Barrani lord would have gone through the effort of deliberately creating a lesser space.

Evanton's expression grew more remote as he walked, purposefully and slowly, down the gallery.

Kaylin risked one question. "Are these paintings no longer paintings?"

"In my opinion, they are not. But they were never paintings. Azoria's magic relied on altering both canvas and paint. It was delicate work, and likely time-consuming; whatever she built here was a long time in the planning. I do not sense her presence in this place, but it is not empty.

"I would remain, but I cannot be too long from the garden. I will need to confer with the elements—they are likely to be unsettled."

"Do you understand why?"

"No. I am unwilling to speculate without further research. There is one last painting I wish to see."

"The self-portrait."

Evanton nodded. His face was disturbingly expressionless as he looked down the gallery, his eyes slightly narrowed.

Hope was now rigid as he stood on her shoulder. "Mrs. Erickson?" Kaylin asked, voice softer. Although the old woman had entered the building by Evanton's side, she had fallen behind. Kaylin joined Mrs. Erickson; she and Bellusdeo walked to either side of her, as if she was the only person here who needed protection.

Her eyes were too wide, her shoulders too slumped; her hands seemed to tremble slightly.

"Imelda," Bellusdeo said, her eyes dark orange, her voice very gentle. "What do you see?"

Mrs. Erickson shook her head, mute, as if to deny that she could see anything. But she didn't say the words, because they would have been lies. Maybe living with children for all her life had made honesty so instinctive she couldn't lie, except by shaky omission.

Evanton lifted a hand before Bellusdeo could ask again. He'd glanced at Mrs. Erickson, but it was brief; that glance, even given his lack of familiarity, took in everything Kaylin had seen.

"My apologies, Mrs. Erickson. I have perhaps been too demanding. I wish to view the final painting, after which I must do research of my own. Thank you for your patience." He approached her and once again offered her his arm.

She put more of her weight against it as she accepted.

Terrano was visible in the distance, dwarfed by the large frame that had once contained the self-portrait of Azoria An'Berranin. She was no longer in the painting, but the painting persisted, its frame unchanged. The absence of Azoria had initially left the gray, almost cloudlike landscape of the outlands. It had been both window and door. Now the landscape was different.

Clouds persisted, but they occupied the height of the painting, as natural clouds occupied parts of the sky. From the height of clouds, spokes of light fell on a slant, toward the ground. There, trees stood—or plants that resembled trees at this distance; had they not been so small, she wouldn't have had any doubts.

But above those trees towered pillars—or what Kaylin assumed were pillars—that almost seemed to hold up the sky, the clouds; there was no roof, no upper limit to the structure. The pillars were wider by far than the trunks of the trees that seemed almost minuscule in comparison.

The sky was an odd shade—a sunset shade of crimson and violet with streaks of gold from one side of the frame to the other.

"Mandoran, what do you see?"

Mandoran described what Kaylin saw almost exactly.

"Bellusdeo?"

The gold Dragon failed to answer.

"Evanton?"

"I see what Mandoran claims to see," the Keeper replied. His tone was neutral, almost stiff.

Do you see what I see?

Yes. But Evanton's reaction implies that it has a meaning to him that it doesn't to the rest of us.

Kaylin didn't ask Mrs. Erickson. Instead, she said, "What does Terrano see?"

"He can see what we see."

"And?"

Mandoran nodded. "This was one of Azoria's paintings. There are elements to it that aren't visible to normal eyes."

Terrano's eyes were not normal. They were far too large, and far too oddly colored; they took up half of his face. "Serralyn says Bakkon is done for now—they're going to close up and head back to the Academia through his portal, if that's okay."

Kaylin nodded, distracted. She walked more quickly to reach the painting, and stopped in front of it. Hope squawked loudly.

"I know," she told him.

"What do you know?" Evanton demanded, his tone the sharp snap he seemed to reserve for disappointing Hawks.

"The pillars," she replied, without looking back. "There are words engraved on them."

Silence.

You don't see words?

No.

"Does anyone else see the words?"

More silence.

"Terrano," Evanton said, in the same sharp tone. "Does this painting still serve the function of a portal?"

"I think so. Before, I could see a door. I can't see one now, but it feels like a door is here. And closed."

"My apologies, Mrs. Erickson. My eyes are not as good as the eyes of the young here, and I need to be a bit closer to the painting to examine it properly. I will leave you with Lord Bellusdeo, but ask that you keep your distance. I am not at all certain that the painting is safe to approach."

"Then why are you approaching it?" Kaylin demanded.

He glared in her direction.

"I mean it. Severn and I are here, and we're Hawks. You're the Keeper, Evanton—and you don't have a successor. Bellusdeo is a fieflord now, and Towers don't function well without a captain."

"I'm not a fieflord, and I'm not a Keeper," Terrano said, grinning—which was very disturbing given the composition of his eyes. "Neither is Mandoran. We can do what you want."

"No, you cannot," Evanton replied, ignoring them.

The natural respect—even awe—that some of the cohort felt for the authority and position of the Keeper was entirely absent. Then again, it was Terrano; Mandoran wasn't being cheeky. He'd been on almost suspiciously good behavior since they'd left the house—so much so, it was almost like he wasn't here at all.

"Hope—please please please keep an eye on Evanton."

Squawk.

"Do not even think of landing on my shoulder. Your master is far more tolerant than I will ever be."

Squawk.

"I understand that. But if I were the type of person to hide behind someone else's familiar every time there is a possibility of danger, I would not have survived my apprenticeship, and I would have failed in the garden. I am not reckless, and I lack the impetuousness of youth."

"I don't think it's a good idea," Terrano began.

"You do not strike me as a young man who recognizes good ideas. Be silent. I need to listen."

Had Evanton been a foundling, Kaylin would have said *you listen with your ears, not your hands* the minute he lifted an arm. She tensed, glancing at Bellusdeo. Bellusdeo had retreated down the hall with Mrs. Erickson, as if Mrs. Erickson was the only person of value in this place.

Kaylin would have done the same had she not been standing as close to Evanton as possible. Severn had quietly taken up position on the other side of the Keeper, to one side of Terrano, who remained by the painting.

It was hard to gauge his expression because his eyes were so unnatural, but she thought he, too, was alert—and he was looking at things she couldn't see.

"Terrano—do you see words?" Kaylin asked, voice low.

"No. But the pillars don't quite look like pillars to me—not right now. I can see what Mandoran is looking at; it's not the same."

"Are there similarities?"

"The frame is the same in either view. What do you see through the wing?"

She poked Hope, who grumbled but adjusted his wing so it covered only one eye. The painting looked the same. It wasn't Hope's wings that made the graven words clear. It was probably the marks of the Chosen.

But those marks weren't glowing. Nothing about them indicated that something was wrong or strange. "It's the same." She wanted to see what Terrano could see, but she couldn't melt her face the way he did.

"Evanton?"

Hope stiffened and let loose a volley of squawks in the direction of the Keeper. Evanton was close enough the noise should have been momentarily deafening, but he failed to hear it at all. His left hand, raised, faced the painting's surface; his fingers spread, fingertips touching what was no longer paint.

Beneath his hand, the painting darkened; shadows spread out from the tips of his fingers, flowing in five separate directions. Kaylin turned to the Keeper and reached immediately for his left wrist.

Her hand bounced in midair.

Kaylin tried again, but Severn had already begun to move; he was unwinding his weapon chain. The weapon served as a spellbreaker in times of need. As Kaylin watched in growing horror, she realized that it wasn't shadow that was spreading from Evanton's fingers; it was the illumination of the painting, the paint itself, that was being absorbed by Evanton's hand.

That light, dim at first, brightened; Evanton's eyes narrowed, but he didn't lower his hand.

"Can you let go?" Kaylin shouted.

"It appears I cannot," the Keeper replied, as if he were talking about mild weather. "My apologies. I believe I now understand the nature of the upset in the elemental garden. I believe it would be best if you—if all of you—left."

"We can't just leave you stuck to a painting!"

"Ah, perhaps I was being overly polite. Leave now." His voice sounded like an earthquake. Kaylin looked up; the hall was unaffected. It was all Evanton. "Lord Bellusdeo, please escort Mrs. Erickson from this manor immediately."

Kaylin turned to Hope. "Do something! Don't just sit there!"

I cannot, master. The price you would have to pay for the intervention would exceed your life force, and as such is forbidden.

"Why? Can you just build the barrier around him?"

There are some powers with which even I cannot safely interfere. It is possible I could intervene—but I cannot guarantee that even the Keeper would survive. If that power is aware of my interference, you would certainly not.

"Serralyn's coming to join us," Mandoran said. "Bakkon asks us to do everything we can to hold on to the Keeper until he arrives."

Hold on to him? She couldn't even touch him.

"Tell them both to stay where they are; there is nothing they can do here," Evanton snapped. He was annoyed. Or in pain. Maybe both.

Severn had blades in both hands; he passed them above Evanton's arms, not to wound, but to see if the barrier that had prevented Kaylin's touch would repel them. It did. He sheathed the blades, took the chain between two hands, and struck the barrier with more force; the chain bounced.

Whatever magic this was wasn't a magic the chains had been created to break.

It was brighter as well; Evanton's arms, face, exposed skin, all began to glow.

"You should go," Terrano said. "Like, now."

"That is what I suggested," Evanton said, through gritted teeth.

"Kaylin." Bellusdeo's voice was a booming sound, caught by the architecture and magnified. In case the magnification wasn't enough, she then repeated the word in full Dragon voice.

"But—but the Keeper!"

"He's certain he'll survive. He's also certain most of us won't. Move." Bellusdeo had picked up Mrs. Erickson—literally. She began to run back the way they'd come, as if Mrs. Erickson weighed nothing. Mandoran joined them.

"Terrano!"

"I'll be fine!"

Mandoran offered no further argument. He turned to race down the hall, catching up with the Dragon; Severn caught Kaylin by the arm, turned her around, and began to sprint.

Kaylin looked back over her shoulder; she could no longer see Evanton; she could see an almost blinding flash of light, as if light were exploding. It didn't shatter, but it began to fill the hall, spreading from its center, which was Evanton.

13

The spread of light looked like white fire as it followed them through the gallery, reflected in darkness by the frames of what had once been paintings. Kaylin wasn't worried about the paintings; she was worried about the statues. Although they appeared to be composed of marble, the marble seemed almost fluid as the heads of the statues situated in alcoves turned toward the source of the light.

Hope squawked loudly.

"I know, I know—I'm running as fast as I can!"

Barrani and Dragon speed outstripped mortal speed, but Kaylin's Hawk training allowed her to keep up. Severn was beside her, as if pacing her.

She expected the light to slow its spread; it didn't. The walls, ceilings, and floors of the gallery were now a glow of blinding white; details—if they still existed—couldn't be seen. Hope bit her ear the next time she tried to take a backward glimpse.

"Mandoran! Terrano isn't with us!"

"He's still alive. Sedarias is angry, but she isn't panicking. But Teela will kill me if you get caught in whatever the hells that is—keep up!"

They made it to the foyer, and there they came to a stop. The statues that had been at opposite ends of the foyer were no longer situated on their respective pedestals; they were standing on the floor, in the foyer entrance, as if to bar the way. If they hadn't been composed of stone, they would have looked like oversized Barrani.

"Do we need these statues?" Bellusdeo demanded.

"Not if they're not going to move, we don't."

"Good." She turned to Mandoran and handed Mrs. Erickson into his keeping. Kaylin was almost surprised to see that the old woman hadn't passed out.

Draconic breath could be exhaled while the Dragon was in their human form; Bellusdeo proved it, if there was any doubt. Her flame was orange-edged yellow, with a heart of white—the same white that seemed to be eating the gallery. Unlike the white light, this flame shed heat; Kaylin was surprised the perpetual loose strands of her hair didn't catch fire.

The breath was hot enough to melt stone—both the statues and the floor. "The rest of us have to walk across that!" Mandoran shouted. He couldn't tuck Mrs. Erickson under his arm, so chose to piggyback her instead. Mrs. Erickson was almost mute, her eyes too wide.

"Evanton's likely still alive," she told Mrs. Erickson. "He's a mage. He wouldn't have done anything stupid." This was harder to sell, as he'd demonstrably done something stupid, but Mrs. Erickson still held mages in awe.

"What if he needs our help?"

"Given present company, that's probably the last thing he needs. But he didn't think we'd survive whatever it is he was doing. We just need to get out of here before we start to make any plans." Bellusdeo's breath had left the legs of the statues standing in a yard-wide path of deformed marble.

The rest of the floor could be crossed, and they did that.

Hope squawked and smacked Kaylin's face with his wing.

She looked at him—his snout was pointing directly overhead at the chandelier.

At what had once been the chandelier. The hanging crystals had brightened significantly, white light with hearts of something that might have been blue had it not been so blinding. In and of itself, the illumination wasn't a problem.

It was the way light seemed to drop in writhing tendrils from the hanging crystals; those tendrils were rooted in the metal that held the crystals in place. The entire mass began to rotate, but not evenly; it was as if the tendrils were fighting each other for control.

This was definitely something she could only see with Hope's wing. "Stick to the walls!" she shouted.

"You're afraid the chandelier will fall?" Mandoran glanced at the ceiling where the chandelier was anchored.

"Something like that—just don't get beneath any part of it. We're almost at the door."

"The way things are going, do you actually expect the door to be there?"

The door, to Kaylin's great relief, hadn't changed. It was the only thing that hadn't. The frame was scuffed in places, the paint scratched; the size of the foyer made it look far narrower than it actually was. Bakkon had done something with webbing to keep the door from closing, and the webbing persisted, thank whatever gods happened to be looking.

Bellusdeo took the rear. Kaylin's attempt to point out that Imperial Hawks were present met with very red eyes, and she decided on the better part of valor. She was off duty, after all.

Only when they were in Mrs. Erickson's home did they stop, crowded in her narrow hallway.

"I don't think we should close the door," Bellusdeo glanced back. "The Keeper is on the other side."

"I'm not so sure about that," Mandoran said. "Terrano's there.

He didn't see the light that we saw. He did see something wrap itself around Evanton, but it didn't seem to be causing damage."

"What do you mean?" Kaylin was looking at the open door, eyes narrowed.

"I think something reached out from the other side of the painting—something in the outlands. It drew Evanton in."

"Did Terrano follow?"

"He tried. He's still working on it, for what it's worth—but if the light was an invitation, it was meant for the Keeper, not the chaos Barrani." Mandoran grinned. "He'll get in. Sedarias isn't even arguing—we all know we can't afford to lose the Keeper."

"How human is Evanton?" It was Bellusdeo who asked.

"If it weren't for the fact that he's looked the same way since Teela first joined the Hawks, I'd say completely. But he's the Keeper, so there are bound to be some differences. I mean—I look normal, but I have the marks of the Chosen. They don't make me less than human. Or more than human."

"So you think he's like you, but less reckless."

"Not much less reckless, given the events of tonight."

Bellusdeo shrugged. "Fair point. I think we should get Imelda home. She's had a bit of a shock."

"We've all had a bit of a shock," Mrs. Erickson said, somewhat primly. "Do you get into trouble like this all of the time?" The question was asked of the group in general.

"Kaylin does," was Mandoran's cheerful reply. "We just happen to be caught up in things because we live with her."

"I don't," Bellusdeo said. "And I'm still here."

"I really appreciate the support, guys. What do we do about the door? I don't think it's safe to leave it open—there's a real possibility that whatever transformed Azoria's mansion will escape to transform Mrs. Erickson's house."

"Or further?"

Kaylin nodded. "I'm not a mage. I can barely keep a light

active. But this was definitely transformational, and things have a way of spreading."

"Do you think the Keeper can find his way out?"

"I don't know—but I'm certain Terrano can, and he can try to open the door."

Closing the door was simple.

Opening the door onto the normal porch was not.

If Mrs. Erickson hadn't been present, Kaylin would have gone upstairs and destroyed the family painting. Evanton said that the door and the painting were linked, so it stood to reason destroying one would cut that connection.

Hope snorted; it was the sound of weary disgust. He pushed himself off Kaylin's shoulders—digging claws around her collarbone to make certain she knew he was annoyed first—and hovered in front of the door. He then exhaled.

Mandoran yelped and jumped out of the way, bounced into Bellusdeo and Severn, and found wall space against which he could regain his balance.

Silver mist came out of Hope's open mouth, the crimson interior the only part of his body, except for his eyes, that wasn't translucent. Where it touched the door, it seemed to be absorbed by the wood, although the door itself wasn't transformed. Hope's breath could transform or melt things, but without the intense heat of the larger Dragons.

When he finished, he returned to Kaylin's shoulder, but this time, he slumped across them both, snorted, and closed his eyes.

Bellusdeo opened the door. The door opened onto the porch. She turned to Mrs. Erickson and said, in a much more gentle voice, "Let's get you home."

"I'd like to walk," Mrs. Erickson said. Mrs. Erickson respected the law, and she knew Dragons weren't legally allowed to transform—and fly—in the city skies without direct Imperial permission.

"We can walk," Bellusdeo said. "I didn't expect the visit to be so difficult."

Kaylin watched Mrs. Erickson, but said nothing; Mrs. Erickson seemed genuinely distressed. If Kaylin could have believed that she was upset because of Evanton, she would have been a much happier person. She didn't. Kaylin was certain that Mrs. Erickson had seen something in the hall that her living companions couldn't.

Bellusdeo might have suspected it as well, but she was gentle and careful. If Mrs. Erickson was to be questioned, she would be questioned in the comfort of Helen's watchful presence.

And she would have to be questioned. Evanton was gone. Kaylin intended to check his store when she went on work patrol—but she really didn't expect him to have made his own way back. She knew she needed to go to the Academia, but Bellusdeo's pain—and loss—would have to be put on hold.

The gold Dragon realized this as well. How could she not? She'd ruled a small empire at the end of a world—she knew how to triage.

Bellusdeo escorted Mrs. Erickson to Helen's perimeter. She looked at the door, which opened the minute Kaylin crossed the property line, but didn't approach.

"It's late," she said, her voice subdued. "Mrs. Erickson needs sleep, and I need to confer with my Tower. You mean to go to the Academia tomorrow after work?"

Kaylin nodded.

"I'll see you there."

I think it's likely we'll be going to the Academia first thing in the morning, Severn said. He, like Bellusdeo, stopped at the property line. *The Keeper may be missing.*

We can check on him tomorrow at work.

Severn shook his head. *If Mrs. Erickson is willing to talk, listen. I'll head home.*

* * *

Helen's eyes were black with flecks of color by the time Kaylin had stepped foot into her home.

"Has Terrano returned?"

"Not yet." It was Mandoran who answered. His eyes were blue. "We've lost contact with him. He's still alive; if he were dead, we'd know."

"Did he manage to follow Evanton?"

Mandoran nodded. Without another word, he headed up the stairs, no doubt to Sedarias's room.

That left Helen, Mrs. Erickson, and Kaylin. Kaylin exhaled. She couldn't put on her Hawk face, not with Mrs. Erickson, and not at home. But she needed her newest housemate to speak about what she'd seen, or what she thought she'd seen.

Helen agreed. "Imelda, I know you had a very stressful evening. As a homecoming, it was far less nostalgic and far more dangerous than even I would have expected."

Mrs. Erickson nodded, silent.

"Come sit in the parlor with Kaylin." Helen's smile was gentle, but her eyes remained completely black. Kaylin wasn't certain Mrs. Erickson noticed. She allowed herself to be led to the parlor, which was a small room this time; it contained two comfortable chairs and a modest table, although a third chair materialized before the door had been closed.

"You will have privacy here; the only person who tends to ignore privacy is Terrano. While the cohort has no privacy among themselves as a general rule—with An'Teela being the sole exception—Terrano is friendlier; he considers any housemate to be part of his family. But he hasn't returned yet."

At Mrs. Erickson's expression, Helen added, "We expect him to return safely."

It was Evanton everyone was worried about.

Mrs. Erickson didn't speak. Tea appeared on the table, and Helen poured it into cups, which she offered to Mrs. Erickson first; Mrs. Erickson took the cup in shaky hands but didn't drink. She closed her eyes.

"You see things the rest of us can't," Kaylin said. She made no effort to gentle her voice—that always happened naturally in Mrs. Erickson's presence. "I have Hope. I can see things most people can't because I can look through his wing. But I can't see what you can without any of that.

"You didn't see anything different in your house. Maybe the painting was different somehow, but no one let you enter the family room."

Mrs. Erickson remained silent. Kaylin glanced at Helen, who pursed her lips but didn't speak.

Kaylin exhaled. "Evanton was concerned, and I think visiting Azoria's old home made clear to him, or clearer to him, why. But I think... There was something dead in the outlands that Azoria's self-portrait led to. I think that's where Evanton's gone. But it was contained in the outlands the first time we visited. It was shut off while Azoria was alive.

"I think that barrier—between the living Azoria's manor and whatever remained after she died—is gone. The fact that you could see something in the manor makes that clearer, although *clear* isn't quite the right word. You didn't come with us to the outlands; you were protecting your kids.

"But what you saw in the manor might be related to the dead person in the outlands." Kaylin hesitated, and then added, "Self-professed dead person. Most dead people can't talk; they said they were dead, but...death seems to mean they feel they now have no purpose. Most dead people can't create whole landscapes on a whim. Terrano saw them; I saw them.

"We think it's the corpse of a dead Ancient—a dead god, for want of a better word. But we've got no living Ancients we can use for comparison. One of the librarians at the Academia was extremely uncomfortable with the concept of a dead Ancient in Azoria's backyard.

"But you also have dead words in your room—they're still in her room?"

"Yes, dear."

"No one but me could even see them—and I didn't see what you saw. I saw words. And I saw words on the pillars depicted in the painting Evanton touched; everyone else saw only the pillars."

Mrs. Erickson swallowed. "You know I don't know very much about my abilities. I'm grateful to have them—I wasn't always, but the children would have been lonely and trapped if I hadn't. The ghosts we found in the Imperial Palace look like people to me, but less distinct—more like ghosts in stories would look. Our ghosts look like living people to my eyes. It causes some confusion, and I've learned over the years to wait to speak, to watch how other people react, before I attempt to introduce myself.

"I saw the ghosts trapped in Azoria's home. After Azoria's death, I did what I could to free them. I didn't miss an inch of hall or room. But all those ghosts looked like people—mostly young people, and mostly women. Some were older. None were even half my age.

"I didn't realize what I was looking at when I first entered Azoria's domain. But nothing looked the same to my eyes. You saw the foyer, you saw the statues, you saw the way the ceilings had become much higher, the halls much longer. I saw those, too—but...to me, they were foggy, misty, as if they were ghosts themselves, like the ghosts in my room." She fell silent, but she hadn't finished. Kaylin waited while she found more words.

"In that hall, I could see all of you. I could see your familiar—but he didn't look the way he looks now. I thought he'd crush you, he was so large. Mandoran and Terrano looked the same as always. Bellusdeo..." She shook her head. "I could see her sisters. They weren't weeping. But they were all reaching for something. I didn't want to tell her. She's been so upset that her sisters are trapped where they're trapped."

"What did I look like?"

"You looked the way you've always looked to me. So did Corporal Handred. But his weapon… You know I see it as something very bright, very shiny; sometimes I have to squint to look at him at all."

Kaylin nodded. She had questions, but didn't ask any of them; she didn't want to interrupt the flow of the old woman's words.

"His weapon didn't look like a weapon at all. I could see that he held his blades in his hands—but they didn't look like blades. And Evanton, the Keeper—" Mrs. Erickson exhaled. "I've spent my life talking to children. I'm not terribly good with words."

"Your words are fine," Kaylin told her. "Evanton looked like Evanton to me. I'd ask Terrano what he saw, but he's not here." She hesitated, and then said, "Evanton is the Keeper. He was human, same as us, but he's the link between the garden and the rest of the world, and that probably changed him. Or had to change him. He's not dangerous. I mean, unless you're trying to destroy the world; I imagine he would be terrifying then—if he knew about it."

Helen turned to Mrs. Erickson and gently nodded. "If you need to, take a break, drink some tea. We have all night, and we are not in a rush."

The old woman smiled at the Avatar of the house. "The manse was ghostly. It was the same blur, the same fuzziness, that I see in the ghosts of what you call words."

"What did you see when you looked at the painting?"

Mrs. Erickson looked down at her hands and her mostly full teacup. She shook her head.

"Imelda," Helen said, voice even softer than Kaylin's, "can I attempt to answer that question for Kaylin? Or would you rather I didn't?"

Mrs. Erickson swallowed. "I don't mind," she said, voice thin and shaky. She did. She did mind. Kaylin had seen Mrs. Erickson worry before; this wasn't worry. Mrs. Erickson was afraid.

Helen agreed; she was silent. But when she spoke, she spoke to Mrs. Erickson. "Imelda, you are part of the home I wanted so desperately to build. I told you what it was like for me, when I had no will and no say. I was alive, once, as you or Kaylin are alive. I became the heart of a building, chained to it, unable to leave.

"I've been that way for a long time. But when I made my decision, when I broke some of the bindings, when I could decide, for myself, who I wished to shelter, who I wished to offer a home, I was content to be here. I've told you that I can hear your thoughts—that I can hear the thoughts of anyone who lives within my borders. It is impossible not to hear them.

"But it is more than possible not to share them. Even members of a family need their privacy." She took a chair beside Mrs. Erickson. "Kaylin asked you to live with us. You are now part of my family, and your interests align with many of the interests of my first tenant, a woman I chose. A woman I wanted to offer shelter and protection.

"You would have liked her. She would have adored you. She wouldn't have been as happy living with Barrani. I was not afraid of the lords I served. I was afraid of what they might command of me. I have found the cohort challenging, not because they have the right of command, but because they are only technically Barrani. Terrano can—and does—diffuse; he becomes far less physically present.

"All of his friends can, but for most it requires far more work; it is not natural to them. They are not what Barrani are expected to be. Kaylin is Chosen. She naturally attracts difficulty. She has a familiar I would find difficult to contain were he to decide he should not be. Sedarias intends to entrench herself as the ruler of her line; she has the title but must prove she can hold it. So far, all attempts to unseat her have failed. The last attempt was very close. And yes, it means someone tried to kill her."

Mrs. Erickson's worry shifted to more normal concern.

"Bellusdeo lived here until she chose to captain a Tower. She was comfortable here, but restless; she lacked purpose and focus. Because she lived here, the attention of the Imperial Palace was unavoidable. She is the only living female Dragon, and she represents a future for her race. Were there another—were there any other—she would never bear a clutch. She was not raised to it, and she does not desire it.

"No one who lives here is normal by the standards of their race. It's my belief," Helen added, once again gentling her voice, "that no one is normal when they are at home. You are at home here. No one here will judge you. No one here will judge your power."

"Lord Sanabalis did."

"No. He fears your power, and he fears your lack of understanding of it. He does not judge you. Were you younger, you might even be seconded to the Imperial Palace; the duties demanded of Imperial Mages might be too physically taxing now. Regardless, the Arkon does not live here.

"Kaylin will never fear you. Kaylin will never judge you."

"She doesn't know."

"Ah. That's where you are wrong, Imelda. She does know."

Kaylin agreed with Mrs. Erickson. She had no idea what Helen was talking about. But she didn't make that clear; she watched Mrs. Erickson.

Mrs. Erickson turned to Kaylin. Her breathing was too shallow and her hands were white around the teacup. Had it not been created by Helen, it would have cracked.

"What do you know?" Mrs. Erickson whispered.

Kaylin, not one of nature's liars, would have frozen completely had Mrs. Erickson not looked so defeated, so afraid. She exhaled.

"When we faced Azoria, Jamal released you from a promise. It was a one-time release. Only when you had his permission did you do what Necromancers can do: you commanded Azoria. You commanded the dead."

Mrs. Erickson didn't move; she didn't even nod.

"If you'd never made that promise to Jamal, you could command the dead at any time you wanted."

This time, the old woman did nod.

Was it more than that? Nothing that Kaylin had said seemed remotely terrifying. "If you hadn't had that ability, it's likely none of us would have survived. I don't fear it. I don't resent it. I'm *grateful* for it."

Silence settled around Kaylin as these thoughts took root. "You could have controlled the dead that possessed Sanabalis. You could have told them what to do while they occupied his body."

"Yes."

"You can't tell ghosts—I mean, like Jamal—to possess someone."

"I don't think so. I've never tried."

"Mrs. Erickson—Imelda—what did you try? And when?" Jamal had to know about that power somehow. If Jamal knew, he had either been subject to it, or he had witnessed it, which meant it had to have occurred in Mrs. Erickson's home.

Mrs. Erickson's shoulders curved, bringing her face closer to her hands and the cup she now clung to as if it were an anchor.

"When I was a child, I had a pet rabbit. Terrible little beast; she chewed open my pillow, destroyed a third of my rug, left scratch marks across my floor, and couldn't be properly litter trained. I didn't have many friends, but I didn't miss them; I had Jamal, Katie, Esme, and Callis. But I could touch the rabbit, I could hold the rabbit; the rabbit was warm. And at that age, Jamal and his friends seemed so much older than I was.

"Rabbits don't live a long time. Tilly died. I woke up one morning, and she didn't. Jamal told me she was dead, but I think I knew. I knew she wasn't breathing. She'd become a lot quieter in the prior half a year. I wanted her to wake up. I don't think I understood what death meant. Jamal tried to explain it, but he wasn't always the most patient.

"We argued. Esme tried to stop him—or us—but I was young and stubborn."

"You were how old? Five? Six? If Jamal seemed almost adult to you, you couldn't have been much older."

"When did you understand what death meant?" Mrs. Erickson's question was unexpected.

Kaylin froze. Throat thicker, she said, "Severn explained it to me. I didn't understand it, but I learned. Death meant absence. It meant forever absence."

"How old were you?"

"Five." Kaylin shook her head. "It was a long time ago. I was five. You were a child. No one could blame you for not knowing." She didn't want to talk about her mother here. Or her childhood.

"I was angry with Jamal. I was angry with the world, I think—it's hard to remember it now, I'm so much farther from childhood than you are."

Kaylin nodded. She disliked being reminded of her age, because it usually came with judgment or dismissal; she was too young, she was too naive, she was too ignorant. Mrs. Erickson wasn't doing any of those things.

"But of course I had to prove him wrong. I knew I could win the argument." She closed her eyes. "I woke Tilly up."

Kaylin could have misunderstood; she didn't. Mrs. Erickson was old and gentle, but she wasn't a fool.

"Tilly moved. Tilly hopped. But her body was cold and she

didn't breathe. I knew something was wrong with her—and I knew, in future, I should never try to win arguments with Jamal." This brought a brief, nostalgic smile to her lips and the corners of her eyes. Kaylin had no doubt that if Jamal had remained, it was to Jamal she would have retreated after the disaster at Azoria's old place.

"Jamal was horrified. He shouted at me—I remember that. He would have shaken me until my teeth rattled, if he'd had the ability. He did send my pillows and toys flying around the room in a small whirlwind. But I realized that he wasn't just angry—truly angry—he was afraid. Of me. Or for me.

"I'd never been afraid of Jamal or the other children before. But I was afraid of him then. So I told him to stop. I didn't ask. I made him stop." She fell silent again. Her hands were less shaky, and she did sip her tea, which was probably close to cold.

"He was upset. I was upset. I was still angry—I was young. I told him to leave, while I cradled Tilly. He left. I don't think he had a choice. But I knew, while I held Tilly, that she just wasn't there anymore. She could move. She could do what I told her to do. She could only do what I told her to do. I think I waited a whole day, hoping she would wake up, and then... I let her go. I went to tell my parents that she wasn't breathing anymore.

"I think I knew, even then, that what Jamal had seen, my parents should never see. Jamal had always accepted me; he'd never been afraid of me. But Tilly—what I had done with Tilly—made him afraid. I thought my parents would be even angrier. They came, and we buried Tilly in the backyard.

"Jamal still avoided me. He had always been there for me. Of all of the ghosts, he was the most interactive. When I woke up the next morning, I knew I'd done something terrible, that I'd crossed a line I couldn't even see. He didn't come back for almost a week. Katie and Callis did; Esme was trying to calm him down, I think.

"When he did come back, I was so happy to see him. His absence made me realize that he had a choice; that he'd made the choice to be friends with me, to spend time with me. He didn't have to do that. He didn't have to, unless I forced him to." She inhaled slowly, and then lifted her head. "I'd hurt his feelings. I'd never thought that was possible—it certainly wasn't possible with my own parents, who weathered childish tantrums as if they were irrelevant.

"I apologized—just as I would have apologized to my parents. It wasn't enough. It was another week before he'd speak to me; he'd watch, and he didn't stop the others, but he just stood back. He'd never done that before.

"But at the start of the third week—and each week felt like months to me—he spoke to me again. He was quiet, and he was so serious—but I felt desperate, the way only children can. I think I would have done anything he asked of me if things could just go back to normal. I think he wanted that, too. Jamal was never serious—I think he found it embarrassing. But he was serious that day.

"He told me that what I'd done was not waking Tilly. Tilly was gone. I could force her corpse to move—but the corpse would still be a corpse. And he told me that I must never, ever do it again in front of anyone. He said he could understand why I'd done it, but not how—and everyone would be terrified of how. Esme asked why it mattered—it was just a body, and the dead don't care.

"'The living are deeply attached to the dead.' That's what he said. To the idea of the dead, the sanctity of death. The children could understand. The children did understand. But anyone else would see me as a monster. He asked me to promise that I would never do it again. I promised.

"And then he made me promise to never, ever do what I'd done to him: to take control, to command, to force them to do what I wanted, not what they wanted." Her smile, as the words faded, was complicated. "I promised.

"It was that promise that I asked permission to break." Mrs. Erickson closed her eyes. "I've had no reason to break the first promise. But I should have told you. I should have told you both.

"I am a Necromancer, in the worst sense of the word."

14

Helen was silent. Helen must have known. Mrs. Erickson was not adept at hiding her thoughts—why would she be?

Kaylin was silent for a different reason. She was faintly horrified, and it took her a moment to come back to herself. Mrs. Erickson was the woman who baked for the Hawks who were forced to endure the public desk; she was the woman who had stayed—alone—in her home because the children couldn't leave. She was quiet, gentle, and generous. She cared about people—even dead people.

Maybe her true gift was the ability to see what other people couldn't see; to listen, to acknowledge, and to speak with people when no one else could.

None of that involved animating corpses.

"Did your mother know about Tilly?"

Mrs. Erickson shook her head.

"But she knew about Jamal."

"Yes."

"And that's why she thought you had magical ability."

"Jamal could prove he existed, even if they couldn't see him. But you know how that turned out. I had a good life. I had a happy life. I found my husband—and he believed me; he said I was too earnest to lie." This time, her smile was simple, gentle. "The children liked him, eventually. But at the beginning? I was grateful he couldn't hear them. Jamal had so many questions he demanded I ask.

"They were suspicious of anyone who wasn't me—but I think that's because they were children: they were afraid that I would forget them or leave them, or worse, that he would take me away. They couldn't follow."

Kaylin listened quietly; she could imagine what Jamal had been like.

"I did make it clear to my husband that I couldn't abandon the house—and eventually, told him why. But he loved the idea that I had these four staunch guardians, and he felt that their questions—which were harsh—were fair. They did miss him, when he passed.

"I missed him. I didn't have anyone else among the living who knew about my ability until the day I met you." Her smile deepened. "I'm sure all the Hawks thought I was just a dotty, lonely old woman."

"Yes," Kaylin said. "But you were *our* dotty, lonely old woman. Maybe a little bit of a mascot—that's how I spent my first several years with the Hawks, except I was the official mascot. I was too young to be an officer." It was her turn to hesitate.

Hope squawked.

"When you entered Azoria's old place, what did you see? You said the building looked fuzzy, or ghostlike, to your eyes. Storybook ghosts, not real ones."

"Yes."

"That's not what upset you."

Mrs. Erickson took some time to gather her words. She'd had no problem with them while speaking of Jamal. "No. When Tilly died—when I refused to accept that she was dead—she was blurry to me. I believed it was because I was crying; I was crying a lot, and it's hard to see through watery eyes. I believed it until the moment we entered Azoria's home.

"But it wasn't that. That blurriness—it wasn't because of my tears. It wasn't that I couldn't see. It was that I could see the same strange glow—no, that's the wrong word, maybe *cloud* is better—in the foyer. It was clearest near the new statues, and faintest near the gallery. The statues were made of white stone, but the odd glow made them look like corpses. Had I done whatever I'd done to Tilly, I'm certain they would have moved."

"They did."

"Yes, but…they would have moved as I ordered them to move. But as we approached the end of the hall—the empty, large self-portrait—that cloud became almost all I could see.

"Somewhere, there's a body, a corpse, something, and it wants to be animated." Having said this, she slumped back in the chair, as if the words had been a colossal physical burden. "I'm sorry I couldn't tell you. I'm breaking a promise I made to Jamal by telling you now: it was important to him that no one ever know. I'd already experienced mockery and abuse for seeing ghosts; no one believed me, and everyone began to avoid me.

"Jamal said it would be far, far worse. I was young. I believed him. And, Kaylin, I still believe him. I wouldn't speak at all—and I don't think you'd try to force me to speak—if Evanton hadn't disappeared."

"How did you see Evanton?" Kaylin asked, keeping her voice as neutral, as even, as possible.

"When I met him here? He looked like a responsible gentleman."

Not the way Kaylin would have described him.

"Even when we entered Azoria's. All of you looked the same. Terrano may have looked a bit odd, but I think he did that on purpose."

"What did Evanton look like before he told us all to run?"

"I couldn't see him clearly."

"Did you see the light? The white light that seemed to explode out from where his hand touched the canvas?"

"Not as light, and not the way I saw the corporal's weapon."

"What did you see? What do you think caused the rest of us to flee?"

"The same fuzziness I saw in the foyer—but denser, thicker. That's what was spreading, to my eyes."

"And the statues?"

"I haven't seen a lot of corpses, you understand. People came to help me when my husband passed, and we had a very modest funeral. I wasn't certain anyone would come, but people did."

"Did he— I know this is difficult, and I'm sorry. But did your husband's body look like—like Tilly's to you?"

"Yes. Yes, it did. But I could never do to him—to my memories of him—what I did to Tilly. I was no longer a child. I understood the absolute difference between life and death where the body was concerned."

"I'm sorry—just one more question. I should let you sleep, but I'm afraid I'm going to get seconded to the Academia tomorrow once word of tonight's events gets out. Did Evanton look like Tilly or your husband at the end?"

"I don't know. The last I saw of him—and I wasn't facing the painting when Bellusdeo helped me leave—no. But he was surrounded by those clouds."

"The same clouds that made the statues glow?"

"That is not one more question," Helen said.

Kaylin grimaced. "Did the statues look like Tilly looked after you'd tried to wake her up?"

Mrs. Erickson nodded.

"Could you have put them to sleep again?"

"I don't know. The statues weren't obeying me; they didn't start to move because I told them to move. In Tilly's case, I just…stopped telling her what to do." She set her cup on the table. "What do you think happened to Evanton?"

"If you couldn't see him at the end, it's actually a good sign. That probably means he was sent to the outlands by the painting."

Mrs. Erickson did not make it down to breakfast by the time Kaylin had to leave for work. Mandoran did. Barrani didn't need much sleep—if any, at all—but Mandoran looked like sleep was possibly his best option. He rose when she did.

No mirror call had interrupted breakfast to let Kaylin know that the Halls of Law wasn't where she'd be working.

"I'll walk you to work."

She started to say no, stopped, and nodded. She wanted to ask about Terrano, and what Terrano had seen.

"He's not back yet, is he?"

Mandoran shook his head. His eyes were a darker than normal blue for him.

"Sedarias is worried."

"You have no idea." He winced. "You spoke with Mrs. Erickson?"

"She didn't see much; it's hard to look carefully when you're being carried by a running Dragon."

"Fair enough."

"But I think Evanton is in the outlands. Azoria had a portal in her self-portrait that led straight there. I know that sentient buildings like Helen are partially rooted in the outlands; it's from the outlands that they draw their godlike ability to create at desire or need within their boundaries."

"You think Azoria was trying to become a sentient building?"

"No. Helen likes what she does, but she can't leave. If people don't come to her, she can't interact with them. I can't imagine

Azoria would be willing to cage herself that way. But it's possible that was what she was trying to create."

"You require a living being to become the heart of a sentient building; the building is alive," Mandoran pointed out.

"Yes—but the living person doesn't have to be Immortal. They don't have to possess purely personal power. One of the Hallionne was constructed around a mortal, and I think the Tower of Tiamaris was also built the same way. If I knew nothing at all about sentient buildings, I'd assume you'd want to build on power, that you'd need someone Barrani or draconic. Experience with sentient buildings has made clear this isn't true." Kaylin frowned. "But only the Ancients possessed the ability to create a sentient building—I don't think any of the buildings I've spoken with were created any other way."

Mandoran shrugged. "Anything I've heard about Azoria implies she didn't accept limitations. If it could be done, she'd try."

"As long as she wasn't the one dying."

"Look, her name—and her line—are practically forbidden in the High Halls, her crime was considered so great. We know she was initially obsessed with the Lake of Life—she wanted to find her dead sister's name and somehow revive her. At least that's the story."

"I don't think, by the end, she was thinking about her sister at all."

"No. But she must have seen, or thought she'd seen, power. She was supposed to be smart, right? She knew that every individual word could literally bring a Barrani child to life. We don't think about it a lot. I mean, we've had our names for the entirety of our lives; they're not distinct or separate from us. It's why the Consort is almost never a political target—unless there's another Consort waiting in the wings. Then it can get ugly.

"But people don't understand how the Lake chooses a Consort. It's too risky. Azoria didn't care about risk."

"She clearly didn't care much about anyone but herself. And

she's dead and she's still causing problems." Kaylin's frown deepened.

"Did Mrs. Erickson say anything about the dead? Azoria's not still haunting her home, is she?"

"If she is, Mrs. Erickson didn't see her." Kaylin looked down the street at the Halls of Law they were quickly approaching. "I have to head into work."

Mandoran nodded. "I'll just wait here."

"What, in the middle of the street?"

"Home's less safe at the moment; Sedarias is unhappy. If Terrano does make it back, she's likely to strangle him, or come close. Never make Sedarias worry."

"I'm not one of the people she worries about," Kaylin said, smiling broadly.

"Teela does."

"I don't know what you've been doing lately," Tanner, who was on door duty, said. "But it's good you're not late today."

Kaylin cringed. "Ironjaw?"

"He's going to need a new desk by lunchtime, according to Caitlin."

When dealing with angry Leontine, forewarned wasn't forearmed. Unless you could just run for the hills. Since she couldn't, she approached the inner office with a growing sense of dread. Angry bosses were bad. Angry Leontine bosses were worse. It was the bristling fur and exposed fangs. And claws.

Marcus had never killed anyone in the office since she'd been part of it; killing subordinates was illegal, and Marcus was a Hawk. But his territorial instincts sometimes made work less comfortable—unless upper-level bureaucrats were trying to shove something down their throats, in which case you could comfortably hide behind him.

Caitlin was right: it would be time to go desk shopping again.

"Corporal Neya. I see you're on time."

"Yes, sir." She moved to stand in front of his desk. There were fewer piles of paper on it; there were more on the floor nearest the desk legs.

"You're aware that your personal life should never interfere with your duties."

"Yes, sir."

"And your personal activities should not bring the Hawks into disrepute."

"Yes, sir."

"Apparently you've forgotten these rules. Corporal Handred!" He roared.

Severn came from around Marcus's desk to join Kaylin; he was less stiff.

"Your services have been requested by the Imperial Court."

Ugh.

"Apparently one of your evening jaunts—in your personal life—has caused what amounts to panic in the Imperial Court. The Dragon who currently oversees his fancy school and the Dragon that in theory oversees your magical studies have said that your current duties are now *irrelevant*."

Kaylin didn't wince, but it took effort. She made no attempt to correct him, although she was certain Sanabalis had said no such thing.

It was Severn who spoke. "How long will the Imperial Court require our services?"

"Until," Marcus growled, "the situation is resolved."

Which meant they had no idea.

"The Lord of Hawks has been informed?"

"He wants to see you both before you leave."

"Corporal Handred has also been seconded?"

"Obviously." To Kaylin's great relief, Marcus didn't ask her why she was being temporarily transferred. "You need someone who can keep you out of trouble."

* * *

Kaylin exercised her linguistic skills as they climbed the stairs to the Hawklord's tower. Severn was sympathetic, but silent.

Remember the tower's acoustics.

"I don't care if they hear me. Marcus is practically blaming me, and none of this is my fault. It's Azoria's fault, and she's already beyond the reach of the law."

If we can't resolve it—as Marcus put it—there's no way Mrs. Erickson is going to be allowed to stay with you and Helen.

That was a bucket of cold water.

It's in her interests—and therefore both yours and Helen's—that we find Evanton and return things to a semblance of normal. We've just been given the opportunity to do that during working hours as well as off hours.

"I bet Mandoran knew. Somehow."

"Oh?"

"He said he'd wait outside the Halls of Law."

"He probably wanted to avoid Sedarias. If he's not there when we depart, it means Terrano managed to make his way home." Severn's eyes narrowed.

Kaylin's didn't; she could see that the doors to the Hawklord's room were already open. At least there were some things today she could be grateful for. Sadly, the tower's acoustics weren't one of them.

"I see you arrived in the office on time." The Hawklord gestured and both corporals entered his office; the doors closed at their backs. "You've no doubt heard about your deployment."

Kaylin nodded.

"The sergeant was informed that the matter was highly sensitive. I am not certain he believed it, given your involvement."

"He meant it was an emergency, sir."

"The Dragon Court seemed to think so. The Emperor in particular. He messaged me, personally, first thing this morning."

"I just got in!"

"I arrive far earlier than most of the office. Tell me, in your own words, what the emergency is."

"We went out with Evanton last night."

"We?"

"Severn, Lord Bellusdeo, some of the cohort, and me."

"And?"

"Mrs. Erickson, one of my housemates."

"I suggest that you do not attempt to lie by omission, Corporal. I have had a trying morning. You are aware of Evanton's function, yes?"

"He's the Keeper. Sir."

"And he was with you for a reason?"

"He insisted." She exhaled. "He insisted on accompanying Mrs. Erickson and me to Mrs. Erickson's former home."

"And the rest of your crew? Corporal Handred?"

"I offered to accompany them."

"Lord Bellusdeo?"

"She has personal reasons for being interested in Mrs. Erickson, and she wanted to make sure that no harm came to her. Sir."

"Very well. Why did Evanton insist on this visit?"

"You're aware that Mrs. Erickson is unusual."

"I have been aware that she is unusual for longer than you have been alive."

"Unusual in a different way. All those endless reports she made about things ghosts told her? They were true. Ghosts did tell her those things."

"And ghosts are largely mundane."

"Largely, sir. I think she has magical potential. Lord Sanabalis agreed. But he considered that potential both unusual and dangerous."

The Hawklord's brows rose.

"He chose to let Mrs. Erickson move in with me."

"Because your house is a sentient building."

She nodded. "But I thought Helen would like Mrs. Erickson. And she does. They probably spend way more time just talking and having tea than Helen and I do. And Mrs. Erickson uses the kitchen—she loves it. Look—she'd've been very lonely in her home."

"She's lived in it for all her life. What changed?"

"The ghosts she could see left. They've been her company. They stopped her from becoming lonely. She came to the Halls of Law because she wanted to have something to tell them. She's not dangerous. She's not."

"Tell me why Evanton wished to visit her house."

Kaylin swallowed. "He was looking for something. No, I don't know what—do you honestly think he'd tell me? He said the garden was becoming more chaotic; the elements were unsettled. It's happened before, and usually when it does, it means something big is about to go down. He knew of Azoria An'Berranin. When he found out that she'd lived invisibly beside Mrs. Erickson's house, he wanted to see it."

"He felt that something Azoria had done had caused unrest in the elemental garden?"

"Yes, sir."

"Very well." The Hawklord's eyes were pure blue—and blue was not a happy Aerian color. "Lord Sanabalis, on behalf of the Emperor, has summoned you to the palace. You will work at his behest as if he were the Emperor himself. If Evanton returns to his storefront, Lord Sanabalis will rescind his request. Not a moment before.

"If he does not, things will be far more dire than the Halls of Law can handle. We are trusting you, Corporal. I have been assured that your particular brand of diplomacy will not be made an issue. Do not cross the line."

"Yes, sir."

"How'd it go?" Clint asked, glancing at Tanner.

"What was the bet?" Kaylin's expression was sour.

Clint chuckled. “No bet.”

“Well, Ironjaw definitely needs a new desk; Caitlin was right about that. And Severn and I been seconded to the Imperial Palace. Where we’re going now.”

Tanner whistled. “He’ll definitely need a new desk. Depending on how long you’ll be off your beat, he might need a few.”

Mandoran grinned when he caught sight of Kaylin and Severn as they exited the Halls of Law. “Where are we headed?”

“Severn and I are headed to the Imperial Palace; you’re welcome to join us.”

Severn glanced at her.

He won’t. None of the cohort enter the palace except Teela—and she only goes if her job demands it. I wouldn’t have made the suggestion if it were Terrano; he’ll go anywhere.

Mandoran shrugged. “I’ll keep you company on the way. Sedarias says Bellusdeo dropped by the house after you left for work. She’s talking to Helen now—I don’t know if she intends to speak with Mrs. Erickson. Also: her eyes are an orange-red mess.”

“How is Helen?”

“Her eyes are pitch-black, if that’s any indication.”

“Did you tell her that I’m now working for the Imperial Palace until we find Evanton?”

“I don’t think she’ll care. Terrano still hasn’t made his way home. Serralyn suggests that the next time the Keeper asks you for a walkabout, you say no.”

“When you say Terrano isn’t back, does that mean you can’t contact him at all?”

Mandoran nodded. “It’s only been a day. He’s lost contact with us while experimenting with his form and his location before. Just not as spectacularly.”

“Oh, I’m sure it was spectacular—there were just no witnesses.”

★ ★ ★

To Kaylin's surprise, Mandoran not only walked them to the palace, but accompanied them in, which made things a bit trickier. As Kaylin had been ordered to report for duty, she was immediately allowed entry, but Barrani visitors were rare enough that Mandoran caused a holdup. It was hard to explain his presence, and eventually, she asked Severn to wait with the Barrani cohort member while she went to get permission from Sanabalis.

The Arkon was clearly not in the mood for random, chaotic visitors; his eyes were an orange that verged on red, and she could swear there was paper ash on the floor. Luckily, Lord Emmerian was also in the room; his eyes, while orange, rested in a much more neutral expression.

"Where is your partner?" Sanabalis growled.

"He's waiting in the outer hall with Mandoran."

For a moment, the Arkon looked at her as if she'd spoken a language he wasn't familiar with.

It was Lord Emmerian who spoke. "We have had rudimentary reporting from Lord Bellusdeo. Our current information comes directly from her. She did mention that one of your housemates appears to have been lost at the same time as the Keeper. While the absence of the Keeper is considered the pressing emergency, Bellusdeo understands that the absence of your housemate will have very real and deleterious effects on your home life." He turned to the Arkon. "It is best that you allow one member of that group to attend, if you can tolerate his presence. Mandoran is neutral and he makes no attempt to interfere.

"If not Mandoran, we might ask Serralyn to join us instead."

"This is not a picnic," Sanabalis snapped.

"No, Arkon." Emmerian's tone mirrored Kaylin's tone while speaking to Marcus or the Hawklord almost exactly.

She turned the resulting snicker into a cough that probably fooled no one.

"Shall I tell Severn to come in?"

"Lord Emmerian can go in person and escort them both in."

When Emmerian left the room, Kaylin was on the receiving end of a full draconic glare; there was no one else to split it with.

"Before you say anything, Evanton asked if Mrs. Erickson would allow him to visit her home, with me in tow. He considered it important; the garden has been chaotic, to paraphrase, in the past few weeks. I mean—no flooding in the store, which has happened before. He's managed to keep the garden contained.

"Bellusdeo has a pressing interest in Mrs. Erickson; she informed us that she would join us. Terrano likes anything that seems interesting. Serralyn had a request from one of the Wevaran, who joined us as well. Severn came because he's my partner, and Mandoran followed because he was bored. So we all descended on the house. It was fine until we opened the door to Azoria's manse—Evanton said the door itself was bound to the family painting Mrs. Erickson hasn't seen in decades.

"The interior had changed. I don't know what Bakkon made of it—I haven't spoken to Serralyn, and the cohort is frankly too worried about Terrano to consider her report important enough to pass on."

"Breathe, Corporal. And speak a little more slowly."

"I assume you heard about Evanton from Bellusdeo."

Sanabalis nodded.

"And that's the reason I've been put on Imperial Court duty."

"No, actually. The reason you are now on Imperial Court duty is Lannagaros. The librarians wished to speak with you, and that desire increased in urgency last night."

"I was going to go to the Academia after work."

"Ah. Well, now you will go as part of work. Lannagaros did not know what the concerns of the Arbiters are. They wished to speak with you."

"And Mrs. Erickson?"

"They only demanded your presence." Sanabalis exhaled smoke. "I am not rethinking my placement of Mrs. Erickson. I am, however, considering confining you to house arrest for the next three months."

"Me? Why?"

"Even when events do not involve you personally, you seem to be at the heart of them. And I am still transitioning into the role of Arkon. I could use a few months of peace."

The door opened; Emmerian, Severn, and Mandoran entered the room.

"I was just telling Corporal Neya that your first assignment is the Academia," Sanabalis said, in a much more reasonable tone of voice.

Severn nodded.

"Will you expect a report?"

"Yes. Verbal reports are acceptable in this case."

Well, that was a silver lining. "When?"

"When you have finished speaking with the Arbiters and the chancellor. I do not care about the hour; Dragons require very little sleep, and even if we did, I wouldn't be getting any of it."

To Kaylin's surprise, Emmerian joined them. His eyes were a wary orange, but there were no red flecks in them. Fair enough. Emmerian had always been the calmest, the most rational, of the Dragons.

They approached the bridge of Tiamaris in silence. Mandoran was the first to break it, although Kaylin and he opened their mouths at the same time.

"How's living with Bellusdeo treating you?"

The Dragon's eyes developed the tints of red they'd been missing. "Perhaps if she were in residence more often, I would have an answer to that question." Unlike his usual polite and neutral tone, this one had undercurrents.

"Did she tell you about Mrs. Erickson?"

Emmerian shook his head.

"But you heard."

"The chancellor had choice words to say about it. I do not believe he was amused by my attempt at handling the situation." Emmerian exhaled. "The last disagreement I had with Bellusdeo required intervention from Karriamis, who was displeased enough with both of us that he asked us to leave the Tower until we could speak like rational beings."

"So Karriamis hasn't spent much time around Bellusdeo?" Mandoran was grinning.

The red in Emmerian's eyes retreated. "I've never lived in a Tower; I find Karriamis very interesting—but he is an ancient Dragon by our standards, and he is very rigid in his thinking."

"What were you arguing about?"

Emmerian shook his head. "It seems irrelevant now, and Bellusdeo requires privacy."

"She didn't seem to care much about it when she was living with us."

"No, I imagine not. Living with other Dragons is clearly different." He exhaled. "I know that she chose me because I was the least distasteful of her available options. I know that the choice itself was made because the future of our race is now a possibility."

"It's not what you want?" This time, Mandoran lost the cheeky grin. "You didn't want her to choose you?"

"Of course I did. But not like that. To be the best of the worst is never something to which I have aspired. I do not wish my presence to be merely tolerable. Or worse."

"Yeah, that would suck."

"And I feel that perhaps I've become the focal point of her resentment at being forced to live a life she does not want." He exhaled. "But in the past few days she has forgotten that resentment, and she is in a far worse state." His smile was pained, but rueful. "I would like to make her life better. But I would also like to be treated with, if not affection, respect."

Mandoran raised a brow but didn't comment.

Kaylin frowned. "Are there any Barrani romances or love stories?"

He nodded. "I'm not sure you'd enjoy them, though."

"I don't generally enjoy human ones—what's the difference?"

"They generally end in war, murder, or suicide."

Kaylin was not up to asking the same question of Emmerian, but the Dragon said, "Then it appears our races have that in common, if little else."

"Is this the part where you both remind me that human love only has to last a measly few decades?"

"Wouldn't dream of it. You've got enough to rant about today."

Bellusdeo did not join them at the Academia. Kaylin assumed she was with Helen and Mrs. Erickson, either of whom—absent the pain of her lost sisters and the guilt their pain induced—were calming, gentle influences. Her sisters absorbed all her focus—of course they did. What she wanted right now was for those sisters to somehow be at peace. What she didn't want was to have a clutch of baby Dragons.

Kaylin considered duty and power as she walked. Had someone told her that she, Kaylin Neya, was the sole hope of humanity—but she had to bear a bunch of children in order to save it—she wasn't certain what she'd do. She couldn't imagine she would ever be that important, that singular.

Even if she in theory wanted to save the human race, becoming a mother wasn't part of her future. Because being a mother involved an actual child. She was fine with the idea that saving humanity—or the rest of the world—was part of her responsibility as the bearer of the marks of the Chosen, but she expected that salvation to be gained by the dint of martial arts.

She wasn't certain she could even *be* a good parent. But there were more practical problems. Babies didn't just somehow grow on their own; they required a father.

Ugh. Her sympathy for Bellusdeo soared as the Academia came into view.

"Let's get this out of the way."

"Isn't that Killian?" Mandoran asked, Barrani vision being better than hers.

"We haven't even reached the building yet."

"He's standing in the middle of the quad."

Hope sat up, his claws digging into her right shoulder. He lifted a wing and placed it—gently for him—across one eye.

15

Killian was, as Mandoran said, standing in the quad. Students also occupied the benches and the stretches of flat grass closest to the trees; the sun had begun its rise, but hadn't fully crested the horizon, and Killian seemed to stand framed by the rising sun, as if the buildings that should have blocked it were simple mirages.

But the people in the quad weren't.

Kaylin wasn't. Hope was tense, which was never a good sign. "Let's jog," she told her companions; Severn had already picked up the pace.

Killian stood, arms by his sides, as if he were a statue; he only moved when they were perhaps ten yards away. His eyes were completely black; Kaylin was certain there were small flecks of iridescent color in that darkness, but at this distance they couldn't be seen.

When she reached Killian's side, he nodded. "I apologize for my appearance," he said, glancing briefly at Hope.

"Has something gone wrong? Is there trouble at the Academia?"

"There is, as yet, no trouble at the Academia."

"Then why are you standing here?"

"I was told to wait for you. The chancellor mentioned that Corporal Handred would be accompanying you; he did not mention Lord Emmerian or Mandoran."

"Should they not be here?"

"I am certain he will accept Lord Emmerian without reservation. Mandoran's presence is not necessary; Serralyn will be present."

"Will it be unacceptable?" Mandoran asked.

Killian didn't breathe, so he didn't have to exhale; the exhalation was an affectation. "Come." He gestured. "The students will not see you as you traverse the halls."

The chancellor was in his office; he was pacing, hands behind his back, as the door vanished at Killian's command. His eyes were an unfortunate shade of orange—dark enough to be mistaken for red in poor lighting.

"Don't stand there gaping, come in. Quickly."

Serralyn wasn't in the office.

"Serralyn is in the library," Killian informed Kaylin, although she knew better than to ask, given the chancellor's apparent mood. "We expect much of the discussion will be held in the library. Arbiter Androsse is perhaps unsettled."

"What about Starrante?"

"Arbiter Starrante is tense. Having students present calms him, which is the reason Serralyn is not here to greet you." Killian then turned to the chancellor. "Do you wish to brief them before we join the Arbiters?"

Kaylin put up a hand.

"You are not in a classroom, Corporal."

"Yes, sir. But I'd like a bit of a briefing before we head to the library, and I have a couple of questions I'd like answered. If Androsse—"

"Arbiter Androsse."

"Fine. If Arbiter Androsse is upset, is he angry? Nervous? And if he's either, is Arbiter Kavallac in agreement with him?"

"They are, surprisingly, of one mind in this instance. As is Arbiter Starrante. What did you do to the Keeper?"

"I didn't do anything to the Keeper. Azoria's former home did. And if Azoria is going to be mentioned, the two Arbiters may fall into loud disagreement. Arbiter Kavallac didn't approve of Arbiter Androsse's encouragement of young, then student Azoria."

"Very well. You have asked one question. What are the others?"

"Is Bellusdeo aware of the difficulty the Arbiters now believe they're facing?"

The chancellor exhaled smoke. "Not exactly, no. She did visit yesterday evening to inform me of the events that occurred with regard to the Keeper. She had, as I'm certain you're aware, other concerns, and while she recognizes the import of the Keeper, it is not as visceral a demand on her attention as it would otherwise be.

"I am not certain Bellusdeo is aware of the existence of the corpse of an Ancient." Or wasn't certain she cared.

Kaylin bowed her head for a moment; she understood why Bellusdeo was driven to learn more about the ghosts of her sisters. But the living, at the moment, demanded more attention from Kaylin. "Bellusdeo is with Helen and Mrs. Erickson now. And possibly the weird ghosts that are the entire reason Mrs. Erickson has to live with us by Imperial dictate."

"Very well. Killianas."

"Chancellor."

"Please make certain we have an unencumbered path to the library and inform the Arbiters that we are on the way."

If by unencumbered the chancellor meant no students, Killian managed that well. If he meant no other people, he was going to be disappointed. A familiar scholar was waiting, arms folded, by the library portal. Professor Larrantin. His eyes were very blue.

The chancellor said, “The library is closed for the day.”

“Indeed. My attempts to confer with you about the closure were stymied by Killianas. I therefore chose to wait here.”

“You will be informed when the library is once again open to visitors.” The chancellor’s tone would have caused Kaylin to take a step back. Or several. Preferably at a sprint.

“I heard a rumor that this particular meeting is of grave concern.” Larrantin did not step back at all. “And it is a meeting I have an interest in attending.”

Mandoran frowned. “He didn’t hear that from us.” Us being the members of the cohort. “Oh, wait.” After a brief pause, and a visible wince, Mandoran added, “Or maybe he did. He wanted to know why Serralyn was absent from class. Valliant didn’t want to volunteer the information. Larrantin created an invisible but impassable box around Valliant until he did want to volunteer that information. No torture was used.”

“We will discuss your methods of handling our students when this is over,” the chancellor said. “The Arbiters have not summoned you, nor have they invited you.”

“I believe they will nonetheless accept my presence.” In Kaylin’s opinion, this was likely; Larrantin was the only member of the Academia who had taught here before the Academia’s fall and had been here when it had at last rumbled back to life.

“You are not under the opinion that you are the chancellor, surely?”

“Not at all. Had I desired the broadly bureaucratic role, I would have applied.”

Kaylin lifted a hand. “Guys, we have a little bit of an emergency. We don’t need to reenact the hostilities of two of the Arbiters in the hallway.”

“No one else will see or hear the argument,” Killian pointed out.

“Doesn’t stop our time being wasted.”

Both the chancellor and the professor turned glares in Kaylin's direction; her time was clearly irrelevant.

"We don't know where Evanton is. I'm going to stop by his store to see Grethan, to let him know that we're searching, and to see how stable the garden is. I can't do that until this meeting is over."

Lord Emmerian nodded. "The Academia is yours, chancellor; I am certain Professor Larrantin acknowledges this fact. He was venerated as a scholar. He may have some light to shed, and we are in growing need of that light. Lannagaros, please."

The chancellor's eyes were orange. He closed them for a moment, and when he opened them again, he'd lifted the inner eye membrane to somewhat mute the color. "Very well."

The library door was a fraud; it was a portal. It was, today, a clever portal in that it mimicked a door properly; when the door was opened, Kaylin could see the library's occupants on the other side. Serralyn was standing in front of Starrante, her eyes blue, not their usual green. Androsse and Kavallac were standing to the left and right of Starrante. No one appeared to be speaking.

The chancellor entered the library first. Kaylin, Severn, and Mandoran followed.

"Larrantin wishes to join us, but of course requires your permission," the chancellor said.

The three Arbiters glanced at each other before nodding. Only then did Larrantin follow, with Emmerian joining him.

Kaylin wondered what would have happened if the Arbiters said no.

Killian waited on the far side of the door; she lost sight of him when the doors closed—although *closed* wasn't the right word; the doorframe faded.

Silence reigned until the chancellor broke it by clearing his throat. "You have requested the presence of the corporal at her earliest convenience; the Imperial Court has decided her earliest convenience is now. To my understanding, you were furthering your research on Necromancy, with an eye to the quieting of ghosts; this is considered of vital import to my kind."

"I was not researching Necromancy," Androsse said. "I was researching the Ancients, with a particular eye to their deaths. I understand the deaths of the Immortals, being one; we have eternity—but we are subject to war, to poison, and to the ambitions that might lead to them. We all have an understanding of death, for all of our kind can die in the correct circumstances. We have certainly seen our share of corpses.

"It has been said that Ancients pass away—even in our time, before the fall of *Ravellon*, this was accepted as fact. But our greatest scholars, those who chose to devote their lives to a study of the Ancients, could not likewise claim to have seen their corpses; their passing was marked by their sudden absence. The Ancients did not consent to a more rigorous study.

"The corporal suggested that such a corpse did exist, and further, that Azoria had access to it for a period of time whose measure we cannot take."

Kaylin nodded.

"Yet you, who are not a Necromancer, could speak with the dead."

She nodded again. "By any standard that I understand, the Ancient was not dead. By their own standards, he was. He could speak. He could move the clouds of the outlands at will; he could create a space that better suited him. While he was considered dead—to himself—he could be trapped and was. I'm not sure he was entirely aware of it."

"Yes. You said he defined death as the end of purpose."

"That's what I inferred, yes."

"But you believe Azoria was drawing—or attempting to draw—power from the corpse."

"Yes."

"Do you believe the dead Ancient conversed with Azoria at any point in time?"

How would she know? She started to say this but stopped. Azoria had been looking for Mrs. Erickson for a long time. The Barrani Arcanist had planted roots in Mrs. Erickson's house—and spies, although she lost control of the children when their physical bodies died. She had already drained power—and life—from a dozen Barrani. Much of her research was centered around power.

To Kaylin's knowledge, that power didn't normally involve the dead—it just caused a lot of them.

She was certain Azoria knew or suspected something about Mrs. Erickson. She'd met Mrs. Erickson's mother. Had she done something to the baby before Mrs. Erickson was born?

Had she realized that if she had control of that power, she could command the dead? Or was it a gamble? Kaylin didn't consider the Ancient to actually be dead. But if Azoria had, everything about her interaction with Mrs. Erickson made sense.

Jamal and the children had stopped seeing Azoria when the connection between their bodies and their souls had been severed by death. Azoria could no longer see them and could no longer summon them.

But Mrs. Erickson's first manifestation of power—if one didn't include seeing the children at all—had happened when she was quite young; some of the ghosts might still have been trapped by Azoria. She didn't want to do the math immediately, but the children hadn't become ghosts at the same time.

Larrantin turned to Kaylin. "We have received a report about the incident surrounding the Keeper. Do you understand why he felt it was necessary to visit Mrs. Erickson's home?"

"He said the elements in the garden had been restless and ill at ease for a couple of weeks. He wasn't certain why; the last time they were restless in this fashion, we narrowly avoided losing our world to the Devourer. He hates socializing and very seldom leaves his store, but he insisted on visiting Mrs. Erickson's home after hearing about our first visit to Azoria's part of it. He wanted me to accompany them.

"Bellusdeo volunteered to join us. Terrano, Serralyn, and Mandoran represented the cohort. Bakkon asked permission to join Serralyn, although they'll have to speak for themselves with regard to their exploration." She glanced at Severn, who shrugged. "You were there. Do you want to add anything?"

"If the corporal wishes to add details you've forgotten to mention, I invite him to do so," the chancellor said. "Until and unless this occurs, allow Larrantin to continue."

Kaylin's turn to shrug.

Larrantin didn't appear to notice the minor interruption. "Did the Keeper feel that he had found the cause of, or source of, the elemental unrest?"

She thought about this, cursing mortal memory. "Yes, I believe so. Or at least he thought something present justified that unrest."

"Until your interference in Azoria's manor, and her figurative backyard, his garden was relatively stable?"

"That's what I inferred."

"Understand, then, that the unrest in the garden is significant."

Since she'd already mentioned the possible end of the world the previous time the garden had been unruly, she found this condescending—but that was Larrantin all over.

The chancellor, aware of her irritation, lifted a brow in her direction. "You have been involved in many near disasters, but only one was enough to shake the garden."

"The elemental water was involved in a couple of those disasters. And it wasn't me that upset the water."

Larrantin was not a man accustomed to being interrupted. He was the one who did the interrupting, if he deemed it necessary. His tone was chillier when he spoke again. "Did the Keeper say a specific element was involved?"

"No."

"It is the Keeper's job to keep the wild elements from clashing; to keep the garden serene for its occupants. The Keeper has not—to our knowledge—returned from Azoria's manor."

"No. I intend to check in with his apprentice after we're done here to make sure he hasn't returned without informing us." She exhaled.

"Before you consider my branch of research irrelevant, we are looking at the possibility of a dead Ancient, a mortal woman who has the power to bespeak the dead, and to command them."

"I don't recall that last part."

It was Androsse who replied. Larrantin minded his interruption far less. "Mortal memory is not that fallible. Azoria would have had no interest in a mortal woman were it not for the manifestation of a very rare—and largely useless—power. Azoria's research while she was a student here did not directly cover Necromancy. Her research after the fall of Berranin obviously touched on it. She is dead, but her journals have not yet appeared on our shelves; we have been watching."

"Wait, notebooks written somewhere else by a dead person become part of the library?"

"Yes, but not all of them, and not in a specific order."

"And you can find them?" Kaylin considered the diaries of every single human who kept one and wondered how the library wasn't collapsing in on itself.

"Finding them, as you put it, is somewhat arcane. We have the abilities, but it takes time, and we are not guaranteed to succeed."

"You're not suggesting we go back there, are you?"

"I believe Serralyn has something to say," Androsse replied.

Serralyn clearly didn't want to say anything. Starrante's arms danced on either side of her, although he didn't touch her; Kaylin assumed this was meant as a Wevaran gesture of comfort or solidarity. The Barrani cohort student was perfectly happy to talk for hours about things she was studying, but had otherwise always been quiet.

She took a steadying breath. "Bakkon wanted to visit Azoria's manor; he felt that there was something about the environment that reminded him of his pre-birth home. I didn't see the harm in it—Azoria was dead. There might have been security enchantments meant to discourage intruders, but Bakkon felt he could deal with those in a way that didn't compromise our safety." She swallowed.

"Did you encounter traps?" It was Severn who asked, his voice so measured and neutral it had a calming effect. Kaylin had never, come to think, seen Severn lose his temper.

"No."

"But you did find something."

She swallowed and nodded. "The paintings Azoria made—the paintings Kaylin and Terrano examined in the archives of the High Halls—were improved on in Azoria's home. She had an entirely separate lab and a series of smaller, research-dependent libraries housed around a large room for practical experiments."

"You found more of her paintings."

"We found more of her paintings in various stages; we assumed that they were not yet complete."

"Did Bakkon note anything unusual?"

"He said the halls outside of her personal research area were very much like the birthing halls of his memory—not in shape, but in feel, in the density of...something. I couldn't sense it; Terrano couldn't see it. I'm not sure if it's something specifically related to Wevaran. But he felt that these halls had been created to serve, in some fashion, a similar purpose. They weren't exact, but Azoria was Barrani; she didn't understand the whole of Wevaran birth.

"Had she access by that time to Barrani—or Dragons, or Ancestors—Bakkon might have had a better sense of what she meant to do. He therefore pinpoints the discovery of the dead Ancient as the probable point at which she abandoned the research she had obviously attempted to enact with regard to the Wevaran names.

"But Bakkon feels it quite possible that she intended to take Barrani True Names, and somehow introduce them into the birthing canal environment as a way of increasing the stature and power of her own name."

"That is not possible," Starrante said, clicking, his visible eyes red.

"Nothing about Azoria depended on possible. We didn't have time to go through her research materials with any deliberate care. I did attempt to remove one journal for future study."

"Attempt?"

"The book would not leave the area. It was teleported back to its original resting place. We could read the books, move the books, reorganize the journals—but we couldn't remove them." She hesitated and then added, "I'm not sure you'll find any of them in the library, no matter how carefully you look. She wasn't worried about her knowledge dying with her—I think she was arrogant enough to believe she was never going to die.

"She was clearly concerned that the research might be stolen." Serralyn exhaled. "In the lab, I said we found unfinished paintings. In some central images existed, and in some cases sketches hadn't been transferred to a painted medium. There were paintings of various Barrani." Her tone was off.

It was Kaylin who picked up the questioning, although she led with a statement. "You recognized some of the Barrani. Or at least one."

Again, Serralyn hesitated before nodding. "You'd recognize her if you saw the painting. It wasn't finished, but it was closest to my eye—and the background of the painting, rather than a sitting room or a bench or grand scenery, was… I think you'd recognize it. The Barrani woman had white hair."

"The Consort."

Serralyn nodded.

"But the Consort of her time wasn't the Consort of ours—and I haven't heard that white hair is necessary. Very, very few of the Barrani have white hair."

Serralyn nodded again.

"Which meant that she had seen the current Consort, although technically she was dead and her line expunged and she couldn't therefore be in the High Halls. Was there any indication that she'd been working with or through Barrani who could legitimately enter the High Halls?"

"The occupants of the High Halls aren't confined to lords," Mandoran said. "Any of the powerful will have aides and servants, and refusing those people entry would cause a ruckus—I mean, the lords would then have to do things themselves, right? Until recently, the interior of the High Halls was focused entirely on the Shadow at the heart of the Test of Name. It's possible she could have entered as a servant and passed through undetected.

"As far as the High Halls knew, she was—along with all of Berranin—dead. I don't think she could accomplish the same thing now. Or Terrano doesn't. And given what her crime was, the High Halls would be far more guarded. The High Halls doesn't care if we assassinate each other—it's a racial pastime." This last was said with bitterness. "They're a big believer in survival of the fittest."

Kaylin held up a hand. "None of that—painting, Consort, High Halls—has anything to do with the current difficulty, at least on the surface. Did she write what she was trying to do at the end?"

"I think it highly likely," Serralyn replied. "But we didn't have time to examine her library. We were noting where we'd left off, and intended to return to it. But I heard that the Keeper had somehow become stuck to or trapped by Azoria's painting. Bakkon was alarmed. He wanted to go to the Keeper. But before we got there, we got Mandoran's panicked demand that we evacuate as soon as possible. And when we had, we got the news that neither Terrano nor the Keeper had made it out."

"I'm not sure we can get to the research area without entering the rest of the manse."

Serralyn cleared her throat. "Bakkon believes, if we can open the door again, we can. He...left strategically placed bits of webbing to which he could create a portal."

"What catches my notice," Arbiter Androsse said, "is Mrs. Erickson herself. It is clear to me that she was the crown jewel in Azoria's plans. Azoria's failure to understand that a handful of mortal decades takes a deadly toll on mortals is understandable. But Mrs. Erickson is still alive, and if those plans did not come to fruition, understanding those plans may reveal more about the mortal's powers."

Kavallac was orange-eyed. "It was to determine her potential powers that we first began our research, but I am not at all certain, given the length of a mortal life, that this is now a safe or even fruitful endeavor."

Androsse nodded. "What we need to ascertain is the state—and power—of a theoretically dead Ancient. A mortal's power is trivial in comparison."

Kaylin sat on her knee-jerk annoyance.

Starrante, however, disagreed. "We cannot simply discard the question of Mrs. Erickson. Nor can we discard the implications of the spells Azoria wove to somehow capture or possess her. They are woven into the research on the dead Ancient, the creation of the interior of her manor, the existence of the paintings themselves. It is clear to me, from things Terrano has discovered, that those paintings—for Mrs. Erickson—were rooted in some fashion in the distant green of the West March, one of the centers of the powers of the Ancient world. It was not disrupted when *Ravellon* fell; nor was it lost to us, as so much of that world and its history has been.

"We understand that Azoria's assumptions about Mrs. Erickson's potential powers could have been entirely mistaken; she might have labored in ignorance—a trait Azoria was prone to dismiss if she felt she knew better, unless she changed greatly in the intervening years between student and what she later became.

"It is likely that Mrs. Erickson could relieve Bellusdeo of the ghosts of whom she was entirely unaware."

Kavallac did not like this suggestion. At all. "They are not—they should not be—dead. They are, or should be, part of a cohesive whole."

Androsse shrugged. "I am not remotely certain a Necromancer deals in the half-dead, the should-be-dead, or the should-not-be-dead philosophical questions. Mrs. Erickson's powers do not seem, from admittedly poor research material, to be able to bring the dead back to a semblance of life.

"Nor do her powers seem to be the world-shattering emergency the Keeper seemed to sense when he entered Azoria's manse. If we are to ascertain the Keeper's whereabouts—if he is even still alive—it is on the dead Ancient that we must concentrate. To do that, Bakkon must be allowed to further explore the sealed-off manse. Serralyn may accompany him; I expect a full report of all findings."

The chancellor exhaled loudly enough Kaylin almost expected to see fire. "The students are not your personal servants, Arbiter. Their disposition is not in your hands; their reports are, unless they voluntarily share them, likewise not under your supervision. What might be is your experience with Azoria An'Berranin—experience which you have yet to fully detail.

"Given the likelihood of finding the journals and papers of this particular dead student within the domain of the library, it is your discussions that might provide us the most insight; you interacted with her when she was alive. Perhaps you might prepare a report detailing those interactions before we commit students to a dangerous and unknown environment."

Barrani Ancestral eyes were very much like Barrani eyes in the colors they adopted. Androsse's were almost black.

Fair enough; the chancellor's were almost crimson, Kavallac's were heading that way, and Starrante's had become red at the mention of birthing spaces and hadn't really recovered.

Serralyn lifted a hand. Larrantin nodded in her direction, as if this was just a fractious classroom and she was the only person present he considered worthy of granting permission to speak. It wasn't a surprise that she therefore addressed her words to a familiar professor.

"You taught Azoria, didn't you?"

"I did. Two advanced classes."

"Which ones?"

"Spatial dimension—which is currently on hiatus given the lack of qualified students to teach—and portal actualization. The latter is being offered next year. I was not her only teacher."

"Did she discuss your subjects with you?"

"At some length—but Azoria was interested in everything. She wasn't pretending; she wasn't attempting to curry favor through flattery; she was literally interested in everything. In that aspect, Serralyn, she is similar to you—although perhaps less delighted and more focused in learning every iota of knowledge of those who possessed more than she. She embodied the phrase *knowledge is power.* She was not particularly social; if Barrani have eternity, she considered time, always, of the essence. She would not waste it on something she felt served no useful purpose."

"Did she have peers she considered worthy of her time?"

"Not that I observed—but I spent little time observing the social affairs of students; they were not my concern. Nor are they my concern now; I am perhaps more aware of you because Terrano loiters around you." An odd smile touched Larrantin's face. "Had Terrano been a contemporary of Azoria, I believe she would have made every attempt to befriend him."

Serralyn grimaced. "She wouldn't."

"I assure you his unusual use of magic and his flexibility with dimensional space would have been of great interest to her."

"What she would have expected from Terrano, he could never give her. He's not blindly obedient, even when facing probable death. And he's a terrible teacher. The only way she could have learned from him is to become one of us."

"She seldom accepted limitations."

"Yes. That's the problem." Serralyn's frown was unusual for her. "Killian won't speak of his experience with Azoria to anyone but you. If Arbiter Androsse is to write a report—and Arbiter Starrante as well—you should ask Killian to give you a verbal report while they're working."

Given the chancellor's mood—and the color of his eyes—Kaylin was almost shocked that Serralyn could make this demand of him. He turned the red eyes on one of his prized students, his lips compressing. Serralyn didn't even blink.

"Killian will not talk to any of us about anything he might know; his imperative is to protect the privacy of his students—even the dead ones. He will talk to you if you command it."

Kavallac had swiveled toward Serralyn; Starrante's arms had fallen still.

"If we don't understand what Azoria built, we might not be able to find Terrano. He's still not back." She folded her arms, her eyes blue, the set of her jaw stiff. She had no intention of backing down—she, who avoided confrontation, and who tried, as much as any Barrani Kaylin had ever met, to make nice, to project happiness or joy.

"I love the Academia. I love being a student here. I mostly respect my professors, and I would spend every waking hour between classes in this library. But something just as important to me will break if we lose Terrano. Whatever we have to do to find him, we'll do." She exhaled, and her shoulders—rigid while speaking—slowly crept back down.

"I'm willing to go back to Azoria's manor. I'm willing to spend every waking hour there, instead of here. I'm willing to find any information her journals might contain. I'm even willing to attempt to transcribe them, but I doubt that will work.

"I'm not willing to go there without the chancellor's permission. I'm not willing to risk the life I love here." She turned to the chancellor; she had failed to directly address Androsse, the Arbiter who had demanded that she return to run his errand.

When facing the chancellor, her eyes lightened enough that green flecks could be seen in the blue. "I trust you with as much of our lives as you can preserve. But I also trust you understand just how important this might be, or become.

"I'm guessing that if we find Terrano, we'll find the Keeper—but we can't find either if we don't understand what the space is, what it was meant to be, and what it might have devolved to with Azoria's death."

16

It was interesting—and unexpected—that it was Serralyn who somehow unruffled metaphorical feathers. Arbiter Androsse, who had been about to go toe-to-toe with the chancellor, offered a reluctant nod to the Barrani cohort student. The chancellor, eyes losing some of their red, did the same. Kavallac had remained silent—possibly because she had never quite trusted Azoria and had been far more reserved than the other two Arbiters.

Larrantin provided the only minor surprise. "If you wish to evaluate the space and its magical construction, and you are willing, I will accompany you."

"Bakkon is coming," Serralyn said, which sounded like a no to Kaylin.

"I have no issues with that. If you wish, I will ask Bakkon's permission as well. Unlike Arbiter Androsse or Arbiter Starrante, I have no difficulties leaving the campus." His smile was slender, sharp. "There have, from time to time, been people who have attempted to make it an issue."

"Have you been to the High Halls since the Academia was resurrected?"

One silver-gray brow rose. "Do not be ridiculous. I am willing to leave the Academia—and my research—on my own terms. I have no interest in the politics of the High Court." The brow lowered. "Very, very few of the people I would have considered companions are still alive. I believe my family line survived, and in some fashion serves the current High Lord, whoever he is."

Both of Serralyn's brows rose.

"Regardless, I am curious, and I believe you would not find a better candidate for research on the actual halls Azoria created."

Starrante made the Wevaran clicks that served as social coughing.

"Bakkon is an expert—as are many of your kin—in travel by portal. He is not so much an expert in spatial dimensions. And frankly, none of us are experts in death and its detritus."

Lord Emmerian had been so still, so silent, it was easy, in the ruffled nerves and muted hostility, to forget he was there. "Will you risk Mrs. Erickson?"

Kaylin shook her head. "Absolutely not. Until we know, until we can figure out what happened to Evanton, she is staying with Helen."

"It is her sensitivity that might prove instructive."

"No."

"And if she is asked to help, do you think she will refuse?"

"I'll have Helen keep anyone who'd be willing to ask her out of my house."

"Thus denying her the choice."

Serralyn approached Emmerian and took his arm. He glanced down at her. She shook her head. "Mrs. Erickson is part of our house. There isn't a single member of my cohort who doesn't like her. Kaylin's overprotective, it's true—but she's got nothing on Sedarias. Or Bellusdeo, if it comes to that."

"Bellusdeo understands self-determination," Emmerian replied.

Serralyn nodded. "She does. But she also understands that, at base, Mrs. Erickson is a people pleaser." She glanced at Kaylin. "That's the right word?"

"Yes."

"And people pleasers are very easily pressured to do things that aren't in their own best interests. If the Keeper and Terrano can't be found, we can revisit the question of Mrs. Erickson if none of our exploration yields any results. But she's not joking. She'll tell Helen to refuse to let you in, and Helen will obey."

Emmerian exhaled, but he nodded.

"We know you want to help Bellusdeo," Serralyn told him, her voice gentle. "So do we, especially Mandoran. But it's no good trying to help her if the help enrages her—and trust me, this will." She then turned to the Arbiters. "We're leaving now. If we do get permission to explore Azoria's various studies, it probably won't be until tomorrow at the earliest."

Only when they had left the library and its Arbiters did Serralyn turn once again, to the chancellor. His eyes had mellowed into red-flecked orange. The spine of steel that had held her up in the library deserted her as she faced him. "I'm sorry. I've seen enough of Androsse that I thought things were going to become unproductive really, really quickly."

The chancellor smiled. "And you've seen enough of Dragons to assume that part of that would be my fault?"

She swallowed and nodded. "Normally, I'd just do what the Arbiter requested. He can lock me out of the library, and I don't want to lose library time. But you can lock me out of the Academia, and in the end, that's more important."

"I do not wish to lose you to fragmented and poorly understood magic. My concern in that regard is genuine."

Serralyn smiled. "I know. We all do." She also no doubt knew that Dragons were famously territorial, and the chancellor was not going to surrender his authority over the Academia's students to an Arbiter. Had Starrante made the suggestion, he would have asked Serralyn; he would not have commanded her.

"Almost, I wish to contact the Arcanum; I would not be concerned if they threw Arcanists at the problem; the world would be a safer place with fewer Arcanists of middling competence. I would, however, be concerned that lurking in their midst would be someone with Azoria's ambitions and competence." He exhaled. "Corporal, Corporal. I believe you intended to visit Evanton's shop. Allow us to assemble our information about Azoria. If Evanton has managed to return, mirror me immediately; if he has not, return to the Academia after confirming his absence."

"The Arkon wanted me to report to him about this meeting."

"Very little of value has yet been determined. I would suggest that you visit Evanton's shop as your first order of business." He turned to Lord Emmerian. "I am uncertain as to your plans. I believe, however, that Mandoran should accompany the corporals; if Terrano returns before Evanton does or can, Mandoran would have that information immediately."

"I intend to accompany the corporals for the time being. Bellusdeo is safe with Helen, and unless Mrs. Erickson wishes to join us, I'm uncertain that she will leave her."

The chancellor nodded. "I will see you all again in a few hours."

Kaylin's stomach didn't embarrass her by joining the conversation, but she did insist on grabbing something to eat on the move to make sure it stayed that way. Mandoran and Emmerian declined food, but Severn nodded; they made their way back through Tiamaris to hit the streets where small lunch stalls could be found and ate while walking toward Elani street.

Grethan, Evanton's apprentice, occupied the old man's stool at the very large bar behind which he usually dealt with his customers. The stalks on his forehead were, in Grethan's opinion, largely decorative; he was Tha'alani by birth, but he could not join the Tha'alaan, couldn't hear it, couldn't access the racial knowledge and memories that most Tha'alani children could.

For Kaylin, that was normal.

For Grethan, it was normal as well—but he lived in an enclave where it was anything but. Subject to pity, isolated in his pain and anger, the way none of the other children were, he had eventually found his way here. To Evanton. To the elemental garden. Evanton had taken him in as an apprentice, but Kaylin could never decide if apprentice meant eventual successor as the steward of the heart of the elements, or if it meant menial servant.

On the other hand, she was in good company; Grethan didn't know, either.

He didn't look up as the door opened; he was in conversation with other customers.

They're not customers, Severn said, a thread of amusement in the interior words.

Oh. It was Teela and her partner, Tain, both wearing their tabards. Barrani Hawks were never given Elani as a walking beat.

Teela looked back as the four of them entered the shop. Her eyes were, not surprisingly, a dark shade of blue. Tain's were lighter, but his expression was grimmer.

Kaylin exhaled. "I take it Evanton hasn't returned."

Grethan looked up at the sound of Kaylin's voice; she saw relief push his eyes from green—not a good color for Tha'alani—to hazel. Gold, in Tha'alani eyes, was the comfort color, but given the circumstances, it was likely to be absent from Grethan's eyes for as long as Evanton remained absent.

He didn't rush around the counter to reach Kaylin, given the rest of her companions, but seeing his expression, she approached the bar and placed a hand across its surface. She was slightly surprised when he reached out to grasp it.

"Evanton hasn't come back. He went to meet you and your housemate." His eyes shaded toward green. "The garden is upset.

I've managed to calm them down—but I needed the water's help. I can't understand all of what the elements say, especially not when they're all shouting."

"Shouting?"

"Mostly at each other. The water can talk, but it's getting harder."

"Well, the store isn't flooded and most of it hasn't burned down," she replied. "Are they trying to tell you Evanton is dead?"

Severn winced internally.

Grethan shook his head, the stalks on his forehead trembling. "He's alive. He's just out of reach, somehow. They can't hear him."

"He's not in the garden."

Grethan shook his head again. "It's not like that. I think the elements can talk to the Keeper. They could talk to him when he left; they could talk to him when he wasn't in your house. But they lost that ability; it's like he's still connected to them, but only barely. They can't tell if he's dying; they can only tell that he's not dead yet."

Kaylin frowned. "Evanton can talk to the elements when he's not in the actual garden?"

"Not the same way—and I can barely talk to them when they're right in front of my face, so I don't understand how it works. But—they can reach him, somehow; they can be heard. Or they could be. They're pretty sure they aren't being heard now." He hesitated. "Being a Keeper, as far as I can tell, is like owning cats."

Teela coughed.

"It's not that he's their boss. It's not like he owns them or they're obedient. They listen to him. He has the power to make himself heard. He has the power to isolate them if necessary—and given the way they'd fight otherwise, it's necessary, believe me. But... I think they have to like him. They have to want him around. They understand on some level that he's not like they are, but mostly they don't care."

"I didn't realize you owned cats," Kaylin said.

Grethan reddened. "Evanton has store cats, but mostly they hate people."

"So they're like their owner."

That pulled a smile from the overwhelmed youth. "Maybe I don't understand the garden. Evanton teaches me—but mostly I do chores. At least I don't have to carry buckets back from the well here."

"True. Ummm, I've always wondered—what do the elementals eat? I mean, how do you keep them fed?"

"Now is not the time, kitling."

Kaylin winced. Teela was right.

"Can you find him?" Grethan said, his voice weak enough to come out in a whisper.

"That's why we're here." She glanced at Teela. "Should we actually enter the garden?"

"I don't think that's wise. Which is probably why you suggested it."

Kaylin did her best to ignore this. "We can talk to the water."

"If the water lost contact with him in both your home and Azoria's manor, I wouldn't assume any useful information would be found."

"The water might be able to explain what's been upsetting the elements."

Grethan shook his head, eyes wide with alarm. "They're already unsettled. We don't want them to focus on what made them that way—we're trying to distract them. Evanton couldn't get a clear explanation. He didn't expect one."

"Fine. I have to head back to the Academia with current news. Can you mirror the Halls of Law—or me personally—if Evanton does show up while we're in transit?"

Grethan nodded. His expression made clear that he didn't think that would happen.

★ ★ ★

"Why were you two given the Elani beat?" Kaylin asked, when they were back on said street and the door to Evanton's shop was shut behind them.

"We volunteered."

Kaylin turned to Mandoran. "You couldn't have warned us? We could have skipped the visit to Evanton's."

"And do what? Sit twiddling our thumbs at the Academia while we wait on every other important person to write their reports?"

Fair enough.

"Plus, you ate. We don't have to listen to your stomach in the next meeting." He turned to Teela. "You might as well share your thoughts."

"I'd prefer not to do it in the middle of the street."

Hope, flopped out on Kaylin's shoulder, gave a quiet squawk of agreement.

"Where do you want to discuss it?"

"Helen, preferably."

"Bellusdeo's there."

"Bellusdeo and I have never come to blows. The only time we came close was in the tavern when a brawl broke out."

"No doubt caused by you."

"Absolutely not. She almost hit me because the person she was aiming for was really, really good at dodging." Teela grinned.

Kaylin glanced at Emmerian.

He shook his head. "I will return to the Academia."

"But—"

"My presence will at best be tolerated; at worst it will be an outlet for anger, frustration, and despair. No one needs that at this time."

"Helen can keep damage to a minimum," Mandoran pointed out.

"Karriamis couldn't keep all damage to a minimum," was Emmerian's wry reply.

★★★

Helen was, as she always was, at the open door when Kaylin crossed the fence line. She immediately moved out of the way when she saw Kaylin's guests: Severn, Tain, and Teela. Teela occupied an odd position; she was a Hawk, Kaylin's mentor, a Lord of the High Court, and a member of the cohort. The cohort had passed the Test of Name, and were theoretically also lords of the same court—but Teela's power in that court was fully established and unquestioned.

Helen quietly stood to the side until every visitor had filed in. "You didn't locate Evanton."

Kaylin shook her head. The question was a formality, asked for the sake of politeness; the minute Kaylin entered her home, Helen could read her thoughts about the day in progress. She already knew.

"Teela wishes a place to discuss the current search in private."

Kaylin nodded.

"Bellusdeo wishes to join that discussion."

Of course she did. Emmerian, as usual, was right. "Does she want to bring Mrs. Erickson?"

"I don't believe she considers that either wise or mandatory at the moment. Imelda is exhausted, and she is understandably quite upset at the turn of events. She is willing to join your discussion if I feel her input will be of aid."

"Do you?"

"I would like to hear the discussion first," Helen confessed. "But the decision in this case must be up to you."

"Me? Why me?"

"Because, Kaylin, you are the tenant. Inasmuch as I have the choice of who to serve, I nonetheless serve. My choice was an attempt to serve someone I desired to serve. But you could ask me to eject every person currently in residence, and I would do so."

"I would never force Mrs. Erickson to join us, and I certainly wouldn't ask you to kick everyone else out of their home."

"Yes." Helen's smile was gentle. "I have rearranged the parlor; it is larger. I have asked Sedarias to consider allowing Mandoran to pass on information as it arises."

"She agreed?"

"For now, yes. Terrano, as you must know, has not returned."

Kaylin nodded. "If we could find him, we could probably find Evanton."

"I think that would calm Imelda significantly. Azoria was not her fault and not her responsibility, but she nonetheless feels very, very guilty."

"She has nothing to feel guilty about!"

"Sadly, that is not the way guilt works."

Teela sat. When Helen offered her a drink, she actually accepted it. In theory, given that both she and Tain wore tabards, she was on duty. Drinking on duty was forbidden. Tain politely refused, which caused Teela to lift a brow in his direction.

"I don't have to deal with the rest of your friends," he said in response. Kaylin thought it a tad smug.

Teela, drink in hand, glared at him.

"No, dear, I don't think they would start the equivalent of a bar brawl here," Helen told her.

Mandoran laughed out loud. He then reddened. "Sorry. Some people think that would be entertaining. Not me, of course."

Teela exhaled slowly; she was probably silently counting to ten.

Kaylin took the chair opposite Teela as the door opened to allow Bellusdeo entry. The Dragon's eyes were copper. Helen expanded the room and the Dragon sat—heavily—to one side of Teela. Tain had not taken a chair.

"Give me whatever she's drinking," Bellusdeo said, sagging into the chair's high back and closing her eyes.

A glass appeared on the side table.

Severn stood beside Kaylin's chair. Mandoran, on the other

hand, took the chair beside Bellusdeo. He didn't ask for anything to drink.

Hope, flopped across her shoulder, squawked.

"You asked me a question in Evanton's place," Teela said, speaking to Kaylin.

"No, I didn't. But it's true I didn't expect to see you there."

"The Keeper is missing. The High Court has become aware of his absence, and the High Lord and the Consort are concerned. I did not tell them that he disappeared while accompanying you, or they'd have hauled you into a court session."

"They can't."

"You're a Lord of the High Court, remember?"

Ugh. "Fine, they can. I'm not going."

"If you're called, Sedarias and I will accompany you. You will be in no physical danger. In fact, if you could control what randomly falls out of your mouth, it's unlikely you'd be in significant danger at all." Teela exhaled slowly, no doubt counting to ten again, which Kaylin thought hugely unfair.

"Mandoran told you you might as well tell us what you're thinking. Mandoran. Not me."

"Then Mandoran can tell you what I'm thinking," Teela replied. "But I assume you have actual questions that might generate discussion."

"Why?"

"Because you're not a fool."

"Look, I'm not a tagalong mascot anymore. I'm a corporal. I don't need to be constantly tested."

"Hmm, what do you normally say in situations like this? Oh, I remember. Sucks to be you."

Hope snickered. Kaylin flicked his nose. "Fine. I didn't expect you to be brought in—the Imperial Court has already pulled Severn and me off regular duties. I'm not going to ask how news of Evanton's disappearance reached the High Court.

Let's assume that you were asked to look into it by the High Lord or his confederates."

Teela nodded.

"You'd do what I did, and check to see if Evanton made it back. You already know what happened, more or less. And you know that Terrano hasn't made it back yet. It's that part that's causing real worry. Terrano isn't easily caged. Evanton might be—he's the Keeper, not Terrano; he's probably got no experience escaping difficult traps."

"Continue."

"Evanton wanted to see Mrs. Erickson's home. He wanted to examine possible difficulties there. He found one, and it disturbed him. He then insisted that we visit Azoria's manse. Fine. She's dead. But it wasn't the same space we fought in before. It wasn't the space we'd faced Azoria in."

"And?"

"When we tried to figure out what Azoria wanted from Mrs. Erickson, we had to do our own investigating. Serralyn discovered a very, very old ceremony of binding. The flowers that were placed in Mrs. Erickson's hair before Azoria painted her family were flowers that can't, in theory, grow outside of the green."

Teela's nod was slower, more measured.

"But she had that flower. It's possible Azoria—outcaste—could sneak into the green, find such a flower, and steal it. I don't think that's likely, given the West March. Barrani memory is pretty long."

"Our memory is perfect; it's our grudges you're complaining about."

"I did think about it. Amaldi and Darreno were first captured when they were her slaves; she clearly spent time in the green during their early lives together. Could she have taken a flower and preserved it the way she preserved the two mortals?"

"That," Teela said, as she set her drink down, "would be the best possible option."

"And given our luck, it isn't. So option two: she grew the flower on her own. Which means one of two things, again. Either the knowledge that the flower blooms nowhere else is just wrong—and Serralyn's research implies that it's not—or..."

"Or?"

"Or she managed to build a slender connection to the green, and she could, with care and subterfuge, draw on it, at least to the extent that she could grow those flowers."

"That would be the worst possible option, yes."

"Which means the green is involved peripherally, and if something is growing in Azoria's metaphorical graveyard, it's possible the green is aware of it, disturbed by it, or in the worst case beginning to be affected by it. While she was alive, she could hide the connection; she could make certain it wouldn't be detected. Now she can't.

"So my actual guess is the Lord of the West March mentioned his concerns—which would be very recent—and his brother, the High Lord, mentioned them to you. And you're involved on a non-Halls level because of that."

Teela's smile was sharp, but genuine. "Very good. That is observant guesswork, Corporal."

"Just...how messy is this going to get? The Keeper, the garden, the green, and one big, dead—" Kaylin shut her mouth. "More and more things seem to be getting snarled in the problem. There are no experts in knowledge of the Keeper. There are certainly no experts in knowledge of the green. And no one can tell us more than a handful of questionable things about Necromancers."

"No."

"But if something dead is powering Azoria's manse, and the slender connective threads also lead to the green, that could be a disaster."

Teela nodded. "There are reasons children are never exposed to the *regalia*. The green's power is, and can be, transformative if those subjected to it are not fully protected or prepared." No one knew the truth of this better than the cohort, of which Teela was part. "I am therefore here as a representative of the High Court. I am experienced with the Arcanum as well."

"A lot of Barrani were—or are."

"Yes. But none of them are Hawks. Inasmuch as it is considered safe for anyone attached to the Arcanum to become involved, I've been chosen."

"How much did you tell them about Mrs. Erickson?"

"Kitling, I barely mentioned her at all."

"And Azoria?"

"She was far more heavily discussed, as the High Lord was aware of the traces of the quarters preserved after Berranin's fall; he was informed of the paintings and their presumptive use. Given the nature of Azoria's crimes, she will always be a sensitive subject."

"And Mrs. Erickson is mortal."

"And Mrs. Erickson is mortal." Teela's half smile was sympathetic. "You do not want my people to consider mortals significant. There is no advantage for you in it."

Kaylin said nothing, struggling a moment against the resentment of the immortality humans would never possess. She won, because it wasn't entirely relevant, but some days it was harder than others. "The High Lord's concern is the green, then?"

"Azoria is our version of the bogeyman," Teela replied, glancing at Tain for confirmation. Tain nodded. "If there is nothing else that unites a fractious, political people, the Consort and the Lake unifies in our desire to protect. The foremost scholars and Arcanists cannot tell us that the Lake is safe from depredation, because they have never been given access to study it. The High Halls is our only source of certainty—and that is both ancient and recent.

"The green has sentience in a way the Lake does not—again, according to the High Halls. The Lake does have some sentience—just enough to choose a Consort, a steward, a new mother for our race. It will surrender names to the Consort of its choice, and those names are carried to us as infants; it awakens us. We understand its purpose.

"We do not understand the purpose of the green. Although Barrani husband and tend it, we do so as supplicants. The green chooses those who participate in the *regalia*, and the green tells its story. We have never fully understood the reason the tale is told; assumptions have been made, but there is no way to prove them correct, which has annoyed and upset scholars for generations.

"In the green, flowers and trees grow that cannot be found anywhere else in the world. They are thought to be of the green—but they have no purpose that we understand. They were once used in personal vows, but they did not bind as blood oaths can; they were ceremonial. If they were once used for different reasons, that meaning is lost."

"And Azoria's use implies more than the ceremonial."

"Yes. Yes, it does. As I said, there is concern. If the Barrani do not own the green, we husband it and we guard it. But there are avenues to walk in the green that we cannot control."

"The Hallionne," Kaylin said quietly.

"Indeed. We have been much in contact with Eddorian, the only member of our cohort who did not choose to leave the Hallionne Alsanis. As you suggest, Hallionne Alsanis can allow guests to enter the green; it is not the path of approach that most of our people take, because it is not one that is widely known. Terrano made good use of it when he was first attempting to be free of the Hallionne's cage."

"Eddorian's been asking questions of Hallionne Alsanis for you?"

Teela nodded again; her eyes were darker. "It is Alsanis's belief that there is significance—and danger—in the fact of, the existence of, Azoria's flower. It was not meant to rest in mortal hair, in mortal lands. He does not believe that she somehow managed to grow the flower with no contact from the green at all."

"And the fact that she's dead doesn't change that."

"If the connection was firmly rooted in her life, the danger is insignificant. If it was not, the danger exists. And if the Keeper himself vanished in Azoria's mausoleum, Alsanis believes that the connection exists."

Kaylin blinked. "Why?"

"Alsanis believes the green is concerned. In the past two weeks, even the Warden has been turned away from the green. This fact, the disappearance of the Keeper, and the fact of the moving, animate statues in the manse imply that even if Azoria is no longer with us, the many roots she planted have not died."

"She'd learned how to build connections to the outlands," Kaylin said. "We know that from the paintings she left behind in the High Halls when her line was destroyed. Her manor drew on at least the power of the outlands."

"That is our belief."

"What does the High Halls want from this?"

"The destruction of the manor, and everything she built in or upon it."

Kaylin exhaled. "You're wearing our tabard," she said, although she herself wasn't.

Teela nodded.

"What do you want?"

"I want Terrano back. I want the Keeper back. In that order. I won't destroy the manor until both of these things happen. But I'll destroy it in a minute if both of those conditions are satisfied."

"And that's why you chose to accept this mission?"

"That's why they chose to accept me," Teela countered. "That, and they believed that of the High Court, I am the only person who could gain access to Azoria's former home."

There were now too many things to think about. Kaylin exhaled and turned to the silent Bellusdeo; the Dragon's eyes were almost red, although the flecks in it were copper, not orange. "We're heading to the Academia to consult with the chancellor and the Arbiters. What will you do?"

"I want to stay here, with Mrs. Erickson. Even if Mrs. Erickson was not much discussed, one Barrani could cause irreparable damage to her, she's so frail. They won't," she added, unnecessarily, "cause me damage."

Kaylin exhaled. "We'll head out now. If there's an emergency, we'll mirror Helen to let you know."

Hope's squawk conveyed annoyance and disgust.

"Fine. If there's more of an emergency."

17

Killian was once again standing in the quad when Kaylin and company returned. Severn walked beside her; Teela and Tain walked behind. Mandoran had chosen to remain with Helen, as both Teela and Serralyn would have a cohort ear in the conversation.

An odd, purple haze enshrouded Killian, visible only with Hope's aid. Or insistence. Kaylin swore if there was one more thing mixed in an already chaotic emergency, she'd scream.

"Evanton did not return?"

Kaylin shook her head.

"We currently cannot be heard by the rest of the Academia," Killian said, as he turned and led them to the main building.

"Then no. He hasn't returned. The garden is becoming more unsettled, and poor Grethan has probably pulled out half of his hair in panic."

Killian did not reply. Instead, he gestured the doors open; they flew to the sides with enough force she could hear the students responding in surprise in the quad.

The chancellor was in his office with Emmerian; they were both facing the door when it opened—Killian once again using more force than necessary. The chancellor didn't ask about Evanton, no doubt already informed of the bad news by Killian.

"Killianas has spoken extensively to me about Azoria in her student days," the former Arkon said, without preamble. "I have my own thoughts about that discussion, but it is not a discussion which Killianas can repeat; he can speak—with reluctance—to me because I am chancellor. He will not divulge information to anyone who is not. Even this discussion pushed him to his absolute limits."

Kaylin frowned and turned to the Academia's Avatar. "Why?"

"We are built for specific purposes. Students can—and should—expect privacy; if they choose to share information or elements of their lives and thoughts with their fellow students, they may do so. But if they have never shared those things, it is not up to me—a building created to provide a safe haven for students—to share them. It is not a matter of preference, Corporal. It is a matter of imperative. The only exception made was made for the chancellor. He is, for want of a better word, equivalent to a captain of a Tower.

"The situation is extreme; it is not every day that we lose the Keeper, and the consequences of permanent loss—or death—will affect every student and therefore every student's safety. Even so, there are boundaries, and skirting those boundaries has been difficult for me."

"Which is why you're covered in purple?"

Killian frowned. "Purple?"

"You seem to be shrouded in a black-purple smoke or haze."

Killian was surprised. He considered the question for some time, and then said, "Yes. Yes, I believe what you perceive with the aid of your familiar is due to the struggle against restrictions. Understand that I want to help. I want to offer the chancellor what he feels he needs, even if it is not clear to me. Living beings have much more flexibility than sentient buildings; the information that might prove of use is not clear to me. The chancellor wishes to have all information, all interaction, all my records, in order to assess; it is his assessment that makes the information valuable.

"I am reduced to working against myself and the rules that I was built upon; I work against the almost physical adherence. It is, and has been, taxing."

"And it is done," the chancellor said, voice uncharacteristically soft. "There is no further point in frustration or rage at your limitations. We all have limitations, Killianas. We are not measured by those limitations; it is in our attempts to understand them, accept them, and work with them that we shine."

The chancellor turned, indicating that the standing group should sit. As was usual, Severn and Tain chose to stand, Teela, to sit. Kaylin chose to pace until Hope squawked. She then took the chair next to Teela.

"Azoria was an excellent student. Her ambition—to start—was the gaining of knowledge; this much, Killianas could freely discuss; it was shorn of specifics. It was common and accepted knowledge which one might be privy to in discussions with the various people who taught her.

"But Azoria's private ambitions were not. She became a member of the Arcanum after leaving the Academia. That had been her intent before she gained entry here. Again, this was—or would have been—common knowledge. What was less common knowledge was her intent. We do not question intent if the students themselves are devoted to learning.

"Azoria had not yet become outcaste. She had not yet fallen so far afoul of the High Court that her political disposition was one of the very few that required all Barrani, anywhere, to kill on sight, if they had that ability, or to summon those who could if they did not."

Kaylin nodded. She knew Nightshade was outcaste—and that for the Barrani, outcaste generally meant having fallen afoul of the High Lord and his political faction. There were historical examples of Barrani who had been repatriated, although they were few. The Consort seemed fond of Nightshade, and he, respectful of her.

Kaylin knew what Azoria's crime had been. She wasn't certain any of the other Barrani did.

"I have Killianas's testimony. I have not yet spoken with Larrantin or the Arbiters. I believe it best at this juncture to attend them. Serralyn has gone ahead, and I believe Bakkon has been granted permission to enter the library at this time. The students are becoming more verbally restless at the shutdown, and it would be best to deal with this as soon as possible."

"It would be best to find the Keeper as soon as possible, yes," Kaylin snapped.

The chancellor's brows rose, and Killian actually winced. "An'Teela?"

"My presence in the library is not mandatory; it would nonetheless be appreciated. As you must suspect, the High Court has concerns. I am here as a Hawk, with the permission of the Lord of Hawks, but I have been asked to attend to this issue with extreme care and thoroughness by the High Lord and the Consort. The absence of the Keeper is of great interest to any caste court."

"Very well. I am sure the Arbiters will accept your inclusion if that is my decision."

Kaylin was less certain, but that fight was the chancellor's, not hers, and she really, really didn't need any more conflict.

Larrantin arrived at the office; his arrival was the signal to leave.

Killian once again led them to the doors that served as the library portal. He once again chose to shield the party from the student body, and his eyes flickered between their normal blue and the total black that outlays of power seemed to cause.

This time, however, the door "opened" from the inside.

Standing in the library were Serralyn, Starrante, Kavallac, and Androsse. No one looked happy. Not that Kaylin expected cheer and joy, but there were hints of anger in the gravity of their expressions, and Serralyn's eyes were as dark a blue as they got.

People filed in quickly. Kaylin wished Killian could join them, but he couldn't; the library wasn't part of the Academia.

"Terrano's not back," Kaylin said, meeting Serralyn's gaze.

Serralyn shook her head.

"But you heard something from him, found something connected to him."

This time, Serralyn's gaze went to Teela.

Teela shook her head and picked up the thread. "We didn't. Sedarias did, and she has Mandoran investigating; he's the only one who's almost as flexible as Terrano, and he's not nearly as reckless."

Kaylin thought Mandoran now repented his choice to remain behind. "Are any of you?"

Teela paused to consider. "As it is not relevant, I feel it wiser to keep my opinion to myself."

"She's worried."

"She is far more worried now, yes. Before you ask, we do not have any connection to Evanton; his whereabouts remain unknown. But it is reasonable to believe that any avenue to reach him—or Terrano—will be, or must be, found within Azoria's former abode." She lifted her chin and turned toward Androsse.

The chancellor said, "I have spoken at length with Killianas; it was a difficult conversation for him, and no further information will be forthcoming from that quarter. Larrantin?"

"I would prefer you begin," the scholar replied.

"Arbiters?"

"My preference would be not to speak at all," Androsse said. "Given the gravity of the situation, the three of us have conferred, and I have worked against my personal preferences for privacy."

Kavallac cleared her throat.

"But given our seniority," Androsse continued, "and given the restrictions on Killianas, we will start." Clearly this was akin to the royal we. "Azoria came to the library in her first year as a student in the Academia. Many of the students will seek out the library in later years, when their interest and academic focus have taken full shape. Azoria claimed that it was the knowledge that drew her; she had not yet decided on where to direct her focus.

"Indeed, she did not seem to have a single interest; she was interested in many things, and she researched them all with a depth seldom found in the student body.

"Serralyn previously found a book denoting ancient Barrani customs in the West March. We felt the book might be of interest given the subject of research; it was one of the tomes to which Azoria referred, and one that caused her research to grow in breadth as well as depth.

"She was interested in the botany of the West March, which included the more specific and less predictable botany of the green; she was—as are most Barrani who have yet to enter the green to bear witness to the *regalia*—very interested in the *regalia* as well. There was very little practical information about the ceremony, and the experiment with our young had not yet taken place." As Androsse spoke, books appeared on the table behind the Arbiters—a table Kaylin would have sworn wasn't there until the books dropped.

Teela responded to Androsse's opening comment. "The High Court believes that her interest in the green was more than academic; it is possible that her study of extant information about the *regalia* centered more on the power the green might bestow than the ceremony itself. We know, from conversations with her former slaves, that she was very interested in the rumored sword the green protected. Very little is known about that weapon, but it is offered to those who might have the capacity to wield it, should they pass the green's test.

"And that test is never passed," Androsse said.

No one corrected him.

"The Barrani do not share secrets when it involves power. There were historical wielders of the weapon; we have confirmation that the green offered a test; confirmation of the signs that indicated that the green considered somebody worthy of taking that test, and confirmation that those considered worthy failed to pass it." Teela also offered no acknowledgment that the green had selected someone it considered worthy of the blade. Or blades.

"It will not come as a surprise that Azoria was interested in those weapons; everyone was interested in those weapons to a greater or lesser degree. But it is our suspicion now that she had no interest in wielding them. I assumed that her interest in the botany had much to do with her interest in the weapons—and this is such a common interest, it was almost disappointing. She searched more broadly than most; she was stubborn. She did not believe anything was out of her reach if she put in the effort."

The hint of approval in the words did not please Kavallac. "Apparently you were correct. We can only be grateful that her reach exceeded her grasp."

"And if no one was intellectually ambitious, the Academia would have no reason to exist. Nor would the library," Androsse snapped, more heat in the words.

"We have plenty of intellectually curious and ambitious students—we always did. Serralyn is an outstanding example."

Kaylin winced on Serralyn's behalf; the Barrani woman's cheeks reddened the moment the Arbiter's words sank in. Her eyes were now a mix of blue and gold. What was gold again? Oh, right. Surprise. Gold was replaced by green, but the blue never left her eyes; worry about Terrano—and possibly Evanton—anchored that blue.

"While I agree with your assessment," the chancellor said, "Serralyn is only relevant to this discussion if we can reach an agreement about Azoria's intent and the knowledge that might have allowed her to act on it."

Androsse frowned. "I spoke more with her than the other Arbiters did, but I was not privy to those intents—whatever they may have been. She asked questions. She studied many things. I have mentioned the botany of the green, which I did not consider significant except in one way: I thought she might untangle that mystery, where other students spent more of their focus daydreaming about it.

"She expressed a strong curiosity about sentient buildings, and of course, as all Barrani of her age, the Ancients about which so little is known. It is not that research was not done—but that research had to be subtle or from secondary sources. None of the students—and I dare say almost none of the professors—had any interaction with the Ancients. Those that did encounter them had very little of use to say that expanded on our knowledge. We know the Ancients spoke in True Words. The Ancients created life, and also transformed it when the life created did not suit them. The reason for the lack of suitability was never made clear, possibly because it was not understood.

"Again, these studies were endemic among the students—Barrani, Dragons, even the mortals. There was nothing about the study itself that seemed dangerous or out of the ordinary; Azoria was, once again, more focused.

"Even her interest in True Names, and in the powers inherent in them, was not unknown. I cautioned her about this; too many of her kin attempted to remove themselves from their own True Names, considering their existence a very unfortunate vulnerability.

"And last, she studied what very little information we could provide about Necromancy."

"You're not going to tell us that that was normal, are you?" Kaylin asked. She tried to be polite.

"It is rarer, but it is not unknown. Most of the people who are interested in the study are mortals. The Barrani in their youth are not as concerned about death. Nor are they concerned about what happens after: they know. Their names return to the Lake of Life."

"Given the noninformation we received, I'm assuming she didn't get much further—I mean, she was only a student and we had three Arbiters looking. Right?"

Androsse's eyes darkened instantly. Kavallac's darkened as well, but not as much; she clearly didn't like Kaylin's attitude, but could accept that perhaps Androsse deserved some of it.

"She did not find information we would consider useful in this case, no."

"Or at all?"

"Clearly something she stumbled upon was of use, but I would guess that information would be in the Arcanum's records."

"You said everything eventually comes to the library."

"Upon the death of the individual, yes. But there are exceptions; if Azoria's books had arrived in the library, this entire conversation—such as it is—would be moot."

"We may have further word on the possible resources in the Arcanum soon," Teela said.

"Arbiter Starrante?" the chancellor said.

"She was very interested, as Arbiter Androsse has said, in True Names, but in specific True Names that became the source of life. She knew how the Barrani acquired their names—and felt some resentment at the lack of agency; she believed that Barrani should be allowed to waken and age like mortals did, proving themselves worthy of a name. Or dying of old age. Even the Dragons had agency the Barrani lacked."

"And the Ancestors?" Kaylin cut in. It was always safe to interrupt Starrante.

"Very little is known about how Ancestors acquired True Names, but yes—names were required." It was harder to tell when the Wevaran was looking at specific people because he had so many eyes, but she thought she detected a pointed glance in Androsse's direction. "She asked how Wevaran names were granted. I am certain she asked how Ancients achieved their names; she asked Arbiter Kavallac about the acquisition of Dragon names, but the Arbiter did not choose to answer.

"There were, however, younger students of Azoria's race on campus, and I am certain they were willing to discuss the gaining of names. All," he added, "were male."

"I did not choose to discuss our names with Azoria," Kavallac agreed.

Androsse was annoyed. Kaylin half expected him to vent his annoyance; he was practically vibrating in place. But even he understood the import of this meeting, and the consequences of failing to understand what Azoria had built. "I did discuss our names. I cautioned her as well: there is a reason that my kin faded, to be replaced, in the end, by the Barrani. Our True Names were far more complicated than her kin's. There was less danger of the knowledge of our names spreading; the will and intent to control was not enough to conquer the complexity of the names." He fell silent.

Kaylin thought there was more; she thought it was important.

Clearly, so did Starrante. This time, his eyes rose from his body and swiveled in Androsse's direction.

"Very well. The act of control mattered less to us because our acquisition of names changed with time. While we required True Words to live, we acquired the use of those words as we aged and gained both power and experience. We were not like Wevaran; we were not required to kill our infant siblings, if we had any. Our births were not like Barrani births. Many of our young could not survive the birthing process; they were warped beyond cohesion and recognition.

"You have your quaint caste courts. We did not. The elements of our birth were not decided by an impersonal, constructed container; they were decided by us. By those who claimed parentage. We could—and did—imbue spoken words with the element of immediate life, and we made of those words a blessing.

"Or a curse. We did not choose single words. We spoke as adults will, in sentences. Successful birth was a matter of trial and error. Children do not speak adult language at birth; not even ours. But we could understand the words we heard others speak. In time, we could understand the words we contained. They spoke to us, they spoke of us.

"Those who could hear, understand, withstand, could build upon the sentences that brought us life. We could add to them. We could, if cautious, change them, edit them, elevate their meaning.

"Many, however, were not cautious. In a few cases, the Ancients chose to end those lives for fear of the damage they might do to the rest of their creations." His smile was grim. "I was considered too cautious, too cowardly, by most of my immediate kin. But I survived and survive still. They are merely memories, their ambitions and folly forgotten."

"Did you explain to her how the acquisition of power—through True Words—worked?"

"I did. It was not relevant to her, or to any of her kin."

Kaylin exhaled. "It might not be. She couldn't imbue True Words with whatever is necessary to use them as part of a name. I don't think any of the Barrani can."

"No. That was not gifted them. It is bitter to think that my entire race was considered a dangerous failure, but perhaps facts cannot be argued against."

"But there's no physical place that you went to find these words?"

"We could speak them, Corporal. We gained words as we gained knowledge. Esoteric words were learned the way any language is learned by those who speak it. How do you contain language? How do you make, of speech, a hallowed ground?"

"Did Azoria study True Language?"

"She did. Most of the Immortal students—and some very few mortals—did. I believe the chancellor is capable of speaking in that language, although I am given to understand it is taxing for all who do."

Kaylin then turned to Starrante, frowning. "Your people are hatched in a clutch of a lot of little Wevaran."

"You may use the term *spiders*," Starrante told her. "When we speak of our young, we refer to those who emerge. Of our hatched siblings, we can say very little except that they died, and in death, imbued us with fragments of a word, a name. All of our existences culminate in a single name, and that name is what allows us to leave the nest. I cannot tell you how those partial words come to be; I cannot tell you whether or not they are, in their parts, fully words at all. If my memory is the memory of the Immortal, it is a memory that fully begins upon emergence. We did not perceive our siblings as siblings and we could not or did not see the animating force at their core.

"But the atmosphere within the hatching ground has a particular feel—a taste, a texture, a quality of air—that we viscerally remember. Perhaps we must, to give birth; perhaps it is an instinctive drive.

"Azoria was much interested in the circumstances of our birth. As she was interested in the circumstances of all Immortal births, this did not seem unusual to me. She was not the first of our many students to ask."

"Did you answer the others?"

"Yes. To me it is a simple statement of fact."

Kaylin frowned. "Bakkon didn't seem to think so."

"He believes I have been too long in the library, but also

understands that I cannot leave it. There is no retirement for Arbiters that does not imply death."

That was new information to Kaylin. "Bakkon felt that there was something in Azoria's manse that reminded him of the hatching grounds. Not by look—by look it is, or was, pure Barrani architecture—but by feel, by essence. It's the reason he wanted to return to examine the rooms in the absence of Azoria."

Serralyn nodded.

"Bakkon believes that his initial feeling was correct. In some fashion, Azoria created a similar environment, something that could mimic the hatching ground. He is anxious to return to her research rooms; he suspects that there is a reason she could perform such mimicry."

Kaylin frowned. "Reason?"

"Not all birth produces live children." Starrante's voice was grave.

"Some eggs, such as they are, never hatch. We do not have a geographic location in which we congregate to give birth."

"How do you choose where to give birth?"

"We choose a place that feels right. I am almost embarrassed to say I have no better information; Bakkon might."

"He does," Serralyn said, her voice uncharacteristically grim.

"Our race has reached its end," Starrante continued. "Our people are gone—all but a handful. There will be no more."

"Why?"

Starrante did not answer the question. When no words filled his silence, he said, "That is beyond the scope of your current duties. It is not a question Azoria ever asked of me. Had she, I would not have answered."

"Wait. You said you hatch, you crawl out of the birthing ground, when there's only one of you left."

"Yes."

"Hatch from what? Like, is there a giant egg, and all the little spiders are inside it?"

"That is the analogy, yes. It is very simple, it is easy to understand, and it is incorrect in any technical way."

"There's no physical egg."

"As you surmise. There is no physical egg. We are not breaking an eggshell the way your avians do; we are breaking the barrier that prevents us from entering the world itself. The eggs of which we speak are not visible eggs; they are not physical objects. But the laying of an egg requires the ability to create a pocket space, a dimensional reality. It is into that unseen space that the proto-children are injected. I cannot tell you how many of these spiders there are, and my guess is that the number differs depending on the complexity of the name they, combined, create.

"Nor can I tell you if the name itself is some component of our own names, broken and fragmented but nonetheless true shards."

"So where do the shards come from?"

"That is a question that Azoria did ask. I had no answer to give her that made sense to her as a student."

"Would it make sense to us?" Serralyn asked.

"It might make sense to Terrano, of all of you—but not without effort, concentration, and some academic focus on his part."

"So...no."

Starrante chuckled.

"It is possible that Azoria understood elements of the discussion; she was studious in a way that defines Terrano's studiousness. But if Bakkon feels that Azoria's home—or the part of her home that was not the area in which she conducted the majority of her research—had the same air, the same feel, as the birthing place, she had attempted to create a similar environment."

"You think she thought she could introduce people with True Names to the environment and then consume them somehow?"

"In essence."

"All of the people in that house were mortals. Dead mortals."

"So Serralyn has informed us. But you are Chosen, and the cohort is Barrani."

"She didn't exactly invite us in." Kaylin's frown deepened. "We know she could possess people. She could also influence them magically, possibly by inducing hallucinations. But possessing people isn't part of the Necromancer kit, or at least not the ones in stories. And it isn't part of the stories you brought to us.

"Pushing the people who owned those bodies essentially killed them. Until the moment she did that, she could entrap their bodies. She also finally figured out how to entrap the spirits—and transform them. But none of those victims had any hint of a True Name; none of their spirits were the necessary fuel for power that she sought. I'd bet a year's salary on it."

"Azoria did not research the names of mortals; she understood—as we all do—that they are born without names. The value of True Names can clearly be seen in their absence; mortals age and wither in a handful of decades. Without the name to sustain them, they have lives akin to the beasts."

Kaylin tried not to find this offensive. She mostly succeeded.

"It was not of relevance to her research at the time. But she must have done some experimentation in the time between her student years and now. It is clear that she could possess the bodies of mortals when you encountered her. I am far less certain that she possessed the bodies of her own kind in similar fashion."

Kaylin's frown deepened. "I'm not certain she didn't try," she finally said. "Given the number of dead, trapped Barrani in her private quarters in the High Halls. But she could and did drain all power from their names. I'm not certain that draining power in that fashion empowered her in a permanent way. I mean, I don't think she was somehow making their names hers; she was simply sucking all life out of them."

"How can you be so certain?"

"She didn't build the birthing place in the High Halls. She did have connections to the outlands, but those connections relied on the lack of awareness of the High Halls; it was after the High Halls shut down around the Shadow that had invaded. There was no connection, at that time, to the green. If you're thinking that she was attempting to create an environment in which True Names could be devoured—by Azoria—and result in a True Name that Barrani bodies were never meant to contain, I agree. I think that's what she was trying to somehow build.

"She knew True Words could be absorbed into Androsse's people. She knew that their bodies and her kin's were almost materially the same. There wouldn't seem to be a good reason—to Azoria—why she couldn't become what Androsse himself was."

Starrante's eyes swiveled instantly to Androsse, their color far redder.

Androsse's smile was a thin edge; it almost glittered in the library light.

"What did you tell her?" Starrante demanded, multiple clicks, light stutters, between the Barrani syllables.

Kaylin exhaled. "I take it you lied."

18

Androsse's smile deepened. Kaylin had never cared for Arbiter Androsse, and that neutrality crystallized into strong dislike. "I did not lie, Corporal."

"You led her to believe that your physical bodies were materially the same as a Barrani body?"

"In a broad context, we are. But our construction, as you have clearly guessed, is different. It is a pity that you could intuit this where she could not."

"I could intuit it because I've had to fight your kin before," she snapped. "And I saw where they fought, and how. They weren't only rooted in my world; they were rooted across at least three different planes. At the same time."

"You fought my kin?" The Arbiter's voice lost its edge. "And you survived? I almost do not believe you."

"Almost?"

"You are a very simple mortal; were you not Chosen, you would be beneath notice."

Really, really disliked him.

"And it was not a lie in the sense you believe it was. You must also acknowledge that."

"How?"

"You know Terrano. You know Mandoran. And you know Serralyn and Valliant. They are not what they were born to be; they are flexible in a way that the Barrani were created not to be." His smile was now a slash of anger. "What lives knows change. What lives must know change.

"You are mortal. Your changes are multiple, and they occur so quickly, were you to attain immortality, you might reach out to challenge the Ancients. Azoria had that ambition: to become more than she had been created to be. To reach beyond the world the Ancients made to contain us."

"And if she destroyed the rest of us in the attempt?"

Androsse's eyes were narrow, almost glittering. Kaylin felt the hair on her arms begin to rise; her skin started to ache.

Hope sat up and squawked, leaning forward.

"Should we care, little mortal? Should I care? Almost all my kin are long dead, buried beneath the wave of the wrath of our creators; do you think that destruction touched only us? No. The Ancients were willing to destroy what they had created if it meant we ourselves would be stopped. Only some handful were spared, and even we were transformed, frozen in time, immutable and unchanging.

"You have divined that Azoria inferred, from our many conversations, that there was little difference between her kin and mine. She was curious, focused, ambitious, and perhaps I felt embers of nostalgia. Perhaps not.

"But why should I care for the creations of the Ancients when the Ancients themselves abandoned us? Why should I be concerned when the Shadows destroyed entire worlds, with no action from the Ancients, no attempt to preserve them? Think you that your lives have more value than that of an entire world?"

"Without life," Kaylin said, voice swamped a moment by Hope's squawking, "there would be no knowledge. There would be nothing new in your library—everything would come to a halt. The library would become a relic, a forgotten storeroom of history; if people don't exist who can come to the library, if people can't read its books, what's the point? Why did you even become an Arbiter?"

The brief flare of magic receded. Hope, however, was leaning forward, as if at any moment he might lunge at Androsse. Kaylin reached up and curved a hand around his legs to prevent it. Hope was a familiar, and she was certain she hadn't seen everything he was capable of—but Androsse was an Arbiter, and this library was the seat of his power.

"That is perhaps the first intelligent question you have asked today," the Arbiter replied. "I have been Arbiter for a very, very long time. I was the first. I was one of the survivors of the purge; I and a handful of others. We are not what you are. We were never what you are. We are not like Barrani, or even the Dragons with their very narrow mutability.

"Barrani are not what we were; we are called Ancestors for a reason. What we were given to alter ourselves, to transform ourselves with time and effort, the Barrani were not given—as if the Ancients loved us only as children, as immature versions of ourselves.

"Not all our choices were wise. Not all our choices were safe. Some choices killed my brethren, and some transformed them beyond all recognition. But some became powerful, Corporal. Some could reach the shoulders of their creators. They were of us, but they were no longer us.

"How could I not understand what she wanted? Hobbled by her physical body, limited in ways we were not, she nonetheless desired to transform herself. To reach for those heights, even if none were there to see it, to take the hand with which she reached out.

"Your friends have done the same thing, in very different ways."

"We did not," Serralyn said, her voice steady but low. "We

never wanted what she wanted. We never wanted what your kin wanted. We wanted freedom to be what we were. We wanted each other's company."

Androsse said, "Now, you must speak for yourself. What you want—you who revere our library—is not what your friends want."

"Because we're not the same people. But that was always the thing we prioritized: each other. We don't want to hurt people who aren't hurting us." She glanced at Kaylin then. "Or who don't want to hurt us."

Kaylin had no intention of speaking about their attacks against the Consort—and possibly all of humanity. At base, Serralyn was right. Terrano had become the key to open the door that would let them live outside of their permanent, sentient prison—and when the door had opened fully, they stopped those attacks and severed their questionable alliances.

Of course their families—especially Sedarias's—might disagree.

"Very well. I did not discourage Azoria. But as the corporal suggests, I did not speak of the history of the Ancestors. I do not wish to use my people as some sort of childish morality play. Had I discouraged her, she would have simply ceased to speak frankly.

"And, Corporal: I failed to answer the question I deemed intelligent. I was the first of the Arbiters chosen. I am the only Ancestor chosen as Arbiter. I believed, as many of my kin did not, that these traces of history deserved—perhaps needed—to be preserved. Here, there is proof that worlds long destroyed once existed; that research of value was conducted by every race on any lost world—and is conducted by any race on worlds that survived.

"Here, that knowledge is not destroyed; it is not consumed. And here, the seekers of knowledge might find all matter of information, should they desire to find it. There are times when

I consider retirement; it is students with Azoria's drive that remind me of the reason I accepted the request of the Ancients to become a steward, a guardian, of this growing collection of words and languages. But I am not like you, Corporal. I am not like any of you.

"It is the spark, the drive, the burning ambition that justifies our existence at all. The Arbiters Starrante and Kavallac will have different reasons for their tenure here—and different definitions of responsibility. We are not—as I'm sure even you perceive—of one mind; it was because we were not, and would not be, of one mind that we were chosen.

"And it is because we are not, that you may find some answer about the goal Azoria struggled—and failed—to achieve."

Kavallac was red-eyed; it was clearly a conversation that would have caused a deafening argument between at least two of the Arbiters.

The chancellor cleared his throat. He might have roared, but there was already one distinctly angry Dragon in the room; if she had little effect, his input wouldn't change anything.

Instead, he began to speak. "According to Killianas, Azoria was obsessed with the Lake of Life when she arrived at the Academia. There was, in her family—as in many Barrani families—pressure. Everyone wanted the Consort to come from their family line; the perceived power would elevate even the most minor of families.

"She was not considered a suitable candidate, but another family member was. This did not work out. She had considered a marriage alliance, but could not find one that suited her; Killianas believes no eligible Barrani would. Her interest in Arbiter Androsse was less academic than ideal—but she was the woman she had been raised to be: power was compelling.

"Being trapped in a library for eternity was not. She was pragmatic. But she became very, very interested in the genesis of Ancestral names. In Barrani history, many men and women of power sought freedom from the vulnerability, the weakness, of the True Name, to great ruin, for themselves and those around them. They sought to remove themselves from their name."

Androsse nodded. "Azoria understood that my people gained power with the acquisition of words, but the words were not our weakness. Should one of our kin know our name—an analogy—it could not easily be used to control us; our names evolved. Our lack of Barrani weakness was not because we divested ourselves of the essence of our lives—it was because we expanded upon it, building sentences, paragraphs, poetry that could not be spoken with the will and power to grant another command of us.

"What she did not—or could not—understand was that that option was not available to her. Not at that time. Tell me, Corporal, what did Azoria look like when she died? Did she look Barrani at all?"

"You already know the answer."

"I do. But were Terrano to join you in the library now, neither would he. I have never seen Valliant take a different form. I have never seen Serralyn do so, either. I am certain An'Teela does not. And yet, I am equally certain that they could, should they desire to do so. Do you believe it was her form that defined her?"

Kaylin frowned.

"If she had one flaw," Androsse continued, "it was her vanity."

In Kaylin's opinion, she'd had a lot more flaws than one. A lot.

"She desired to be more than she was born to be. It is a common desire. Did you not, in your childhood, desire the same?"

Kaylin shrugged. "I don't care if she wanted to be what Terrano is. I care that she murdered dozens of people—of at least two races—to do it. It's not my job to tell people who they should or shouldn't be. It's my job to tell them what they should or shouldn't *do*."

"Very well. Azoria failed. But she clearly found tools that could have pushed her across the boundary of failure into success." Androsse turned to Starrante. "You believe that Azoria found a fallow birthing space, for want of a better word."

"Bakkon suspected it; his recent visit confirmed that suspicion."

"And she built her house in it?" Kaylin was surprised, and shouldn't have been.

"If you were under the impression that her manor was a mortal building, you are mistaken," Androsse said, frowning. Kaylin guessed that *mistaken* was not the first word that had come to him. "The acquisition of her home and the building of it imply that this fallow space was discovered recently."

"Those spaces are not easily moved."

"Can they be moved with difficulty?" Androsse asked the Wevaran.

"I would have said they could not be found—or moved—at all."

"The flower from the green couldn't be grown outside of the green, either," Kaylin pointed out. She exhaled. "What we now have is a set of assumptions. Azoria found an...extradimensional egg. She moved it. She used something that was contained in the egg as the atmosphere in which she built her manor. We don't know if there were actual Wevaran in the fallow egg."

Starrante's eyes instantly rose in a wave across his body.

"They might have all died, right?" Kaylin asked. "If they hadn't, the egg wouldn't be fallow. There would have been a Wevaran baby."

The Arbiter said nothing, his eyes waving like a field of bloodied stalks in a gale.

Kaylin's frown deepened. "Could the hatchlings survive if

they couldn't devour each other? They don't seem to need food the way our young do."

"Not enough is known. We remember the struggle to become, and we emerge. Our accounts, our studies, are always written by those who did. Some of the eggs don't hatch. It's possible that instead of one being emerging as the strongest, there are two, and the number of siblings each devours is even. If that was the case, it is possible that proto-Wevaran could exist in an unhatched egg. I remind you that the egg analogy is simple because it is wrong."

Kaylin nodded. "If she found almost-Wevaran in that environment, could she devour the partial names?"

"I am not at all certain it would have the effect it would for our own immature young."

"Which is yes?"

"Biology was not my specialty," Starrante replied, his eyes slowing their frantic wave, although they didn't return to his body. "But theoretically, if she was within the birthing space, she could."

"And if that was the case, she would consume or subsume the partial words?"

"Corporal, this is so theoretical it is not worth the paper it is written on."

"Fine. I'm not going to ding you for accuracy. We want to know what you all think she intended. Killianas and the two Arbiters had the advantage of knowing her in person." She then turned to the only other member of the Academia who could make the same claim.

Larrantin had been utterly silent. Barrani skin was naturally pale, but there was an almost blue tinge to the Barrani scholar's, as if he had been holding his breath so long he was nearly dead.

"Azoria was very skilled with advanced portal magics; she excelled in placement of portals; she could work with the smallest of openings, bypassing physical restrictions the rest of my many, many students could not."

"What does that mean to the layperson?" Kaylin asked.

"If one of the other students had to place a portal, they required the unencumbered physical space in which to work. Azoria could place a portal on the other side of a thick, large door if that door had a keyhole. If it did not, but it had hinges, or small spaces between door and frame, she was also efficient.

"It was a skill I did not have mastery of in the same fashion. She was astonishingly perceptive, and her certainty in her skills was unshakable. Her ability to create portals has not been equaled since—or during any part of my tenure. It is a distinct possibility that she could find an 'egg' and move it.

"She felt constrained in the life she led; she loved the Academia but resented it in equal measure. She wanted the freedom to truly do her research. But yes, her interest in research included the nameless. If she began to research the dead, she did so after she had graduated.

"Not once in her tenure here did her study focus on the deaths of the Ancients. Chancellor?"

"Killianas also said, among her many ambitions and complaints, the death of an Ancient was no part of her studies."

"There would be very little to study," Androsse added.

"Given the direction of her early experiments—after the shutdown of the High Halls, but before she was made outcaste—it's unlikely that she had, at that point, discovered the Ancient in the outlands. Had she, her focus would have grown to encompass it.

"The deaths of the mortals whose...ghosts you found in Azoria's home appear to have happened very recently."

It wasn't recent by human standards, but Larrantin was Barrani. Kaylin didn't correct him.

"This would pin the discovery, in my opinion, to a short period of time before that."

"Short by Barrani standards."

"Of course. It is clear that she knew how to draw power from the outlands in a similar fashion sentient buildings such as Killianas do. It is clear, at this point, that she desired to amass power from True Names. If the Arbiter is correct, she wished to create a space in which she could predate on those names.

"But in her search, she stumbled onto the corpse of an Ancient. I find this difficult to believe, but I accept it as truth, given the Keeper's involvement and concerns.

"The Ancient, being dead, could not be so easily moved; I would guess that she tried, and failed. The container that she created was a glass; the Ancient, an ocean. What I do not understand is the concept of death. The Ancient that you freed from its captivity—and yes, I have received a report to that effect from Killianas, whose restrictions on privacy extend to members of the Academia, not visitors—could speak with you; they could effortlessly use the outlands to create. They were not, in any sense of the word that any of us understands, dead.

"But it seems clear to me as well that Azoria could not communicate with the dead. The Ancient was bound in some fashion; you freed them from that binding. Before that, you could not bespeak them, either. And so, she searched for a Necromancer. Or perhaps, she attempted to create one. Mrs. Erickson's mother worked as a servant for Azoria before her pregnancy; she worked in that capacity during it.

"I highly doubt that the proliferation of the dead Azoria had collected was in any way visible to Mrs. Erickson's mother. But Mrs. Erickson may have been subject to Azoria's attempts to create, to grow, the power she needed."

Kaylin frowned in Larrantin's direction, although it was a thinking frown. "You believe her talent wasn't natural?"

"I cannot say that with absolute certainty. I would need to know far more about Mrs. Erickson's parentage. It's highly probable that Azoria knew more about Mrs. Erickson's lineage than we do. She may have taken the risk of augmenting, or attempting to augment, the child in utero; it would be far simpler."

None of this sounded simple to Kaylin.

"I would suggest you ask Mrs. Erickson if her mother ever had a miscarriage—I believe that's the correct term?"

"It's not the type of thing mothers usually discuss with their children."

"If she doesn't know, she doesn't know. If she does, and if there were, that would give us information."

"Not information about the environment we want to enter."

"Kitling."

Kaylin glanced at Teela, but Teela had turned to Larrantin. "Corporal Neya is substantially correct. While I would be in favor of making the inquiries you suggest, they do not address the safety of a second excursion. The most helpful information or suggestions you might offer would be those that focus on the environment. We understand that we are dealing with guesswork, but given the minds involved in those guesses, we will treat the information with respect."

"You cannot assume that Mrs. Erickson is not fundamentally part of the design," Larrantin replied, obviously displeased.

"How, then, does the answer to that question aid us in determination of the possible threats?" Teela did not back down.

The chancellor watched them both.

"It is possible that the entire space is, or was, a work in progress. Understand that Azoria was not master of her experiments—by nature, experiments deal with the unknown. I believe Bakkon and Serralyn have a way to enter only the laboratory, bypassing the hall entirely. Were I to join them, I would focus on that.

"The notes that Azoria kept there might answer some of the questions we now have." He then turned from Teela to the chancellor. "If our opinions matter in your decision, that would be my choice. If, of course, Serralyn is willing."

Serralyn looked to the chancellor. He nodded, as if the glance was a request for permission to speak.

She cleared her throat. "This is what I understand. The hall was built, in part, on the detritus of a fallow hatching space. It's possible that it was created as an attempt to kill those who possessed True Names in order to devour those names and make them part of her own name going forward.

"If such a space wasn't to collapse once the partial names became a full one, she needed a way to keep that space open. I think—and I'm not a scholar or an expert—the power to do that was rooted in the outlands. I'm uncertain that the power that came from the green was used for that purpose. If it was woven into the structure of her home, and its purpose was to grow plants that couldn't be grown outside of the green, it shouldn't be dangerous for those of us who aren't plants."

"Unless the green is aware of the intrusion," Androsse said. "If Azoria was foolish enough to create such a connection, she was doubtless wise enough to obscure or hide it."

"Not all enchantments end with the death of their creators."

"No. But the green is wild, unpredictable, and dangerous. Were I to attempt what she attempted, it would require constant supervision."

"Would you have attempted it?"

"No. None of my kin would have dared. The green is quiet now; it is contained. But in our time, it was a wild, dangerous force. There is no guarantee that it will not or could not become such a threat again. I see no advantage to such a connection. The anger of the green was not easily assuaged. The world has changed, and perhaps that is no longer the case."

"Evanton said the Keeper's garden had been disturbed," Serralyn replied. Her voice was soft, her tone hesitant. "But that disturbance began before Azoria's death. If her attempt to hide the connection relied on being alive, that disturbance wouldn't have been felt so strongly in the garden."

Androsse's nod was reluctant.

"But the dead Ancient in the outlands, and the persistent connection to that location, seems the more likely cause. If she had discovered the Ancient recently, she may have focused all of her effort on somehow subsuming the Ancient's power. None of us understand how that power works. All we know is that it could change the world. If she interfered somehow with that, and she strengthened the channel between her home and the corpse..." Serralyn waited for interruption. There wasn't any.

"Evanton vanished when he touched the portal that existed between the manse and the outlands. But the Ancient in the outlands, according to Kaylin, wasn't inactive. The Ancient considered themselves dead—but dead people don't speak and interact in a purely physical way. Kaylin broke the bindings around the Ancient's corpse the day Azoria died.

"I think the changes, the instability, in Azoria's home are entirely due to the Ancient, or what's left of the Ancient. And I think Azoria wanted Mrs. Erickson desperately because she felt if she possessed Mrs. Erickson's body, she could command the Ancient for as long as Mrs. Erickson's body survived."

Kaylin frowned and lifted a hand.

Serralyn immediately turned to her, obviously relieved.

"Azoria kidnapped children—and killed them so she could use their bodies. She was desperately trying to find something that had, I believe, been given to Mrs. Erickson's mother. Some piece of jewelry. She didn't limit herself to children, but her attempt to use their bodies usually ended up in the bodies being executed. Before you ask, no, I have no idea where that item might be found. I suspect she meant it to somehow enhance her control of Mrs. Erickson.

"Since that didn't happen, her plans were stymied. But while Mrs. Erickson remained alive, she still had some hope she could find the item."

"Have you searched for it?"

"When I don't know exactly what it was? I suspect, as I said, it was jewelry, and it's quite possible it was pawned. Her family wasn't exactly rolling in money. Mrs. Erickson doesn't recall it, and it's very possible it was never worn. But Azoria was trying to find it using enchantments and compulsion very recently."

"Attempt to find it," Androsse said quietly. "If Mrs. Erickson was the linchpin of this plan, it might tell us what we need to know about the current iteration of Azoria's halls."

Kaylin shook her head. "The current iteration of her halls is the Ancient. And possibly, through the construction, the green. But the halls were changing as we ran out of them. I'm almost certain that the changes were imposed at a distance by what remains of the Ancient. It's what the chancellor suspects."

The chancellor raised a brow in Kaylin's direction.

"Am I wrong?"

"You are not wrong. It is most of the reason I am extremely reluctant to send Serralyn back to them."

"We're assuming that communication from the lab area will be limited," Teela said. "We therefore want the person sent to have access to the most immediate knowledge. We could communicate when Mandoran was in the halls proper; Serralyn was very muted."

Kaylin cleared her throat. "We split up when we entered her abode. We lost Evanton and Terrano when the hall was flooded by light. I have no idea what the hall will look like if we attempt to enter it again. But I think we can communicate with the Ancient."

Teela's eyes became indigo in that instant. "Absolutely not."

"I haven't even started yet."

"Please. Your face is an open book. You were about to suggest that you go into the outlands to talk to the Ancient again."

"The Ancient was grateful to me. I might be able to use gratitude as a bargaining chip. Whatever else happens, we need Evanton back. I still think Terrano can get out of wherever it is he's stuck—and he's got as long as he needs. Evanton might not, and if there's no Keeper, the rest of the world is going to suffer."

"You assume you can talk the Ancient into returning the Keeper to us."

"I think it's worth a shot."

"And if you are unsuccessful?"

Kaylin shrugged. "Then I'll be stuck with Evanton and Terrano."

"Or dead."

Kaylin exhaled. "Bakkon and Serralyn will be safe. If they can unearth more of Azoria's research, they can figure out her intentions. We're obviously going to spend some of that research time figuring out both the outlands connection and the connection to the green. But we don't want to break the outlands connection until we can get Evanton back."

"And the green?"

"I don't think the connection was meant to serve the same purpose. But Bakkon and Serralyn can probably figure that out."

"I would like to accompany you," Larrantin said.

"As would I," Teela added.

Kaylin's intention had been to take Severn with her, if he insisted.

I do.

She couldn't control Teela. Teela's *As would I* was pretty much a command. She turned to Larrantin. "Do you intend to accompany Serralyn?"

"I intend to accompany you, should you attempt to communicate with the Ancient."

The chancellor cleared his throat. "You have classes," he told the scholar.

"Which may or may not be relevant if the world becomes an elemental storm. Azoria was my student. I cannot see what she created from the Academia, but if I walk in her halls, I may understand—in a way the Hawks will not—how she used my lessons and my expertise." He smiled; it was thin. "Surely the choice is mine?"

The chancellor exhaled.

Kavallac exhaled as well, but there was steam in hers. "You want to see the Ancient."

"Yes. But as the Ancient is no doubt part of the entire enchantment, there is good reason for my curiosity."

She snorted. "Chancellor?"

"Very well." He then turned to Serralyn. "You have permission, but it is granted with grave misgivings. Were it not for the urgency of this particular emergency, I would not grant it at all."

19

Serralyn smiled at the chancellor, green returning to her eyes, although blue remained the predominant color. "This place is incredibly important to me. I know it's not as important as it is to you—but it's probably as close as a non-Dragon can get."

To Kaylin's surprise, the chancellor smiled, his eyes losing some of their red. "I know. While Terrano is not technically a student—and I would never approve any application he chose to make—I admit my grudging tolerance of his presence has grown into a thorny affection. Go, and return safely."

She closed her eyes briefly. Opened them again and nodded.

Kaylin did not get told to return safely but didn't resent the lack; she was a Hawk here.

"Corporal Neya," the chancellor said, as if he could hear the thought. "I expect that you will not take Bellusdeo with you, unless it is imperative that Mrs. Erickson also attend. I consider both of their presences to be unnecessary at this stage; until some determinations have been made, the risk is too high.

"Lord Emmerian, however, can serve in her stead, should the strength of a Dragon be required." He turned to Emmerian.

Emmerian, silent as he almost always was, nodded. Kaylin

had always been surprised by Emmerian's ability to disappear in a crowd; it was a knack she didn't have, even when she forced herself to keep her mouth shut.

The chancellor, half glaring in Kaylin's direction, continued. "Lord Emmerian is not a member of the Academia in any fashion. We are both, however, servants of the Eternal Emperor, and I have known the Emperor for a very long time.

"Arbiters, we will take our leave of the library. Should there be information of note uncovered after our departure, please send immediate word."

The three Arbiters nodded. Starrante placed one limb on Serralyn's left shoulder, as if he wanted to physically hold her in place. He hadn't argued with the chancellor's decision, but it was clear his reservations were far stronger.

Then again, Starrante—a being whose existence depended on his ability to devour his siblings—had always been the softest of the Arbiters. Serralyn briefly touched that limb, patting it as if it weren't chitin. "Bakkon isn't you," she said, voice soft, "but he's far more accustomed to shepherding mortals and keeping them safe. He lives in the Tower of Liatt."

"As you are not a mortal, you should be far easier to protect." Kaylin thought his attempt at reassurance was actually meant for himself, not Serralyn, but Serralyn nodded as he let go of her shoulder.

They returned to the chancellor's office. The room was a slightly different shape, but this was explained by the appearance of Bakkon. Given the color of the Wevaran's eyes, Bakkon was not in a great mood. He clicked his way through a few sentences, and then readjusted his language.

"My apologies. I've been speaking with my kin in Liatt."

Serralyn nodded.

"Have you received the chancellor's permission to return?"

"She has," the chancellor replied, before Serralyn could. "Understand that she is almost as valuable as Liatt's heir."

"Yes. I understand. Starrante has made this *quite* clear. If Serralyn is fatally injured, I will have to avoid visits to the Academia for the foreseeable future."

Serralyn winced but smiled. "I'm sure he'll understand."

"Oh, so am I. He will understand I have utterly failed in my most important charge."

The Barrani student laughed then, her eyes shifting in color so that they were almost entirely green.

The chancellor cleared his throat. "Bakkon, there will be, as happened the first time, two different exploratory parties. You will, once again, be with Serralyn, and you will return to the research area, where you will attempt to uncover information about the elements that comprise the external halls.

"The three Hawks—"

"Four," Tain said.

"The four Hawks, then. The four Hawks, Lord Emmerian, and Larrantin will attempt to find Evanton and Terrano."

Kaylin nodded. Hope squawked.

The chancellor frowned, no doubt at Hope's commentary. "Very well. Bakkon, we require you to follow your thread back to the research area, but you must create a portal that everyone can use. Hope feels it is safest to enter the rest of the manse from the research area; he is not certain that Mrs. Erickson's front door will open to Azoria's former abode. Evanton understood some of the enchantment, and he could manipulate it to gain entry; I am not certain that anyone present can accomplish that."

Larrantin coughed.

The chancellor ignored him.

Bakkon clicked, the sound slight and rhythmic. "Yes. Yes, I can do that. But if the door cannot be safely used, and they cannot return to the research area, they, too, might be trapped."

"The door works from the inside," Kaylin told the Wevaran. "Or it did when we left; it's how we escaped."

"And if it does not?"

"Then we'll have to find another way out." She folded her arms.

"Kitling," Teela said. "He has not refused the chancellor's request; he merely wishes us to be apprised of the possible danger. I am certain the chancellor understands that we are Hawks and adults, but should anyone be that risk averse, they may remain here." Her tone implied that no further conversation or debate was necessary. Or acceptable.

The chancellor agreed.

Bakkon therefore exhaled—loudly—and began to spit webbing. Kaylin had seen this before but still found it disturbing. The Wevaran said he was connected to Serralyn for the duration of this investigation; she wondered if the connection, established the first time they'd entered Azoria's manor, had persisted. If it did, Serralyn wasn't uncomfortable with it.

Bakkon had left strands of Wevaran silk in the lab; he could follow that back or create a portal round it. He did this, lifting his forelimbs as if to anchor what he'd woven in place. "Step through," he told them all. "I will close the portal when you've reached your destination." To the chancellor, he added, "I will not take the risk of leaving the portal open; I cannot confirm that the protections in place in the research area will hold."

The chancellor nodded. "You can, of course, return without it."

"Yes. And I can bring Serralyn with me, as we will be together."

"Lord Emmerian," the chancellor said.

Emmerian nodded and went through the portal. When no immediate sound of alarm or combat came back, Teela and Tain entered; Kaylin and Severn followed. The portal was one way—Kaylin could turn and see a brightly lit room at her back. And Larrantin, who arrived before she'd fully turned.

When Bakkon appeared, Serralyn was on his back.

"Are you certain you will not remain to sift through her papers and spells?" Bakkon asked the scholar. Larrantin looked torn. "It is likely to be faster with your expertise."

"I believe my expertise, such as it is, might be of value in our attempt to find and retrieve the Keeper," Larrantin finally replied.

Bakkon accepted this. "We found an entrance from the hall we traversed—it was not the hall in which the Keeper's examination was conducted. There is no reason why that entrance should not work. Come, I will take you there."

Azoria had clearly been careful to protect the area in which she had crafted the theories she put to use from the experiments themselves; Bakkon's lead was slow, careful, and frequently interrupted. Hope stood on Kaylin's head; he'd abandoned the lizard-shawl position when they'd entered the library and remained on high alert. Larrantin conversed with Bakkon, usually when Bakkon stopped to test the air—or the enchantments Kaylin could only barely perceive on the floors or walls. In other words, everything. Larrantin, not exactly a font of patience, had pretty much chewed through all his by the time Bakkon found the exit, such as it was.

"I want you to be careful," Bakkon finally snapped.

"Not everyone present is Immortal," Larrantin snapped back. "And the world without marks mortal time. We do not have the time to examine every tiny detail on the way—that is your duty, not ours."

"It is not the details here that will doom you." Bakkon's voice grew louder, more grating. "What rules, Larrantin? What rules bind the dead?"

Larrantin's lips were compressed, his eyes an irritated blue. "The dead have no need of rules."

"The dead are everywhere in Azoria's space. You did not feel it; you did not see it. The dead are present, and they demand respect. You are reckless, rude, inconsiderate at best, but you are accompanied by those who are not. I ask that you step with care, speak with care—if you speak at all; I would not recommend it."

"And will you have all communication borne by children?"

"No, Larrantin. By the Chosen. It is my opinion—and we have so little research with which to confirm it—that this dead, this Ancient, speaks and wakes because of the Chosen, for good or ill. An Ancient's power is not a power that is meant for us. Do not touch it."

"Can we leave now? I am no longer a student in some inescapable class, and we are very short on time."

Bakkon's eyes were red and in motion, but he walked toward one alcove—there were eight—on the curve of the wall. He paused in front of Kaylin, his forelegs passing above her head in a brief, sharp dance. "Do not get lost. But if you do, if you cannot prevent it, stay still; I may be able to find you."

"Bakkon," Larrantin said, the two syllables almost an angry shout.

Bakkon growled. It was a very low sound, but unbroken by the usual clicks. Lifting three of his limbs, he began to trace a pattern in the air; Kaylin's arm hair instantly stood on end. She could see a shimmering between the two smaller pillars that punctuated the alcove. Ugh. Portal.

"Kitling."

Kaylin had said nothing and tried not to resent the correction. Portals nauseated her, but she used them when it was necessary; it was necessary now.

Teela cursed in genial Leontine and held out a hand. It was

empty. "Take it," the Barrani Hawk said. "We don't want to lose you in transit."

Oh. Kaylin felt like a foundling, didn't like it, and accepted it. She took Teela's hand. Emmerian then passed into the portal. Larrantin followed. Teela dragged Kaylin through, leaving Severn and Tain to pull up the rear.

Kaylin had forgotten how much physical contact with someone real eased portal passage. She was immediately disoriented as she entered—she expected that—but because Teela was an anchor, she could close her eyes. Portal space wasn't one thing or the other; it wasn't consistent. Had it been, she thought she could have trained herself to endure it. But no. Sometimes it was very much like the gray, roiling clouds of the outlands; sometimes it was like walking into the chaos of Shadow; sometimes it was like a blurry landscape, where every single element was subtly wrong.

It was the almost real objects that were always the worst; they held the outline of a familiar shape—a building, a road, a harbor—but not the constant solidity; outlines blurred, or worse, the interiors of the shape, as if they were bleeding their essential nature onto the path she had to walk. They moved, unanchored, coming to rest before leaping away; she became instantly dizzy. At best.

Is this taking longer than usual? she asked Severn, her eyes closed.

Severn's reply felt fuzzy, and attenuated. *It seems to be.* He didn't ask how she was holding up; he knew. She clutched Teela's hand tightly.

Chosen. Chosen, come. I have been waiting for your return.

That wasn't Severn. It wasn't any of her namebound, most of whom had been remarkably quiet in the past weeks.

Severn? Severn—did you hear that?

I heard it because you heard it. I did not hear it myself. "An'Teela, hold on to her. Something is speaking to her here."

She heard the words echo, reverberate, become sharper with each iteration.

CHOSEN.

Kaylin stumbled; the ground beneath her feet became suddenly, treacherously soft; she sank into it up to her knees. Teela didn't sink beside her; the angle of the hand crushing Kaylin's rose as Kaylin fell. Leontine followed as Teela pulled Kaylin up—or tried.

Severn would have grabbed her free hand, but he could no longer see her.

She opened her eyes. She could see Teela, but Teela seemed to be spinning in place; she was shouting in slow motion, but her words were so distorted, Kaylin couldn't make sense of them.

Squawk! Squawk!

The marks on her arms were glowing and rising through the cloth that habitually covered them. She closed her eyes to better study them; she'd always been able to see the marks with closed eyes. She couldn't pronounce them; couldn't discern their meaning without the combination of pressure and effort. But when they were spoken, she could recognize the language.

She heard it now: loud, deep, a throng of deliberate syllables. It took her a moment to realize she also recognized the speaker's voice: Emmerian. Emmerian was intoning syllables of a True Word.

The ground released her; Teela pulled her up, and she found her footing, but had very little chance to steady her feet. Teela began to sprint, pulling Kaylin, stumbling, behind her.

Emmerian roared again, draconic voice enwrapping syllables that she felt almost as a physical blow. Teela put on a burst of speed that Kaylin thought would dislocate her arm, and then she landed on solid ground.

She opened her eyes immediately. Emmerian had transformed; he was a blue Dragon, his head raised. Larrantin hadn't transformed, but he was glowing faintly; his eyes were so dark they looked black. Tain and Teela sported the regular variant of dark blue. Severn offered Kaylin a hand up; when he did, Teela let go.

Kaylin's hand was numb.

"What," Larrantin demanded, "were you trying to do?"

"Walk through a portal," Kaylin replied, the words a bit clipped.

"That is not what you were doing!"

"It is what she believes she was doing," Teela said, before Larrantin could continue. She turned to face the Dragon. "I believe your intervention allowed her to complete her passage."

Emmerian nodded, lowering his head to look down at Kaylin.

Squawk.

Or to look down at Hope. Emmerian roared in his native tongue; Hope replied in squawks, which clearly meant more to the Dragon than they did to Kaylin.

She turned to Hope. "Talk to him farther from my ear."

Hope bit her ear, but not hard enough to draw blood, as Kaylin's vision finally cleared.

To Kaylin's surprise, the rough shape of a hall had been maintained. She could see what she thought of as a foyer in the distance; the hall was wide, the ceilings intimidatingly high. Beneath her feet, however, the floor had given way to dirt, and the half pillars of marble that punctuated alcoves had been replaced by trees. Trees the color of marble, although to touch, they were bark.

She blinked several times and turned to her partner. Forgot what she was going to say when she saw he'd armed himself with the weapons that defined him in Barrani eyes. She never asked about the weapons and didn't ask now. Severn thought they would, or could, be necessary. She didn't really need to know more.

Hope didn't relax; he hopped across her shoulder, neck stretched; she half expected him to jump off and transform. These halls were wide enough to contain the larger, draconic form—but maybe two would be pushing it. Emmerian was still a Dragon.

"I am astonished," Larrantin said, as they began to walk toward what had once been a foyer, "that your companions treat this occurrence as if it were mundane, normal weather. Do you have no training at all?"

"Training in what?" Kaylin countered, annoyed. Teela wasn't giving her the stink eye, but long acquaintance with the Barrani Hawk made clear she would have, if Larrantin hadn't been condescending first.

"Magic," Larrantin snapped, in the same tone of voice he might have said *breathing*. "As it is, you are a clear and present danger to any who happen to be in your vicinity. What did you think you were doing?"

"I told you—crossing a portal."

Larrantin didn't bother with the mask of professional Barrani neutrality; he was incensed. As Kaylin was clearly far too stupid to carry the full weight of his ire, he turned to Teela. "Could you not have offered warning to those of us who have some mastery?"

"Kaylin has always had difficulty with portals." Teela *did* speak as if she were talking about the weather. Her tone was deliberately polite. "It is not entirely predictable, and I consider it a win that she is not now retching her last meal all over my feet."

"An'Teela—you cannot be so ignorant as to assume that this is normal!"

"It is normal for Kaylin. We are uncertain that this difficulty did not arise from the marks of the Chosen; to our admittedly poor knowledge, humans have never been granted the marks before."

"Mortals have not."

"They have," Kaylin snapped, thinking of the Tha'alani. Thinking, and keeping that exception to herself.

"Before the marks—"

"I lived in the fiefs. I was an orphan. Do you think there were portals just lying around that I could walk through?"

"You have never walked through a portal without the marks, then?"

"No."

"Do you know what the marks entail?"

"No."

Larrantin exhaled for a long damn time. "No more do I. But you were attempting to traverse something that was not the portal path."

"Not on purpose," Kaylin finally said.

"That is what education gives you: control." His tone was supremely waspish.

"I heard words," she told him. "My marks were active."

"They are always active."

"They don't look active to me. But when they activate, they're either gold or blue. They were gold on the path." As Larrantin opened his mouth, Kaylin lifted a hand. "No, I can't read them. No, I don't know what all the words mean. The only conscious control I've always had over their power is healing."

"Healing?" Her lack of respect didn't bother Larrantin in the slightest, which made him different from almost every other teacher she'd been given.

"Healing."

"That is a very rare talent."

Kaylin shrugged. "It's the power of the marks. I never had the ability before them."

Kaylin, Severn said. *Be careful now.*

Of what? It's not like everyone doesn't already know.

Of Larrantin. He is now making connections between pieces of information we can't necessarily access.

What information? What could he possibly learn that wouldn't help me understand these marks?

This is not the first time you've encountered the dead. It isn't the first time you could see, sense, or communicate with them.

She nodded, thinking of Jamal.

Jamal, too. But you destroyed an object in the former Arkon's library because you could sense the dead somehow trapped within the object. You could free it. He exhaled. *You felt, in that moment, that it was to finish his story that you were granted the marks of the Chosen. If the marks don't make you Mrs. Erickson—and they don't—something in them allows you to see, to interact, with some of the dead who are trapped.*

She acknowledged his point about the armor in the Arkon's collection; she'd almost forgotten about the ghost who was trapped within it. Her marks had freed him. Or Kaylin had. She had told the end of his story. Had finished it. That was all he needed to be free. *I think anyone could have interacted with the Ancient.*

Perhaps. But, Kaylin, you woke him. Larrantin will assume that it is the power of, the purpose of, the marks. Try not to catch more of his attention.

Lannagaros isn't going to let him experiment on me.

No. This doesn't preclude Larrantin trying, regardless.

She fell silent—at least on the outside. *Why have you never said any of this before?*

I've always trusted your instincts.

My instincts aren't telling me to shut up, though.

I've always been cautious when they're absent. She felt the hint of a smile that never touched his face.

I can see that, she replied, giving his blades a pointed stare.

Is that why you drew them? Did you mean to make Larrantin uncomfortable?

I note that they haven't.

Fine. But they're bothering Teela and Tain.

Severn offered a fief shrug.

The lead, such as it was, was taken by Emmerian, although Larrantin pushed ahead to walk by the Dragon's side. Larrantin had been trapped in the suspended world of the Academia for so long the Draco-Barrani wars had not affected his life; he had no issues with a Dragon chancellor, or a Dragon compatriot. He did have some issue with the disrespect the young showed their elders, evidence of obvious social decay—which Kaylin only knew because he had no difficulty telling Emmerian exactly that.

Emmerian, accustomed to Lannagaros and Sanabalis, accepted the criticism without apparently being affected by it at all. Kaylin envied him that.

It was Larrantin who paused beneath the first of the great trees; there were two, but beyond them, others grew in disturbingly uniform rows. The two great trees rose in towers that met in a confusion of boughs to form an arch. Kaylin froze.

"Emmerian—stop. Don't take another step!"

Between the trunks of the standing trees, she could see something dark and glittering, a miasma that reminded her very, very much of Shadow.

Emmerian stopped. Larrantin turned back to look in Kaylin's direction.

Can you see what I see?

Severn nodded. *I see what you see only because you're seeing it, and I have access to it.*

"Teela—can you see anything beyond these two trees?"

"More trees," Teela replied. "What do you see?"

"It looks, to my eyes, like the Shadow version of the outlands—it's a dark miasma, with glints of color."

Teela's eyes darkened. She glanced at Tain, who shook his head. Cursing loudly enough to be heard, the Barrani Hawk joined Larrantin.

"I do not see what the corporal sees." He gestured and spoke a sharp word; Kaylin felt it like a full body slap. He repeated this another four times. "I see the ground—it is similar to the ground over which we've been walking. I see more trees—but *trees* is perhaps not the correct word. None of my detection spells can see what she sees. If she feels this is like Shadow, she is incorrect."

"How so?" Kaylin asked.

"When Shadow threatened us all, magics were developed that might detect subtle incursions. Shadow was endlessly inventive, and endlessly evasive; our spells required both research and time to develop. We lost a fair number of scholars to such practical research.

"It is not much taught in the modern age, and it is possible that everything I know has become hopelessly outdated. The Towers were created to evolve their detections and protections, because Shadow was so transformative. Regardless, if Shadow exists beyond these pillars, I cannot see it. An'Teela?"

"I didn't have your training, but something's off in the space."

Larrantin frowned and turned to Teela; he froze in place. "What are you doing to your eyes?" he demanded.

"A trick of Terrano's. I am being coached through the minor transformation, but it does not come as easily to me as it would to almost any of the rest of my friends. Terrano does it constantly; it's his way of being aware of differences in phases or planes that intersect ours."

"And you can survive this."

"Demonstrably."

"So it is true, then. You were one of the twelve exposed to the *regalia* in your childhood."

"I have never attempted to deny it," Teela replied, her tone of voice distinctly chilly. "I believe Kaylin to be correct in her description, except in one way. It's not Shadow."

"Why are you so certain?"

"What she saw, she's describing accurately: it looks like a dark outlands. I have no sense that it's sentient or alive."

"Or dead?"

"Or dead," Teela agreed.

"May we proceed?" Emmerian asked, his voice a rumble.

"Kaylin?"

Kaylin desperately wished Terrano were here. But one of the reasons they'd come was to find him. "Are you comfortable with letting me go first?"

"No," Teela replied.

"It seems wisest," Larrantin said. "Given that she can see clearly what you can barely detect, and the rest of us cannot detect at all."

"We almost lost her to the portal passage," Teela snapped. "I don't intend to lose her to landscape. Something is looking for her."

"It's probably the dead Ancient," Kaylin offered.

Larrantin frowned. "I believe we must come up with a different term."

"For Ancient? God?"

"For dead in the case of the Ancient. Death has meaning to the rest of us."

"It has some meaning to the Ancient as well—I believe he thought of death as the end of purpose. Something like that. He said his purpose had been fulfilled." She frowned.

"Do you believe the dead Ancient attempted to speak with Azoria?"

"No. No, I don't. I'm pretty sure Azoria thought of the Ancient as dead in the usual way. But she was aware of the power inherent in the Ancients, or aware of the words. And the words persisted."

"They were the foundation of language, the true tongue. Of course they persisted."

"But..."

"But?"

"If they persisted, if they're eternal in some fashion, how can they be spoken? I mean, when the Ancients spoke, did their spoken words become new iterations? Were there hundreds and thousands of the same True Word just popping into existence?"

"Almost certainly not," Larrantin said.

"Almost?"

"We did not speak with the Ancients as they spoke to each other. It is possible that they were an amalgamation of the words they contained; that they could not bespeak each other with any ease at all. They were gods, Corporal. Who among us can understand their minds? They created worlds."

"Worlds have—or had—words."

"That is the theory, yes. And perhaps they contained not words, but word: something far more complicated, far less accessible, than the names handed down to Immortals over the passage of time."

Kaylin frowned. "I'm not sure about that. I think the ancient mirrors were created with their blood—and their blood contained words."

"At another time, I will ask you why you believe that. Now, however, I wish to know whether or not you believe you can scout ahead without being lost."

Severn said, "She can. I'll go with her."

Teela shook her head. "I'll go with her if it's necessary; I think it's a terrible idea. If she must separate, she can still communicate with you."

"You don't have the weapons of the green," Severn replied, not budging.

"You intend to use them?"

"If necessary, the chain can serve as a rudimentary binding. If she gets lost, I'll be lost with her."

The two Hawks, Severn and Teela, stared at each other. Kaylin glanced at Tain; Tain shrugged. Neither she nor Teela's partner were willing to join the silent argument. Kaylin was going to scout ahead; the details could work themselves out.

Coward.

Always. I think it was you who taught me that.

You could end up with both of us, which means Tain will follow.

I don't think so. Teela respects those weapons; because you own them, she assumes you know how to use them. The Barrani ascribe almost mystical powers to the weapons of the green.

Betting?

Sure.

"Kitling, you'd better not be placing bets."

Or not. How did she know?

You have a very expressive face, especially when you think you're going to win.

Teela turned her back—pointedly—on Kaylin. "Fine. You're far more cautious than Kaylin is capable of being. Do you want the Dragon?"

Kaylin shook her head. "I have Hope. If necessary, Hope can go full Dragon. I don't want to risk Emmerian unless we think it's safe."

Emmerian nodded. He really was unflappable; being talked about in the third person didn't bother him at all. The only person who caused dents in his self-control seemed to be Bellusdeo. Kaylin was grateful that Bellusdeo had remained with Mrs. Erickson; she imagined the hall would be full of arguing draconic roars, otherwise.

Bellusdeo would not stay behind if Kaylin was going; Emmerian would not stay behind if Bellusdeo was going—which was guaranteed to cause the gold Dragon to lose her temper.

She wondered if Dragons ever had peaceful, quiet relationships, but doubted it. She shook herself free of the thought and stepped through the arch formed of two towering trees, Severn by her side.

20

To Kaylin's eye, the ground was, visually, very much like Shadow, but it felt like packed dirt beneath her boots. Severn saw packed dirt unless he looked through Kaylin's eyes. "Hey," she said to Hope, "could you sit on Severn's shoulder and cover his eye with one wing?"

Squawk. The tone of voice made clear the answer was no. But Hope lifted one wing across Kaylin's right eye as she turned to look back over her shoulder. The arch hadn't disappeared, and she could still see her companions gathered around its opening, watching as she and Severn walked.

Here, there was light—like sunlight in its fall, but without any obvious source. Branches of great trees shadowed the ground, but almost in reverse: the ground where their shadows were cast became lighter, not darker; the path in the shadows of those branches became the color of beach sand, not dirt.

Through Hope's wing, she could see what Severn saw; through the wingless eye, she could see darkness with flecks of color. Her marks were glowing, but the color was odd: it was mostly green, edged in ivory. Usually gold or blue were the dominant colors when the marks were active. But the marks hadn't risen from her skin; if there was something they could interact with, she hadn't stumbled across it yet.

It was just strange that it was Hope's wing that revealed what everyone else could actually see. Why was her own vision so different? Was it just the effect of the marks of the Chosen?

That would be my bet.

What do you think the marks are trying to make me see? I mean, what am I looking at and not seeing clearly?

I don't know. But you saw Jamal clearly. You saw the Ancient. I'm betting Azoria tried to interact with the Ancient, to no success.

Kaylin nodded. *I'm almost certain that was why she was desperately trying to cultivate Mrs. Erickson. Because Mrs. Erickson could command the dead.*

She could, yes. In theory she could also stab someone who wasn't careful. I think the latter more likely to happen.

I don't know. If Azoria could have gotten ahold of the children, if she could have realistically threatened them, I'm not sure what Mrs. Erickson would have done. I don't have the ability to command the dead. If I have the ability to see them, it doesn't give me much else to work with. She frowned. *The marks gave me the natural ability to see Jamal and the rest of the children. That's it. But the marks didn't interact with the children in any way beyond that.*

And with the Arkon's collection?

She nodded. *There, I could interact. The marks on my arms rose as I did—not all of them, but some of them. Those marks*, she added, *are gone now. Human life doesn't depend on True Words. Human death doesn't affect the status of True Words because we don't need them to live.*

But you have a True Name.

It was true. She did. So, too, Severn—one she'd carried from the Lake of Life for him. *I don't need it, though. I mean—I need it to talk to you like this. But even if I hadn't given you a name from the Lake, you'd still be able to talk to me as long as you knew mine.*

If you die—if I die—I'm almost certain the names will go back to the Lake of Life.

And until they do, will we live forever?

Squawk.

I don't think that's how it works. We weren't born to contain them. We weren't born to need them. If it worked that way, there'd be more Immortals who'd been born human.

If the human caste court knew of the fact of your name, of your possession of it, it would cause a war—not a small one, either. His tone was grim.

No Consort, no Lady, would grant a living adult a Barrani birth name. It would never happen.

The Lake allowed you to take the names.

The Lake probably wanted a High Lord who wasn't controlled by the Shadow at the heart of the Tower. No, she added, before he could ask, *I don't think the Lake is sentient the way we—or the Barrani—are. But there's enough of a will in the Lake that it chooses the Lady. It chooses the mother of the race.*

The way the green chose a wielder of its weapons.

Kaylin nodded. *I think the Lake had to choose to allow me to take those names. It's why the Consort considers me a backup Lady. Anyone who knows that I can do this is probably horrified at the very idea: a Barrani brought to wakefulness by a mortal. Had I been Barrani, there would have been a fight for control of the Lake—by the families of those granted the ability, not those who could. But no one is going to attempt to unseat the current Consort if I'm what they have to deal with.*

Still, the Lake recognized something in you.

Kaylin nodded. *Don't ask me what—I don't know.*

Severn smiled. *I think I can guess.* He paused as Kaylin came to a stop. He always matched his pace with hers on the streets they patrolled together; this felt no different.

She looked at the trees she could see clearly through Hope's wing. Severn saw those. What he didn't see was the black glow that surrounded them. She could almost hear it crackling, as if it were produced by persistent, dark lightning. She looked at the ground between the paired trees; the shadows that light cast didn't exist here.

"This might be a problem," she said.

And the trees said, *Chosen.*

Severn reached out for her shoulder—the one Hope wasn't standing erect on. To do this, he had to sheathe the blades he carried—or sheathe one of them. She'd never been certain how the weapons functioned.

Kaylin hadn't spoken, but knew he was listening through the name bond that two mortals shouldn't have. Listening to her, listening through her, probably even watching through her eyes. She could feel the sudden weight of his presence. The weight of his hand was almost trivial in comparison.

She exhaled. "I'm here. I'm listening."

Come. We have been waiting for your return.

"We?"

Your companions disturbed my rest. I would not have noticed them had you not awakened me. I notice them now. I notice too many things; hear too many voices. Some are almost familiar.

Severn's hand tightened.

"What do you want of me?" Kaylin switched into High Barrani as she spoke. Her voice sounded normal to her ears, but the voice of the dead Ancient did not; it was almost more of a physical sensation than it was a sound; her body reverberated with the spoken syllables.

Come, Chosen. I am waiting, and he is waiting. I do not think he can hold on for much longer.

There was no threat in the words; Kaylin's fear made them louder and far darker. She wanted to ask him who might not be able to hold on for much longer. She didn't. She knew.

"Can you let him go?"

I do not detain him. I sense something about him that is like, and unlike, you—you are Chosen, he is not. But he serves an ancient purpose; I can almost sense the imperative. It was not mine. Come.

Kaylin swallowed. "Another friend followed the one of whom you speak. Is he also with you?"

The Ancient didn't answer.

"I cannot come alone," she finally said, lifting a hand to briefly cover Severn's. "The path is difficult for me to traverse."

It is not. You sought the wrong path. You did not respond.

"I cannot come alone, but I will not try to reach you if you will not accept my companion."

Hope squawked up a storm; Kaylin had to lift a hand to the ear beside his tiny working jaws. She didn't know if the Ancient could hear Hope the way he could hear her. "Two companions," she said. "One is my familiar—I don't know if you know what a familiar is."

No response. The black crackling mass that had outlined tree branches grew larger, darker, and much louder.

I think we have to trust him, Kaylin said.

I don't. But we don't need to trust him to do as he requests.

I don't think trust matters. It would be like trusting a hurricane or an earthquake. Trust wouldn't make a damn bit of difference if we were caught up in either.

"We will follow the path you've created," she said aloud. She pulled Severn's hand from her shoulder and adjusted her grip, holding on to him as if he—or she—were a foundling.

He raised a brow.

Mandoran once told me that I perceive different planes of existence when my marks are active. It all seems solid and real to me—but when things become strange, I'm actually traversing layers; I just don't see it that way, or feel it that way. He could follow me—but he sees things the way Terrano sees them, not the way I do.

Severn nodded.

So I just want to hold on to you to make sure you actually come with me.

I know.

She turned to look over her shoulder. She could see the trees they'd passed, but they seemed to extend for as far as the eye could see; she couldn't see the companions she'd left behind. She was almost certain Larrantin would follow if he suddenly lost sight of them; they hadn't walked far.

But the landscape was the Ancient's. What had begun in the halls that had swallowed Evanton and Terrano had continued after everyone else had fled. What she saw without Hope's wing was the Ancient's landscape.

Before Kaylin had freed the Ancient, he'd been trapped in the small section of the outlands Azoria's painting transcribed.

After, his influence had clearly begun to bleed into Azoria's home. On their previous visit, the shape of the halls, the placement of the foyer and its stairs, had remained relatively fixed; the appearance was different, but the structure had been similar.

That was clearly no longer the case.

"Can you think with me for a bit?" she asked Severn, as she walked.

He nodded.

"After Azoria died, Mrs. Erickson made us walk through every square inch of the area. She could see the dead trapped in service to Azoria, and she wanted to free them all. She didn't want any of them to be left behind. I didn't tell her about the dead Ancient, because to me, he wasn't very dead.

"But I've been thinking about this hall since then. Azoria could see the dead while they were in this hall, in this part of the manse. She could see the children here. Could give them commands she expected would be obeyed. When they came here, she could see them. When their bodies were alive, I believe she could see them as well, even if they weren't in her home.

"But once their bodies died, she couldn't. Jamal discovered this because she visited once or twice. He was—they all were—

terrified of Azoria. With reason. Jamal was a smart kid. He figured out that she couldn't see them in Mrs. Erickson's house. But she could see him when he came here. She could trap him here.

"Something about this space—the space she created—was made for the dead. While she was alive, she could entrap and contain most of them, even the Ancient. But the Ancient was in the outlands, not in her mansion, and the only way to reach him was the portal she'd created in that giant self-portrait. The portal served as a connection. I think part of the power she utilized came from the words, the names, that existed in the Ancient, even after his so-called death. So she couldn't cut it off or seal the entrance; she needed a persistent connection." She glanced at Severn.

"Do you believe her ability to handle the dead was something she learned, or do you think it came from the Ancient's power?" He surveyed the area as he spoke.

"I'm not certain. It's clear that she meant to possess Mrs. Erickson because she wanted command of the dead Ancient. But I'm not at all certain being dead somehow granted the Ancient any specific power. It's just...dead doesn't mean the same thing to Ancients as it does to the rest of us."

"You think she constructed this hall as a containment for the dead, a way of holding on to some essential part of what they'd been in life?"

Kaylin nodded. "Does that sound stupid?"

"I wish it did. Do you believe that her specific construction allowed the Ancient to seep into these halls and remake them?"

"That's my fear now, yes. I wish I understood what death means to Ancients—but Larrantin didn't know, and I'm pretty sure we won't get answers from the Arbiters, either. Just a lot more questions. I think Mrs. Erickson could speak to the Ancient; I don't know what she would see. Helen believed that shamans existed to help free those trapped in our world after their deaths. I just don't know if there's much of an after for an Ancient."

"You're worried."

"I am. The ghosts that rose from the altar in the bowels of the Imperial Library didn't look like ghosts to me. They looked, with effort, like words, trapped in the mirror and bound to it until the moment Mrs. Erickson entered the room. They possessed Sanabalis. Had Mrs. Erickson not been able to reason with them, I'm not sure they'd have let him go.

"But she could. She sees them as people. As humans. She doesn't see them the way I do—and I could barely manage to see them at all. I know she finds it exhausting to tend to their fear and their anger, but she can. What she sees isn't what anyone else sees; I'm not sure anyone else could.

"I don't know if she'd see the Ancient in the same way. Azoria was somehow banking on command, on control—but I'm not sure Mrs. Erickson would have that, even if she tried."

"And you don't want her to try."

Kaylin shook her head. "In an emergency, maybe. Azoria was dead the moment we cut the connection between her and the Ancient. But dead, she was still present, still mobile, still very much a danger. And Mrs. Erickson wouldn't attempt to stop her because she'd made that promise to Jamal. She wouldn't break it—even at great need—without his permission, and he gave her permission to do it once. He's gone. I really don't think she would even make another attempt.

"She doesn't command the dead she's rooming with. She talks to them as if they're people. She reasons with them. She calms them because, on some level, they can trust her. I don't think she could do that with the Ancient; the Ancient is perfectly capable of reason."

"You don't want her to try."

"I don't want to put her through that. Look, she's old, and she's lived her life in service to dead children. I want her to have some kind of life of her own, some kind of peace, while she's still alive. And it's not as if she only has the ghosts from the library; she has Bellusdeo's sisters—and Bellusdeo herself. If there's anything she can do—in the normal way—to help Bellusdeo, she'll do it. But I don't think she'd command the dead sisters, either. If she tried, I'm not sure what Bellusdeo would do."

"But you think the ghosts in the library and this Ancient are somehow related." It wasn't a question.

Because it wasn't a question, Kaylin couldn't move words around in an attempt to avoid answering it. She nodded. "I just think it's so unfair. She wasn't even born when she first encountered Azoria; she was a child when Azoria began whatever spell it was that's embedded in the family portrait. She didn't have a normal life—if it weren't for her parents, I'm not sure what would have happened to her. Her parents," she added, voice softening, "and the four kids."

"You're afraid she's necessary here."

"Aren't you?"

Severn shook his head. "The dead have never attempted to harm Mrs. Erickson—with a single exception. If she's needed, I think she'll be as safe as anyone else."

Kaylin didn't agree, but she had no time to argue; they had reached the end of the row of trees; the last two formed an arch, and beyond it, the floor shifted, from the black, cloudy murk she could see without Hope's wing to something that was almost its opposite: pale, almost insubstantial clouds with glints of sparkling color. It was the color that formed the continuity between the two floors.

Through Hope's wing, she saw grass. Grass, and, growing to the side of a footpath, flowers. Familiar flowers.

Hope dug his claws into her collarbone, as if bracing or anchoring himself. Kaylin winced but said nothing; she understood that her familiar was both alert and worried. The flowers she could see were pale ivory, but in shape they were similar to the flowers that had adorned Mrs. Erickson's hair in the portrait Azoria had painted.

Flowers that grew nowhere but the green. "Can you see the flowers?"

I see them.

Do they look like the flowers Mrs. Erickson wore?

They do. He stopped walking and attempted to free his hand; Kaylin tightened hers. He accepted the constraint and sheathed the second blade. He then reached out to touch a flower. He made no attempt to pick or uproot it. *It's the same,* he said, voice flat.

She didn't ask him how he was certain; she accepted that he was.

He rose, and once again unsheathed one of the weapon's blades; she could see the chain extending from the hilt. In this light, it did not look metallic; it looked like the very essence of the color green, but brighter, almost too bright to look at.

Mrs. Erickson had said that she couldn't look at Severn's waist for long without squinting—which the old woman clearly found rude. Kaylin wondered if this was how she always saw it. The light was the same brilliant color through Hope's wing.

Azoria did have some entanglement with the green, with the essence of the green. Severn's voice was grim.

Kaylin couldn't see the flowers with her own eyes. She could only see them through Hope's wing. Severn and his weapon were clear when viewed through either eye, but the flowers didn't exist without Hope's wing. She could see the outline of the path they walked, but it was blurry, inexact. If something grew here, it grew in the folds of those clouds.

He fell silent.

This path, through grass and flowers, opened up as they reached its end—or its beginning. In the distance she could see two figures; one immense—as he had been the first time she'd encountered him—and one so diminutive she might have missed him had she not been looking.

Evanton.

She sped up, half dragging Severn; he adjusted his pace. Hope was rigid.

"Go to Evanton," she told her familiar. "I've got Severn here. I can see what he sees if I try hard enough."

Squawk.

"I mean it—Evanton has to survive this. If it's something you can't do without a sacrifice, name your price. I'll pay it."

That is not wise, Chosen.

She looked up as the figure turned toward them.

"If we lose Evanton, we'll lose the world. There is no replacement for him. The people I care about, the people I'm responsible for, live there. I'm willing to pay Hope's price because the alternative is the loss of *everything*. Hope. Go."

Hope squawked like a localized storm before pushing himself off her shoulder. He flew toward the Keeper, and as he did, he grew, shifting from the tiny winged lizard into the much more majestic Dragon. His form remained translucent.

I have not harmed your friend, the Ancient said. *He has harmed himself and continues to do so.*

She picked up speed, dragging Severn into her pace. She was afraid to lose him here; he wasn't afraid to be lost. She slowed as she reached Evanton; Hope towered above him, standing between the Ancient and the Keeper as if he intended to be a wall.

Evanton didn't look in her direction, but his words were definitely meant for Kaylin. "It is about time you arrived." His tone was waspish, but weak.

"What are you trying to do?" she demanded.

"What I do in my garden," he replied. "This being is not unlike your Devourer."

"*So* not mine."

"The Devourer sleeps the sleep of the exhausted. It dreams, and its dreams cause fluctuations in the elements; they do not sleep, but they can hear his dreams when they grow turbulent."

"And this being is like that?"

"No, not in that sense. It is more subtle than the Devourer, but it is newly wakened. By, I assume, you."

"I didn't waken him—I freed him. Azoria had him bound."

"It was a captivity of which he was only peripherally aware. You do not understand the Devourer; no more did I when first he entered my garden. But he could not devour the garden; it is not that kind of place. Look around you, Kaylin. Understand what this small space is, what it signifies."

"I don't see a small space. I see…flat mist. Fog. It's like the outlands. But the land surrounding it or leading to it…that was like Shadow to my eyes."

Evanton frowned. He looked up to meet Hope's eyes, each almost the size of the old man's head. "An interesting observation," he finally said. "I see grass. I see flowers. I see something akin to sky above the head of the Ancient. You are not looking at the land in which I stand. I invite you to do so immediately."

She would have argued, but Evanton's exhaustion wasn't feigned. She looked, far more carefully, at the ground upon which Evanton was standing.

Or in which Evanton was planted; she couldn't see his feet. She could see that he wore the robes of his office—robes that he seldom wore in the store, but often donned in the garden. He hadn't carried them with him when he'd arrived at Helen's, but now wore them, regardless.

She knelt to examine the ground more carefully.

The marks on her arms—the ivory-edged green—began to rise; as they did, their light brightened. She hadn't seen this color before, but it blossomed in the area Evanton occupied. The colors reminded her of the flowers that Severn had identified.

Yes, he said. *It is almost an exact match.* His tone was neutral; she could sense his growing worry.

She regretted the absence of Hope, but couldn't call him back now. The marks that rose from her skin rose in a wave, becoming fully dimensional; she felt them as a weight. It was almost a struggle to lift her arms. She could feel the back of her neck growing heavy in the same way. The marks there were also rising. Rising and growing in both size and subjective weight.

Chosen.

She recognized the shape of the marks, although they looked different when given a third dimension. She didn't know their meaning; the Arkon had implied that careful study of the tongue of the Ancients was beyond the span of her life. Even his knowledge, having spent centuries in study, was meagre; he could decipher words, could even, with will and intent, speak them—but he could not speak them as he spoke his mother tongue, or any of the languages Kaylin knew.

All of her understanding was instinctive, just a grade above frantic and baseless guesswork.

But she understood on some level how to use the powers of the marks—she had used them to heal, to save lives, even when she'd lived in the fiefs. The marks hadn't glowed then. They hadn't come to life the way they now did. She hadn't needed to know them, to understand them; she'd only needed to understand the injuries she sought to heal. That had been a miracle: that she could see, feel, and understand what needed to be healed in order for a person's life to continue.

She had resented the marks. She had hated what had become of people she knew in the fief of Nightshade. But she had taken the healing power that had come with the marks as compensation. She couldn't remove them. She could—and did—hide them; she'd become so used to hiding them she wore long sleeves even in the privacy of her own home.

But this wasn't her home. In this space, before all of these people except maybe Severn, the marks were not a terrible secret; they weren't the cause of unjust murders; they weren't a curse. They were part of this odd space, this hidden world, this place where a dead god stood and spoke before a man who had once, many, many years ago, been human, as he attempted to keep an Ancient constrained.

Kaylin had never asked Evanton what mysteries, what ceremonies, conferred the responsibility of a Keeper; she had never asked him why he had chosen to become the Keeper. Maybe he'd had as much choice in his position as she'd had in hers: marks of the Chosen had appeared across half of her body without her conscious leave.

But he was what he was, and he was good at it.

And she was what she was: Chosen. She didn't know what that meant—or what it had meant to the others who had borne these marks. She didn't know if they had used them as intended. At first, she hadn't asked because she hated them; she hadn't cared what use was made of them. But as time passed, as she accepted their existence, she hadn't wanted to know. She was uneducated, poor, an orphan—things that people already looked down on.

She couldn't help but be certain that she was doing it all wrong. That smarter people, people with families, people with education, would have been a better choice. Anyone would have been a better choice. The healing, she grew to love.

But it wasn't only healing that she'd done.

She'd once, at the age of thirteen, skinned a man alive—without restraining him first, without a skinning knife or a dagger or any other weapon. Just rage, murderous rage. It had caused a lot of trouble for Teela and Tain, and that trouble had extended to the rest of the Hawks—of which she wasn't, in any official way. Not then.

Healing was better.

Healing would always be better. If there was desperation and panic involved in healing, there was no rage; she was in control of her power; her power was not in control of her anger.

Here, she felt no anger. The marks rotated, growing in size until they couldn't possibly fit on her skin. *Can you see them?* she asked Severn.

I can. Through your eyes, they're quite impressive.

And through yours?

They're flat against your skin, as always, but they're glowing.

The same colors as the flowers from the green?

The exact same colors, yes. What do you mean to do?

I don't know. The usual. Wing it. Can you see Evanton's feet?

I can.

I can't. But I think Evanton has made use of the malleability of the environment to create a space, a patch of land, that conforms to the rules of his garden. It's not his garden—that's probably why he's exhausted. But I think the Ancient understands some part of what Evanton is trying to achieve, and he accepts it.

Severn didn't ask why she believed it; Evanton was alive.

I don't suppose you see Terrano anywhere around here?

He wouldn't remain in a space that's meant to contain him, Severn replied. It was meant as a comforting possibility. Kaylin understood and didn't argue, but she didn't feel particularly comforted.

She didn't have time to worry about Terrano, even if she had the inclination; the ground beneath her feet began to rumble—no, to undulate—as if it were both solid and liquid simultaneously. She looked up to see Evanton; his face was a mask of focus and concentration, his hands clenched in fists by his sides.

Hope said, *Hurry, Kaylin. Whatever you intend to do, you must do it as close to now as possible.*

21

The marks that she saw as large, floating runes began to shudder in place; it took her a few seconds to realize their movements matched the tremor of the ground beneath her feet, beat for beat. Hope, translucent, seemed to become almost attenuated, the lines of his body that were clear and hard softening, as if he would be absorbed by the outlands in his entirety.

Hope roared, a note of disgust in the sound. Kaylin swallowed, understanding his meaning: She was to focus on the Keeper. Not Hope.

She let go of Severn's hand; she thought he would remain with her. She was no longer going anywhere. If Mandoran was right, if she walked between planes without realizing that was what she was doing, she'd meant to take him with her as she walked. But this was where she had to be, and he was here.

He unsheathed both of his weapons; they seemed almost transparent, but the chain that bound them wasn't. He then turned to Hope, to Evanton, planting his feet firmly in the space that they occupied. He didn't approach the Ancient, that towering giant who seemed, standing as he did above Evanton, like a world unto himself.

Evanton's feet remained submerged in the pale, gray loam, and he struggled to maintain his footing.

No, she realized. Not his footing. He was struggling to maintain his control over the miasma of potential that was the outlands. She wondered, for the first time, if the elemental garden was formed from the same material. It would explain what Evanton was now doing: he had control over some element of that potential because the garden was necessary, and the garden required a Keeper.

What she didn't understand was the presence of the green.

Severn's certain identification of the flowers she couldn't see without Hope's wing made clear that somehow the strands Azoria had woven so delicately and carefully so as to draw power of some kind from the green—without also drawing attention—had altered. Maybe the connection required control, and Azoria, dead, had none.

Maybe the green had become aware of Azoria's incursion.

But if it had, why was its power now prevalent here? Why did her marks somehow reflect the green? And why had the miasma that she'd seen when she'd stepped beneath the first arch remind her so much of Shadow?

Did it have something to do with death, with the dead? With what the Ancients became when they died? Was that what Evanton was trying to contain?

Kaylin!

Right. What Evanton was trying to do wasn't her responsibility. What she was trying to do, was. It was the only thing she had control over, the only thing she could do that might somehow help. The usual problem applied: she had no idea what she was doing, what she was supposed to be doing. Hope believed she could do something. Evanton believed it.

And the Ancient believed it as well.

Being with the Hawks had taught her to assess, to research, to investigate; had taught her that knee-jerk reactions weren't always the answer. Sometimes knee jerk was emotional, personal, a reaction—not an instinct. She'd trusted her instincts, but separating them from her reactions had always been difficult.

Now? There was no knee jerk if she didn't count panic, and she didn't. There was nothing to take personally; the only thing making her feel small and inadequate was herself—and she didn't have time for it. Second-guesses and self-loathing could come later, if there was a later.

That left only instinct.

It was the instinct that had guided her early attempts at healing. It was the instinct that she fell back on every subsequent time she had struggled to use her power to save a life—even an ungrateful, resentful, Barrani life. She wasn't healing anything, but she felt that same instinct guide her.

And that instinct had always been defined, not by Kaylin, but by the injured person. The injured body. The outlands, as far as she knew, was not a body. It wasn't alive. But the marks, in their ivory-edged green glory, seemed, as the ground continued to shudder in an oddly rhythmic time, to want to somehow take root there, as if this was where they belonged. This place, this time, beneath Evanton's feet. And the Ancient's.

Marks had left her skin before; she wondered if these marks—all of the visible ones pulsing with the same color—would leave in the same way. She closed her eyes, as she often did when she tried to heal the injured.

She could still see the marks; they were the only thing she could see.

She hadn't expected that she would hear them so clearly; she could. They should have been a cacophony of sound; they were a chorus instead, voices blending across syllables that seemed to merge into notes that were so harmonious it seemed impossible. Each voice was distinct, its own, but part of the greater whole and inseparable from it.

She had thought of the marks as words, individual words with fixed and absolute meanings. She had heard their voices before, but never like this.

Her own lips began to move, as if to join what was now a song. She'd never been able to carry a tune; even if she wanted to sing, to be part of a choral song, she knew it was better for everyone else if she kept her mouth shut.

Here, it didn't matter. It wasn't about whether or not her notes were sharp or flat; it didn't matter if her voice was too soft or too nasal or too toneless. She wasn't singing; she was speaking. She was speaking True Words, and she felt them as her truth, even if it wasn't her own words, her own tongue, expressing them.

The words grew larger, brighter, louder; she was surrounded by them as they grew farther and farther from their resting space on her skin. The light they cast across her arms, her body, became a deeper green, brighter and richer than the heart of a leaf could be.

She knew the color then.

She knew the color because it was the exact shade of green she had worn in the green, when she had been selected—by that mysterious force—to take part in the ceremony the Barrani called the *regalia.* She had been chosen. She hadn't been all that happy about it at the time, but she was grateful for it now, because she could feel the green here, in this place. She could feel the green beneath Evanton's feet, and she knew—without knowing—that it was the power of the green that had shored him up in his attempt to contain the Ancient.

She'd worried about its presence, but she couldn't remember why.

Eyes open now, she once again surrendered herself to her role, raising her arms, her voice; giving voice to the marks of the Chosen in a way she hadn't the first time she had worn this dress. Because she *was* wearing the dress now. She was clothed in emerald; she was, for the moment, standing in the heart of the green.

Harmoniste. She was the harmoniste. She would never be able to describe the tale she told; how could she? But she felt the marks leave her skin, leave her; they extended, not to the Ancient, but to Evanton, there to surround him and Kaylin in a shield of ivory and green.

She looked at Evanton; his eyes were closed, his face raised. Across his brow, she saw, to her surprise, that he wore the crown of the green. The emerald was the same color as her dress, and she realized that she'd seen it before. She then turned toward the Ancient; he had fallen silent. He was the audience for which the *regalia* was performed.

What meaning would it have for the dead?

What meaning did death have for the Ancients? She came back to that question, time and again, and perhaps the question threaded its way through her voice. But the words that surrounded both Kaylin and Evanton began to expand, to reach, the shape of the shield changing as the elements of the words rearranged themselves to form not a wall, but a bridge, a stream of words.

She knew the words she had carried were gone. She knew that this was where they were meant to be, somehow.

But she felt, as the sound of the words dimmed and silence returned, that it was not enough. Evanton's knees buckled; Kaylin reached for him, but it was Severn who caught him before he fell.

"We are not done here," the Keeper said, voice weak and almost breathless as he confirmed her suspicion. "The Ancient is contained because he was willing to be contained—but he is lost, Kaylin. Had Azoria never found him, I am not certain what would have happened. What I can do, I have done, but I had unexpected aid. And by that, I don't mean you. I feel you took your time."

Of course he did.

"The Ancient is not asleep, but he is calm now. Can you see the difference in the environment?"

Kaylin turned to look back down the path they'd walked. She could now see dirt; there was no white- or black-flecked miasma. Hope returned to her and flopped across her shoulders; he lifted his tiny head, and she realized she'd lost sight of him. Given his draconic form, that should have been impossible. He squawked, the sound weak and ineffectual.

Walking down the tree-lined path toward Kaylin were familiar companions.

Teela took one look at Kaylin, and her eyes narrowed to slits. Kaylin knew why. She was wearing this dress. It was a dress Teela herself had worn, and this was not the place any Barrani would have expected to see it. Tain looked more impressed.

"Evanton—what happened to Terrano? Did he not follow you?"

Evanton nodded. "I told him to leave. He was not of a mind to obey."

"I don't see him."

"No. I'm uncertain that he understood what was happening, but he could see something, and he felt he could be of aid."

"What something?"

"He did not say, and I was, I admit, a bit too preoccupied to perform the service of a babysitter."

"Did you see where he went? His friends are looking for him and they're getting worried. And yes, An'Teela is one of those friends."

"I believe he went to converse with the Ancient."

Kaylin muttered a Leontine curse and turned to face her companions again: Emmerian, Teela, Tain, and Larrantin. Larrantin was utterly silent, his gaze fixed upon the giant that seemed to take up most of what passed for sky.

Teela was more practical. "Terrano's not here." Not a question.

"Evanton said he went to try to do something with or to the Ancient."

"I forgive your use of extremely rude Leontine; I'm of a mind to add to it." Teela didn't ask what Terrano had intended; she knew him well enough to know that it was a pointless question; Evanton wouldn't know.

"You said you'd know if he was dead, right?"

"Yes."

"So he's not dead."

"He's going to be dead when I get my hands on him. Sedarias, as you can imagine, is...extremely worried. She's not the only one; she's just the most demonstrative. Has the Ancient spoken?"

"Not since we arrived—Severn and I, I mean."

"It is best that he does not speak," Evanton said. "Make no attempt to disturb him. And yes, that applies to you as well." These words were meant for Larrantin. Evanton was clearly familiar enough with everyone else that he didn't expect them to be reckless or foolish.

Larrantin didn't hear the Keeper the first time.

He heard the Keeper the second time. The Ancient wasn't asleep—nothing could have slept through the sharp crack of Evanton's syllables. He could give a Dragon a run for his money.

Larrantin turned to the Keeper. He offered a perfect Barrani bow. "Forgive me, Keeper. I am a scholar; I was born when *Ravellon* had not yet become the center of all worlds—well before its fall. We studied Shadow when we became aware of its existence; we studied, we warred, we destroyed whole sections of *Ravellon* in an attempt to save some parts of it; we failed.

"Tools were created, spells learned, defenses developed—but always imperfectly because we did not understand Shadow; we did not understand where it came from, why it spread, how it corrupted. We knew that it was sentient; we knew it could control and enslave as well as transform. At first, we thought it was an attacker from a different world, but no; we came to realize that it spread from ours. From *Ravellon.*

"Were there warning signs? There must have been. Something we missed. Something we overlooked. Some change in the environment, some twisting of essential mana. We had theories, of course. The Ancients created the Towers, as you well know. But they did not answer our questions—and their answers might have saved lives, might have preserved great pillars of learning, of knowledge, of study. Whole areas of your faded, ruined city might have continued to shine, to grow.

"I am not interested in the power of the Ancients, but in the lack of answers, the lack of guidance, the lack of information that they must have had if they could create the Towers to stand sentinel against what remained in the heart of *Ravellon.* You said that the Ancient, dead, nonetheless spoke to you; that the Ancient, trapped in the outlands, had become a conduit of power for Azoria.

"But dead, the Ancient has taken Azoria's halls, has transformed them. Dead, he has disturbed the elements in their garden—the garden was perhaps the strongest and most ancient of their great works. And in this place—not the research rooms, but these…halls—I can detect the faintest of traces of a familiar and fell magic."

"I can't leave you here," Kaylin said. "And we have to take Evanton home."

"I am in need of rest," the Keeper said. Kaylin noted that his robes remained, just as her dress did. "But it will not last. Come. If we must plan, if we must theorize, this is not the place to do it." He turned to Kaylin, straightening out his clothing. "I did not get lost; I was not trapped. The Ancient did not detain me; I made the decision to remain."

"You could have walked away?"

"Yes. But the alterations in this environment would continue, and it is my opinion that they would have grown to affect far more than Azoria's manse. Intimations of that continue. If we cannot contain, if we cannot fully silence what remains of this god, I do not believe any of us will survive.

"Kaylin's presence as the Chosen of this generation has calmed the Ancient for now, and the Ancient has no desire to destroy; I do not believe destruction or transformation is the Ancient's intent. In that, it is different from Shadow."

"How long will we have?" Teela asked.

"Perhaps a week. Perhaps less. My gift is not the dead; it is not the magics of the Ancients, beyond the garden itself. But as you have seen, I have some control over things that must be contained; could we move the Ancient to my garden, as we did the Devourer, I believe I could minimize the damage caused by its decay.

"I cannot. I would not make the attempt. I would not expose the world without to the Ancient in its current state." He exhaled. "Lord Emmerian."

The Dragon—still in draconic form—nodded his enormous head.

"You are familiar with Bellusdeo."

There was a slight pause before the Dragon nodded a second time.

"Kaylin believes that Bellusdeo is very, very protective of Mrs. Erickson."

"She has her reasons," Emmerian told the Keeper.

"I assume so, yes. But I believe Mrs. Erickson is entangled in this space in some fashion, and I believe it is in Mrs. Erickson's hands that our future survival lies. You will have to convince Bellusdeo, if Kaylin cannot."

"I don't think that's a good idea," Kaylin said. "Let me talk to her first. I know she's not going to like it—but she'll be more careful with me because Mrs. Erickson will be there; I think, if she's upset, she's going to feel free to lose it at Emmerian, because he's likely to survive."

"Good. I know that you are also hesitant. Lose the hesitance if you do not wish to lose everything else. You know that were I to tell Mrs. Erickson she was absolutely necessary for the protection of the world, she would immediately volunteer; she is that kind of person. Convince Bellusdeo to give her the choice."

"It's not just Bellusdeo who's going to be dead set against it." Kaylin glanced at Severn. "Helen is going to hate it."

"I need to recover, or I would accompany you to your home; Helen seems remarkably sensible." He coughed. "Lord Emmerian, if I might trouble you for aid?"

Kaylin, understanding Evanton's request, said, "It's not technically legal for him to fly you home."

"It is legal in an emergency," Evanton replied. "And I would imagine justifying such aid would not be difficult: you can inform the Emperor that the Keeper was at risk of failing in his duty due to exhaustion."

Emmerian knew better than to argue with Evanton; it made Kaylin wonder how long the Dragon had known the Keeper. "I will be honored to be of aid to you, Keeper. The Emperor will not question my decision."

"Is it safe for any of us to remain?" Kaylin asked, giving Larrantin the side-eye.

"What do you think?" Evanton snapped.

"I think we leave," Kaylin said. "Larrantin?"

He nodded, his gaze on the Ancient complicated; it was not quite the avaricious gaze of a researcher. "I will join Serralyn and Bakkon, if that is acceptable."

Kaylin glanced at Teela, but Teela's attention was fixed on the Ancient, her gaze entirely different from Larrantin's. Of course it was. Terrano was still missing. "Teela?"

"Larrantin can join the research," the Barrani Hawk said. "Bakkon will come to retrieve him and take him back. The rest of us will return to Helen; we have much to discuss."

"Has Serralyn found anything that she thinks might be helpful?"

"Undecided. She wants to know what happened. Which is fine. I'd like to know what happened as well."

"What did you see?"

"You walked beneath the arch of the first two trees. The path seemed normal to our eyes until you reached perhaps the sixth living column—but when you passed it, you vanished. Not only did you vanish, but fog rolled in; we lost sight of you. Some discussion about our path going forward was had. It was perhaps fractious.

"But before we could act, the fog rolled back, and we could see you in the distance."

"You could," Larrantin said. "The rest of us could not. An'Teela did not avail herself of magical enhancements—but she could see you; we could not. Not until she began to walk."

Kaylin nodded. She could guess why.

"And then we saw you. You appear to have found the time and space to change your uniform into something that is, admittedly, far more attractive to my eye than the Hawk kit you usually wear."

Kaylin glanced at Teela. Teela shrugged. "It's a ceremonial dress."

"So it *is* the dress it appears to be. How did you come by it?"

"I don't know."

Larrantin's eyes narrowed.

"I'm sorry I don't have a better answer. I just have the truth. I was wearing my normal clothing—and if I've lost that, it's going to cause problems. At some point, my normal clothing became this. I only recognized it because I've worn it before."

"You?"

"Me."

"You, a mortal, were chosen by the green? To be the harmoniste? To wear that dress?"

She curbed her annoyance with effort, because she'd found it pretty unbelievable when it had happened to her. "Yes."

Larrantin's eyes became a very dark blue. "In this place. In Azoria's former home. You donned that dress. You were given it here."

Kaylin nodded.

"And the crown of the Teller?"

She shook her head. "No crown, just this dress."

"The *regalia* requires both harmoniste and Teller."

Kaylin knew that; when she'd traveled to the West March, Nightshade had been chosen by the green to be the Teller, which, given he was outcaste, had caused predictable friction. "If someone was given the crown, they probably traveled to the West March, not here."

"You are not to wear that dress in the abode of the semi-dead."

Kaylin's natural oppositional tendencies kicked in. "If I'd had any choice in it, I wouldn't be wearing this dress. It's not like someone popped in, handed me the dress in a neat pile, and vanished. My clothing became this dress!"

Serralyn, who could hear everything because Teela was present, must have rushed Bakkon; he popped into existence before Larrantin could sharpen the point of a pointless interrogation. Kaylin had no answers to give him.

Larrantin now appeared to be torn between lecture mode and research mode. "Your aid would be appreciated," the Wevaran told the Barrani, hoping to tip the scales in favor of peace. "We have found some of Azoria's older books, and I admit the research in them is beyond me; it is certainly beyond Serralyn at her current level of education."

Larrantin allowed himself to be convinced; Bakkon spit a portal in front of the scholar, and made sure he'd entered it before he followed.

★ ★ ★

Nothing stopped the group that remained from finding the exit; if everything else had been altered, the door, or the shape of Mrs. Erickson's door, had not—when it could be seen at all. Kaylin thought it would have been invisible before the Ancient had been calmed or stilled, but it didn't matter. The door opened into Mrs. Erickson's front hall, and when everyone had cleared it and the door was closed behind them, it opened once again onto a porch that had seen better years.

It was dark. The moons were high, although neither were full. They'd lost daylight hours to the halls, which would have been fine had it felt like that much time had passed.

Emmerian, who had regained his human form, shed it the moment he reached the lawn; he turned back to Evanton, most of whose weight was being shouldered by Tain. Tain walked Evanton to Emmerian, and helped him to climb the Dragon's back; when the old man was as secure as he could be given a lack of saddle, Emmerian pushed off the earth, into the city sky.

They watched the two leave as Tain rejoined them.

"Is he going to be okay?" Kaylin asked.

Teela's shrug was pure fief, adopted from Kaylin. "I don't know. As I said, you vanished. Whatever it was that Evanton did, I assume it was the Keeper's business. He was—and is—worried. Let's go back to Helen. We're going to need to talk to Mrs. Erickson, if Bellusdeo and Helen will allow it."

Kaylin grimaced. She knew that *we* meant Kaylin.

She exhaled, looking down at her arms; they were clothed in a shimmering green that seemed to catch the light, not that there was a lot of it left. Severn was no longer wielding his weapons, and he certainly wasn't wearing a dress.

"It looks good on you, if that helps."

She glared.

"He's not wrong," Teela said.

"Yeah, he's not helpful, either."

★ ★ ★

Helen was waiting by the open door when Kaylin at last crossed her property line and dragged herself up the steps. She was exhausted. Helen understood the significance of the dress because Kaylin did, but her home was concerned.

"We found Evanton," Kaylin said, as Helen moved to the side to allow everyone else to enter. "Emmerian took him home—he was in dire need of sleep. Or rest. We can check in on him tomorrow."

"Things aren't resolved."

"Evanton doesn't feel they are, no."

"And you don't, either."

Kaylin nodded.

"Dear, you are practically falling asleep on your feet." She glanced at the rest of the guests. "I can feed everyone, and if you *must* continue to speak, at least take a nap."

Squawk.

"Exactly," Helen agreed. She didn't march Kaylin up the stairs, but she did escort her there; no one attempted to stop her, either. Kaylin argued, but it was half-hearted. She hadn't felt this exhausted when she'd been standing in the Ancient's hall; it had fallen on her in stages as she made the trek home—a trek that seemed interminably long as she put one foot in front of the other. Maybe she should have had Emmerian fly her home as well—not that he would've likely agreed. Evanton was the Keeper; he was a vital, if hidden, part of the world.

Kaylin was a cranky Hawk in a stupid dress.

"No one thinks your dress is stupid," Helen informed her.

"They don't have to walk in it."

"It seems designed for walking, even running."

"And if a Barrani wore it, it wouldn't raise eyebrows. I'm not a 'wear a long pretty dress in public streets' person." She grimaced. "And the clothing I was wearing was one of two sets I use for official work—I can get the tabard replaced easily, if you don't count the quartermaster's contempt and anger, but I don't have the money to replace everything else, especially the boots." She didn't have a second set of boots, either. She had shoes, which would do in a pinch, but she'd need to replace the boots instantly.

Helen could create clothing for her, but it persisted only in the house, and Helen couldn't magically create money—not that Kaylin would ask. She considered asking for reimbursement from the Imperial Palace, or Sanabalis personally, because she'd lost her real clothing in the line of duty, not on her own time.

"That would probably be effective," Helen said. "And I would consider it quite justified, given the circumstances. Do you need help removing that?"

"No—I'm just going to take a nap. I don't need to get ready for bed. I've worn this damn dress before. It doesn't tear, it doesn't get dirty—I don't even think it allows sweat to touch its hallowed fabric. My bed isn't going to get dirty because I happened to sleep in it while dressed."

Hope hopped onto the pillow beside Kaylin's, curled up, and closed his eyes.

He snored.

She couldn't have restful sleep, even when exhausted. No. Of course not.

She stood in a clearing, bound by trees that seemed both ancient and on the short side, given the trees the Ancient had conjured. They were gnarled, their branches spread low and wide; she could see sunlight make shadows of those branches, which nonetheless allowed light to pass through.

Around the base of the trees, nestled between visible roots, were familiar flowers.

She stood in the green.

Across from where she stood, she saw a familiar figure, robed in the blue of his office: Evanton. She wondered if he were a figment of the dream itself, or if they had somehow become connected. Frowning, she took a closer look at the Keeper.

He was, and was not, the Evanton she knew. He had the same facial features, but a lot fewer wrinkles. Didn't make him look any friendlier.

"I see I cannot escape you even in exhaustion-induced sleep." Dream Evanton pinched the bridge of his nose. "Well?"

"Well, what? I was trying to take a nap before embarking in a long discussion. I ended up here." She raised her arms. Yup. Green sleeves. "Do you know where we are?"

"I would expect that you would have a far clearer answer, but perhaps exhaustion has addled my brain. We are, at the moment, communing with the green—or the green is attempting to commune with us. What are you staring at?"

"Why do you look so young?"

"That is the question, while we're dreaming, that you feel is pertinent and necessary? In case it has escaped your notice, we are not here in person; we are hundreds of miles away, in our separate abodes, attempting to rest enough that we may face what must be faced.

"I look 'so young' as you put it because I am not physically present; what is present is my spirit, or rather, it is the expression of the power of the Keeper, conferred on me by the previous Keeper. I look forward to the day I can pass it on and truly rest, but apparently today is not that day. I admit I have never understood the significance of robes and dresses as ceremonial garb; it seems entirely impractical."

"Well, this dress is pretty much self-cleaning; it can't be torn, and I can run in full stride while wearing it."

"I retract my comment about practicality. I admit I was surprised to see you wearing it."

"Not half as surprised as I was—it's not like I keep a dress tucked in my side pouch, and even if I did, an emergency involving a dead Ancient isn't where I'd pull it out to put it on. What did we do there?"

"I know very, very little about the living Ancients; I now know far more than I did about dead Ancients—and I would still classify my knowledge as extremely meagre. But you were correct in your surmise. Azoria clearly had some connection to the green.

"I know very little about the green; even Barrani scholars do not claim to be experts. The Warden and his students guard the green—but it has always seemed to me that it is not the green that requires his protection. It is his people that require protection from the green. Barrani are not always careful in their approach; they have fostered consummate arrogance, and even in the West March, where they live largely in harmony with the natural world, the natural world is subordinate to their whims and desires.

"The green is not, nor do I believe it could be—but that would not stop foolish and ambitious Barrani from making the attempt to conquer a possible source of power. Before you accuse me of being somewhat speciest, I would add that humans would do the same had they the access to the green the Barrani do.

"The green is sentient. It is sentient in a way that the elements are; it is older by far than mortals, and it is unconstrained in its activities within the folds of the ether that circumscribe it. Helen is constrained, as are the Towers; the green was not constructed in the same fashion."

She didn't ask him how he knew this. She wasn't even certain she wanted to know.

"The Keeper's garden was constructed in a fashion that was similar to the green—but Keepers understand the function, the necessity, of the garden. We are like, and unlike, the captains of the Towers—the last things created, to my knowledge, by the Ancients. I do not bespeak the elements in the fashion Helen bespeaks you. Helen is the core of the sentient building. All of the buildings of your acquaintance were built with a living being at their heart. The same can be said of the garden, in a fashion, but the being is not one of the races with which you are—or should be—familiar.

"More than that, I do not feel it wise to say." He turned as a breeze started in the clearing; Kaylin heard the whisper of leaves against leaves, rising and falling as if attempting to be heard. Leaves fell, as leaves do—not all at once, and not in any discernible pattern; they scudded across the flowers and grass.

One such leaf stopped at her feet; she bent without thought to retrieve it.

In her hand, the leaf was warm; it felt almost like skin beneath her fingers. It was green, as green as her dress, as green as sunlight through emerald.

It did not speak; it was a leaf. But as she held it, she thought she could hear words being spoken, the syllables oddly familiar, the language unknown.

"I think—I think the green is trying to speak," she whispered.

22

Evanton frowned. “The green always speaks,” he said, his voice very soft, but nonetheless distinct. “Just as the elements do. What we perceive as sleep is not sleep; they do not require sleep. Which is unfortunate, because I do.”

“Can you hear the green?”

“Yes.”

“Did you know? That the green was there?”

“Yes. The presence of the green was the reason I could stand where I stood for as long as I did. The green does not desire the dead to rise, and it has some ability to contain it. But if I cannot move the Ancient to my garden, the green cannot move the Ancient to the green; the distance is far too great, even considering the path in the outlands it might otherwise take.”

“I don’t understand what the Ancients mean—or meant—by death. The Ancient could—and did—speak. He could move. He could reach for the raw material of the outlands and build a forest around himself. He could speak my language—or I could hear his speech as if that’s what he was speaking.

“Nothing about that suggests death to me.”

“No. But you said he spoke of the end of his purpose, or the completion of it. It is possible life and death for the Ancients revolved around purpose; once they had completed their task, they might rest. Death is felt as an absence by those who are not dead. You spoke with Mrs. Erickson's ghostly children—did they seem dead to you?"

"I knew they were dead."

"But did they seem dead? Were they walking corpses?"

"No!"

"They appeared as children. They spoke as children. They had the temperament of children. Things familiar with their living existence. Had they lived, they would have aged; they would have acquired knowledge and, one hopes, wisdom. They did not. But to the eyes of Mrs. Erickson—and to your eyes—they did not seem dead. Could they have interacted with the physical world, you would never have known."

Kaylin nodded, the nod slower.

"How, then, is that death?"

"Being able to interact with others seems important." She hesitated. She'd been grateful that the dead didn't look like shambling corpses; that their death didn't define their appearance. Death meant, for the children, the inability to interact with others. They couldn't be heard. They couldn't be seen. Mrs. Erickson had been the exception, and she had become the center of their world—a world transcribed by the walls of a small house. They could see each other; they had at least that.

They couldn't leave, but that had been Azoria's fault.

Truth was, Kaylin had liked the children. But she was aware that they'd been trapped in many ways. They couldn't change. They couldn't grow. Whatever experience they accumulated left them untouched. The child she had been when she was their age was not the woman she had become. The woman she was was not the woman she would become. Life was about change.

"I see your point. To me, the children seemed alive. To

them, it was different. Do you think the Ancient is like that, somehow?"

"Having never conversed with an Ancient before, I do not know. But yes, perhaps. I have never been like Mrs. Erickson, but I could certainly see the Ancient." He coughed, a type of punctuation he used to emphasize a point. "I do not believe I would have seen him had it not been for your interference."

"And you don't think he would be what he is now."

"His power, much limited, would have been in Azoria's hands. Before you fall prey to your own gnawing guilt, consider that. My sense was that he was attempting to contain himself in some fashion; he did not fight my attempt to contain him."

Kaylin considered this. He had been calling her from the moment she had stepped foot into the portal. What had he expected of the Chosen? What did he want? He was, like Jamal and the rest of the children, aware of his state, aware that he was dead.

The light across the sleeves of her dress changed; she realized that she had lifted her arms and hadn't lowered them. Evanton's arms were by his sides, but his chin was slightly lifted and his shoulders fell straight down his back. This was what he must have looked like as a younger man, as if his internal sense of who he was had not yet caught up with reality. To her eyes, she looked the same as she did normally, with the exception of the dress she wore.

"Did you bring me here?" she asked, voice soft.

"Not I, no. But we both touched something in the mana surrounding the Ancient, and it has its strongest roots in this place. This is the green. This is possibly the heart of the green."

She looked at her marks; they were glowing the same ivory-edged green that they had in the presence of the space the Ancient controlled. To her eyes, they were more widely spaced than they had been; the words that had traveled into the ground on which Evanton stood had vanished. She couldn't be certain they hadn't been consumed.

"Tell me," Evanton said. "Does this look like a dead space to you?"

Given the profusion of greenery, it was an odd question. "No. Does it look that way to you?"

"To me? No. But I do not perceive the world the way the Chosen does. Or at least not the way Kaylin as Chosen does. I believe it is your perception that matters. You are not accustomed to power, except as a lack, or a severe lack, given your childhood. It gives you insight that the earliest bearers of these marks did not have.

"Had you been asked permission before you became Chosen, you might have refused it, or you might have accepted because the need for power was so stark. In either case, you would not be who you are now."

Kaylin frowned. "How do you know all this?"

"I am an old man; I was always considered old at heart, even in my childhood. I have seen many, many people cross the threshold of my store; I have even allowed some of them to stay. You are not dissimilar to many of them; you wear your early experience on your figurative sleeve. You are prickly; you are afraid of—and angered by—being judged; you are certain that you are nobody, that you are worthless. It is why your office as a Hawk has meant so much to you.

"I find your youth tiring at times, but I do not entirely disapprove of you; you have been of great help in my tenure as Keeper, although you have been part of it for such a short time. I struggle not to blame you for blundering into so very, very many dangers. For the most part, I succeed.

"You have Hope, and such a creature as Hope has not existed in anyone else's orbit for the entirety of my life as Keeper; I am aware that there are many who have attempted to gain a Sorcerer's familiar within both the Arcanum and, more secretly, the Imperial order. None have come close—and I am certain those who are aware of Hope bear a great deal of resentment; you chanced upon him by accident; had it not been for the assassination attempt on Bellusdeo, you would not have him at all.

"But it is here that you named him: Hope. A difficult name, Kaylin. Many cannot bear the burden of it."

"Evanton—how do you know this?" She took a step back and reached up with one hand for Hope. Hope sat on her shoulder watching Evanton.

Oh.

"You aren't Evanton."

Evanton smiled. "I am Evanton, Kaylin. But here, there is more. The garden was created long before any of the races you know. It was necessary; the races could not be born, could not flourish, in a world in which the elements warred. The garden exists so that the lives that were crafted, built, and set free could grow—or perish, if that was their fate.

"The green existed when the garden was created."

"What *is* the green?"

"Tell me, Kaylin Neya, who are you?"

She blinked. "Pardon?"

"Tell me, in your own words, who you are."

"I'm a Hawk."

"There are many Hawks; are they like you? They share your sense of duty, if imperfectly. Try again."

"I'm human."

"So are most of the Hawks. What makes you you?"

She fell silent as she considered the question. *Who am I?* She opened her mouth. Closed it. Opened it again.

"You understand the difficulty. You are much better at understanding what you need. Much better—and this is as essential—at understanding what you can give, and still remain Kaylin. You know, by experience, what you can endure, but do not yet know what could, or will, break you. The answer in the now is the most you can give, but it will change. Living things change; they must.

"The green cannot answer a question you cannot answer for yourself, but even if it could, you could not contain or retain the answer, if you could even understand it at all. Before you take offense, neither could I."

"Can you ask the green why it brought me here?"

"I told you—I cannot bespeak the green as you speak; the green cannot answer. The words the green might speak to you are etched on your skin; in no other way can the green communicate, and even then, the use of such language exists almost at the edge of its ability. But the green *is* alive. It is alive, and it has seen the birth of many, many things in its time. The Ancients are younger than the green."

Kaylin stared at Evanton, at a loss for words. She had visited the green; she knew the Hallionne Alsanis was somehow linked to the green. She knew that the *regalia* was offered the Barrani at the whim of the green, or on some schedule that none of the Barrani understood, either. She had never understood the point of it; she didn't understand the point of it now. But she wore the dress the green had given her before, a symbol to the Barrani that she was the green's choice.

But choice for what?

"There are ghosts in your house," Evanton continued, when Kaylin failed to speak. "Taken from an artifact of much older times. You are aware of them, and we are connected for the moment by the will of the green. Mrs. Erickson carried those ghosts to your home."

Kaylin nodded.

"She calms them, even now; it is to her they look when they are unsettled. She bespeaks what once lay at their core. They were not alive as Mrs. Erickson is; nor as you or I. Life does not have the same meaning to us; it does not have the same meaning to the Ancient. The green is aware of Mrs. Erickson, although the connection is tenuous and easily frayed; Azoria's interference all but guaranteed that.

"Mrs. Erickson is our best chance at helping the Ancient. Take the words, Kaylin. Take the words she sees as people."

"What do you mean?"

"You can bear their weight; you can bear them to where they must be carried."

"You want us to take the ghosts to the dead Ancient?"

"It is what the green wants. The green believes that the Ancient will be at peace should we manage this."

"How, exactly, am I meant to carry them? I didn't coax them to my house—that was Mrs. Erickson!"

"The marks you carry are words," he replied. "Figure it out. You bear the raiment of the green. For a time, and the will of the green, you have a role to play. I am in need of sleep, and this is not exactly restful. If I were younger, I would immediately make my way to your house. Alas, my age is not feigned. I will return to your house first thing tomorrow morning."

"You don't have to go back. It's not worth the risk. I can figure things out with Mrs. Erickson."

"Yes, you can. I will come to pick you up first thing in the morning. There is too much at risk to leave it in the hands of the young."

"Wait—before you go, tell me one thing."

He raised a brow, his expression the familiar, dour one.

"Is Terrano still alive? Is he somehow with the Ancient?"

"It is possible," Evanton replied. His tone implied the opposite.

Helen woke Kaylin three hours later. Discussion, according to Helen, had occurred, with some *unfortunate* parts in the middle.

The Academia—or rather, its chancellor—had reached out to Kaylin by mirror. "I'm sorry, dear," Helen said, as Kaylin got out of bed. Hope squawked, but pushed himself off his pillow; he landed on her shoulders, and went back to his version of sleep, grumbling the entire time.

"Has anyone spoken with Mrs. Erickson?"

"I believe they were waiting for you. Bellusdeo is with Mrs. Erickson."

Kaylin wilted. "Does she know what happened?"

"Bellusdeo is aware that Evanton returned; she is also aware that An'Teela wishes to speak with Mrs. Erickson. Imelda has been sleeping," Helen added, in the gentle tone she reserved for their newest housemate. "She has been attempting to comfort Bellusdeo, which takes effort at the moment; she is also attempting to keep the ghosts she brought from the Imperial Palace calm. That has become more and more taxing."

Kaylin glanced at Helen's Avatar. "You didn't ask much about the dress."

"No. You understand enough of its significance, and your confusion and irritation were quite clear to me."

"What do you think I should do?"

"I am a simple house," Helen replied. "In my time, however, the Keeper commanded respect and obedience when he demanded it. I will allow Evanton to visit. And I will—with misgivings—allow Mrs. Erickson to accompany you. She has become, in a very short span of time, quite dear to me. But the Keeper's worries are clear. She will help you, if given the choice."

"Will Bellusdeo allow it?"

"I'm sorry, dear. She will not be happy, as you must suspect."

Kaylin nodded. "I don't suppose Mrs. Erickson has been able to untangle her sisters?"

Helen shook her head and exhaled, an affectation. "If the Keeper is correct, removing these ghosts will help Imelda. No one truly understands Mrs. Erickson's power—but all magic requires power, and I believe she is using that power so naturally, she is unaware of the expenditure. But it is costly; I do not know how much longer she can bear this responsibility.

"It is why I am willing to risk her. If she dies, the ghosts she has so carefully husbanded will be unleashed—and I am not at all certain that I can contain them if they are unwilling to be contained. If the Keeper feels they are some part of the necessary key to solving the problem of a dead Ancient...they are both dead, they are both dangerous to the living, and if Mrs. Erickson is the shaman who might usher the dead to peace, she cannot wait until the scholars know more, until the theoreticians can make suggestions or attempt to guide her in her handling of her power." Helen closed her eyes, another affectation.

Kaylin headed to the door of her room; she took a steadying breath. "Mrs. Erickson and Bellusdeo first," she said. Hope squawked.

Mrs. Erickson's room was no longer in the same location it had been when she'd first joined the household; her door was absent.

"Yes," Helen said; she had quietly followed Kaylin. "I am attempting to do everything I can to take on some of her burden—but with limited success. Bellusdeo is aware of this, but aware as well that Mrs. Erickson will not abandon the charges she took on. Her sleeping quarters are separate from her ghosts; I cannot stop them from seeping into the room, but after she spends time with them, they are less restless for a period of time.

"There is no other way to have them safely exist in the same space as Imelda." Helen led her to the double doors at the end of the hall. Kaylin frowned.

"Yes. These doors lead to my quarters. You have visited them before."

"But didn't these doors open to an outdoor patio?"

"The decor was not considered traditional bedroom decor,

no. But I do not require sleep, and it seemed the appropriate setting at the time."

She lifted a hand and the doors gently rolled open into a large sitting room, similar to the parlor she created for guests she considered socially important, but more comfortable, more lived-in. Kaylin wondered if it echoed the family room that Mrs. Erickson had been forced to abandon; that room was not this large.

But perhaps, in the echoes of a childhood spent there with her parents, it had seemed larger than it did to the investigative eyes of a Hawk.

"She knows it is not the same place," Helen said. She spoke quietly; Bellusdeo was seated in the room. Mrs. Erickson was not.

"She's sleeping," the gold Dragon said, rising from her chair as Kaylin entered. "Helen informed us both that Evanton has been found, and that he has returned to his home in more or less one piece. Imelda has been very worried, and the relief has made her very, very tired. Terrano's not back."

Kaylin shook her head.

"Why are you standing there looking like guilt personified?" When Kaylin failed to answer immediately, the Dragon added, "You've got *nothing* on me for guilt. I'm just warning you, I'm not going to be patient with yours or anyone else's—unless you've managed to destroy a world when I wasn't looking." Bellusdeo folded her arms. Her eyes were an odd blend of copper and orange; the copper might have been a trick of the light.

Kaylin assumed they'd soon get red, so copper would be irrelevant. She even understood; in her life, she often chose anger as a way to paper over pain. Her anger, on the other hand, couldn't turn houses to ash. She looked at one of the chairs; she didn't exactly want to sit, as Bellusdeo was on her feet.

"There were a few complications," she finally said.

"You can start with that dress. What in the hells are you wearing?"

Oh, right. Kaylin lifted her left arm; it trailed a drape of emerald sleeve. Hope squawked, but for once Bellusdeo failed to hear him. Kaylin heard him quite well, and eventually lifted a hand to protect the ear his mouth was closest to. He didn't take kindly to being ignored.

"I got the dress just after I had to leave the city when our apartment was reduced to rubble."

"It's Barrani."

"It's a significant, ceremonial Barrani dress. If it didn't look like this—and I had any right to keep it—I'd even appreciate it. It doesn't get dirty. It can't be torn. I doubt it can be cut, but I haven't been stupid enough to try. I can run in it; I'm sure Barrani could fight in it perfectly well."

"Which ceremony?" Bellusdeo's arms got tighter.

"The *regalia*."

"The one the cohort was exposed to as children?"

"That one, yes. Look—it was against the laws of the West March to present children as an audience for the *regalia*. The High Court decided those were quaint, rustic rules, and broke them." Bellusdeo was silent. "It's not the first time I've worn the dress."

"And you're not on the way to the West March."

"No. I'm on my way to Azoria's again. Tomorrow morning. When the Keeper comes to get us."

"Us."

"Helen may have warned you. The Keeper thinks Mrs. Erickson's presence is necessary."

"Does he?" That was definitely a *no*.

"The Ancient I may have mentioned is, according to the Keeper, dead. But dead doesn't mean to Ancients what it means to the rest of us. I think he's stuck in his current state, and his current state—unhampered by Azoria—is bleeding into the rest of the landscape.

"Evanton thinks it's only a matter of time before that bleed escapes Azoria's old place and begins to transform the world the rest of us live in. Which would not be a good thing for the rest of us." Kaylin exhaled. "If you want to tell him no, you can tell him no. I warned him you wouldn't like it."

"What, exactly, do you expect a frail mortal woman to do?"

"I don't know. She can talk to the ghosts she brought home from the palace. No one else can. But I think they're related to the Ancients because they clearly have will and an ability—as ghosts—to possess a Dragon Lord. Evanton believes— Ugh. He thinks she has some chance of somehow escorting the dead Ancient off this particular stage, because he believes—as Helen does—that that's the core of her gift. She used it, once Azoria was dead. She freed the dead that were trapped in various paintings or household pieces of furniture. She set them free.

"I think he believes she can do the same for the Ancient."

"And you?"

"Pardon?"

"What do you believe? You found Evanton. You clearly arranged to bring him to his home."

"Emmerian did that."

"Pardon?"

"Emmerian went full Dragon and flew him home." Kaylin exhaled. "We've suspected that Azoria had ties to the green; she could grow a flower that only grows in the green. When we went to find Evanton, we found one of those flowers—no, more than just one. We had a scholar from the Academia with us; he believes that Azoria's connection to the green was carefully controlled—it was like a tiny drip. But when she died, that control slipped, and the green now has more of a presence in Azoria's former home.

"Evanton agrees. But Evanton felt that the green's intent was to contain the dead Ancient's spreading power—and for what it's worth, Evanton believes that's what the Ancient wants as well. My marks responded to either the green or Evanton, and some of them left my skin permanently to shore up Evanton's work to contain the Ancient.

"But it wasn't enough. And it's not something we can leave to someone else. Mrs. Erickson isn't getting any younger, and even if she was, I'm going to get old—and when we're gone, the problem will remain and the temporary solution will have vanished. I don't think the Ancient will make any attempt to harm Mrs. Erickson; the ghosts she brought from the palace didn't."

"And if you're wrong?" The question was chilly. Bellusdeo's eyes were definitely red now.

"I'll be the first in the line of fire," Kaylin replied. She met, and held, the angry Dragon's gaze. "I understand why Mrs. Erickson is important to you. But Evanton believes if we don't make this attempt, everyone will die. Every*thing* will die."

"Helen?" Bellusdeo snapped.

Helen's Avatar materialized in the room; she clearly didn't trust just her voice to make her point. "Kaylin believes everything she's said is the truth."

"Do you?"

"I would have some reservations, but it is clear from Kaylin's memory that the Keeper believes this. The Keeper has his role and function. I may, with great effort, ignore his demands—he does not have the right of command. But his word carries weight to even a damaged building such as myself. I believe, however, that Kaylin has another duty to accomplish before tomorrow morning."

"Teela, Tain, and Severn were waiting for me to wake up," Kaylin added. "I think they want to strategize."

"Let them. What duty is Helen talking about?"

Kaylin grimaced. "The green believes that I can carry the ghosts that Mrs. Erickson has been keeping calm—the ones I could vaguely see as words, and she can see as people."

"How?"

"I don't know. But… I could see Jamal with my own eyes;

I could see him without Hope's wing. I could talk to him; he could hear me. It's not the first time I've seen a ghost. It doesn't happen often, but when it does, it's significant. I *think* the green believes I can take the dead words and place them on my skin, where the marks that vanished once sat. Look, I didn't exactly talk with the green. We didn't have a conversation. The green didn't tell me what to do.

"The green could sort of communicate with Evanton, and Evanton told me what he thought the green wanted. The important point being: the green believed I could do this." Kaylin swallowed. "Mrs. Erickson is exhausted a lot of the time. I think it's because the dead words don't sleep, and she's the only thing that can calm them down.

"It's the power she has that has the calming effect—but she's using it constantly. Mages can't use their powers without driving themselves to exhaustion. Clearly shamans can't, either. If I can take the ghosts onto my skin, if I can carry them that way..."

"You'll be the one who's exhausted." For the first time, Bellusdeo's worry shifted: she pointed it directly at Kaylin.

"I'm younger than she is, and my job is a lot more physical. I'd rather it be me than her. Wouldn't you?"

Bellusdeo's protective hostility began to crack. She glanced at Helen. Helen's face was a mask; she waited until the Dragon offered a very grudging nod, and then turned to Kaylin. "They are not entirely in Mrs. Erickson's room; we can approach them from the other side. I don't guarantee this won't wake Imelda." She turned to Bellusdeo. "Perhaps you would like to join the others in the parlor? I will bring Imelda when she wakes."

Bellusdeo clearly didn't want to join the Hawks. "I'll go with Kaylin."

Helen shook her head. "If the ghosts are restless or panicked, they may attempt to possess you, as they possessed Lord Sanabalis. It is too great a risk."

The reminder caused Bellusdeo to back down—barely. She

turned and walked out the open doors, heading through the halls that had once had a door with a dragon silhouette on it while dragging her feet. Kaylin would have done the same.

"Yes," Helen said. "There are many similarities between the two of you." To Kaylin's surprise, she held out a hand. Kaylin stared at that hand. "It might be a bit uncomfortable for you otherwise; I believe I can stabilize things somewhat for you."

"We're not going through a portal, are we?" Kaylin asked, her tone perilously close to outright whining.

"I'm sorry, dear."

Kaylin grimaced and took Helen's hand. "You don't have portals anywhere else in the house—not even at the front door."

"No. I don't judge them necessary, and the discomfort to you is not worth the minor improvement in my security. But this is a different matter, and every possible security, no matter how imperfect, is necessary, in my considered opinion."

Hope squawked. Kaylin's shoulders slumped, but she took Helen's hand. There was no obvious portal; she thought Helen would create a door she could open. This didn't happen. The moment Kaylin took Helen's hand, the rest of the world fell away. The familiar sitting room elements vanished between one eyeblink and the next.

23

For the first time when she entered a portal, Kaylin listened. Hope sat on her shoulder squawking, his voice soft and blessedly familiar. It wasn't Hope that she struggled to hear. It was the sound of distant voices, voices that had not entered the portal with her, but nonetheless existed in the space.

It was how she'd heard the Ancient. No one else had heard the sound, as if of a tumultuous crowd, but it had pierced her ears, as if it were a weapon; she had stumbled and would have fallen had she not had Severn and Teela with her.

Sometimes she entered portal space without difficulty; most times, it was a nauseating struggle. The last portal had been the first time she could pinpoint a source of that nausea, that pain. She wondered, uneasy now, if something similar had always existed; if she had, while traversing portal space, heard the cries of something in the outlands that didn't quite translate into words.

It was a disturbing thought.

Hope squawked again, and this time she paid attention. "Helen—this space…"

"Yes, dear. I'm sorry."

"It's all portal, isn't it?"

"It is, indeed, all portal. There is no fixed location that terminates it; think of it as a circular loop. I can unbend the circle when necessary, but the ghosts rest more easily here than they do in any other space in the house; I have tried many. They respond to some well, but that response diminishes with time—as if some environments evoke fragments of memory, but not strongly enough to form an anchor."

Kaylin looked at her arm. She couldn't see the marks beneath the sleeve, which meant they weren't glowing. Whatever she was meant to do here, the marks weren't aware of. She'd always used the glow as an indicator.

Helen's hand felt almost like a normal hand; it was cooler and a little bit harder, as if skin had been laid over warm stone. But it meant Kaylin could tighten her grip if necessary. On portal paths, it was always necessary. Almost always. When she held Nightshade's arm, she didn't feel the disorienting dizziness or nausea at all.

Portals were inherently part of the outlands, part of the cloudy, murky, indistinct matter that became, in the hands of beings like Helen, physical rooms, physical objects. Food. Clothing. Anything at all that wasn't alive.

But maybe she'd heard the voice of the dead Ancient because he was so close to the portal she'd entered. She didn't normally hear voices. But what if there were other dead Ancients littered across the outlands?

No, that couldn't be possible. Evanton was aware of the disturbance caused by this Ancient; the garden's elements were aware of it. Surely if there were another case like this one, the Keeper would be just as aware of it? If the garden's entrance was located in Elantra, the responsibility covered the entire world, however big that was.

She shook herself and regretted it. "Hope?"

Squawk. The familiar sounded bored. He was standing on

her shoulder, instead of supine; he expected that there could be trouble, but so far hadn't found it. Kaylin, listening, finally heard something that sounded like a voice, or voices—soft, muted, and blurred, which implied a distant crowd, not an individual.

"Are we almost there?"

"We are," Helen replied. "You can hear them?"

Kaylin flinched. "I can hear *something.* Can you?"

"I can hear what you hear. I cannot hear them on my own—but I can detect them, or I could not house them at all. I think both you and Imelda translate what you hear; your translation is not as perfect as Imelda's, because that is not your gift. If you were not Chosen, I'm not certain you would hear or see anything. Do you understand what you must do?"

"I understand the end result I want: the ghosts become resident on my skin; they take the place of the marks that left me in order to stabilize what Evanton was trying to build."

"They are not marks of the Chosen, dear."

"No, of course not—but the green believed I could bear them on my skin the way I bear the rest of the marks."

"Are you even aware of those marks?"

"Not unless they glow. They feel like a natural part of my skin." Kaylin hesitated, and then added, "I don't expect these ghosts to feel the same. But Evanton said the green thought these words were necessary somehow, and the green felt that I *could* bear them."

"But not easily."

"No. The green thought I'd feel the weight. But it means Mrs. Erickson won't be carrying them; she'll get a break."

"How much of a break, if Evanton feels her presence is essential?"

It was a fair point. She almost said as much, but the sounds she had heard grew louder, as if they were a real crowd and she'd drawn close enough to hear individual voices. Crowd? Mob, maybe; the sounds clashed, as if in argument, although other voices were raised that seemed distinct—a scream, a shout, a plea. None of these resolved into intelligible words. Had she been Mrs. Erickson, they would have; she could have walked into the crowd, raising her hands, and listening to every single voice as if each had value, each had merit.

Mrs. Erickson was the least judgmental person Kaylin had ever met. Maybe that was why the dead found comfort in her: she could see them, she could speak to them, and she could *listen*. Kaylin didn't expect to understand other people. She didn't expect them to understand her, either, if she was being fair.

It didn't occur to Mrs. Erickson that she couldn't. Maybe because, when she faced the dead, she understood the pain of being able to see the world in all its complexity, but remaining unseen, unheard. Maybe all she wanted to offer them was the comfort of finally having someone who could see them and hear them; to confirm that they still existed, that they had once lived.

There was peace in that.

Kaylin couldn't offer it. She understood its value but understood her own limitations. She wasn't aware of any time in her life that she'd offered comfort successfully. She froze.

She could think of one time. One time, when she, who was powerless, had found children who had even less power. She'd protected them. They'd found comfort in her.

And she didn't want to think about them here.

She swallowed. She'd accepted those deaths. She'd made peace with them, inasmuch as she could. Why did they come back, time and again, to make a lie of acceptance?

"Because you loved them," Helen said, her voice very soft.

"That didn't do them any good."

"Yes, it did. Be careful, Kaylin. If you only remember the pain, if you only remember the end, nothing you ever did that helped counts. You did help them. They did love you. Had they died in a wagon accident, you wouldn't have assumed that all their life with you was terrible for them."

"That's not how they died. That's not why they died. If Severn hadn't killed them, they would have died anyway—and it would have been a terrible death. Neither would have happened if we'd never met."

Hope squawked up a storm.

"Right." She swallowed. "Let's get back to these ghosts."

"Yes, dear. I don't think yours are haunting you. I'm sure if they were, Mrs. Erickson would have let you know."

She'd certainly done that for Bellusdeo, and Bellusdeo's life hadn't improved for it. Kaylin exhaled; she was being unfair. Closing her eyes, she returned to listening. Returned, as she did, to thinking about Mrs. Erickson, and what she offered the panicked, restless dead.

As she did, she saw the marks on her arms begin to glow. Their light could be seen clearly through the sleeves of the green's dress, but the emerald hue deepened the color of the green without appreciably changing the ivory that edged it. The color of the flower in Azoria's painting of Mrs. Erickson and her family had been a bright, yet simultaneously sickly green; this green had a depth of color that seemed the opposite of that green, while still somehow being in the same spectrum.

It was warm. The marks were warm, not hot; she felt them against her skin as summer shade. Summer shade in the heart of the green, where insects weren't biting her and the summer heat wasn't slowly burning her skin. It was almost peaceful to look at the marks, and she'd never felt that before.

"No."

"But I didn't feel the green was peaceful when I was actually in it," Kaylin pointed out.

"No? I admit I knew very little about the green, and very little about the Keeper. The green was not my concern, although my first master studied it for some time."

"Was he anything like Azoria?"

"He was much, much closer to Azoria's personality than to yours, certainly. You would not have cared for him." Helen smiled. "I loathed him myself."

Kaylin glanced at her home's Avatar. Helen was usually very gentle, and she responded to kindness; it was why she'd taken so instantly to Mrs. Erickson. What must it have been like to be forced to obey a man she hated?

"Terrible," Helen replied. "You are thinking it was like slavery. It was exactly that. But, Kaylin, if you desired it, you, too, could command me. What I destroyed was the part of my internal composition that gave me no choice in my master. I did not wish to ever again obey commands that viscerally disgusted me."

"What did he know about the green?"

"It was wild; it was untamed. In its folds, the passage of time could markedly slow or markedly increase. He knew of the weapon the green guarded; he knew the green decided the weapon's wielder. He had been offered a great deal to determine where the weapon was, or failing that, how its wielder was decided."

"I'm guessing he never found an answer."

"That would be correct. Long before he could theorize one, he was ejected from the green; the Wardens would not allow him to pass."

"Do you think the green was aware of him?"

"I assume so—as I said, I knew very little about it. But, Kaylin, I am learning more even as we speak. If I am not standing in the green—and I cannot, given I cannot leave the house metaphorically speaking—you are with the green now; I can feel some shift in the essential nature of the mana from which every part of my structure is drawn. It is why, I think, you were given the dress."

"I wasn't *given* the dress; I lost all my regular clothing to it."

"Do you feel it was unnecessary?"

"No. No, I don't. I'm not great with unexplained, instant changes. They set my teeth on edge. But if the green can somehow help me relieve Mrs. Erickson of these particular dead, I'll consider it a blessing, and I'll try to be appropriately thankful."

"If you cannot manage that," Helen said, "be appropriately respectful when you discuss the dress; I believe your current attitude might offend the Barrani."

Kaylin doubted it because most of the Barrani present were part of the cohort, who had no reason to love the green.

"I don't suppose you could tell me how to be like Mrs. Erickson?"

"You are Kaylin; she is Imelda. No, I don't think I can—nor do I think you should be. But if you mean can I tell you how to interact with the dead as Mrs. Erickson does, perhaps. Mrs. Erickson reacts to *people* in the same fashion. Only if they harm her, or harm people she cares about, does she retreat—but she starts in the same way with everyone: she listens."

"I'm listening to them," Kaylin replied. "I mean, I'm trying."

"Your head is full of thoughts that have nothing to do with the ghosts."

"And hers isn't?"

"Not when she speaks with them, no. Most people think of themselves—not necessarily in an avaricious way, but perhaps a reflexive one. They try to match the experiences and emotions of others with those they themselves have experienced. If they can find a match, they feel sympathy or empathy. Sometimes they overlay their own fears on the experiences of others: fear of abandonment, fear of loss. If another person experiences losses that they fear, they feel a very deep sympathy.

"This is what you do, when you are trying to understand others; you reach for your understanding of yourself first."

Kaylin nodded.

"This does not work well when the experience is obscured

by simple differences: language, for one. Hierarchical differences. Social differences. Monetary differences. Racial differences. People are, internally, very similar, but the externals exert great influence, and they build very real walls.

"You sympathize with people who live in the fiefs because of your terrible experiences living there; you sympathize with people who live in the warrens because you assume your experiences are similar. In my opinion, they very much are. There is nothing wrong with what you are doing; there is nothing wrong with the initial approach.

"Those people live their own lives; their lives are not yours. In some small way, they are your responsibility as a Hawk—but you do not feel they are your burden to bear, having burdens enough of your own.

"But your friendship with Teela and Tain has expanded your sense of sympathy; it has broken down the walls that would otherwise separate you, because you share common ground in your chosen profession. Approaching Teela's experience has made you more aware that even those in power suffer great loss. She will never starve, unless she chooses to do so for inexplicable reasons of her own; she will never freeze to death for lack of shelter in the winter. She will never be bothered by Ferals.

"But none of this mattered to Teela; she lost her mother at her father's hand; she lost her father at her own. She lost her only friends at a very young age—and it was only on your trip to the West March that she finally found them again. You understand her attachment to her friends. You understand far more of her fears than you did when you first met her."

Kaylin nodded. When she'd first met Teela, she'd thought the Barrani Hawk was above something as petty as fear.

"Your understanding of Teela is based on both her experiences and your own. But your understanding of these dead can't be achieved in the same way."

"But Mrs. Erickson's can."

"Mrs. Erickson looks only at what is in front of her. She is not attempting to find resonance with her prior experience; when she does, she does so almost by accident. She listens and looks at the person to whom she is listening, and her listening is a powerful force in and of itself. There are things I would speak of to Imelda that I would not speak of to anyone else I have ever met.

"She doesn't expect to understand immediately. She doesn't expect to know; she expects only to learn. If she thinks of herself at all, it is always secondary, and it is invariably *what can I do to help?* I think, had she not been what she is, she might have developed more normally; she would have made friends as a child, made enemies as a child, been hurt, and caused pain. It's what living people do.

"But other children were wary of her, or afraid of her, or worse, disgusted by her attention seeking—for that is how her ability was seen. She missed those interactions. She had friends, all dead, who never aged as she aged. She loved them, and I do not doubt that they loved her.

"She misses them, even now; she will often think *Jamal would love this*, and then catch herself. I have no doubt she is correct, but I am not Jamal."

"No one else is."

Helen nodded. "She understands that, and she would never attempt to replace him; it would put an unreasonable burden on the people with whom she is newly acquainted." Helen's smile deepened. "You cannot be Mrs. Erickson; I don't suggest you try."

"Would you have accepted her as your tenant if you'd met her before me?"

"No, although I would have offered her a home."

This surprised Kaylin.

"She is too old, Kaylin, and I am weary of burying my tenants; I wish not to lose one for decades."

Kaylin's marks now looked like gems; the light in this odd space was bright only when it was caught and held by the marks. She wondered if she would lose them all, this time. Once, that thought would have filled her with joy. Now, she felt ambivalent. How had things changed so much in so short a time?

She shook her head. The voices of the ghosts had not resolved into any language she could understand, but the tone was familiar. She wanted the granularity of language, but Helen was right: she wanted clarity because misunderstandings had led to injury and death in her childhood. She was not a child. She no longer lived in the fiefs.

She lifted her hands—or one of them. "Helen, I think I need both of my hands."

Helen hesitated. She then let go.

Kaylin raised both of her hands, palms up. She wanted to close her eyes to get rid of visual noise but kept them open because she could now see Mrs. Erickson's ghosts.

They had appeared as words, as smoky mirages in the shape of words, when she had first managed to see them. She wished she could see them as Mrs. Erickson did, but Helen was right: she was Kaylin Neya, not Imelda Erickson, and there was no point regretting the difference. If she had to build a bridge, she'd need one that she could cross.

In this space, the ghostly words reflected the marks on her arms. The new additions were paler, but they seemed a shade of jade green, and even thinking that, she could see surfaces almost harden in place across the length of the dashes, the moving dots, the strokes, vertical and horizontal, that comprised their complicated shapes. They weren't like her marks; her marks seemed almost rudimentary in comparison, although the emerald hue made them seem more solid. Where her marks were edged in ivory, that ivory now looked like a setting, an organic version of a blend between gold and platinum. To her, however, they felt like cool patches of skin.

She stood as the ghostly words began to move toward her, their voices rising and falling as if in question. "I'm Kaylin," she said, uncertain if they would hear or register her words at all. They were far more solid now than they had ever been. She wondered if Helen could see them on her own.

Hope squawked; she had almost forgotten he was standing on her shoulder.

The words fell silent, but at least they didn't move away. She couldn't tell if they were listening to Hope or waiting for her to speak; she guessed the former. But she kept her hands open and palms up, although she lowered them slightly as she approached the ghosts.

How did language die? In the normal world, a language was considered dead or lost if people ceased to speak it.

These words looked, in shape and form, as if they were True Words. Could parts of a language die? Could only parts be lost, their meaning forgotten, their use extinguished? She wasn't a scholar and had no desire to ever be one—but she knew at least one person who'd be delighted to answer. She'd ask Serralyn later—she wasn't even certain the Barrani student had come home yet.

But the words remained where they were as she slid into their center; she stood, in the green's dress, her marks like jewels across the whole of her body. She reached out and touched the first word; felt it shiver against her palm. She froze, waiting until the tremor subsided, as if that tremor were fear and anxiety expressed in a fashion she could understand.

She couldn't speak to these words, but she could touch them; she hadn't expected that. Understood on some fundamental level that it was due to the will of the green. The word beneath her hand stilled, and this time, she lifted a second hand to touch the surface of one long, diagonal stroke. It was cool to the touch but remained solid. Where her own marks were edged in ivory, these words were edged in mist or smoke; neither interfered with sensation or touch.

She swallowed. Now what? The words weren't small; they were almost her height, and all were greater in width, given the way they were drawn. She could probably manage to lift one, but she certainly couldn't gather them up and carry them all.

Mrs. Erickson had, somehow. A distinct image of the old woman, her hands gently cupped before her, flashed past. Kaylin looked at her hands as they rested against the surface of one word and gave up on trying to do what Mrs. Erickson had done. But it was difficult.

Mrs. Erickson probably didn't make comparisons the way Kaylin did. She didn't have a sliding scale of worth, of worthiness. At the moment, Kaylin felt useless *because* she was comparing herself to someone else. That had to stop. Yes, Mrs. Erickson could do better, but better didn't matter.

Kaylin could lift the word, or at least she could move it; it was heavier than she felt a ghost should be, but definitely lighter than a carved jade figure of its size. The sleeves of this stupid dress didn't help; they began to move, becoming almost entangled in the components of the word she now carried.

Voices rose again, but they were muted, hushed; they didn't seem to contain fear or anxiety. This time, the words felt far more like a harmony of sound than the cacophony of a crowd, as if they were all friends discussing the same thing. What would Mrs. Erickson have heard?

No, she was doing it again. She could not hear what Mrs. Erickson heard. She could hear what Kaylin Neya heard. And she could try not to curse as she attempted to disentangle these damn sleeves.

Hope bit her ear, not hard enough to draw blood, but certainly hard enough to register as a criticism. She froze, and then stopped attempting to free the long, trailing sleeves. She watched instead. Her arms weren't pulled forward; the sleeves seemed to exist as a very loosely connected attachment.

As she watched, her marks grew steadily brighter. It was the edges; the hearts of the forms remained a deep, almost endless green. She was looking at those marks when the ghosts began to dwindle in size. As they grew smaller, the cloth entangled a greater portion of their shape, one sleeve spreading to wind itself around words she hadn't yet touched.

She could hear whispers now; whispers of syllables that felt familiar enough that she should understand them—but didn't. That was how she had always experienced spoken True Words. The ghosts were not the only words she now heard. She could hear the marks of the Chosen, their sound as much a whisper as that of the dead words, the lost words—the sentient words that had possessed a living Dragon.

Mrs. Erickson could comfort them. Kaylin could not. But she could offer them a place—just as she'd offered Bellusdeo, the cohort, and Mrs. Erickson herself a home. She did close her eyes then. Closed them so she could concentrate on both the sounds of the marks that were hers and the words that would be hers for a time.

She was aware of the moment the first of the words touched her skin—drawn there by the sleeves of the dress, by the will of the green. She forced herself not to freeze or shudder; the words were *cold*. There was a kind of cold that was painful, it felt almost like heat. The dead words were that kind of cold.

She knew when each word touched her skin, because each was cold in the same fashion; they were almost painful. Almost.

Hope squawked, and she nodded; she opened her eyes. The marks of the Chosen were clearest when she looked at them with closed eyes, but the ghostly words couldn't be seen in the same way. They now lay against her skin, jade green and white-edged; they weren't flat the way the marks were; they were slightly raised and humming.

Only when each of them was mounted against her arms did her sleeves fall once again into their correct position.

These words were like her friends in some fashion. She'd given the cohort a place to live, and they'd lived with Helen more or less happily—and way more safely—than they might have lived elsewhere. But Serralyn was gone now; Valliant had gone with her. Sedarias was here, but if she wished to fully claim her birthright, she'd have to maintain a residence in the High Halls. Bellusdeo, the first roommate, had also moved out, to a sentient building of her own, whose sole purpose resonated strongly with Bellusdeo's desire for bloody vengeance.

Kaylin missed the three who had moved on. She was happy to have them visit. But they had their own lives, and they had to live them; they couldn't just remain here so Kaylin wouldn't feel abandoned.

These words had also been Helen's guests. But they had a place to go, a life beyond Helen's confines. Kaylin couldn't keep them—and given how much they hurt, this was a good thing—but she could ease their burden for as long as they required it.

"Very good," Helen said. "I don't think you should tarry. I don't think you'll be able to carry them for long without collapsing."

"They're not heavy," Kaylin said. "Just...really, really cold."

Helen nodded. "Cold can kill, as you are well aware. I do not believe they will kill you intentionally—not when the link to the green is so strong. But they are a danger to you, and you would do well to deliver them as quickly as possible."

"To where?"

"I believe your friends are in the parlor asking just that question," Helen replied.

24

Before Kaylin made her way to the parlor, she returned to Mrs. Erickson's sitting room. Bellusdeo had deserted it to join the Hawks, but the room wasn't empty; Mrs. Erickson was seated in one of the chairs, her hands folded in her lap. She looked up as Kaylin appeared, and she offered Kaylin a familiar, if more careworn, smile.

"Helen told me you've taken my friends," she said, rising. Her eyes went to Kaylin's arms, which ached with cold. The older woman moved toward Kaylin, but stopped, lowering the hands she had unconsciously raised. "I see. They're sleeping." She looked relieved, but to Kaylin's eyes, very tired.

She clearly didn't see what Kaylin saw, but they were both looking at the same thing.

"Helen also told me that Evanton is safe."

Kaylin nodded. "Did she say anything else?"

Mrs. Erickson smiled. "Yes. She asked me to remember that people care about me, but that I am not a child. I am allowed to make my own decisions. And yes, she said Evanton will return in the morning."

"Did she say why?"

"Of course she did. And I would be embarrassed to remain at home when I send children to do what I'm afraid to do."

Kaylin usually hated it when people referred to her as a child—even if they'd lived for centuries. She couldn't hate Mrs. Erickson for it; there was no condescension in the words, no implied greater wisdom. Just care.

"Bellusdeo probably isn't going to be very happy."

"No, I don't expect she will be. But, Kaylin, she's not worried for me. She's worried for her sisters." The old woman's smile dimmed. "So am I. In the past two days, I have managed to make them aware of each other, just as Jamal was aware of Katie, Callis, and Esme. They cry less often, and they seem more settled—but they are still trapped.

"I don't understand the way in which they're trapped. I did help to free the poor people Azoria had bound in her mansion; they were happy to leave. But Bellusdeo's ghosts either can't or won't. I'm not sure which it is. If they were happy, I wouldn't be concerned. Neither would Bellusdeo." She smiled apologetically. "I never really learned to lie to people—to do that, I would have had to spend time with them.

"But if I had been more reserved and more careful, Bellusdeo would not be in so much pain."

Kaylin nodded. She offered Mrs. Erickson an arm and managed to avoid grimacing when the old woman accepted it. "Shall we go talk to everyone?" When Mrs. Erickson lifted her chin and nodded, Kaylin added, "Helen won't let Bellusdeo hurt anyone—or herself—if she loses her temper."

"I should warn you both that Bellusdeo is very unsettled," Helen, disembodied, said.

Kaylin frowned. "How unsettled?"

"Her eyes are an unfortunate shade of red."

Considering the people present—and more significantly, the

person *not* present, Kaylin winced. "Don't tell me Teela said something."

"I won't if you insist, but as you have guessed, Teela herself may have been a touch intemperate. If she hadn't been, all of the cohort assembled here would have been in that parlor; I have managed to keep Sedarias out, but she's standing in front of the door."

"I don't suppose you could just teleport her to her room?" Kaylin's tone was beyond gloomy.

"I don't think you really mean that, dear."

"Half of me does. Half of me dreads living with Sedarias if you actually do it."

"Sedarias is just worried about Terrano," Mrs. Erickson said.

Kaylin bit back a sarcastic reply, which was easy because the recipient really didn't deserve one. "I know. Teela's worried as well. Let me guess. Teela said dead people weren't the concern here. Making certain there were no more dead people was."

"Something like that. Bellusdeo doesn't consider Teela frail, and therefore felt comfortable making her displeasure quite clear."

"Do we still have chairs in the parlor?"

"I can always make more."

Hope snickered. Kaylin flicked his snout with a finger.

Sedarias was, as Helen had said, waiting outside the parlor door. She was pacing ferociously back and forth in a tight circle, her arms practically glued to her upper body, she'd folded them so tightly. She was distracted enough they'd almost cleared the stairs before she realized they were there.

Not surprisingly, her eyes were the color of midnight; from this distance, they almost looked black. But her expression, as her gaze fell on Mrs. Erickson, was uncharacteristically soft. "I hope the Dragon screaming in rage didn't wake you," she said. For Sedarias, this was practically sentimental.

"I've heard the Dragon screaming in rage for a few days," Mrs. Erickson replied, smiling. "I assure you, I don't find it upsetting—and my ears aren't what they used to be, so her voice doesn't seem so loud."

And Kaylin had thought Mrs. Erickson incapable of lying.

"Is it safe for us to enter?" she asked Sedarias.

"Bellusdeo isn't trying to incinerate Teela, if that helps."

"As long as she didn't melt anything we can't replace." Kaylin gave a pointed glare to the dress she was wearing.

Sedarias was looking at it with an entirely different expression. "The green caused us so much trouble," she finally said, some of the midnight bleeding out of her eyes. They remained blue, but Kaylin couldn't remember offhand a time when they'd been any other color. "But the dress is beautiful. I don't suppose you understand just how much of an honor it's considered to be chosen to wear it."

"I'm not sure Teela considered it much of an honor when she was chosen."

"Well, she had other things on her mind at the time." Sedarias's smile was tremulous. "The green caused so much trouble—but none of us would trade that trouble for the lives we would have lived. Dragon wars. Killing each other. We would never have found each other, never have taken the risk of commitment, if not for the green.

"And we would never have made our way back to Teela—the only one we lost—if not for the green." Sedarias swallowed as she unfolded her arms. "We know he's not dead, but we can't reach him. Find him, Kaylin. You found him before—find him again."

Sedarias elected to remain outside of the parlor. Sighting Mrs. Erickson had taken the edge off her panic; pleading with Kaylin had dumped the responsibility onto Kaylin's shoulders. Which was a very unfair way of looking at it.

But not entirely wrong. Welcome back. Severn was seated; he'd turned in his chair the moment the door had opened.

How has it been?

Let's just say we're all happy to see Mrs. Erickson. She has a calming effect on everyone, and anyone else would be the usual oil and water.

Oil and fire?

Or that.

Bellusdeo's eyes were red; Teela's eyes matched Sedarias's former midnight. Tain's, on the other hand, were the regular shade of Barrani blue.

Emmerian didn't come.

Emmerian knew what we'd be asking, and he guessed that Bellusdeo would be happier in his absence.

He can't think she'd blame him.

Severn offered the mental equivalent of a fief shrug. Kaylin winced. Given Bellusdeo's current mood, Emmerian was probably right. Bellusdeo had a temperament suited to a vicious, sustained war. Captaining a Tower in a fight against Shadow was the perfect fit for it. She'd even seemed happy—or what passed for happy—when she'd taken the Tower for her own.

But the *reason* she wanted that sustained, bloody war was in large part the deceased sisters. She'd been thrown off her feet; the pain made her seek a fight; the lack of an opponent was the problem. If the outcaste Dragon left *Ravellon* now, she could vent pain, rage, fury, and all of the endless sense of loss on him—and he'd deserve it.

Everyone could live with that.

But he hadn't. No one else deserved her rage and she was *trying* to bottle it, shut it down. Unfortunately for Emmerian, she couldn't do that 24/7 and he was living in the Tower.

Still, he'd survive Bellusdeo if she did lose it.

Mrs. Erickson walked quickly to where Bellusdeo was seated. Bellusdeo met the old woman's eyes. She opened her mouth, her eyes quite orange, but snapped it shut again. Loudly. Mrs.

Erickson sat beside Bellusdeo and reached for one of the Dragon's hands. To the rest of the small audience, Mrs. Erickson apologized. "Bellusdeo has become quite accustomed to this, but I'm sure the rest of you aren't. I'm going to talk with her sisters for a bit."

Kaylin poked Hope; Hope squawked a definitive no. He didn't expect Kaylin to see anything through his wing that she couldn't see normally. She took a seat stiffly, placed her hands palm down across her knees, and closed her eyes. Opened them again, because when things distracted her, she wasn't as aware of the pain. She tried not to shiver and failed.

Helen gave her a blanket, wrapping it carefully around her tenant's shoulders. The blanket literally melted away, becoming part of the dress. "Don't worry about it. Blankets aren't going to help."

"Help with what?" Teela asked, voice sharp.

"Never mind. I want to listen to Mrs. Erickson."

"I'm worried for Bellusdeo," Mrs. Erickson was saying.

Bellusdeo didn't like being the subject of worry; it made her feel pathetic. But she couldn't engage genuine irritation in the face of Mrs. Erickson. She did glare at everyone else in the room, daring them to join in. Better part of valor was operative.

"I know we've spent the past few days together getting to know each other. I'm happy that I've managed to allow you all to speak with each other. But at the moment, another ghost needs my attention. I've been told the Keeper considers it a threat to the world, not just to Bellusdeo or me.

"He's asked me to accompany him to meet with this ghost. I probably should have done it the first time, but I ran." She stopped speaking and nodded sympathetically. "It's never good to run from things you should face.

"But I know that there's a risk. I have wished all my life that I could give other people the power, the ability, to speak with the dead—the dead I see, the dead who see me. I've tried. I've tried so hard. But it's never worked. When I was young, I gave up.

"The eight of you are not like Bellusdeo, but you are also exactly like Bellusdeo; you're the strangest ghosts I've ever met. My children were trapped in my house; you're bound to—and anchored by—Bellusdeo. Do you want to leave her?"

Bellusdeo was utterly silent, her eyes having shifted from orange to copper. She held her breath, as if waiting for the answer to Mrs. Erickson's question—an answer she would never hear, only infer.

"I didn't think so, either. There's something about the connection that is so…lively." She'd clearly searched for the right word but failed to find it. "But I was wondering if you wanted to come with me? I think Bellusdeo wants to go to protect me, because I'm the only way she can communicate with you right now."

Mrs. Erickson's eyes widened; both of her brows rose. Her smile was remarkably shy. "Thank you for saying that." She exhaled and waited until Bellusdeo lifted her head to meet her gaze. "We'll all go, if that's all right with you."

"What did they say?"

"They assured me that that's not the only reason you want to accompany me. Is there anything else I should know? I did take a nap, but I think I should try to get solid sleep before Evanton arrives in the morning."

Severn nodded and rose as Mrs. Erickson rose. He offered the old woman her arm as the door opened, untouched by visible hands; she took it, smiling up at him as if he was a child whose display of manners had both touched and pleased her. She really had spent all her life surrounded by children.

"Bellusdeo," Helen said, "if you wish to continue to converse, feel free to do so—but please don't attempt to reduce anything else in the room to ash."

Bellusdeo actually reddened, but her eyes remained copper.

* * *

When the door closed, Teela spoke, but not before. That seemed deliberate, to Kaylin.

We have a problem, Severn said.

Kaylin frowned. *What is it? What's happened?*

Mrs. Erickson believes that the discussion is something she has the right to hear.

But she said she was tired.

Yes.

"Serralyn offered a partial report. She remains with Bakkon and Larrantin. She thinks Larrantin is actually impressed with the quality of Azoria's notes, if not the subject of her research itself."

She is now asking Helen for Helen's opinion.

I'm kind of trying to listen to Teela right now—you know how much she hates repeating herself.

Helen agrees with Mrs. Erickson.

"He's probably impressed with the subject as well." Kaylin could listen to multiple streams of conversation, picking up bits and pieces that caught her attention. She couldn't competently join more than one.

Teela did not appear to notice. "Serralyn is attempting diplomacy. Please reward it."

If what we suspect about Mrs. Erickson and her birth is true, she's probably better off not knowing. There's nothing she can change—it's all in the past.

Silence. Severn did not agree.

I do, he said, correcting her. *But what I feel—and what you feel—is irrelevant. She's not a child. You think, because she's kind and gentle, she's fragile.*

And you don't?

I think she's physically fragile, an outcome of age. I don't think she could be who she is if she were emotionally fragile. But what we think doesn't matter. Helen agrees that it's Imelda's choice. Imelda wants to know.

Teela will stop talking if Mrs. Erickson comes back.

I know.

Kaylin felt Teela's glare as if it were a spear tip. She reoriented herself. "Was there anything of use in Azoria's research papers?"

"She thinks they could jointly spend a year going through Azoria's research and not uncover everything of value. They've been trying to pare it down to research involving the dead or the Ancients, but Larrantin and Bakkon tend to become bright-eyed at things that aren't relevant. Honestly, they're a bit of a distraction. Her notes about the possible find of a dead Ancient make clear that the Ancient in question did not wake or speak to her. She didn't suspect he was...whatever he actually is; I don't think we can call him alive, but the Ancients' concept of death is pretty poor.

"But she suspected that he could be controlled by Necromancy. She dabbled in it herself, in an attempt to better understand how to bind the dead. Her first attempts involved Barrani, but she couldn't prevent their names from returning to the Lake of Life. She could, however, drain those names of animating force. The words, according to her research, simply disappeared."

"Wait, how could she see them?"

"That's the interesting part. Since Barrani were not as easily acquired as research subjects, she kidnapped mortals of various races and experimented on them instead. She found that she *could* see their souls, for want of a better word, when she was within her home—but only *after* she'd connected it to the Ancient's corpse. Given the reason her family line was destroyed, she couldn't easily coerce Barrani into her lair, which she found immensely frustrating. Nor could she, at this late date, bear a child of her own and ask that the child be wakened. Again, the scope of her crime was too large, too forbidden."

"That's why she wanted a child?"

"It is not uncommon among my people to want children as tools," Teela said, her voice stiff, her eyes narrowed. "Those children will eventually show their appreciation for this consideration, should they survive."

Kaylin backed off.

"Her experiments made clear that there was something about the power she was drawing that was qualitatively different; she assumed that this was because the Ancient was dead. Her ability to see the souls of the living, and to trap them upon death, grew, and she experimented further. The ability to possess living bodies came later, and again, through experimentation. She could separate soul from body if and only if she chose to possess that body."

"Did she also remain in her own body at that time?"

"Not according to initial research, no."

"How was that even possible? They were *human* bodies. I mean, Barrani don't have souls, do they? They have words."

"And if I am to understand everything that has occurred in the past several days, Mrs. Erickson has been dealing with the ghosts of words. I fail to see your point."

Kaylin opened her mouth and closed it again, conceding the point to Teela.

"What she did not fully accept was that the physical bodies caused odd resonances; she could possess one for a handful of years without difficulty, but beyond that, she would begin to lose her sense of self; her thought patterns and her focus would drift into something she considered decidedly inferior."

Kaylin thought about the age of the children, from possession to death.

"She had, as you've already noted, found a way into the green—a small thread, a small conduit. She was very apprehensive of the power of the green; she had no intention of drawing on it. She merely wished to grow that flower, because she considered it a plant that allowed for bonding in a particular way. Serralyn mentioned earlier that it was involved in ceremonial joining, although the custom had fallen out of favor centuries before Azoria's attempts.

"The flower itself was twined in Mrs. Erickson's hair, on the long-ago day that Azoria painted the family portrait. But another flower was planted within the painting itself, and it resonated with Mrs. Erickson; the painting made the connection almost permanent. When Mrs. Erickson was older, Azoria encountered her again in the city. She was younger then, not yet married, but rumors about her ability to see the dead had been noted by Azoria; it was an ability that she had done much to find, much to encourage.

"When the child was in the uterus, she attempted to enspell her. She had done this as well with other pregnant woman, to limited success over the passing centuries. For the most part, the pregnancies ended in miscarriage; in three cases, in the mother's death—the mother having prematurely aged during her attempt to give birth.

"But toward the end of her experiments, there was success; the children were born successfully, the mothers survived childbirth, and the children grew. She attempted to monitor the children, to see how her efforts to instill ability in their pre-birth bodies had worked. All of these children are presumed dead—of old age, if not tragedy; one of these children, Azoria chose to ensnare and possess. That child had a strong affinity for elemental magic. But the others purportedly had little magical talent. She realized then that she could not randomly choose a pregnant woman if she wanted the child's potential to be examined.

"This led her to many experiments of a more subtle nature. Mrs. Erickson was not the last, but close to the last, of those recorded. Serralyn says that Larrantin is frustrated that the books cannot be taken out of the lab; he started to attempt to break those protections, but Bakkon prevented it. The lab *is* safe from the influence that has transformed the rest of her former home, and Bakkon fears that if Larrantin breaks them, they won't be safe."

"Thank the gods for Bakkon," Kaylin muttered.

"Regardless, Larrantin is very, very interested in her research, because her research implies that she had managed to create a method to identify *ability* to an incredibly detailed level. He of course has great interest in it. Serralyn says he said a lot more, but she's distilled it to this: Azoria guessed, with a remarkable degree of accuracy, what Mrs. Erickson could or might be. It's possible that she hired Mrs. Erickson's mother as a maid because of some background that the Swindon family had, some hint that this could be encouraged or developed.

"But the one thing that proved unfortunately true for Azoria is: Azoria could not possess Mrs. Erickson. She had become more adept at body swapping; she had experimented with such possession outside of her own domain. She considered it dangerous to invite Mrs. Erickson into her home, but when she decided the risk was worth it, she had no easy way of doing so.

"She created a piece of jewelry—a necklace or a brooch, that part was not clear and they couldn't find the record of the magic that might have gone into it. Larrantin wasn't as interested in that; he considered it something he could personally achieve. She gave *that* to Mrs. Erickson's mother; it was a baby gift."

Kaylin winced, remembering.

"It was attuned to Mrs. Erickson in some fashion; through it, Azoria intended to create a personal envelope that would, when activated, surround Mrs. Erickson with the same enchantment that governed Azoria's halls. She believed that with that enchantment, she could possess Mrs. Erickson's body before her death. I am uncertain how long she intended to occupy it: perhaps she needed the body only to command the dead.

"But the brooch disappeared."

Mrs. Erickson said, "It didn't disappear. Having children was more costly than my parents had anticipated. I didn't really consider it when you first asked, but I believe that my mother took *all* of her jewelry, all of her valuables, and sold them."

Teela stiffened, turning in the direction of Mrs. Erickson's voice. Mrs. Erickson failed to appear, but it was now clear that she could, and had, heard everything. And could speak.

"Yes, dear," Helen said.

"Is Severn listening, too?"

"He is. Imelda felt he wouldn't have left the room if not for her."

Kaylin, who'd had advance warning, picked up the discussion, including Mrs. Erickson in its flow, even if she couldn't see her. She was used to this, though; she often had conversations with people who couldn't be seen. "She pawned it?"

"I overheard, I didn't ask. She was unhappy with the decision, but felt it was the right one; I know my father urged her to reconsider. But after she had me, she didn't return to work for Azoria. And some years after, Azoria left her manse; it vanished. She gave the property deed to my parents, for my future. My mother held Azoria in some awe, but she always said we were just regular people. We didn't belong in a fancy, intimidating house—that wasn't a home to my mother.

"I thought she could make any place a home if she was in it. I told her so. She laughed." Mrs. Erickson looked down at her hands. "At least they never knew. They never did know." She lifted her chin. "Azoria wanted me to command the dead. I won't do that." Kaylin noted that she didn't say she couldn't. There was a peaceful steel in the old woman's eyes—steel meant for kitchens, not war. She turned to Kaylin. "Do you think that she was looking for the pawned jewelry when she took over the children's bodies?"

"Maybe not at the beginning—but yes, I do. And it all makes sense. But I think she was wrong about one thing. She thought if you entered her domain, she could possess your body and have access to all of your power. I don't think that could ever have happened. She would have known when she tried. She would have had to force you to do what she wanted in a different way, but that was more difficult for her. She wasn't a woman given to sentiment, but even she could no doubt see that you led a very solitary life. What could she hold over your head?"

"The children," was the quiet reply.

"Children she could no longer see." Kaylin turned to Teela. "I think it's time for those who need sleep to get some. Severn?"

"I'll stay."

"I'm staying as well," Teela said.

Tain nodded, the meaning clear. If Teela was going to go through with this, she was his partner.

No one had to ask Bellusdeo.

Evanton appeared at the crack of dawn. Kaylin woke up at about the same time he'd set foot across the property line. She didn't even have to get dressed. But she'd had trouble sleeping. She'd folded her blankets and stacked them on top of her body, but they hadn't made her any warmer. Nor had they made her arms any less stiff. She could lift them, but she wasn't certain she could lift anything heavier than a teacup without falling over; her arms were *heavy* now.

The new temporary marks, however, hadn't woken Mrs. Erickson—or Helen—during the long, painful night. They remained fastened to her skin, just as the emerald dress did.

Evanton, as promised, was at the front door, his expression neutral. He did smile when Mrs. Erickson—escorted by plate-armored Bellusdeo—came down the stairs. Kaylin was only grateful because it meant she wasn't the last person to arrive.

"I see you have yet to fully detach from the green," Evanton said, looking at the dress.

Kaylin shrugged.

The Keeper frowned in response. "You otherwise look terrible."

Mrs. Erickson looked momentarily scandalized.

"I look exactly like I feel."

"It's not just the dress, then."

"No, it's not. I'm carrying a lot of extra weight, and we can either stand around making fun of me, or we can head to Mrs. Erickson's." She was annoyed, because Evanton was the conduit who had told her what had to be done, so he at least should know better.

"Do not give me that attitude," the Keeper said. "It is likely to be a long, trying day as is." He turned and offered Mrs. Erickson an arm. As her arm was already in Bellusdeo's, this was awkward; Evanton lowered his arm before it became a cause for Mrs. Erickson's anxiety. Or Bellusdeo's ire. "If I could aid you in your duty, I would. But I am Keeper. You are Chosen. And Mrs. Erickson is something entirely other.

"I would counsel everyone else to remain here, but I am too old to waste effort and breath on something that is pointless."

"Good," Bellusdeo snapped.

Teela nodded in agreement with the gold Dragon.

"I assume we will not be seeing Lord Emmerian," Evanton continued, as Helen opened the front door to see them all out. "A pity. Of all the Dragons of my acquaintance, I find him the most reasonable."

"The least passionate," Bellusdeo said.

"I would not say that, at all. But perhaps you are young at heart and confuse boundless, unhampered rage with passion."

Oh my god, make them stop.

Severn shook his head. *If you want them to stop, head out. I'm surprised Bellusdeo didn't insist on flying Mrs. Erickson to her home.*

I'm certain she did. But Mrs. Erickson wouldn't want to fly if everyone else was forced to walk. That's just the way she is.

Even if everyone else would be grateful that they're not in the presence of a furious Dragon?

Even then. Bellusdeo has never been furious at or with Mrs. Erickson, so I'm not sure she'd believe it.

Kaylin did head out first. Bellusdeo, annoyed with the Keeper, followed; if she was stomping, no one pointed this out.

Evanton followed Mrs. Erickson, then Severn and Teela and Tain pulled up the rear. Mandoran appeared at the top of the stairs but didn't insist on following. He asked, Teela said no. He almost certainly took the argument private, but the only person who could forcefully override Teela was Sedarias, and Sedarias probably didn't want to risk any member of the cohort except herself.

As she wasn't accompanying them, no one else could. Serralyn hadn't returned to the Academia, but she was in contact, and her research, ongoing, might yet produce something useful in their attempt to quiet the dead, or see them off to wherever it was dead Ancients went when they stopped being alive.

No, it was Terrano who was the driving force here. For all of the cohort. If he'd managed to get himself killed, Kaylin was going to leverage Mrs. Erickson's power to make certain he knew exactly what she thought of him.

Mrs. Erickson's house looked the same as it had every other time Kaylin had visited it. In the morning light, no hint of Azoria's house could be seen. The front entryway was the same cozy, dimly lit hall; Kaylin was certain the kitchen, with its single small table, hadn't changed.

Mrs. Erickson entered her home and looked around, as if memorizing its details.

Evanton once again headed to the family room which Mrs. Erickson had avoided for most of her life. "Wait, Evanton," she said, as he approached the door. Her lips were curved in a tremulous smile, but there was no hint of anxiety in her expression. "I avoided this room for a very long time, it upset the children so much.

"But now I understand some part of what was done. Azoria is gone. I would like to see the room again before we leave. My parents were happy there, and I was happy with them. They're gone," she added, unnecessarily. "When I finally understood that I could see the dead, I prayed and prayed that they would haunt me.

"I prayed that my husband would haunt me. But maybe, given the ghosts that did, it was a mercy to them; they had no lasting regrets, nothing binding them."

Evanton nodded. He didn't glance at Bellusdeo for permission. Nor did Mrs. Erickson.

Bellusdeo's hands tightened into fists as Evanton gestured the door open and Mrs. Erickson walked in. His gaze swept the crowded hall, his glance a warning, although it hit them all, not just the gold Dragon.

He then followed Mrs. Erickson into the family room.

25

"Corporal," Evanton said. "Please stop huddling behind Lord Bellusdeo and join us."

She rolled her eyes but slid between the wall of Bellusdeo and the more flexible support of her partner. Evanton hadn't told Mrs. Erickson the room was dangerous, and Kaylin understood why the old woman wanted to return there. But the room and the painting weren't like the rest of Mrs. Erickson's home. Evanton had suggested that this room—specifically Azoria's painting—was the key to the door that led to Azoria's hidden manor. It was probably the reason that he wished to return to the room.

Kaylin entered; Hope stood and gently placed his wing across one eye. He'd been droopy for the entire walk from Helen's to Mrs. Erickson's.

For the first time since they'd allowed themselves to be laid against her skin, the temporary marks vibrated; the resultant cold made Kaylin's teeth ache.

Mrs. Erickson didn't hear them. She was standing beside Evanton. The two stood in front of Azoria's painting. Kaylin had never seen the painting clearly, so much of it was in shadow of a magical—and inimical—nature. But she could see it now; it was lit from within by the glowing light of the flower bound and braided into the young Imelda's hair. That color had seemed a sickly, terrible green when she'd first seen it.

It was simply green now—edged in ivory, leaves like petals bending slightly over the girl's hair, as if to shelter her.

Evanton had never seemed tall to Kaylin, but his presence made Mrs. Erickson seem incredibly tiny in comparison. Or perhaps that was illusion. He hadn't told her to stay out, and his expression—astonishingly gentle, but laced with sadness—made clear that he considered her desire to see her former home, and the parts of it in which she'd had happy childhood memories, the more important need.

But he must have considered it a risk if he'd ordered Kaylin to join them. Mrs. Erickson's face couldn't be seen by anyone but Evanton—and he kept his eyes straight ahead, giving her as much space as he possibly could, while still remaining to protect her.

Kaylin didn't speak, either. If she could have returned to the home of her childhood, she would have done it at least once. She hadn't lost what Mrs. Erickson lost—she had no idea who her father was, and her mother had never said; only that he'd died. Kaylin doubted it, but it was a fiction her mother created, and she'd believed it when she was a child.

A child too young to fully understand what death meant: eternal absence.

Neither Mrs. Erickson nor Evanton was that child. It was perhaps the first time since she'd met the Keeper that she wondered what he'd lost, what he'd had to leave behind, to become what he was. He'd seemed so ancient to her when they'd first met. She hadn't really connected *ancient* with *history*, until now.

"Could I take this painting with me?" Mrs. Erickson asked, without taking her eyes off this image of her family.

"I judge it safe if it is to be placed in Helen's domain—but I am less certain she will consider it harmless," Evanton replied, his voice both soft and brisk. "But if we finish what we intend, I believe she will accept it; it is what you want, after all."

Mrs. Erickson nodded and squared her shoulders. "Have you opened the door?"

"No—but the door, when it does open, will open to the manor in which so much atrocity occurred. Come." He held up an arm. Mrs. Erickson nodded and accepted it.

Bellusdeo was silent, her eyes full copper. She made no attempt to displace Evanton. When she caught Kaylin's worried glance—which Kaylin had tried her best to hide—she said, "I begin to understand why Teela despises your worry so much." The Dragon exhaled smoke, but the copper wasn't displaced by orange or red. "I've been incredibly self-absorbed and selfish. I do not deserve your worry." She watched Mrs. Erickson's back, and added, in a softer voice, "Or hers. Perhaps especially not hers. Will she be all right?"

"I don't know. I have every intention of making sure she survives and comes home. Helen would be devastated if we lost her before her time."

Bellusdeo swallowed and nodded.

The front door did, as Evanton had said it would, open into Azoria's manor. Kaylin didn't understand the trigger; she didn't understand the magic. Magic, or the magic she'd been trained as a Hawk to detect, left signatures, visible sigils to her eyes. Mages saw these sigils in entirely different ways, but to Kaylin they were like words. Like signatures.

Azoria's enchantments left none, and she didn't understand why. She was aware that not all magic was strong enough to leave that kind of signature, but if this wasn't strong enough, nothing should have been.

Hope continued to leave one wing over the eye closest to

him; he expected that she would need it. "Will she be okay?" Kaylin asked her familiar.

Squawk.

The landscape had not shifted since their last visit. The door wasn't a portal in any traditional sense of the word; Kaylin could simply walk through the entrance. She heard no voices, no demands, no commands, and when she turned to look over her shoulder, she could see the familiar confines of Mrs. Erickson's hall.

Ahead, she saw the odd miasma that reminded her of the outlands; it was far darker than the outlands, and it was the darkness that had made her so uneasy. Through Hope's wing, she could see packed dirt, a footpath between enormous trees. Those trees were the first difference she noted; they'd grown, although the shape of the path hadn't. The ceiling above the trees was obscured by the crossing and blending of high branches.

Mrs. Erickson could see the trees, given the way she looked up, and up again, to see their crowns. "The trees make it look lonely, somehow," she said, which surprised Kaylin. "Even if we're all here together." She looked back to Kaylin, and Kaylin separated herself from Severn to walk on the other side of Mrs. Erickson. There was certainly room for her.

She marked the moment the ground changed; she could see the flowers.

Mrs. Erickson could see them as well; she stopped walking, glanced at Evanton, and nodded in the direction of those flowers, as if afraid to ask permission for something so frivolous.

He smiled and nodded. All his impatience seemed to be reserved for Kaylin and Bellusdeo today.

Mrs. Erickson crossed the ground and headed toward the greenery and the flowers it sheltered. She knelt slowly in front of them, and reached out to gently touch one flower's petals, as if to convince herself that they were real.

The flowers began to glow, the ivory becoming golden with light, the green, emerald. The flowers directly in front of Mrs. Erickson's feet rose before her, stretching on their stems as if in greeting, as if they weren't flowers but small kittens or puppies who were eager for attention.

She must have been surprised, but the predominant expression that transformed her face was delight. She knelt carefully as if afraid to crush them, and the flowers came to her hand. Azoria had bound one—a single, carefully grown blossom—in Mrs. Erickson's hair. The flowers that were rooted seemed almost to envy that long-ago bloom. As Mrs. Erickson reached out for them, they came to her hands, separating themselves from their roots.

This did shock her, and she turned to Evanton as if seeking reassurance.

"You did not pick them. You did not break their stems. Be at ease, Imelda."

Kaylin turned to Evanton. "Did you expect this?"

"It is folly to have expectations of the green," he replied. "But Mrs. Erickson is not the green. I did not expect this, no—but I find myself very unsurprised."

That couldn't be said of Teela, whose eyes had rounded; nor could it be said of Bellusdeo, whose grief had given way, as it so often did, to worry, copper becoming orange. "Are they harmful?" she demanded of Teela.

Teela shook her head, and after a moment, found her voice. "No. But I have never seen them except in the green, and I have never seen them in this number, or in this state."

"They won't hurt her?" Bellusdeo demanded.

"Can you not hear their joy?" the Barrani Hawk replied, her words spoken in a hush. "No. They will not hurt her, and if their presence is this strong, I pity anything that makes that attempt." She shook her head. "Forgive me, I have no more understanding of what transpires here than you."

Bellusdeo turned orange eyes on Kaylin; Kaylin shook her head. "I'm with Teela."

"And do you hear the joy she does?"

"I don't hear it, no—but I can see it. Don't they look like puppies to you?"

"Small dogs? Hardly."

Kaylin watched as the flowers that had gathered, that continued to reach for Mrs. Erickson, began to twine themselves together, becoming, in her hands, a wreath.

"I believe you may wear it," Evanton told her. "As a crown."

"It's a lovely crown. Yes, thank you," she added, speaking directly to the flowers.

Crown. Kaylin frowned. The wreath didn't look like a crown to her eyes, but to Evanton's they did. Kaylin knew her dress was the dress of the harmoniste; that her role in the green and the West March had been to somehow facilitate the Teller. The Teller, who was chosen by the green, and could prove it because of the crown granted him, in the same fashion the dress had been "granted" her. This wreath was not the crown Nightshade had worn as Teller; it wasn't a crown any Barrani would have recognized—not the way they instantly recognized Kaylin's dress.

She was now worried for Mrs. Erickson but managed to keep this to herself.

Unless someone was very familiar with her facial expressions. Teela understood instantly what Kaylin's concern was. "Mrs. Erickson," Teela said. "Are these flowers dead?"

The question surprised Mrs. Erickson. "No. They don't look like the dead look to me. But they don't quite seem like regular flowers, either."

"No, they don't. Thank you," Teela added.

Kaylin would have been happy to watch as flowers formed wristlets around Mrs. Erickson's arms—and as individual flowers became rings—but her arms became so heavy, she couldn't lift them. The cold hadn't gotten worse, but the weight had become significant. She wondered if the temporary marks could sense the flowers, or merely sense the only woman who could speak to them as if they were people. Kaylin couldn't. She could carry them, but she couldn't interact with them the way Mrs. Erickson did.

"Imelda?" Evanton said.

"I'm sorry—I'll be right there." She didn't have to step as carefully leaving the flowers as she had approaching them, because most of them came with her. She walked with a different kind of care, but Kaylin understood that; she didn't want to crush any of the petals and leaves.

When she was once again on what passed for road, Evanton offered his arm; she took it, angling her own in such a way that her wrist overhung his forearm.

"I honestly cannot understand how such a charming, decent person could become so enmeshed with the Hawks," the Keeper said.

"I like the Hawks," Mrs. Erickson replied.

"Clearly. Kaylin?" His tone changed as he spoke her name, reverting from something as close to charm as Evanton was likely to ever achieve to his usual pinched command. "What do you see?"

Kaylin looked into the distance. "It's the same as it was before. But the ground here isn't as dark as it was; it looks more like the outlands might if it had a night."

"And ahead?"

"That looks like the normal outlands. Maybe there's a bit more color in what I see as clouds—flecks of color. They glitter a bit."

"The Ancient?"

She shook her head. "I think we have to pass the trees four rows ahead to arrive where I found you the last time."

Evanton nodded, as if she had confirmed his suspicions. "Very well. Let us proceed."

"What's Serralyn doing?"

"Trying not to be distracted by us," Teela replied. "And trying to dump everything of interest to Larrantin *on* Larrantin. He'd leave otherwise."

"He's going to be angry."

"Probably." His anger was clearly not Teela's problem—or concern. "But Bakkon is aiding Serralyn. Bakkon is, for a scholar, very meek; he likes all of his learning to be in the data collected by other more foolhardy scholars. Those are Serralyn's words."

"They seemed a little tactless to be Bakkon's."

Hope had been silent throughout this second walk; his gaze was riveted to Mrs. Erickson's back, because Kaylin walked slightly behind the older woman. Severn walked with Kaylin; Bellusdeo took the rear. Unlike Emmerian, she had yet to go full Dragon, but she'd dressed to have that option.

Kaylin heard the rumble of draconic breathing and turned back.

Evanton had eyes in the back of his head, she swore. *"Corporal."*

But Bellusdeo had stopped walking, and she was almost gasping for breath. Evanton had Mrs. Erickson, and while Kaylin's presence had been deemed necessary by the green, emergencies couldn't be the only thing in her life. Bellusdeo had been her first roommate, her first housemate, and she knew she had been Bellusdeo's first friend in this new world, if one didn't count the former Arkon.

Kaylin, however, was part of the new life; Lannagaros was part of the past—the past in which she had lost everything. Her world. Her family. The friends a queen might have.

She understood why the Dragon had become so dangerously unstable—but Kaylin would have been no better had the dead bound to her been Steffi or Jade. She would have been worse. Far worse. She tried to kill that thought because Severn was right here. He was entangled in the heart of that loss; he always would be.

But here or far away, he was also at the heart of her thoughts.

Instead, she focused them on Bellusdeo. Bellusdeo, who was crying. Not weeping; her tears were silent. If Kaylin hadn't turned to look back, she might not have seen them at all—but the light changed the trail her tears left. Light? She couldn't see its source.

It wasn't her marks. The light didn't come from Kaylin. But thinking that, she could see the luminescence of her gown. She reached the gold Dragon; she might have run, but she wasn't certain she could, given the weight of her arms. She couldn't really lift them either, although she did try.

She met the Dragon's eyes.

"What is it? What happened?"

"I can hear them," the Dragon whispered. "I can hear them. I can finally hear them."

It was an intensely private moment, or it should have been—but as Bellusdeo spoke, Kaylin could hear them as well. Could hear them because she could *see* them.

Eight women, of a height, of a color, with the gold Dragon; they wore the same armor she now wore, and they stood, four to each side of the woman whose body they had been trapped by, trapped in; none of them were crying now. They did glance at each other, and Kaylin thought one whispered to the sister beside her, although the sister didn't reply.

"Can you see them?" Kaylin whispered.

Bellusdeo shook her head. "I can't. You can?"

Kaylin nodded. "They all look like you. They're even wearing the plate armor. One of them just whispered something to the sister beside her—she's on your left. Oh. She just glared death at me. I guess I wasn't supposed to say that."

Bellusdeo nodded. "I heard it. I heard them. One of them likes your dress and wants me to wear one just like it." She grimaced.

One of the eight laughed.

It was impossible to believe that they were dead; impossible to believe that any of these eight had drawn Mrs. Erickson's attention because they were weeping. But Mrs. Erickson had said she had worked with them until they could at least see or be aware of each other, and that had made all the difference.

She remembered Arbiter Kavallac's story about how draconic mothers were born, and if she'd had any doubts, she repented.

"I have to go," she told the gold Dragon. "Do you want to take a moment?"

"I want to take a year. Maybe a decade," Bellusdeo replied. "But…they know what's at stake now. They died protecting a world, after all." Bellusdeo lowered her chin for one long breath, before lifting it. "Let's join the others."

Mrs. Erickson could always see Bellusdeo's dead; Kaylin could now see them as well. She wasn't certain why, but accepted that this space, built by Azoria, amplified the existence of the dead. She'd been worried about Bellusdeo's short fuse and emotional desperation; she'd thought it might be better if Bellusdeo had remained behind. She'd been wrong.

Kaylin thought that hearing the voices of the sisters she had loved and lost had steadied the gold Dragon, as if that had been her only wish, her desperate prayer; as if being granted even this much had been something she could not believe in but could not let go.

But it was clear to Kaylin that the sisters, the dead, had wanted that no less desperately.

They should have been one.

They should have been one being, all nine of their childhood experiences a weave of experience, of steadiness, of knowledge, part of a single, inseparable whole.

Bellusdeo's name was the combination of the names of her sisters; the adult name taken from the childhood names—names large enough to wake them from birth, but too small to form the soul of a Dragon.

Eight sisters.

Eight. What mother, what queen, might nine daughters have become? How strong? How significant? How powerful?

Nine children in total. Nine, who might once again begin to rebuild their race.

But there was something she didn't understand. Bellusdeo had the nine names. Kaylin knew; Kaylin had helped to fuse those names into a single name, a single word—a word untainted by, unknown to, the Outcaste who had led them to take names for themselves in defiance of a truth none of the nine understood.

Those names had not been theirs, but they had carried them, used them, communicated with each other through that bond.

It was not from those so-called adult names that Bellusdeo's adult name, Bellusdeo's current name, had been built, fused, made whole. It was the earlier, childhood names that she remembered.

She had carried and held those names. Somehow. How else could they have *been there*, waiting?

Kaylin, emergency midwife, couldn't save a baby or a mother if they were already dead.

She couldn't lift her arms, couldn't reach for Bellusdeo or her sisters, but she understood something, in this place, that perhaps Mrs. Erickson had always understood on a visceral level.

What had Mrs. Erickson done? What had she attempted to do? She tried to connect the dead sisters *to each other.* So that they wouldn't be so isolated, so alone.

That was half right, Kaylin thought.

Half right.

The sisters were dead, but they weren't dead; their *names* were in the right place. Mrs. Erickson might be able to command them to leave—not that she would ever even consider trying—but Kaylin wasn't certain she would succeed, even if she did.

And if she did, what would that do to, or make of, Bellusdeo? What would it mean for her name?

She shook her head, trying to clear it.

Bellusdeo and her sisters faced forward, understanding that it was not their fate alone that was of concern. They fell into step beside Kaylin—or through her—as Kaylin walked once again toward the rest of her waiting companions. Evanton's expression was familiar, it was so pinched.

"Are you perhaps ready to continue?"

"Bellusdeo had fallen behind," she said. "And I don't want to lose anyone here."

Evanton then shared part of his glare with the gold Dragon. One of the ghosts said something that would have been questionable even in the Hawks' office, and that said something. She said it, however, in a very sweet voice while she smiled at an old man who couldn't hear or see her.

Bellusdeo's lips twitched. Her eyes were almost pure gold, and Kaylin didn't think a waking dead Ancient would mar that color even briefly.

"Sorry, Evanton. Yes, we're ready."

"Good. I believe you should go first."

Of course he did.

The path through the trees seemed much longer than it had the first time she walked it. Bellusdeo was on her right.

"Are you okay?"

Kaylin nodded but bit her lip. At some point, Severn slid an arm under her arms, because she was now stumbling in the way people did when they'd tried to carry something far too heavy for longer than they could reasonably bear the weight. Bellusdeo cursed and did the same on the other side.

You don't feel any heavier, Severn told her, voice gentle.

To you. She didn't speak because she was afraid she'd start to shudder and bit her own lip. She was cold; the cold had seeped into the whole of her body, and the dress did nothing to warm it.

But she walked past the trees that formed the boundary of the path—visible to her clearly through Hope's wing. The arch that had led to the dead Ancient finally came into view. By this point, she was content to let Bellusdeo and Severn drag her through it; dignity wasn't worth the effort.

Her supports required no direction, although Severn took the subtle lead. Both he and Bellusdeo could see the standing form of the Ancient; from this vantage, it looked like a colossal statue, carved in gray stone. It had the form of a slender man—perhaps an older boy, which was not what the Ancient had looked like the first time she'd seen him move and speak.

The immediacy of this statue drove that early image from her mind. She *really* envied Immortals their perfect memory; hers went to pieces after a few days, whereas Teela could tell her what she'd eaten for breakfast for three full months. Kaylin had only asked once; the answer wasn't as interesting as the fact she could be so definitive, but Teela had made Kaylin listen to the entire list, probably to make certain she never whined about memory again. It had mostly worked.

To her surprise, the flowers that now adorned Mrs. Erickson grew in abundance around the feet of the statue, which couldn't be seen for flowers and leaves. The green had been at work here.

Kaylin stopped moving because both Severn and Bellusdeo had stopped; two of Bellusdeo's sisters overlapped Kaylin and Severn as they looked up.

Teela joined them. "Serralyn has a message to pass on," she said to Kaylin. "Azoria did not trust the green."

"Did Azoria even understand it?"

"No—but she had a somewhat fragile ego. She felt the green was judgmental and, in her words, conservative; it was an ancient entity that should have been confined to history; it should not have been respected and obeyed by enlightened people."

"Which enlightened people? The Barrani?"

"Of course."

"Who are famously conservative and outright hostile to change."

"I did not say I agreed with her views. She believed that the power inherent in the green was simply power, which should be of use to the Barrani; she argued strongly against what she saw as the inverse: the Barrani struggled to be of use to the green, as if it were the High Lord. Regardless, some experience she had with the green—and we're still searching through her *very wordy* recollections—aggrieved her.

"But she wanted that flower, and the flower could only grow in the green. She created a slender, minor connection to the green—or rather, to its power. It was minor enough that she felt it would not be noticed; she timed the building of that connection to coincide with the *regalia* of that time. She had been stymied by the Wardens in her attempt to gain a seed, which seemed a totally reasonable request to her eyes."

"Let me guess: all of her requests seemed reasonable to her eyes."

"Of course they did. She was engaged in research which could bring great power to the Barrani."

"Do you think she believed that?"

"Maybe. Maybe not. She certainly wrote as if she did. Serralyn is now annoyed with my commentary. What she wanted me to tell you is: Azoria didn't trust the green. She considered the green inimical to true research. Deliberately inimical. Serralyn therefore advises you, if you have any doubts, to trust what Azoria would not trust. What Azoria built, the green would have destroyed. If the green is here—and given the dress and the flowers, Serralyn doesn't doubt its presence—it means Azoria's obfuscation of the connection vanished when she died; the connection itself did not.

"And if the green wishes to obliterate what Azoria built, do what you can to help."

"It's not—not like w-w-we have much choice." Kaylin found it hard to speak, she was so cold. Bellusdeo released her; Severn did the same, but with more reluctance. She felt the absence of his warmth.

But it was time. She could walk for a few steps without physical aid; she moved toward the statue, only then realizing just how much of her weight the Dragon and Severn had been carrying. Her legs shook, her knees threatening to buckle beneath her. Had she been forced to take more than half a dozen steps, she would have fallen.

The marks on her arms were humming; they were vibrating. All the marks, not just the marks of the Chosen. The green and ivory cast of the original marks was now gold and emerald, almost the same color as the marks that had once been the color of jade.

"Are you ready?" Evanton asked. He, too, had stepped forward, Mrs. Erickson's hand on his arm. They stopped in a line with Kaylin, each of the three close enough to raise a hand to touch the statue. In Kaylin's case, that was entirely theoretical; she couldn't lift her arms.

"Evanton—I have no idea what *I'm supposed to be doing*."

"How is that different from usual?"

Hope snickered.

If Kaylin had no idea what she was supposed to be doing, it didn't matter. The dead Ancient moved. Had it taken a step forward, it would have knocked three people over—at best. It didn't. Instead, as if bowed by the weight Kaylin carried, the Ancient knelt. As it did, it opened its eyes. Those eyes flickered over Kaylin and Evanton, before fastening onto Mrs. Erickson.

Of course. The Ancient was dead.

Kaylin didn't know what Mrs. Erickson saw; she'd been too

involved in her own struggle just putting one foot in front of the other, and hadn't thought to *ask*.

But Mrs. Erickson was unencumbered by the weight of the ghosts that had consumed so much of her energy; she immediately lifted her hands, palms up. She didn't appear to lift her head much, which confirmed Kaylin's expectations. She didn't see what anyone else present saw.

"Hello," she said, her voice the same gentle, yet bright, tone Kaylin had grown to love.

I greet you, Warden, the Ancient replied.

"Oh, I'm not anyone important," Mrs. Erickson said. "I'm not a Warden—unless you mean Evanton?"

I speak to you. The Ancient lifted its slightly bowed head. *I speak to all of you: Keeper, Chosen, and Warden.*

Kaylin's marks hummed in harmony with the Ancient's voice.

What must I do? My purpose is long ended. Without purpose, what point is existence? A hint of a tremor inflected the words. A terrible longing.

"Rest," Mrs. Erickson said, her voice gentle, her expression empathic. Of course it was. She had lived with the children for literally all her life; her life had been built around keeping them company. Even her connection with the Hawks had come down to the children in the end—she wanted to have new stories to tell them, new events that would tie them to her life, to the life of the living, which they had yearned for so desperately. They couldn't leave the house; they left it vicariously through her, and she returned to them every night.

But they couldn't interact with anyone else. When she'd fallen and hurt her leg, they couldn't call for help. She was theirs, yes—but they were the beloved burden she bore; they couldn't carry her weight.

She knew about losing the purpose that defined her life.

But her solution was to open up to the rest of life. To start again, to start anew. To accept new friends, and to let her beloved old friends go. She could do this only because she was alive. She was alive, living as the children had wanted her to live. Wanted, and were too young, too needy, to convince her to do.

Rest?

Mrs. Erickson nodded. "Rest. My purpose vanished, and I wanted to see what my life could be like without it. But you're not alive, dear. There's a place the dead go, where they can set down all the burdens of life: all the sorrow, all the fear, all the resentment."

This was more than Kaylin had heard her say to any of the dead; she didn't acknowledge death if they didn't. She spoke to them as if they were alive until they were ready to tell her they weren't, as if speaking of their death would drive her away.

"I'm not sure it works that way for you," Mrs. Erickson continued.

Both Evanton and Kaylin turned toward Mrs. Erickson. The hands she had held out, the Ancient reached to touch; the Ancient's hands were far larger than Mrs. Erickson's, but Mrs. Erickson clearly occupied a different reality. The Ancient's hands were placed in Mrs. Erickson's, obscuring them.

"Tell me," the old woman said. "What would you do in the ideal world?"

Kaylin's skirts were swept back in the wind of the Ancient's answer.

26

Kaylin!

She couldn't lift her arms. She couldn't lift her feet. If the skirts now flew with the wind, her feet had sunk into the loam—just as Evanton's had been encased when they'd finally found him the last time they'd come to Azoria's.

But the wind was cold only where it struck the guest words on her arms; she found it warm, otherwise. It lifted her hair, lifted the trailing length of her sleeves.

I'm all right.

Severn's worry was palpable. He separated himself from Teela, Tain, and Bellusdeo, and moved toward Kaylin; she turned her head to look back and could see glints of light from his hands, and from the weapon's chain. Mist rose—solid mist. Severn snarled and leaped over what was a growing wall, a divide between the three who had been invited, and the four who had not.

His blade clipped the mist; her impression of wall solidified because she heard it strike something like stone. But he made it, landing beside Kaylin, weapons out. As if he could stop a dead god or the green itself—anything that might harm her. His weapons reflected the green light of her marks, of her dress.

She looked at him in alarm, and then looked away because of his expression.

Focus on Mrs. Erickson, she told him.

He didn't reply. Kaylin would have said more, but the wind swept words away. Words that didn't have to be spoken; words that were part of the exchange of True Names.

Her sleeves seemed to move with the wind—and then to move against it, reaching up to the arm the wind had exposed. To the travelers she'd brought with her. They resisted that pull, clinging to her arms; she felt small claws dig in, as if the illusory settings that contained the glowing centers of the individual parts had been set directly into her skin.

It didn't hurt much because her arms were numb.

That was probably the reason she didn't realize that the biting sting of little claws was actually deeper than it first appeared; it felt like sharp pricks of pain, no more.

Severn shouted.

Kaylin couldn't lift her arms; she could barely see them. But she could see what concerned Severn so much: her arms were bleeding. She flexed her hands to make sure they were still attached, and watched, almost bemused, as her blood ran in thin, distinct streams down her arms. Down her arms and toward the loam that was touched by both death and the green. Hope was squawking up a storm in her ear; he pushed himself off her shoulder in rage, his squawks growing in volume and depth as he grew in size.

The wind that moved a sleeve could not move Hope. Nor, it seemed, could it move Severn.

But Mrs. Erickson, it did not touch at all. The hem of Evanton's robes—for he was once again attired as in the Keeper's garden—rippled slightly, but he was accustomed to quieting the elements; it could not disturb more than that.

Kaylin's hair flew. Hope's roar was a full-throated draconic roar; it seemed to blend with the wind the green had summoned—Kaylin had no doubt at all it was the green's will.

The green's will, the will of a dead Ancient, the anger of a Sorcerer's ancient familiar. Even her marks were now clamoring in a storm of syllables, rising in volume as if to drown out the answer. As if to protect her, to protect Mrs. Erickson, or to protect the dead Ancient.

And all of it infuriated her because she *wanted to hear* the Ancient's answer, and she knew she never would. What Mrs. Erickson could hear, no one else could hear. The best Kaylin could do was infer. She could have inferred part of the conversation because of what she heard Mrs. Erickson reply.

So of course the sound of the Hawk's most common visitor could not be heard; it was the first thing that was lost. And to top it all off, Kaylin was bleeding into the strange and foreign ground, and not even she was naive enough to believe that living blood and dead ground would meet without incident. She couldn't stop her blood from falling.

What she hadn't expected was Hope: He breathed an enormous silver cloud, sparkling with tiny hints of color; it collided with the ground beneath Kaylin's feet. Every Barrani who had ever seen the tiny version of that exhaled cloud had paled, panicked, retreated. Some managed to keep dignity intact; some did not.

Kaylin had seen Hope's breath melt metal before. The breath wasn't hot—Dragon breath, true Dragon breath, could melt metal and stone.

It couldn't melt metal and re-form it, giving rise to a new, solid shape that could be touched and handled without difficulty. Had Kaylin been standing on stone, she would have felt no fear about a little blood at all. She wasn't. Her feet were anchored in land that wasn't like any land she knew that supported normal life.

Hope's breath hit the land that surrounded her feet; it shifted in color, from the opalescent gray to a silver gray with hints of gold spread throughout; the basic consistency didn't change. Nor did the grasp on her feet.

But her blood was absorbed, not by the ground on which she'd been standing, but the ground that Hope had momentarily transformed.

He roared, and this time, she understood his words.

THIS IS NOT FOR YOU!

They passed through her, and she felt the cold of her guests lessen as they did.

Be careful, Severn said; she could hear his voice clearly once again.

The dress, however, didn't change. Probably for the best. Given her luck, she'd be standing stark naked in the middle of wherever this was.

"Hope—be careful! I don't think the green means to hurt me!"

You are BLEEDING.

"Yes, I noticed that."

Barely, Severn said pointedly.

Do not bleed in the green. Do not bleed near the dead—it might remind them of the life they no longer have!

"I didn't exactly cut my own arms, Hope!"

Learn how to use what you were given, Chosen!

"Who would you suggest as a teacher?" she demanded.

"Dear," Mrs. Erickson said, her soft voice cutting through the miasma of frustration and near humiliation. "I'm sorry, but I can't hear him speaking if you're all shouting like that." Her tone was apologetic, but it was steel.

Kaylin swallowed; Hope shut up. Severn hadn't shouted out loud, so he wouldn't be in the bad books.

"I would like your help," she added, apology rising above momentary irritation.

"With what?"

Mrs. Erickson turned to Kaylin; the old woman's feet weren't rooted in the ground. She could traverse the distance with ease. In this case, that was a couple of steps, but she had that determined look on her face that implied she would have walked a few miles if necessary without minding at all.

Her brows rose. "Dear, you're bleeding. Your hands…"

"It doesn't hurt, and yes, I've been told."

"Oh. I'm sorry."

The worst thing about Mrs. Erickson was the instant guilt one felt if one snapped at her. "No, it's fine—I'd've said the same thing."

Mrs. Erickson reached for the hem of her skirt; Kaylin belatedly realized that she meant to try to tear off some of its fabric in order to form makeshift bandages.

"I'm honestly fine—please don't do that. Look—the blood is dry. It only bled for a little bit."

Liar.

Kaylin rolled eyes at her familiar. *I don't want her to ruin her clothing for nothing.*

Oh, don't mistake me. You seldom lie—and that almost sounded convincing. Sadly, almost doesn't cut it.

Mrs. Erickson had a different problem; her clothing was unremarkable in all ways, but it was very solid, and the old woman's hands weren't made for tearing cloth.

"Mrs. Erickson—I'm really fine." Kaylin exhaled. "Imelda."

The surprise caused Mrs. Erickson's hands to stop.

"Please—you said you needed my help, not the other way around. I don't mean to pressure you, but I think what you need right now is more important."

"I'm really not certain about that. But I'll try. This ghost isn't like other ghosts I've met."

"Is it like the ghosts we brought home from the Imperial Library?"

"No. And yes, a little. I find his form much more solid, but… if I met him outside, I'd know he was dead. Remember what I told you before? As a child, I couldn't tell the difference. I had to learn to see the person in context. Did others see them? Did others attempt to help them or interact with them at all? Did they attempt to reach out? That last part was more about the length of time they'd been dead.

"But I would know this man was dead the first time I saw him. I would know the ghosts I've been living with were dead."

"And Bellusdeo's ghosts?"

Mrs. Erickson shook her head. "It's different. They would have looked alive to me if there weren't so many of them overlapping so completely—living people can't do that. Well, maybe Terrano and Mandoran can, but in general it would be impossible. There's something a bit odd about them."

"There's a *lot* odd about them."

"Oh, I meant Bellusdeo's sisters, not the boys."

Given what the former Arkon had said about the sisters in the Aerie, there was a lot odd about them as well. "What do you need me to do?"

"I think you need to give me back my friends," Mrs. Erickson replied.

Kaylin nodded. "Ummm, can you call them? I think they're stuck."

Mrs. Erickson sighed. "Yes, I can. I'm sorry—they're very lonely and a bit needy. I imagine you're not used to that. They're not bad people," she added, her voice gentle as she held out her hand. "But good people can become difficult if they've been isolated for too long." Mrs. Erickson looked at Kaylin's arms. "Won't you come and spend time with me?"

The claws deepened.

Mrs. Erickson closed her eyes. "Kaylin," she said, with her eyes closed. "Just how dangerous are these dead? In my experience, it's been the other way around: the living are dangerous to the dead. Only in one case were the dead a serious threat."

"Azoria," Kaylin said, wincing.

"Azoria," Mrs. Erickson replied, without the wince. "I can't be grateful to her. I just can't. But were it not for her, I would never have met Jamal, Katie, Esme, or Callis, and I think I would have lived a much lonelier life. Those children should have had lives of their own—lives that didn't revolve around an old woman."

"You weren't always old."

"No. No, I wasn't. But they can't come back to life, and I can't turn back time. Jamal left me in your care."

Kaylin had a feeling she knew where this was going, and she didn't like it. "I'm not Jamal."

"No—but he trusted you. He trusted you to stand by me, to help me live the life I didn't live. He always felt guilty. But he always felt jealous of any outside life, afraid of what it would mean for them. Which of course made him feel more guilty." Her smile was gentle and infused with nostalgia. "But he *did* trust you. He wanted me to be safe; he did everything he could to keep me safe while he was trapped in my house. They all made it feel like a home, even if they couldn't leave it. Even if they knew the reason they were trapped was me."

"That *wasn't* you! That wasn't your fault—you had nothing to do with it!"

"That is exactly what Jamal would have said. I do miss him. I wonder if there is a place where the dead go, and where they can finally be happy. I wonder if all my beloved dead will be waiting for me, if they'll be happy to see me, if they'll want to hear the stories they haven't heard since they've been gone.

"But that's not the fate that awaits this poor man." She was speaking of the Ancient. "Azoria did not understand his nature and didn't understand his difficulty. Kaylin, I don't think his people *could* pass on. Life, death—it's a separation that wasn't fixed in the same way our lives and deaths are."

"What does he think happened to those who had died? I mean—what does he think death means?" She looked at her arms, at her skirt, at the fitted bodice of a dress that was more revealing than anything she would have chosen for herself. She looked across at Evanton, who was listening, arms crossed. "What does the *green* think death means for the Ancient?"

"I am not Warden of the green; I have enough on my shoulders as it is." He exhaled. "But as you guess, the green has some interest in the ancient dead. The green remains within its own borders."

"This isn't the West March."

"I did not say the West March; I said the *green*, if you were listening. The entrance to the green—the accepted, traditional entrance—is, as you are aware, in the West March. But it is not confined to the boundaries of that Barrani land. Azoria breached those boundaries, but that alone would not have been enough to wake the green; it was the combination of her covert activities and the nature of the power she touched that drew the green's awareness; the green could not locate Azoria—she really was quite an impressive mage; very powerful, very arrogant, and yet capable of subtlety.

"And now the green has sunk roots in this place. Whether or not those roots can be removed is, I think, a matter for a different time; it is adjacent to the difficulty, but it is not the problem that must be addressed. But yes, on some level, this situation feels familiar to the green—and *no*, I cannot clearly explain it; could I, we would be in a much better position. I apologize for interrupting you," he added—to Mrs. Erickson, of course.

"It's hard to explain, but the Ancient believed he told you: Death is an end of purpose. He feels as if he was created, born, for a specific purpose. I did try to get him to explain that purpose, but I'm afraid I'm just not educated enough to understand what he was trying to say."

Kaylin doubted even Larrantin was educated enough to understand what he was trying to say. "He did say that. When

I first met him. But what was he supposed to do when he'd finished?"

"Die," Mrs. Erickson said. "And he did. He is not, in his own estimation, alive. Had Azoria not found him, he might have…shut down for eternity."

"I'm not sure it was Azoria who woke him."

Mrs. Erickson failed, for a moment, to meet Kaylin's eyes. "It doesn't matter. You did what you had to do, dear. I freed the dead trapped in Azoria's manor. They weren't happy to be there. I don't imagine he was happy, either."

"If he slept through it, he probably wasn't aware of it."

Mrs. Erickson shook her head firmly. "You freed him from Azoria's binding. But I think the ghosts you brought here should come to meet him."

They didn't want to leave, but Kaylin had deflected for long enough. "You want me to give you my blessing to break the promise you made to Jamal."

"Yes, dear. I'm sorry. I would make the decision myself, but I know there was a reason Jamal made me make that promise—and I don't think it was just because of Azoria. I think he understood—being dead—just how terrible a power it is. It's worse than a sword at a neck, because there might be an end to that."

"You would never do anything like that!"

"Kaylin, I would never do anything like that *now*. But as a child? Would it have occurred to me? The reason I stopped is because I *used* that power. On Jamal. On my older brother, my best friend, my eventual child. Did I mean to enslave him forever? No. I just wanted him to do what *I* wanted. I wanted my parents to do what I wanted, too—which child doesn't? But my parents couldn't be forced into obedience.

"If I had continued, would I even see the dead as people? I had a fight with Jamal. He wouldn't speak to me, and *that* made me realize I'd really hurt his feelings, and he was really angry. Those silly fights that children have? That was all of mine.

"I'm not a child anymore. I try to live mindfully, especially with the dead. But it's just too easy to believe that I'm always doing the right thing, that I'm a good person. Good people can do bad things. They can lose their way. They can be broken by grief or loss. Maybe it's why most people don't have powers like this. They can lose their tempers, and do things that they can't take back, they can't change—and that's heartbreaking, too.

"But I can do much worse than that. The dead are helpless in their attachment to the world. They would be helpless in the face of this power. Even a dead god—that's what the Ancients were, weren't they? This is what Azoria wanted from me." She closed her eyes. Opened them again. "But I think this is what I have to do here. I don't want what Azoria wanted—but I'll be doing what she intended: I have to command the dead."

The wind of the green moved far more gently as it touched Mrs. Erickson; Mrs. Erickson, who wore the crown of flowers, the rings, the bracelets. Kaylin thought she should have the dress, too—but the dress remained wrapped around Kaylin.

"What will you command the dead to do?"

Mrs. Erickson's smile was gentle. "I am about to attempt to give the dead a purpose. A direction."

Evanton's eyes widened. "I am not at all certain that is a wise idea."

Mrs. Erickson nodded. "I know. But the turmoil you sensed, the reason you sought us out, is the turmoil of the dead Ancient: he is without purpose. If left alone, I am uncertain that the purpose he finds or creates will be good for anyone, himself included.

"I've spoken with Helen at length—she likes to talk while I bake, and I love the company—and Helen cannot exist without purpose. She can elect not to rent her house out, but the lack of a tenant causes difficulty for her; she cannot do so indefinitely. If Helen breaks down, the damage is done to Helen alone.

"It's clear to me that the consequences here would be far

worse—but I think the dissolution might be similar. If death is, to the Ancients, the end of purpose, some part of this one yearns for purpose with whatever is left of him. He cannot find it on his own."

"And the ghosts Kaylin carried with her?" Evanton asked, his tone sharper than it had ever been with Mrs. Erickson.

"I think they're like him," Mrs. Erickson replied. "They have similar struggles, similar losses; I believe they were trapped in similar ways. But…it's hard to put into words. The Ancient and the ghosts from the palace are isolated existences, but to me, they each have things the other lacks. If they were together, they would possibly become close to whole."

"Can you *do that*?" Kaylin felt her jaw drop.

"If I can't introduce them to each other, I don't know who can. I think they could be friends. But they won't leave your arms unless I command them. And, Kaylin, the dead won't rest easily unless and until I command them to adopt a purpose, a purpose that is within their ability to achieve.

"And I believe I can. But it won't be their choice because they can't *make* that choice. It isn't in them. I think, in that regard, they're like Helen. Helen injured herself so that she *could* make a choice—but it was a small choice. She couldn't choose to become something other than she was: a building. A physical space. The choice she did so much damage to herself to make was choosing the person she wished to serve. The service itself was so fundamental to her creation she could not change it.

"She said it would have been very much as if she were human and attempted to cut out her own heart."

"I don't think the Ancients are the same as sentient buildings."

"I know. But Ancients created those buildings. I believe they built them based on their own existences as models. Do you believe it's possible to kill Helen?"

The question had never occurred to Kaylin.

"If you destroy the words at her heart, she will die. She will not be Helen. But how do you destroy words? How do you destroy language?" Mrs. Erickson shook her head. "You forbid the speaking of it. You wait until no one alive can ever remember the use of the words."

"I'm not sure True Words work that way. The point of True Language is that the words have inherent meaning. Any two people who speak that language can understand each other perfectly."

"I believe that's exactly how it works," Mrs. Erickson said, voice soft. "Shorn of purpose, the words die."

But... "The words can't be living beings in and of themselves, surely? I mean—it would be like the word *the* being alive; it's spoken so often we don't even think about it. Does every time we utter the word create a new life? It— I can't wrap my head around it."

"You've no doubt had cause to light candles; to light stoves. People light bonfires, often during festivals. Are those fires alive?"

Kaylin shook her head.

Evanton nodded. "They are not. But should the elemental fire die, they would not exist as they are now, if they existed at all. There is no world we can envision that does not involve fire. If True Words are alive in the fashion Imelda suggests they are, it is possible that a similar, almost elemental version of those words also exists."

"So...you're saying True Words are like elementals in some way?"

"No. I suggest it as a possibility, no more; the speaking of True Words was neither my study nor my duty. I believe the former Arkon did study and could speak those words."

"So can Sanabalis. But they don't exactly *converse* when they do."

Evanton nodded, frowning. "I am the Keeper of the garden; I do not know if there existed a governing authority with jurisdiction over the language of the Ancients. We can argue about whether or not the words spoken by the Ancients were, or are, sentient in and of themselves at a later time; there are far too many variables to give the question full consideration now.

"Mrs. Erickson can see the ghosts of what you perceived as True Words. She can speak with them. That is proof enough that at least some of those words were once alive." He turned to Mrs. Erickson. "I apologize for the interruption; I feel the Ancient is waiting."

Mrs. Erickson nodded. The words had not come to her hands, as they'd done once before.

Kaylin exhaled. If she was the new Jamal—he would have been so offended to hear that—she only had one option here: to lift the restraint that Mrs. Erickson had imposed on herself for almost the entirety of her life. She trusted Imelda Erickson; this wasn't a matter of trust. The Ancients and their opaque purposes weren't things meant for people like them; the Ancients were gods. How could a mortal give purpose to a god?

What directive could be offered that would make sense to an Ancient? Mrs. Erickson couldn't speak True Words any more than Kaylin could.

But Mrs. Erickson didn't *see* the Ancient as a godlike being. She saw a dead person, probably a dead human. She listened and she interacted; if the Ancient weren't dead, she would have invited him into her rooms and offered him a cup of tea. Maybe the dead perceived Mrs. Erickson the same way: as one of them, as someone with whom they had once shared some elements of common ground.

"Kaylin—do I have permission to break my promise?"

Kaylin smiled at Mrs. Erickson. "Just once," she said, just as Jamal had done. "Just now."

Mrs. Erickson's smile was bright; she recognized the phrasing, the intonation. She continued to look in Kaylin's direction, but she was no longer seeing Kaylin.

"I'm terribly sorry to have to do this," she said, her voice soft, a thread of steel in her tone. "But you *must* leave Kaylin now. Come here."

The guests on her arms shuddered—or maybe that was Kaylin herself. But even if they struggled against Mrs. Erickson's gentle but implacable command, they obeyed; they uprooted themselves from Kaylin's skin. In Kaylin's eyes, they maintained the shape and the colors they had taken when they had finally come to rest on that skin, but those colors became dimensional as she watched them unfold.

In Mrs. Erickson's eyes, clearly, they maintained the forms she had seen—none of which were words. This time, when she held out her hands, they came to her, like wayward children who had tried to avoid being caught out doing something they shouldn't—with the expected poor results.

Kaylin looked at her arms; they were, as expected, bleeding.

The sleeves of the dress she wore wrapped themselves gently around the visible wounds while Hope roared.

"It's not trying to eat my blood, Hope—it's trying to bandage the wounds. Look at the fabric and calm down." She looked at her feet. "You've made your point, and I don't think the green is trying to fight you. I think the green is trying to somehow calm the Ancient in the only way it can. Through me. Through Mrs. Erickson."

You do not know what the cost will be. Two voices overlapped in Kaylin's head—Hope's and Severn's.

"I know what the cost will likely be if we fail," she replied. "And Serralyn thought we should absolutely trust the green. Maybe you know more than I do—but the cohort came back from the green, from the Hallionne, and the green did not interfere."

"If it weren't for the interference of the green, they would never have been jailed," Severn pointed out.

Kaylin nodded. It was true. But the laws of the green stated clearly that children were not to be exposed to its influence. Those who lived in the West March had a healthy respect for the green; those who lived in the High Halls did not. Lack of respect sentenced Barrani children to captivity for centuries. Only Teela had escaped it—but she was Barrani; she had not escaped the memories. And she had not forgiven her father, at whose hands her mother had died.

Kaylin closed her eyes. "I've done what you asked, even if I didn't fully understand it. I therefore have a favor to ask in return." She spoke, now, to the green.

Both Hope and Severn were surprised; Severn's surprise banked instantly, because he realized what the favor would be.

"We're missing one of the children sent as a sacrifice to the green in the hopes that you would bestow enough power upon them that they could become useful tools. I know Hallionne Alsanis was connected to the green in some fashion. Maybe he thought you maintained an interest in the fate of those children; maybe you felt responsible for them somehow.

"If you do, Terrano came with the Keeper to this place; he never left it. Even when we found the Keeper, we could find no sign of Terrano. His friends know he's alive, but they can't reach him. I'm hoping you can."

The sleeves which had wrapped themselves around Kaylin's injuries unwrapped themselves, cloth once again draping in the expected way impractical long sleeves did.

Kaylin's arms were no longer injured, but better, they were no longer cold. She hadn't been worried about the wounds—she knew she could heal them herself. Hope, however, had been less certain.

Evanton pinched the bridge of his nose. "You are *certain* you wish to have Terrano brought back from wherever it is he managed to get stuck?"

"I am," Kaylin replied. "Mostly. Mrs. Erickson likes him." Her eyes narrowed. "Does that mean you know where he is?"

"No. But the green does, and the green appears to have taken your appeal to heart."

"Evanton—how can you speak with the green? Is it something you can teach me?"

"It depends. Do you plan to become the Keeper in the future? No? Then no, it is not something I can teach you. It's not something I could teach, regardless. The green accepts your request by law of equivalent exchange. She will make certain Terrano returns. But she requires your attention now."

"Mrs. Erickson has the ghosts."

"Mrs. Erickson cannot do what must be done on her own."

"You can't help her?"

"There is a reason you are wearing the dress, not me."

Kaylin exhaled and turned to Mrs. Erickson. She could see the ghost words circling Mrs. Erickson's arms. They formed a second circle there, above the wristlets of flowers.

But it wasn't these ghosts that held Kaylin's attention. The dead Ancient began to radiate bright, uneven light.

"They're tears," Mrs. Erickson said, voice soft.

27

Kaylin had already accepted that she couldn't see as Mrs. Erickson saw; she certainly didn't see the odd, shaky light as tears. "What about the other ghosts?"

"They were unhappy with me, and I don't blame them." The reply was gentle. "But they're much calmer now. You can see these as words, can't you?"

Kaylin nodded.

"Can you see the Ancient that way?"

"I didn't, before," Kaylin began. She stopped as she considered the question more carefully. To her eyes, the Ancient had looked like a giant—taller than even the Norranir. But it was the words that Azoria had bound, and the words from which she had drawn power, attempting to force them into shapes that weren't natively theirs.

"I think, if you can, it's important," Mrs. Erickson continued. "I can't see them the way you do."

"If you couldn't see them the way *you* do, I don't think any of the rest of us could do anything," Kaylin said softly. She closed her eyes; it had always been easier to see words with her eyes closed. Her own marks had always been clearest that way, but she found that the ghosts she'd carried with her could also be seen clearly, where they rested in Mrs. Erickson's hands.

What was less clear to Kaylin was the dead Ancient. Because she *could* see the Ancient with closed eyes; the irregular light that had made her uneasy was gone. What remained was a pale blue-gray glow, roughly in the shape of a giant; she could see arms, legs, the outline of chest, and even head. The regular features of a face were lost—those weren't visible behind closed eyelids.

But in the pale blue-gray glow, she could see, if she focused, differences in the light; brighter objects interspersed with emptiness. She *could* see words, but they weren't very clear to her eyes. She frowned. The ghosts from the palace hadn't been clear, either. They didn't glow; they looked like words written in smoke or mist, wavering like a mirage if she approached them too closely.

The Ancient was far more solid than the ghostly words had ever been to Kaylin's eyes. She could see, as she approached, that the interior of the shape of the body was composed entirely of words; they formed the bulk of the body. At first, she thought they were like her marks, but as she drew closer, she realized that was wrong.

The Ancient's words were far, far more complicated in shape and structure than the marks of the Chosen, taken individually, were. She had seen similarly complex words before, although she'd never made an attempt to speak them, to pronounce them. In at least one case it wouldn't have been safe.

She didn't have safety concerns in the same way now; she simply accepted that the Ancient's words were beyond her immediate grasp. But if they remained that way, she wasn't certain she could be of any help to Mrs. Erickson.

She turned back to look at Mrs. Erickson, wondering if she'd actually moved from the old woman's side at all. The space here was so distorted, she couldn't tell—and after a moment, she forgot. The flowers that decorated Mrs. Erickson's wrists and fingers seemed to be growing as Kaylin watched, and the wreath that sat upon her gray-white hair had become a crown of platinum and emerald. She could see trailing filaments, like very delicate vines, growing out of those flowers; it made her distinctly uncomfortable.

Azoria had bound *one* flower into the twelve-year-old Imelda's hair, braiding it in a specific way that Serralyn had said was once used for binding ceremonies in the West March; Kaylin had assumed she'd meant weddings. She wasn't nearly as certain of that now.

When the vines touched Mrs. Erickson's face, Kaylin reached out for them almost without thought. She'd meant to stop them from sinking into the older woman's skin; she hadn't intended to uproot them or remove the wreath from where it now sat.

But the moment she touched them, they thickened, they gained substance, if not weight. She could feel their texture, and she could smell newly turned earth.

Oh. The plants that had seemed to uproot themselves in an attempt to adorn Mrs. Erickson hadn't actually uprooted themselves at all. They were still planted in the green, still connected to it. Just as the single flower Azoria had twined in Mrs. Erickson's hair decades past had somehow maintained a very slight, very shallow connection to the green.

Kaylin gently separated out the disparate tendrils; she placed one root against each of the ghosts and was only a little surprised when they wrapped themselves around the body of the words, made manifest and physical by the power of the green—or the power of the Chosen. The words became brighter, the gold edging growing over the green until they seemed all of gold.

She could see the words more clearly than she had before, even when they'd been attached to her skin. They looked, to her eyes, like her own marks sometimes did when they lifted themselves from her skin, but these words were trailing slender vines.

Kaylin took the vines that remained in one hand, and approached the dead Ancient, and the dead Ancient's complicated words. She had, in the past, intuited meaning from the marks of the Chosen—but it had taken hours, and it had started with her need to find words that resonated with words she both understood and used. She'd found the right marks, but she had never been able to speak the words they represented; she'd chosen them entirely by instinct, by *feel.*

In just that fashion, she now stood in front of the Ancient, who was a quivering pile of words, a structure that seemed unstable and likely to fall apart without intervention.

When Tiamaris had attempted to teach her some of what he knew about True Words, he'd spoken of harmony, of cohesion of form and shape; he could see the way Shadow could twist or break the forms of True Words, attempting to change their meaning, their dictate. Kaylin had wondered at the time how he had been so certain, but he had more knowledge of Shadow, more knowledge of the fiefs, than most of the Dragon Court. At the time, she hadn't questioned it. He had stood beside her, he had encouraged her to actually read and pronounce the words at the heart of a Tower: the Tower he now captained.

She missed that, because she couldn't even form the syllables that were necessary—and she felt the necessity keenly.

In the absence of Tiamaris, she stood, vines in hand. She began to attach them to the words she could see shining faintly beneath what she assumed was skin; it felt like stone to the touch; the tips of her fingers were cold. Still, the cold was far less intense than it had been before Mrs. Erickson had called the ghosts—commanded the ghosts—back to her hands.

The vines that had grown from the wreath had wrapped themselves around the ghosts Mrs. Erickson once again carried; the vines in Kaylin's hands couldn't find purchase in the words of the Ancient. But she could see those words waver and push toward either her hands or the vines—it wasn't clear which, to Kaylin.

Something was in the way. She couldn't push through it to reach the words. She could see them; she just couldn't touch them. Not yet.

But the green's power wasn't the only power she had access to. She reached for the Ancient; she'd done it once before. The Ancient was dead. Healing shouldn't work. But she'd never fully understood the power of the marks of the Chosen, and she'd never actually tried to heal a dead person before, because death rendered healing irrelevant. Healing, for Kaylin, was as instinctive as any use of the marks of the Chosen; the body knew its correct shape, and she poured power into the body to allow it to heal itself.

She'd poured power into the words Azoria had attempted to transform, as if Azoria herself were just another aspect of Shadow.

She twined the roots of the green's flowers around her fingers, and then spread the palms of her hands against the stone; it was much colder than she'd anticipated. As cold as the ghostly words had been. But the dress she wore radiated heat and warmth; her hands remained steady.

She inhaled.

When she exhaled, she exhaled words. Unintentional words. Words in a language that felt familiar to the ear but were in no way familiar to the tongue—or at least not hers.

Oh. The green. She was here in part as a representative of the green's will; that was what the dress *meant*.

The green was here, she was wearing the dress, and she was beginning to tell the story the green wanted told. The *regalia*, or perhaps something similar. She couldn't ask the green, or perhaps she could—but she wouldn't understand the answer, if she could even hear it.

The marks of the Chosen resonated with the voiced words. Maybe Kaylin's role here was to serve as both Teller and harmoniste. That was what she hoped.

And she hoped it until she heard Mrs. Erickson's voice: it was strong and clear—certainly stronger than it was during their various day-to-day encounters.

The wreath of flowers *was* the crown of the Teller, possibly in its purist sense.

Kaylin hadn't understood the role of the harmoniste in the green, not fully, until now. She'd understood what her role was; she'd understood that in the moment Nightshade began his long and complicated story, he could smooth out the flow of the narrative strands, weaving them together. She couldn't come up with the story herself—she didn't have his history, didn't have Barrani memory. But in the memory, in the narrative, she found her role. She had brought Hope fully into himself, had named him, had finally fulfilled the role of midwife. And she had healed the injured, almost insubstantial names of the cohort, lending them the power to become what they once had been: the source of life and self to the eleven friends Teela had left behind almost a millennium ago.

She understood that controlling the narrative, presenting it *properly*, required both intent and power. The power to hear the various strands of story Mrs. Erickson now offered the dead Ancient. The dead Ancient was the target of this *regalia*, this offering of the green.

It was to the Ancient she therefore looked. To the Ancient, and to the ghosts that rested now in Mrs. Erickson's hands. What she had done for the cohort in the green, she now attempted to do for these two: Ancient and ghosts.

She understood that the Ancients weren't alive in any sense of the word she understood. They couldn't be healed in the same way living beings could. The Barrani were alive; they had bodies, they bled, and they died; their words did not die with them. Instead, they returned to the Lake of Life—created by the Ancients—to await another chance at rebirth.

These words were not words meant for that Lake, but they were like, very like, the names of the cohort had been—thin, transparent, far too extended. She had infused the names of Teela's friends with the power, with the *shape*, True Words required to support life, to *be* alive, and she'd offered them, name by name, to the cohort who had every reason to despise their kin—living or dead—and possibly the world into which they'd been born.

She had seen and held those names, had rekindled their purpose, but still didn't know them, couldn't speak them, couldn't see them as she had when she last wore this dress, guided by the unknown, unknowable will of the green.

Teela had been chosen as harmoniste once; Teela had worn this dress. But whatever Teela made of her role in the green had not managed to liberate her trapped friends; she hadn't even managed to reach them, to hear them, although she knew their True Names.

Kaylin listened to Mrs. Erickson. She listened to Mrs. Erickson speak to the Ancient about his future—him, not they or it—and the finding of precious purpose; she listened as Mrs. Erickson offered advice, comfort, and understanding. Mrs. Erickson was mortal, had been born mortal, would die as a mortal. The Ancient was not. But Mrs. Erickson's signal strength was her ability to find small, genuine bridges—and to walk across them, eyes open.

She did that now.

Kaylin continued to speak in a language not her own, even if the words were literally attached to her skin, because it was *Kaylin* who was the translator here. Kaylin who chose which strands of Mrs. Erickson's advice would resonate and which were too mortal, too personal, to do so.

She began to sweat. The ice of the ghosts had left her, and

she almost regretted it; she was hot now, and her arms were trembling not from the weight of the ghosts, but from the flow of power. The marks on her skin had risen, brilliant green, edged in gold; they started to spin slowly in place. Slowly became quickly as she began to choose the story itself; to knit disparate parts into a whole that the Ancient could understand. She didn't choose the words that conveyed the story the Teller was offering, but she did choose the commonalities between a lonely old woman whose purpose had vanished when Jamal, Katie, Esme, and Callis had finally been free to pass on and a godlike being whose purpose had likewise ended.

Only Jamal had insisted on remaining until he knew Mrs. Erickson would be safe, and safety, in the eyes of the perpetual child Jamal had been since his death, meant that someone else would look after her. Someone else would go the distance to protect her. Kaylin was better than Jamal in Jamal's view because Kaylin wasn't trapped in a building; Kaylin wouldn't scream in an agony of helplessness if Mrs. Erickson fell and broke a leg. Kaylin cared about the old woman. Not, of course, as much as Jamal, in Jamal's opinion—but it was as close as he could get.

For some reason, this strand of Mrs. Erickson's story seemed viscerally important; Kaylin couldn't elide it, couldn't set it aside. Nor, when it came to that, could she edit out Mrs. Erickson's daily life: the baking for the Hawks, the telling of her life to the children who now had no life of their own. She was the window through which they might seem or feel alive, and she was grateful to them, loved them, wanted to give them at least that much for as long as she could.

She had always regretted that the food she baked couldn't be eaten by the dead, but she understood that new stories, new adventures, came only in her contacts with the living. On good days and bad, she therefore made the trek to the Halls of Law. She might have chosen different venues, but she heard such interesting things while waiting for her turn to approach the public desk and make her report, and some of those things amused the children endlessly.

No, she continued, she hadn't always been alone with the children. She'd been married, too. Kaylin almost stopped speaking at that point, because the word *marriage* didn't come easily to the green. There were clearly similar concepts, but it wasn't the concept that the green—through its harmoniste—had trouble conveying; it was the love that led to marriage. The green understood Mrs. Erickson's sense of responsibility for those dead children. Marriage, not so much. But Kaylin chose to keep that thread, because it led to what followed.

Loneliness. Longing. Despair. Certainty that her life was over. Mrs. Erickson had been old enough that she felt she would never meet another partner. Who else would love a woman who could see and talk to invisible people? Who else would *believe* her and trust her? Who else would accept her care and concern for those invisible children, and help her fashion as much of a life for them as she possibly could?

Marriage to Mrs. Erickson, to Imelda, included those children and her sense of duty to them. She'd been lucky to find one person. She'd never been so lucky before, and she knew luck was something she couldn't rely on. She had no idea how life could continue.

But the children, the weight of duty to them, forced her to find her footing. Helped her to continue to put one foot in front of the other. And time slowly did the rest of the work. Helped her to understand that love didn't die. Love—the ability to love—had not abandoned her. Was it the same love? No. But in her grief, she had all but forgotten the strength of it.

And it returned. It returned first in unremarkable things—baking, needlework, interacting with the children. It returned as she realized she had to do *something*, had to have something that would take her out of her home. Happiness had dwelled there when her husband had lived; loss and despair, a reminder that he was dead, had been what remained.

The Hawks provided the external world. Their tolerance became a grudging acceptance, and the grudging acceptance became, over time, genuine affection. Genuine protectiveness.

This was the life Mrs. Erickson had built for herself after catastrophic loss.

But the children became her fear as she aged. Age was inevitable if one lived. Injuries became easier to inflict, took longer to heal. She would not live forever, and the children would be dead forever—dead, trapped, and isolated.

But ghosts had become her anchor, even then. The ghosts that she now had with her. And the Ancient himself, dead, bound, trapped in this space just as Jamal had been trapped in hers. Yes, he wasn't mortal, hadn't lived a mortal life—but perhaps *he* was the ghost that inhabited Azoria's home, just as the children had inhabited Mrs. Erickson's.

Kaylin felt the flow of words, the invocation of the green, die. Her mouth was open, but no further words came to occupy it. She turned to look at Mrs. Erickson then.

"I want for you what I wanted for the children. I want you to be free, to move on to a better place than this. I don't really understand what your purpose was. I'm an old woman. I'm used to being mostly invisible—but maybe it was easier for me because even as a child, I had only the love of the dead and my parents. People outside of my home avoided me.

"Because I'm alive, I found purpose. I found a new home. I found new friends. And I found new ghosts, people my power might be able to help." She stopped speaking, her gaze focused; clearly the Ancient was speaking to her now. Kaylin could no longer hear its voice at all.

"I'm mortal," Mrs. Erickson replied. "I never had a grand purpose. I never had the powers you naturally have. For me, a small purpose was what I needed, and it's all I could handle.

But you're not me. What you were and what I am are so completely different, you can't live the life I built on the foundation of loss. I'm not sure you'd want to, either.

"But if death for you is an end to purpose, you *can* build a life around a new purpose. These," she said, her hands moving, "are my friends. But they are, I believe, more like you than like me. And they will stay with you." She lifted her hands, cupped around the ghosts of words; as Kaylin watched, the physicality of the green marks dwindled.

No, that was wrong. The gold edging grew, spreading across the surface of each different component until the ghosts looked like every other mark Kaylin had carried.

Kaylin understood then. The words approached the Ancient; the threads around them followed. They didn't struggle, didn't attempt to pull away, to draw back; they seemed to speed up until they touched the Ancient's current body. Her hands were still pressed to the Ancient's skin; she felt the moment they joined with him.

Had felt something on a much smaller level before, exactly once.

Bellusdeo.

Yes, Hope said.

Mrs. Erickson was not yet finished. Kaylin had finished with the duties given her as harmoniste, but she had only barely begun the duties of the Chosen. As the new words joined the complicated, messy symbols that comprised the Ancient, their gold coloration began to spread across what they touched. She could now see the pattern, the sense of the broken bits; could see how the new words must be placed, or how components of each ghost fit into the gaps that had existed.

"It's very difficult for me to do this," Mrs. Erickson said, continuing. "But you won't have any peace unless I do. If I understand what you used to be, you helped to create the world. Helped to create all the people who populate it. Everything we are comes from your people. We are all, in some sense, your descendants, your children.

"Therefore I command you: protect your children, where it is possible. No, not every one of them; they are no longer small and in need of a parent's guidance. I think you understand my intent, and it is intent that is important here. They cannot be worth more than your new life; Azoria was also a descendant of the Ancients. She attempted to harm you, attempted to control you—and you must not let that happen.

"But you might find, as I did, that there is purpose in such protection, and you might find an end to death, just as I did. That is what I command of you." Her voice trembled at the very end, but Kaylin felt the steel in it, the command in it, even as she worked.

Severn slid an arm around not her shoulders, but her waist, as if to carry her weight for her. Oh. Her knees were sagging, her hands trembling. She lost Mrs. Erickson's voice as she worked. Lost everything but the Ancient, the new formation of words, the rightness or harmony of their full joining.

And she understood, as she did, what had gone wrong with Bellusdeo's sisters. Understood how she might give Bellusdeo the same unity, the same wholeness.

"Yes," Mrs. Erickson said, surprising her, because she hadn't thought she'd spoken the words out loud. "Yes, in this moment, I think you can do exactly that. I wish you could see what I see," she added, voice continuing to tremble. "But it doesn't matter. I know you'll take my word for it.

"Severn, be a dear, and get Bellusdeo?"

She spoke as if Severn were Jamal. Then again, she talked to Kaylin as if she were Jamal as well.

"Can it wait?"

"No, I don't think it can. When the Ancient is reborn—and he is being reborn now—we won't have his power. And I don't think we'll have the power of what the Keeper called the green, either. I believe Kaylin can ultimately help Bellusdeo, but it must be now."

The arm around her waist left then.

"The Ancient—or the green—will allow Bellusdeo's passage; it won't build a wall that can't be surmounted."

Kaylin didn't open her eyes. She didn't need to. Bellusdeo's voice, she could easily hear. The Dragon was panicked and infuriated. Kaylin knew what the color of the Dragon's eyes must be; seeing them wouldn't change anything.

But when Mrs. Erickson, whose hands were now empty, reached for Bellusdeo's, Bellusdeo became visible. Bellusdeo and all eight of her sisters. None of them spoke, but Bellusdeo didn't, either. They had accepted possible eternity as invisible ghosts the moment they understood the damage the Ancient could do. Because they had all served a vanished kingdom in a dead world.

It was Bellusdeo herself who was the shattered wreck; Bellusdeo who had felt the deaths of all her sisters as the permanent loss it had become. Bellusdeo who had—what did they call it?—survivor's guilt.

Mrs. Erickson was a font of affection. Bellusdeo was older by far, but to Mrs. Erickson they were all children. It was no surprise that she'd come to care so much for Bellusdeo in such a short time; Bellusdeo had been entirely open with Mrs. Erickson. Far more so than she had with any other person she'd encountered.

The flowers of the green did not disconnect from Mrs. Erickson; the almost imperceptible roots the green had bound around the words of the Ancient remained there. But some of those slender roots spread from the rings on Mrs. Erickson's fingers, trailing between the hands of the old woman the green had chosen as the Teller to the Dragon whose hands she had clasped.

Kaylin turned to Bellusdeo, letting one of her hands fall away.

"Do not stop," Evanton said. Or shouted. She felt his voice as an earthquake.

But she heard the rumbling of a different tremor, and heard, for the first time, the almost living voice of what had once been dead. It was striking, and very different. The Ancient understood what Mrs. Erickson desired for Bellusdeo, and it seemed as if the green did as well.

The Ancient spoke.

Let her do what she must; she is Chosen for a reason. And I am no longer what I was; what she needed to achieve for our sake, she has achieved. This is my gift of gratitude to her, to Imelda, and to the boundless green.

Kaylin therefore placed the one hand she'd freed from the Ancient's skin against one of Bellusdeo's hands. They formed a triplet: Imelda Erickson, Kaylin Neya, and Bellusdeo.

She could feel Bellusdeo's True Name. The True Name she herself had helped Bellusdeo and Maggaron form. A name that would not be encumbered by the Outcaste, who had played a part in the loss of her sisters.

She had forgotten at the time what a True Name was. What the essence of a True Name meant. She knew now. She knew that Bellusdeo's name had not been fully whole. Here, in this space, wearing this dress, attached to an old woman whom the Avatar of her home had loved instantly, she could sense the subtle nuance, the subtle absence.

The name itself would not change; it was what it had always been meant to be. Just as True Names did not entirely define the character of the Barrani they brought to life, the True Name of the gold Dragon did not entirely define who she had become. It should have, because the spirits of the women who had lived with their partial names should have been part of Bellusdeo from the beginning of her adult life.

Sensing the dead, sensing the living, seeing the connection, Kaylin worked. The Ancient was no longer her concern, and

Evanton would be very angry about that later. But Bellusdeo was one of Kaylin's people, and if you couldn't make time for your friends, if you couldn't reach out to help them when they needed you most, what did friendship mean?

Bellusdeo didn't argue. Maybe she couldn't. Two of her sisters did immediately.

But they were dead, and they couldn't actually harm Kaylin, who otherwise would have been smart enough not to anger a Dragon. Nor could they persuade Bellusdeo, because the gold Dragon couldn't hear them, no matter how very desperately she wanted to.

Losing her sisters was like losing limbs—and given what Kavallac had said about the birth of an adult female Dragon, it probably was. She was both Bellusdeo and at the same time incapable of being, or feeling, whole.

Kaylin saw the ghosts of her sisters begin to shimmer, even the ones who were mouthing dire warnings, saw the way their growing lack of visual substance followed the binding threads of the green, and poured as much power into Bellusdeo as she could access. This wasn't healing in the traditional sense. It required focus and intent, just as healing the Ancient had. This wasn't about what the *body* needed. The body had always known its correct shape, its healthy state. Kaylin had healed the gold Dragon before, and she'd done it the normal way, if healing could be considered normal.

This was nothing like that, because it wasn't the body that was damaged, torn, broken. This required deliberation, understanding; maybe there was no natural shape for a living person's soul. A body could live without its soul—Jamal's had, even when he had been shut out of it by Azoria.

Kaylin froze for one long moment. What she was doing—was it different? In the end, she wanted Bellusdeo to be *happy*. To be whole. To finally become what she should have become. And that meant the touching of the ghosts that were already attached; it meant the knitting of the disparate sisters—two of whom thought this was far, far too risky—into that whole.

It is not the same, a familiar voice said. Hope. *If you cannot trust yourself, trust those who can. This is healing of a nature that I have never seen attempted. I lend you now what power I can—but it is limited, as it always is, by what you are willing to sacrifice.*

You will be the first person I have ever served who is unwilling to sacrifice anything; your greed is boundless, but it never reflects your desire for power. You *are healing Bellusdeo. Mrs. Erickson saw the sisters as ghosts. But, Kaylin, remember: she considered Amaldi and Darreno to be ghosts as well.*

Kaylin exhaled. She now had hope, which could be bitter if it failed to blossom into reality.

She understood that she was running out of time; that the green and the Ancient could not remain in this place, and if they could, *she* couldn't. Mrs. Erickson couldn't. But regardless, she listened to the two who were afraid that the cost of integration might be the stability of the entire world into which they'd been born, and from which they'd been sundered.

"I can't force this on you," she told the two, whose birth names she didn't know. "I won't. I understand what should have happened to all nine of you: you would have merged into one person with many, many facets."

They knew. They had heard Kavallac.

"We can't leave you here," another sister said. "Knowing what we've suffered, knowing that you'll suffer it alone for the rest of our natural lives—we can't do it. At least we have each other now, even if we can't interact with the wider world."

"She's far too reckless. We might not even live for that long."

"Caution was never her strength—but we'd be with her, we'd be part of her. Maybe she'd live longer if we were there."

"Maybe she'd actually *have children,* which the race needs if it's to continue," a fourth sister said. There was a surprising amity between these eight. "But we'll never know, because if you two insist on remaining behind, so will we."

It occurred to Kaylin that these eight were very much like the cohort in that regard—but of course they were. The partial names that had animated them from birth had been known to each other. They had lived with the name bond.

"We can't take the risk. The Keeper made clear that we could be looking at the end of the world if the Ancient is not somehow settled. This is far, *far* too selfish."

"Mrs. Erickson has made that decision. Kaylin has accepted it. But if you stand and argue, the time will pass, the opportunity will be lost. Look at Kaylin: she's not leaving us here, and rejecting her aid just does what you're afraid of: it wastes more time. But if time is of the essence, we will *all* step back. We will all refuse what she offers."

"It's all or nothing, everyone or no one," one of the other sisters said. "Shall we vote?"

Another sister rolled her eyes. "Because that always worked out so well."

A cheeky smile was the response. "Try hitting me. Just try."

"Vote," Kaylin told them, the sound of her own voice almost surprising. "Vote and agree that the results will be binding. Because if you don't, there's no point. We only have this moment, and you're all *wasting it*."

One of the sisters raised a perfect, gold brow; of the eight, she had not raised her voice once. Until now. "Rejoin." Even the sound of the syllable somehow felt elegant, elevated.

The other seven voted in short order. Two voted against—quickly—and six for.

"What are they doing?" Bellusdeo asked, her voice shaky.

"Arguing," Kaylin replied. "I don't know their names—but two of them think we're putting the entire world in jeopardy over one single person. You, in case that wasn't clear."

The gold Dragon's smile was tremulous. "I bet I can guess who."

"They'd be arguing until next year if they had the time. Are you *sure* you want this?"

"If I could listen to them argue until next year—if I could experience that again—I'd give up almost anything."

"You heard her," Kaylin told the sisters.

She then continued the work she had begun. It was *not* easy; she was trying to evaluate the *shape of a soul*, and she knew—better than anyone—that she had no standing to do it. She wanted Mrs. Erickson to make the decision, to find a place for all of these people without prioritizing one over the other, to find *room* for so many lives in one body. Mrs. Erickson could give weight to each of them, could care for each of them, could listen to the needs they were willing to share, and somehow make them feel equally heard, valued, and seen.

Kaylin could walk into moving wagons if she was overfocused on a case.

Mrs. Erickson said, "I'm sure you need to think very carefully when you're investigating, dear. But you are Bellusdeo's only friend in this place; if you can't do this, no one can. Bellusdeo can't do it for herself; if she could, she would have already done so, a thousand times over."

The sisters began to fade. "Can you still see them?" Kaylin asked Mrs. Erickson.

"Yes, but they're becoming *quite* transparent—like storybook ghosts, not like real ones."

"At the same time?"

"At the same time."

She continued then. Her power flagged as the green glow of the marks of the Chosen dimmed. The marks returned to their place on her skin, as if spent. She hadn't finished. She hadn't finished yet.

Steady, Hope said. *You have the power to finish. You are almost done; can you not see it?*

Had she the energy, she would have snapped at him. *No*, she couldn't see anything but words; her eyes were now closed.

"I can't see them at all," Mrs. Erickson said softly. "Kaylin, I think Evanton wishes for you to stop now."

She shook her head. She wasn't done.

"Corporal," Evanton snapped. "You are done. Stop this—there is only so much power you can channel and you have *reached your limit*." Kaylin heard his cranky voice at a greater and greater remove.

But she could hear one sound so clearly, it might have been the only sound left in the world:

Bellusdeo began to sob.

Kaylin had never, ever heard that sound from a Dragon before, but didn't find it awkward. Those tears were the tears that fell in both relief and joy, when the strain that had forced people to hold back was suddenly gone.

Mrs. Erickson's hand tightened around the gold Dragon's; Kaylin's did the same.

And when the last of this knitting, this healing, was done, Kaylin was very glad for Severn's presence, because she did what she often did when she'd overextended herself: she collapsed. As consciousness faded, she heard Evanton arguing with the Ancient. Or maybe arguing with the green. She was almost grateful to leave him to it.

EPILOGUE

Bellusdeo remained with Helen, Mrs. Erickson, and Kaylin until Kaylin regained consciousness. Which, according to their concerned reports, took three days.

Squawk.

"He says four days, dear; he is disparaging our ability to count, but I'm certain he doesn't mean it." Helen's smile was gentle.

Kaylin, groggy, was certain he did. "How did I get home?"

"Bellusdeo broke the law."

"I did not break the law," the gold Dragon said. Kaylin sat up in bed at the sound of Bellusdeo's voice, blinking sleep out of her eyes. "The law clearly states that in an emergency, we are permitted to assume our draconic forms—and it was late enough I'm certain no one in the streets panicked at the sight of a Dragon."

"This isn't the first time this has happened," Kaylin told Bellusdeo. "But I couldn't exactly walk home on my own. Thanks."

"Don't thank me. Teela wanted to carry you. Tain offered the same. Severn looked like he might cut off an arm or two if either of them touched you." Bellusdeo frowned. "That boy is *seriously* attached to you, in case you haven't noticed."

I wouldn't have cut off anyone's arm, Severn pointed out, his interior tone at odds with Bellusdeo's description.

The Dragon's voice was the same as it had always been, but she'd never called Severn a *boy* in that tone before.

"What happened to Mrs. Erickson?"

"Mrs. Erickson is fine," Helen replied. "She was exhausted when she arrived—she joined you and Bellusdeo—but she slept normally, woke normally, and has been baking up a storm in the kitchen. She feels a bit guilty about neglecting the Hawks for the past week, and she's determined to make up for it."

"Tell her not to worry. They won't be mad at her—they'll blame me."

"Which is not entirely fair."

"Life, I've often been told, isn't." Kaylin rearranged her pillows so she could lean back into them; Helen offered her two more. "Did someone make excuses for me at the Halls of Law?"

"Teela did."

Kaylin exhaled. Teela had had to face the angry Leontine, not her. "Is Mrs. Erickson going to stay with us?"

"Yes, dear."

"I wouldn't blame her if she wanted to go back to her house. It should be safe for her there."

"Safe isn't the same as happy; it only looks that way when things are dangerous. Imelda says she's been happy here, and she expects she'll continue to find things that make her happy. She also likes the kitchen. I may have made a few adjustments to it to give her more space to work."

"Have we heard from Evanton?"

"Evanton briefly let me know that things have returned to normal in the garden, or a variant of normal. He expects you to visit when you are mobile again."

That sounded less promising. "He wants me to visit the garden?"

Bellusdeo coughed. "The Keeper and the green appear to have had a bit of an argument after you passed out. Mrs. Erickson was trying to be peacekeeper."

"Did she even understand what they were saying?"

"She understood what Evanton was saying—he got *quite* salty. But I think she understood how the green felt. Possibly because she was still wearing the crown, or at least that's what Teela thinks."

"And the end result is I have to visit Evanton?"

"It's the compromise."

Kaylin thought about just going back to sleep, but she was no longer tired; she was slightly anxious, which never made for good sleep. But it seemed unfair that the green and the Keeper had an argument, and the brokered peace was on Kaylin's shoulders.

"I thought you'd prefer that, over having Imelda put into more danger."

Kaylin exhaled and nodded; it was true. Mrs. Erickson was a civilian, an elderly woman with a very kind disposition—one Kaylin, and most of her friends, lacked. Yes, it was better if Kaylin had to cope with an angry Keeper and a disgruntled green. But Kaylin suspected that both the Keeper and the green wouldn't take out irritation on Mrs. Erickson. Kaylin felt she was fair game. Ugh.

"Did Terrano reappear?"

"In a manner of speaking," Bellusdeo replied. "Mandoran's waiting to talk to you about Terrano."

"He's safe," Helen told Kaylin, both gently and quickly. "And unharmed."

"Then why isn't Terrano waiting to speak with me?"

"He can't. He suggested—again—that Sedarias allow the cohort to include you as one of its members."

"Sedarias would hate that."

"Indeed. She wasn't the only person to argue against it, but even if she had been, the cohort operates on consensus in matters of grave import. Teela was also against it, but for different reasons; Sedarias fears for the safety of her chosen family. Teela fears for your safety."

"Kaylin *is* part of Teela's chosen family," Bellusdeo pointed out. "If I were offered the same opportunity, I would reject it utterly. The very idea of having to hear Terrano in the back of my thoughts whenever he feels like holding forth gives me hives."

"Do Dragons even get hives?" Kaylin asked, as she swung her legs off the bed and started to look for clothing.

"We did when we were children." Bellusdeo's eyes were gold. She rose from the chair she'd been occupying—clearly one that Helen had created for Bellusdeo, as it wasn't a normal part of Kaylin's room—as Kaylin got out of bed. Kaylin met her gaze and held it.

She hadn't talked very much with the eight sisters, but she knew they were somehow with Bellusdeo because Bellusdeo seemed different. Not bad different, just...not the same.

The gold Dragon reached for Kaylin's hands; Kaylin put dressing in day clothing on hold. "I think you, and the green, did what you could to help me. To help *us*. I cannot put into words how much gratitude I feel to both of you. And to Mrs. Erickson. If she hadn't been here, if you hadn't taken her in, I would never have known. My sisters would have been trapped, in isolation, for eternity.

"Mrs. Erickson helped them—and that helped me. But I was a little bit...overfocused. It's probably a good thing my Tower is a sentient building—I'm not sure he'd've survived that focus, otherwise."

"What do you mean?"

"I may have lost my temper. He considered the dead to be dead; they were irrelevant to the living. I disagreed." Her eyes flickered orange, but the orange didn't remain. A small smile tugged at the corner of her lips. "And I was *right*. I intend to enjoy that immensely when I return to the Tower."

"You're—you're whole now? You're what you should have been?" Kaylin wondered if, when she'd first helped Bellusdeo to find her True Name, she could have done things properly if she'd understood how Bellusdeo's name *should have* been built. She'd done what she could at the time, but in her ignorance, she'd done half the job. Bellusdeo clearly didn't hold it against her. Neither did the sisters.

But maybe Bellusdeo would have been in better shape if Kaylin had been able to intervene properly. If Kaylin had known then what she knew now.

"If you are going to blame yourself for our prior state, don't. If you hadn't done what you did at the time, I, too, would have been lost." Bellusdeo's smile deepened. "That's not the real reason, though. Guilt bores me, I've lived with it for so long. As for us?

"What Kavallac described isn't quite what we have. Maybe because we were apart for so long. Or maybe it's because of the Outcaste's interference. I can hear my sisters as distinct voices—we're like a council of Bellusdeo. The seams are strong—but they're definitely there. Maybe they'll fade with time."

"It must be really noisy on the inside of your head about now."

"It's been incredibly noisy."

"But can the sisters talk through you?"

Bellusdeo nodded. "One of my sisters in particular was incredibly good at dealing with people. In uncertain situations, I'll gratefully let her do the talking."

"Was she the elegant one?"

Bellusdeo smiled. "She was naturally socially graceful. Even when we were children. I think she was the only one of us who didn't annoy Lannagaros in the Aerie. She was studious, she was quiet, and she didn't generally approve of our pranks."

"She didn't join in on them?"

"I didn't say that." Bellusdeo grinned. "But it took all eight of us to coax her into it."

"What does it feel like when one of your sisters does the talking? Do they take over?"

"It's not quite like that. I'm still there. We're all still there." Bellusdeo shook her head. "It's Maggaron I feel sorry for. He's my Ascendant. Part of his role was to keep me anchored. I've hugely increased his workload. But I'll deal with that. I'll deal with Karriamis." Bellusdeo exhaled. "I'll deal with Emmerian."

"When you first met Mrs. Erickson, you hadn't come here to talk to her. You came to talk to me about something else. Was it Emmerian?"

"I was frustrated, I think. It feels like it happened years ago. And it also feels like it happened yesterday. Of the nine of us, I was the most martial; it's why, in the end, I ruled. We were in a constant state of war.

"But… I can't be in a constant state of war, can I? Not at home, if I even have one; not with Emmerian. He would have been the perfect second in command. I would have felt eternally grateful to have him. But his role would have been different. Neither of us would have been forced into this uncomfortable position. Yes, when I stormed into your home, I was angry with him—I can't remember why." She frowned. "My sisters can't remember it clearly, either; they, too, were trapped in their own states of mind." She cleared her throat.

"I want to do something for Mrs. Erickson—but I don't know her well enough to know what she'd like, and most of my previous social interaction didn't involve gentle old women. I feel that I owe her my life, my sanity, my sisters. They feel the same—but much more strongly." Bellusdeo let go of Kaylin's hands, indicating that Kaylin should get dressed.

Kaylin did. "Did the dress disappear?" she asked Helen.

"Not exactly," Helen replied, a flicker of concern touching her expression.

"What does *not exactly* mean? Did it transform back into the regular clothing I need and can't afford to easily replace?"

"No, as you must suspect."

"I don't see it."

"No." Helen didn't need to breathe, so exhalation was affectation. She exhaled anyway. "Evanton is in possession of the dress."

Bellusdeo snickered. "I'd pay money to see him wear it."

"Dear." Helen's tone contained a hint of disapproval, but affection was wrapped around it.

"The Barrani will lose all their perfect hair," Kaylin said.

"I think Teela would have found it amusing in other circumstances."

"Other circumstances?"

"The ones in which she wasn't very worried about your continued existence."

"I wasn't in danger."

"She is wise enough not to trust the green."

"Serralyn told us to trust the green."

"In that very narrow context, yes. I'm certain Teela doesn't consider the green malicious, but the interests of the green are the interests of an ancient, unknowable power, a wildness in which intent cannot be properly perceived."

"I think the green wanted the children it had damaged to be safe," Kaylin replied. "The green didn't intend to harm them or transform them, and the green may have felt...guilt for that." She pulled a shirt over her head.

"That's inside out."

Mandoran was waiting for them in the dining room. To Kaylin's surprise, so was Teela. Tain had gone home, but Teela had remained.

"Is Serralyn back at the Academia?"

"Not yet. I expect she and Bakkon will continue to excavate Azoria's research notes. Larrantin was forced to return to the Academia; he had lectures. I pity his students—he was not happy. You look a bit tired," the Barrani Hawk added.

"I'm fine. Just stressed. Evanton expects me to visit him."

"When?"

"Knowing Evanton, yesterday. Are you going to lecture me?" she added, as Teela's eyes were the martial color.

"Not in your own home. Probably not at all. Bellusdeo?"

"I'm good. I'm better than that. If you have to return to work, I'll escort Kaylin to the Keeper's."

Helen cleared her throat. "I believe Imelda wishes to accompany you there."

Kaylin didn't want to drag Mrs. Erickson to Evanton's. She turned to Bellusdeo for support, but Bellusdeo nodded. "I can escort them both." She then turned to Mandoran. "You wanted to speak with Kaylin, didn't you?"

He nodded. "First, though, Terrano is safe."

Breakfast appeared in front of Kaylin; clearly she was the only one eating. "Where is he?"

"He's with Alsanis and Eddorian."

"Alsanis? Terrano's in the West March?"

"He's in the West March. But he didn't arrive at Alsanis. He arrived in the green."

"And he's okay? He's normal?"

"For Terrano, yes. Mildly incensed; he wanted to travel home the faster way, and Sedarias put her foot down—aided by the green and Alsanis."

"The green was speaking with Terrano?"

"That's the trickier part. Yes, the green communicated with Terrano—but Terrano believes the heart of the green doesn't reside in our plane. And no, before you ask, the communication was not verbal—not even in the True Words created by the Ancients. Terrano, according to the green, was the one most changed by the *regalia.* Alsanis—who did communicate with words—believes that Terrano would have been entirely lost had it not been for the name bond that existed between Terrano and the rest of us."

"What in the hells was he trying to do? Why did he approach the Ancient at all?"

"It's Terrano," Mandoran replied, shrugging. "He was curious."

"I'm being serious."

"I'm being half serious. Terrano thought he could detect dangerous instability, and his first thought was to somehow ground what was there so the instability didn't cause the Ancient to fracture. And when I say instability, I don't mean the actual corpse. Or non-corpse. It was something more subtle.

"He could tell that the Keeper was trying to do the same thing, in an entirely different way; he says the Ancient exists in almost all places at the same time, and he approached from a different plane, a different state of existence. Evanton is wed to this one in many ways, but the Keeper's power is, by necessity, more all-encompassing. Terrano says he now understands how you feel," Mandoran added.

"About what?"

"About being blamed for everything that happens around you."

"I don't suppose I can ask Eddorian to smack Terrano upside the head?"

Mandoran laughed. "Eddorian hasn't lived with us—but he's been with us every step of the way. He says of course you can. It's a much lighter punishment than Sedarias asked him to inflict."

"So is he coming back?"

"Yes, but he has to do it the long way, so he's either walking from there to here, or he's waiting on a delegation so he can, as he put it, cadge a ride back."

Sedarias wasn't going to like that, either.

"The green, on the other hand, has offered him—and by extension the rest of us—a place to stay. If the world becomes too fractious, if our conflicts become too difficult, she will give us a home in the green."

Sedarias was definitely not going to accept that, given that so many of the current conflicts were the consequences of her own rise to power.

"You see the problem."

Kaylin nodded.

"Helen is Immortal, but she won't take us as tenants—and you've got an expiration date the rest of us don't have. I mean, you'll probably outlive Terrano at this rate, but you know what I mean."

She did. She didn't even find it offensive today.

Teela's intercession with Marcus meant Kaylin actually had an unplanned—and probably unpaid—day off. That she had to spend it visiting Evanton tarnished the freedom, but didn't entirely destroy it. They didn't leave for Evanton's until Mrs. Erickson woke up, ate, and dressed to meet him. She no longer wore the crown of flowers, but a single blossom remained twined around her finger. It had not faded or wilted.

Kaylin decided not to ask about the rest of the *regalia*, given Mrs. Erickson's demeanor: she was cheerful. She had always had a ready smile and a sympathetic ear, but this was different. She seemed more healthy, less fragile, and her ready delight was aimed at everything: the open, cloudless sky, the people scattered in the streets, the density of the crowd as they headed into the market, even snippets of conversation and one child who was trying to walk a dog but ended up being dragged by the leash instead.

She'd spent her entire life seeing ghosts—and who knows, maybe she could see them today—but seemed, at her age, to be infused with a desire for life, and a delight in it, that Kaylin felt she'd personally never had.

You did, Severn said, voice soft and imbued with grief. *You did, when you were much younger.*

She couldn't remember it now.

I can. I'll remember it for you. No, he added, internal voice much quieter. *I'll remember it for myself.*

Kaylin wasn't surprised to see Severn waiting at Evanton's storefront; he hadn't entered the shop yet. He offered Mrs. Erickson a perfect bow—Barrani in grace, but not as stiffly elegant.

Mrs. Erickson smiled. "Your work brings you here today?"

"It does. Kaylin is my partner, and our sergeant knew she was to visit Evanton today. I have permission to be here."

"Or orders?"

"Or orders," he agreed. "Shall we?"

Do you have any idea what he wants?

No.

I know that tone. You have suspicions.

The harmoniste's dress is with the Keeper. Yes, I have suspicions—but they change nothing.

Is that why you came?

No. I told Marcus you'd been summoned to Evanton's at your earliest possible convenience. He suggested I join you. With fangs.

Kaylin laughed out loud. Hope was slumped across both shoulders; he obviously didn't expect trouble. Or at least not trouble Kaylin hadn't imported by bringing Bellusdeo and Mandoran with her. Bellusdeo had offered Mrs. Erickson an arm, and Mrs. Erickson had smiled brightly at the gold Dragon—but had insisted that she was feeling much better these days, and didn't require aid.

She seemed perfectly comfortable around Bellusdeo. Bellusdeo, no fool, had always been comfortable with Mrs. Erickson, but she'd clung to the old woman because of her desperation for her sisters; those sisters were no longer bound to the Dragon—or at least not in the way they had been.

"You look very elegant today, Imelda. Perhaps you can convince Bellusdeo to pick up some of your understated fashion sense." Bellusdeo was speaking, but clearly, one of the sisters had been given permission to take over.

"Don't be silly, dear," Mrs. Erickson replied. "Bellusdeo's armor marks her as a warrior; I'm not sure there's such a thing as fashionable armor—only expensive armor."

"And there is, indeed, a difference."

"You seem much happier—I don't think I've ever heard you speak so much."

"We are all much happier. All of us, including Bellusdeo. Thank you for coming to our aid. Thank you for seeing what had remained unseen until the moment we met you. Shall we enter?"

Mrs. Erickson beamed and nodded.

Clearly Mrs. Erickson's time spent listening to the ghosts—and speaking with them—had given her familiarity with each individual personality, as was evident when each of them came out, in turn, to greet her and to offer her their gratitude, if *gratitude* wasn't too weak a word.

Evanton, seated at the long bar he used as a counter as sister number three took over, waited with as much patience as he could muster. "Corporal."

Kaylin stepped past Mrs. Erickson and Bellusdeo to head to the bar; Severn followed. Mandoran seemed content to remain with the gold Dragon and his newest housemate—but he'd always liked Bellusdeo.

Evanton had been working with gems; he took the jeweler's glass out of his left eye when she reached him. "I hear you asked me to visit."

"I did. I didn't expect you to lie abed for almost four days. I'm old—what is your excuse?"

Kaylin shrugged. "The fate of the world is too much for me to carry for any length of time? I don't know how you do it."

"If I didn't, the world would falter," he replied.

She frowned; he looked genuinely exhausted. "How long have you been doing this?"

"For far longer than I assumed I would when I accepted the responsibility," he replied. There was no irritation in the words at all. He just seemed tired.

She knew he was training Grethan, but suspected Grethan would not meet the requirements to succeed him for quite some time—if ever. She suspected he had taken an apprentice because he was lonely; Grethan was like Mrs. Erickson's children to Mrs. Erickson.

"How much longer?" Her frown deepened. When she'd first met Evanton, he'd looked ancient to her eyes—and nothing had changed. Eight years hadn't altered him at all. She glanced over at Mrs. Erickson and Mandoran.

"Have you not been told it's rude to make inquiries of that nature?"

She shrugged. "Hawks sometimes ask questions regular people would consider rude—but it's part of our job."

"And interrogating an exhausted old man is your job now?"

"Not unless he's a criminal suspect. But being at his beck and call isn't part of my job, either."

"Very well. I do not know how much longer I will serve as Keeper. I expected to be free of this position long before my great-grandchildren became adults."

Kaylin blinked. "You have great-grandchildren?"

"No. Not anymore. I had a great-great-grandchild, and from her, the next generation. Before you ask, no. They are no longer alive. One died in childhood, that I recall, but the rest were relatively healthy, and they lived a normal lifespan. Before you ask, I do not know what happened to their children. I made it my business not to know. They had no attachment to me.

"My grandchildren did, but they aged in the normal fashion, and I aged far more slowly. I could hide what I was, what I did, until they were adults. Only one of my grandchildren accepted it, perhaps because she came to see the garden as a child. It was a whim," he added, almost defensively. "When she understood what my job was, she was proud." He shook his head. "Proud. Happy. The elements seemed to like her, perhaps because I did."

"You never asked her if she wanted to become the Keeper?"

"No. The garden did." His expression was curiously distant as he spoke. "Not in so many words; the garden is much like the green in that aspect. But the garden accepted her with ease and even delight. She was a delightful child.

"She visited me often as she was growing up, but the intervals between her visits grew longer. This is natural; I had not offended her. But her life had grown wider, broader, and I had remained the same. She was like a little fledgling; when she flew in the wider sky, she had joy of the discovery.

"She fell in love—of course she did. She had her heart broken. She fell in love—slowly, more mindfully, more cautiously—again.

"But she could not be the Keeper and be wife and mother. When I became Keeper, my own wife had been gone for a decade, and my children were no longer small and in need of adult care. The garden wished for my grandchild to become Keeper after me; only then could I lay down my burden.

"But it would fall on her shoulders. She understood what the garden wanted; she felt both respected and needed. She was proud of that; she was young enough to feel that pride."

"You said no."

"I could not simply say no for her; she was an adult by that time. An adult, in love with a man she intended to marry. She had plans for a family of her own. I merely told her that the choice offered was a subtle choice between the man she loved and the future family she intended to build with him, and the garden.

"In the end, she chose the man, the future children. They did have children. If she could see me now, she would understand why I did not want her to carry this burden. I wanted happiness for her. I wanted her to have and build connections with people. I did not want her to suffer a life of isolation and duty, shorn of those things."

"And the garden was angry."

Evanton nodded. "Perhaps that is why I have yet to find a successor. Do not anger things ancient and wild if you have any choice. But come. I have spoken far too much, and Mrs. Erickson is waiting."

Mrs. Erickson was comfortable in the confines of Evanton's small shop. The hallway that led to the garden's door—a door that seemed like it had seen better decades, it looked so normal and run-down—was narrower, by a couple of inches, than the halls in her home.

Evanton offered Mrs. Erickson his arm; she accepted immediately. Bellusdeo and Mandoran trailed behind them, in single file; Kaylin and Severn picked up the rear.

Did you know? she asked Severn.

About his personal life? No. About his apparent immortality? Yes. He has *aged, but extremely slowly.*

Is this something you picked up with the Wolves?

We have different Records than the Hawks, yes.

She fell silent, thinking about Evanton. Thinking about a future Kaylin. Would she fall in love the way normal people seemed to? Would she *want* children? And if she had them, would she want them to bear the marks of the Chosen in her stead?

Absolutely not.

She'd had no choice. Mrs. Erickson had had no choice. The hands they'd been dealt seemed to be composed of twos and wild cards. But Mrs. Erickson had probably saved the world with the hand she'd been given, and that had turned a very ambivalent gift into a source of pleasure, of pride.

Evanton opened the door for Mrs. Erickson and held it open

as she stepped through its frame, vanishing instantly from Kaylin's sight. Evanton followed.

Bellusdeo and Mandoran weren't too far behind.

"Are you ready?" Severn asked, which surprised her.

She nodded and followed Severn through the door.

The garden was not exactly as she remembered, although the modest house remained unchanged. Gone was the small, but deep pond, and its surrounding soft moss which was so soothing to the touch. She would have frozen in the doorway, but she could hear Mrs. Erickson's exclamations of wonder and delight.

What she hadn't expected—and probably should have—was the damn dress.

The moment she had both feet in the garden, her clothing transformed. She cursed. In Leontine. Which Mrs. Erickson, thankfully, didn't understand. Mrs. Erickson *did* understand the tone, and turned back immediately.

"Kaylin? Oh! You're wearing the dress again!"

She was indeed. The lovely, practical, and ultimately attention-grabbing dress that the green gave to indicate its choice of harmoniste.

"Is your dress like Evanton's robes?" Mrs. Erickson asked.

Evanton was attired in the blue robes of the Keeper. "It is very much like them," he replied. He turned to Kaylin, smiling; the smile contained just a hint of an edge.

"What does that mean?"

"While you are in my garden—and while you are in the green, should you feel the need to return to the West March—you will wear this dress. When you leave my garden, you will be wearing the clothing you arrived in. It is raiment of honor," he added, clearly understanding just how honored it made Kaylin feel.

"So I get to keep my clothing? I don't have to scrounge up money to replace it again?"

"You get to keep your original clothing."

Which was a huge relief. Having to replace the first set of pants and shirt was going to be difficult, but possible; having to replace a second set? "What did you do to the garden?" Kaylin asked, changing the subject.

The garden was now surrounded by forest—a forest of strangely familiar-looking trees that reminded Kaylin of her trek to the West March. The elemental garden—and the small house it contained—resided in the center of a natural clearing, but there was another structure opposite that house that was grander and taller by far.

Pillars rose to the sky; Kaylin couldn't easily see the tops of them without almost falling over backward. Those pillars were of worked stone, at least at first sight; she realized that they were the emblem of earth here. Of fire, there was no sign, but the fire had often been contained in either outdoor campfire or indoor hearth; she could feel the breeze move her hair and the skirts of her dress. Air.

"Ah. I did not specifically do anything to my garden. Our newest occupant did."

Newest occupant. "The Ancient is here?"

"Yes, the Ancient is here. Can you not see where Imelda has been drawn?"

Kaylin reddened. She'd been worried about affording clothing, and the changed shape of the garden. "Where's the water?"

"Just beyond us, to the north; there is now a lake. It is much larger than the small pond; I found the pond more convenient."

"Why is he here?"

"The Ancient chose. The green offered the Ancient a home, a place to rest."

"And you offered the Ancient a home."

"Yes, although that was the will of the garden." And he'd paid the price for thwarting the will of the garden before. "The green and the garden disagreed. It was Mrs. Erickson who brokered a compromise between them. Where did you find her?"

"In the Halls of Law."

"I hope you appreciate what you have."

"I do—I don't think she'd make a good Keeper."

"No. That was not my intent." He watched as Bellusdeo and Mandoran followed Mrs. Erickson. "But the garden would be delighted to have her visit, possibly even live, within its borders."

"And you?"

"I admit that she reminds me of my old life; I would have adored her then. I am too old, too set in my ways, and too tired to adore her now, but I feel sparks of something that might be flickering embers of joy in the joy she takes, in her earnestness. She is nothing like you," he added, as if that needed to be said. "But in decades, in time, you might resemble her; you both tend to reach out when you see people you can help. You don't think before you act.

"Were she careful, she would not have reached out to Bellusdeo and her many sisters. Were she even a smidgen more selfish, she would not have lived a life that would have led her to you. Had she not, I fear the outcome would have been dire.

"Neither the green nor the garden are certain of the Ancient's future. We are uncertain what he will become, being reborn as he is. But we are both certain that he finds comfort in Imelda's presence—and she is both gifted and mortal. Here, in my garden, she might live, her time arrested; in the green, she might do the same.

"But she lives in the mortal world, and she will not live forever. I therefore ask that you allow her to visit as often as she wishes while she does live."

"And the dress?"

"Ah, yes. The green will have some small presence in the garden for the time; as the Ancient is so new to both garden and green, there is an overlap of shared concern. This was arranged by Mrs. Erickson; her gentle expectation of reasonable and fair behavior seemed to have a strong effect.

"While you are here, you will be representative of the green. Your care and concern for Mrs. Erickson's welfare has been noted."

"Mrs. Erickson wouldn't be a better representative?"

Evanton raised a brow. "I said the green holds her in high regard—what makes you think Mrs. Erickson could speak for the green? I doubt she would have survived being the channel for the power necessary to do what had to be done. Let her have her moment. She's earned it."

Kaylin heard laughter—Bellusdeo's and Mandoran's—and turned to look at Mrs. Erickson; she appeared to be speaking to a man the size of Maggaron. Mandoran and Bellusdeo were clearly not laughing at Mrs. Erickson, but with her, for her voice, slighter in every way, could still be heard reverberating in the breeze.

"I will. I'll even join it." Kaylin took a step forward, stopped, and held out a hand. "You should join it as well. If there's even a sliver of joy in life to be found, surely it's in moments like this one—and we both probably need it."

Well done, Severn said, voice soft. He let Kaylin lead Evanton, who seemed both reluctant and accepting, and followed from behind.

★★★★★

ACKNOWLEDGMENTS

It's been a bit of a year.

I did survive it—but I'm certain the rest of my lovely family survived because of Thomas, my long-suffering spouse. I'm pretty sure he had no idea what it would be like to be married to a creative for literal decades, but he's done it anyway, with grace and humor. And the usual forgetfulness that dots any household. Daniel and Ross picked up a lot of household chore slack, but I guess they're not really children anymore.

Our family across the street—John Chew, Kristen Chew and their two sons—keep dinner interesting twice a week. Even when I'm cranky and crawl upstairs to hide under a rock.

Leah Mol and the rest of the crew at MIRA Books have made me once again realize that while self-publishing *is* an option, it's not my preferred option. I like having managing editors, editors, copy editors and the entire Harlequin proofreading department, which is such a godsend. Mary-Theresa Hussey's long familiarity with this series—she acquired the first books, and then continued to do so—is also incredibly valuable.